Affairs of State

Phil Whitney

Completely Novel Edition

© 2016 Phil Whitney

Discover other titles by Phil Whitney

Relative Values (2015)
The Visitor's Guide to Florence and Tuscany (1986) Guidebook
Off the Beaten Track in Italy (1990) Guidebook

Find out more about Phil Whitney at
https://www.smashwords.com/interview/PhilWhitney59   and
https://www.amazon.co.uk/Phil-Whitney/
get regular updates at
https://www.facebook.com/Phil.Whitney.Author

Author's Note

This book is a work of fiction. Although I have tried to use real historical facts as background wherever possible, I would like to make it clear that almost all the political figures in my book are products solely of my imagination and any resemblance they may bear to persons living or dead is completely coincidental. The only exceptions to this rule are Romano Prodi and Massimo D'Alema whom I hope I have treated with respect. I have added a short appendix to the novel for those who wish to know a little more about the "real" people mentioned in the book.

The stimulus for the story was a very short article in the i newspaper in December 2014 which informed readers that a number of people had been arrested in Italy after a plot to assassinate Prime Minister Matteo Renzi and several of his ministers and advisors – from there, it was easy to imagine that there had been similar plots against his predecessors.

Acknowledgements

As usual, I would like to thank Lucia for her support while I have been writing this novel. I would also like to thank the many friends, both in England and Italy, who have, either knowingly or unknowingly, provided me with background information and ideas for this story. I would also like to thank those who provided constructive feedback after reading 'Relative Values' – it is much appreciated.

Chapter 1 – February 2004

'Come on, Paul. Get a move on, they'll be here soon.'

'OK – In a minute – I just need to finish this article – Franci won't mind if I haven't finished setting the table when they get here.'

'Franci probably won't, but I do.   She's bringing her new boyfriend with her and it's about time she settled down.'

Paul sighed, 'I've told you, he's not her boyfriend and there's no way that she'll be settling down with him.' He put the paper down on the coffee-table, stood up and moved through to the kitchen where he put his arms round Rosa from behind and nuzzled her neck. 'Mmmm, have we got a few minutes to spare.'

'Stop it. No we haven't – so get that table set,' but she turned her head and gave him a smile and a kiss before pushing him away and returning to her sauce.

Quickly but precisely he laid four oval shaped table-mats flanked by matching coasters on each side onto the smoked glass surface of the dining table, and then, taking care that everything was as symmetrical as possible, he laid out small and large knives and forks to the sides of each mat with medium sized spoons across the top. Then he opened the bottom cupboard in the sideboard and extracted four Burgundy style Bohemian crystal wine glasses and matching water tumblers, which he placed carefully to the right of each place setting. In the middle of the table he placed a larger oval mat on which he positioned a jug of water and the decanter of *Solstizio* that he had put to breathe before he had sat down with the newspaper. Finally, he took four red napkins and folded each into the shape of a rose, one of which he placed on each place mat.

He stood back to admire the effect and then moved back to the doorway and the controls for the light; he carefully pressed the cable adjustment so that the wide red shade moved fifteen centimetres closer to the surface of the table and then rotated the dimmer-switch anticlockwise to create a more intimate effect. Satisfied, he moved back into the kitchen where Rosa had now finished preparing the sauce for the *crème caramel* and was laying out *prosciutto crudo, bresaola,* and two types of *salami* on a large serving plate which she would complete by scattering with quartered cherry tomatoes and small gherkins. He slipped his hands into the oven gloves and, warning Rosa to stand back, opened the oven door and leaned back for a second to allow the wave of heat to escape, before withdrawing and uncovering a large casserole dish. He stirred the large chunks of meat inside and then returned the dish to the oven, without replacing the lid.

'What a lovely smell!'

'I'm probably the only Englishman who can claim that *Cinghiale in Umido* is his signature dish. I'm just going to put the water on for the *polenta*, then I'll get out from under your feet,' said Paul.

'Don't worry. I'm done. I just need a couple of minutes to reheat the sauce for the *crostini* before we eat. You're the one who needs the space, because the *polenta* you've bought will need stirring continuously for about forty minutes – I don't know why you didn't get the instant one that only takes five.'

'Because it doesn't taste as good and I thought you wanted to impress what's-his-name – who is not Franci's boyfriend.'

'We'll see.'

Twenty-five minutes later the door-bell rang and, when Rosa pressed the intercom button and enquired, 'Who is it?' despite being ninety-nine percent certain what the answer would be, the soft but cheerful voice of her younger sister replied, 'It's us.'

'OK Come on up,' said Rosa, pressing a button to open the external door, and opening the door to the apartment.

Twenty seconds later, the smiling face of Francesca Conte appeared and she embraced her sister for a few seconds before pulling away to reveal a tired looking man in his late thirties or early forties dressed in smart casual clothes and carrying a bottle of *Brunello di Montalcino*. 'Rosa, I want you to meet Arturo, my boss – and a friend…. Arturo, this is Rosa, my big sister.'

The man smiled, which made him look less tired, and he extended his hand towards Rosa. 'It's a pleasure to meet you at last; Francesca talks about you and your husband a lot.'

'Oh dear,' said Rosa, 'now I'm worried,' and they both laughed, 'My husband – Paul- will be with us in a few minutes – he's up to his elbows in *polenta* at the moment.'

'Hi,' shouted Paul from the kitchen, 'You'll have to excuse me – I'll be right with you.'

'Come through and sit down – shall I take your jackets – what can I get you to drink?'

'Just a glass of water for me, please. I have to drive later, and Franci has assured me that we'll be drinking excellent wine with the meal.'

'Franci?'

'Do you have any limes?'

'I think so, yes.'

'Then I'll have a *daiquiri* please.'

'OK. I'll be with you in a minute. Help yourselves to olives and nuts.'

When Rosa came back into the room with the drinks, Francesca had slipped her shoes off and was sitting on one end of the settee with her legs pulled up under her and contemplating a garlic-stuffed olive before popping it into her mouth. Arturo was standing by the bookcase that had been built in to the old fireplace and was browsing through a large book. He turned and smiled, 'Francesca hadn't told me that you were both authors – my compliments.'

She gave a warm laugh, 'Unfortunately, almost anyone can be an author these days; I have to publish things regularly – it's part of my contract as a researcher at the university. Most of what I write consists of really boring articles for obscure archaeological journals that exist mainly to provide an outlet for people like me who have to publish regularly – I doubt that anyone ever reads them. That was a little bit different as the Etruscans have always fascinated me and Paul had done some really artistic photographs. Because he'd already done a couple of guide-books that had been reasonably successful, we were able to persuade a publisher to take a risk on us.'

'And did the risk pay off?'

Rosa shrugged her shoulders, 'We enjoyed doing the book and we made enough to cover our expenses and buy a new washing machine – the publishers probably made a bit more but nothing great.'

Paul appeared in the doorway and advanced towards Arturo with a smile on his face and a hand extended which Arturo took and gripped firmly. 'Hi, I'm Paul, pleased to meet you… and sorry I was busy when you arrived.'

Arturo gave a friendly shrug to indicate that it was of no importance, 'I've just been admiring the book you put together with Rosa. There are some stunning photographs in there; congratulations.'

Paul smiled and gestured towards the seats, a gesture that was vague enough to leave it up to Arturo whether he sat on the settee with Rosa, or in one of the matching armchairs. He chose one of the armchairs and Paul took the other, leaving Rosa to drop down on the settee where, like her sister, she lifted her feet up alongside her. 'Look at them. If I had my camera to hand, I'd take a picture of them; they're like a pair of bookends….. Here, help yourself,' and he handed the bowl of olives to Arturo.

'You can tell that you're both artistic; you've made this place really attractive.'

'Thank you,' said Rosa, 'but the pictures that end up on the walls in here are mainly the ones that I haven't been able to sell.' The small talk and pleasantries continued for the next twenty minutes until Rosa looked at the Art-Deco clock that they'd come across in an antiques shop in Whitby several years before and suggested that they might like to go through to the dining-area and start on the *antipasti* in a couple of minutes, and then excused herself to go and prepare the *crostini*.

'I'm glad you managed to find time to come and see us; I come across your name quite regularly in the press, so you must be pretty in demand.'

Arturo gave a little smile, 'I think you English have a saying, "all work and no play makes Jack a dull boy," isn't that right?   And Francesca was very insistent that I should meet you.'

Paul directed his look towards Francesca, 'You do realise, don't you, that your mother will be on the phone first thing in the morning, pumping Rosa for every last bit of information.'

'Don't exaggerate,' said Francesca, colouring slightly.

'I'm not. Somebody's seen you together and the Antinos have already got you married off.'

'Phbbt! The Antinos,' and she shook her head while Arturo looked at them both quizzically.

'The Antinos,' explained Paul, 'live very close to my in-laws, and are probably the worst gossips in Florence, which could be useful except that, they're never satisfied with having just a little bit of information to pass on; if they haven't got the full story then they will embellish what they've got so that it becomes a complete narrative, which any writer of fairy-tales would be proud of.'

'I'll make sure I'm very careful,' said Arturo, trying to look serious although Paul could tell that he was not displeased.

'Ready!' shouted Rosa from the kitchen. They all stood up and Paul ushered Arturo through to the kitchen-diner followed by Francesca.

'It seems strange to be here without the kids,' said Francesca as Paul showed them to their places, 'I can't remember the last time we had any time together without them.'

'It's only the second time that Alessio has been old enough to go on the *settimana bianca* trip with the school and last year he missed out because of a touch of flu, so the last three years, even when we've been without Mati for a week, we've had Alessio moaning all the time about it not being fair that he's not old enough to go. Much as I love them, it's wonderful to be able to get rid of them for a few days, knowing that they're doing something that they'll both enjoy and is good for them.'

'Where have they gone to ski?' enquired Arturo.

'Pinzolo, not far from Madonna di Campiglio. Do you ski?'

'Not very well. I occasionally get away and do a bit on Monte Amiata, where a friend of mine has a share in an apartment – but I'm more or less self-taught, and it's unusual if I get in more than two or three days a year, so I'm not going to improve.'

Paul poured the wine and water and they settled down to the *antipasti*. Arturo picked up his wine glass and gently swirled the ruby liquid around and then held it up to the light before taking a sip and nodding appreciatively. 'Cabernet?' he asked, placing his nose inside the top of the glass and inhaling deeply.

'One hundred per cent, cabernet grapes,' said Paul with a note of admiration in his voice. 'You've got a good nose.'

'My uncle used to own an *enoteca* near the Mercato Centrale, I would have been considered a failure in life if I hadn't learnt to identify all the major grape types before I left school. It was far more important than academic work.'

'I hope you just tasted and then spat it out, or your academic work would have suffered anyway!' exclaimed Francesca.

'That depended how closely anyone was watching,' replied Arturo, and they all laughed. 'Where do you get it from? Is it local?'

'We get it from an *azienda agricola* between Tavarnelle and San Donato; I can give you one of their cards if you like.'

When Paul brought out the two serving dishes of *Cinghiale in Umido* and *Polenta* and placed them on the mat in the middle of the table, there was a gasp of appreciation. 'You shouldn't have gone to all this trouble just because we were coming; we only came for your company, but this is better than going to the restaurant.'

'Don't worry, Franci, it's for us as much as is it is for you. With the kids being away, not only have we got time to do things that we can't normally do, but we don't have to worry about the kids objecting to what we eat.'

'But Alessio and Mati aren't faddy kids, are they?'

'Alessio's not too bad, but Mati has started coming home from school with all sorts of strange ideas. A couple of weeks ago she was going to be vegetarian and never eat meat again; she's been a pescitarian, she's tried to persuade us that it's only ethical to eat road-kill, and she was even a vegan for a couple of days. The joys of having a teenage daughter!' Rosa gave a tragic shake of her head and everyone laughed.

While Arturo clearly enjoyed the food, Paul noticed that he only took small helpings, arranging them on his plate so that it looked as if he had taken more. Francesca, on the other hand, took a good plateful, ate with obvious relish and helped herself to seconds afterwards.

When everyone had cleaned their plates and were no longer going back to the serving dishes for more, Paul removed the plates, put them in a pile by the twin sinks and set out the dessert plates and smaller glasses for the *Passito* dessert wine which he took out of the fridge. Arturo placed a hand over the top of his glass as Paul was about to begin pouring the *Passito*, 'Not for me, I'm afraid; I've got to drive later and I'd rather sacrifice the dessert wine for a taste of one of the malt whiskies that Francesca tells me you have.'

'Of course... Franci seems to have told you a lot about us – you've got us at a disadvantage.'

Arturo laughed, 'The downside of being an Investigating Magistrate is that it's difficult to switch off – you can't help asking questions in continuation. To make up for it, is there anything you'd like to know about me?'

'For now, just let us know whether you like *crème caramel* or not, and how big a portion you'd like.'

When the dessert was finished, Rosa suggested that Paul made the coffee and then brought it through to the others in the living room. Francesca stood up and took her sister's arm as they moved out of the room, while Arturo hung behind and studied Paul who was extracting the little espresso cups from one of the cupboards. 'What do you think are the prospects for the next election? Do you think the left have much chance of finally getting rid of the current Prime Minister?' he asked casually, 'I believe that you follow the political situation quite closely.'

'I do my best, but the left makes it very difficult with constantly shifting alliances and regular changes of party names – blink, and you have to start learning all over again... It's hard to say, if you talk to anyone with any sense they agree that he's a crook and claim that they want to get rid of him... the problem is that they find it hard to focus on an alternative... If the left can agree on a leader and stop squabbling amongst themselves then they should walk it – but that's a very big if.'

'What if Prodi were to come back to national politics after his stint as President of the European Commission?'

Paul did not reply immediately while he lit the flame under the Bialetti Espresso maker, but then turned round and said thoughtfully, 'If Prodi were to come back, and came back in time to re-establish his national profile, then the left coalition could win, provided it can avoid squabbling amongst itself in the run-up to the election.'

'That's my analysis too... and I hear that Prodi has pretty much decided already that that's what he wants.'

'I'm impressed,' said Paul, 'you seem to be very well informed... what else have you heard?'

'Romano doesn't have a Party at the moment, as the one he belonged to before he went to Brussels has split and merged several times since he left and, as he represents the whole of Italy on the European Commission, he hasn't aligned himself with any specific group since then. Because of that, and because he knows that it has to be a coalition of several parties to stand a chance of winning, he intends to propose an American style primary to give him a real mandate as leader.'

'You are well informed... and on first name terms with Prodi... but what I'm wondering is why are you telling me all this... it's the first time we've met and you don't seem the type of person who goes around gossiping.'

Arturo gave a half smile and spread out his hands in an unconscious gesture of openness. 'Francesca said you were sharp and politically astute, and I see she was right. Let me come clean with you... after you've turned the gas off under the coffee, which I think is done.'

Paul turned back to the stove, turned the gas off and poured the coffee in to the four *tazzine* that he'd prepared. 'I'll just take theirs through – back in a second.'

When he returned, Arturo had taken the other two cups off the side and put them on the table, one in front of him and one in front of the seat opposite him. 'OK I'm listening,' said Paul who then tipped the coffee down his throat.

'I'm sorry to say that I didn't come here tonight just to sample your and Rosa's exquisite cooking – I'm afraid I had an ulterior motive.' He looked at Paul who did not speak but returned his gaze impassively, so he continued. 'There are a lot of people who have a vested interest in making sure that we continue to have a right-wing, 'big business friendly' government after the next election... a lot of very influential people.'

'When you say 'influential' I take it that you don't mean that they are good at debating.'

'No,' said Arturo, 'I mean that they are effectively the real power behind the state. They're the ones who've kept our current leader out of jail all these years – he's very useful to them as he's a good communicator with the common touch, but he's an intellectual lightweight who will carry out any policy they want, once they've convinced him that it was his idea in the first place and provided he can see that it will benefit himself. My information is that they would go to any lengths to ensure that the left does not have a convincing leader for the election... any lengths.' He stopped and waited for Paul's response.

'So why are you telling me this?'

'Because, Paul, I need the help of someone I can trust – I need your help.'

'My help! What can I do? And why do you think you can trust me – we only met two hours ago?'

'I only met you two hours ago, but Francesca has known you for nearly twenty years, and I value her judgement more than anyone else's.'

'But... so what? What can I do?' asked Paul, genuinely puzzled.

'Arturo smiled, 'What are you good at, Paul?'

Paul considered for a moment then realised what Arturo was after. 'Cooking,' he said, to be awkward, even though it felt a little childish as he did so.

'Go on.'

'Writing travel guides.'

'And what makes your guides so successful?'

'Oh, alright... photography.'

'Exactly. I can't do anything without incontrovertible evidence – I'm pretty sure that at least one very senior person in the Ministry of Justice is involved, and any evidence that's not cast iron won't be good enough... and these people are not as careless as those in P2 were; they don't leave membership lists lying around. I need photographs and you are both an excellent photographer and someone who is completely outside the system.

'What do you want me to photograph?'

'People, places, meetings... maybe even documents.'

'Tell me; where does Franci fit in to all this? Even if the Antinos have told everyone that you're a couple, and my in-laws are dying to meet you. I don't believe it for a minute.'

'I'm afraid that that little deception was your sister-in-law's idea... partly because it serves a real purpose, and partly, I'm sorry to say, because I think that it amuses her... How did you see through us anyway, just out of curiosity?'

'Not only has Franci known me for nearly twenty years, but I've known her too; I've seen her develop from a cocky but naive teenager into a clever sophisticated young woman. I've seen her infatuated with pop stars, toying with various admirers, getting ready to go out with boyfriends and even considering marriage at one stage. I suppose you could say that the Conte sisters have become my specialist subject. She likes you, she trusts you and respects you but that *je ne sais quois* just isn't there... and... even though I don't know you, I'm pretty sure that if you'd been romantically involved you wouldn't have been able to help looking at her legs when she pulled them up on the settee... How am I doing?'

'Very good. You should have been a magistrate, or a policeman. I contacted Francesca a few months ago, after that piece she wrote about the paedophile Bishop, who everyone thought was a saint – a possible future Pope, they said... do you remember that piece?' Paul nodded. 'I found out that she was freelance, so I asked her to come and work for me. Officially she writes press-releases and checks through my speeches before I give them. Unofficially, she writes most of my speeches and I make good use of her talents as an investigative journalist. She's good... very good.'

Paul looked puzzled, 'But I don't remember her writing anything significant since the paedophile piece.'

'As I said, she writes my speeches. Anything controversial that we turn up, she writes it and I say it – that way – if there's any comeback, then it all comes my way.'

'As does all the credit.'

Arturo shook his head, 'Believe me, Paul, it's far better for Francesca not to be associated with the things that we're investigating. If we manage to put the influential people I spoke of behind bars and the left does win the election, then Francesca's career will take off properly, but even then, it would be better if no-one knew what she'd done. These people will still be dangerous even when they're behind bars.

'So why go out of your way to make people think that you're together – surely, that raises Francesca's profile and associates her more closely with you?'

Arturo shook his head, not, Paul thought, looking completely happy or convinced by what he was saying, 'That was her idea, I'm afraid. In her view, doing it this way makes it look as if her working for me is just the sort of reward for other services rendered that is fairly common in our society. She thinks that if people think that she slept her way into her job that they'll see her as an intellectual lightweight, and that that will make it easier for her to do her investigative work,' he raised his shoulders and gave an apologetic what-can-I-do-about-it look.

Paul thought for a moment. He wasn't entirely happy about the relationship – or presumed relationship – between Francesca and

Arturo, but he had no problem with their objective. He thought of all the times he'd despaired at the lack of real action being taken against the general level of self-interest, exploitation and corruption in Italian public life, and railed against the left's inability to stop squabbling amongst itself and do something concrete about putting things right. Now he was being offered the chance to help do what he had criticised others for not doing. He knew that there were areas of Italian life to which it was safer to give a wide berth, and he knew that Rosa would prefer him to keep out of it, for the sake of the children, but he knew that, if he said "no", he would never be able to look anyone he respected in the eye again. He sighed deeply. 'So what, or whom, do you need me to photograph – and when?'

Paul hadn't been aware of the tenseness in Arturo, but now, the release of tension was obvious as he breathed out and his upper body moved back a centimetre so that he was leaning on the back of the chair rather than holding himself erect with the muscles in his back and abdomen. His hand came out and took Paul's followed by his other hand, so that both his were clasped around Paul's. 'Thankyou,' he said. 'Francesca will let you know when and where. It's probably better if we don't meet again, unless it's absolutely necessary. And now, I think we'd better rejoin the others, or they'll be coming to look for us."

Although it wouldn't have been obvious to an outsider, Paul could tell that Rosa was frustrated when they entered the living-room apologising for not having rejoined the others sooner. Paul guessed that Rosa had been trying, unsuccessfully, to get Francesca to open up about her relationship with Arturo – he would have to explain the situation to her later, after they had gone. For the moment, however, it was best to steer the conversation elsewhere, so he asked Francesca if she'd read the latest *Montalbano* offering by Camilleri, which led to a discussion of the relative merits of Camilleri and other contemporary Italian crime writers. Paul and Francesca both argued the case for Camilleri, while Rosa argued in favour of Carlo Lucarelli on the grounds that the creation of a convincing female detective was more of an achievement. Arturo surprised them all by arguing that, while the leading Italians were all good writers and entertained their readers, they did not portray the faults in the system with the same objectivity as some of the foreign authors who made a living out of crime novels set in Italy. When the others reacted sceptically to this, he smiled and advised them to read novels by the English author Michael Dibdin and the American, Donna Leon. The only Italian crime writer he really liked, he said, was a former colleague of his, Gianrico Carofiglio, who had used his experience of the Italian legal system to write two excellent novels in the past two years: *Involuntary Witness* and *A Walk in the Dark*. Rosa said she was surprised that she'd never heard of the books and Arturo promised that he would send them over.

Soon after midnight, Arturo caught Francesca's eye and said, 'I think we ought to be making a move. Rosa and Paul probably want to catch up on some sleep with the kids being away.' Francesca nodded and, despite their hosts saying that the time was unimportant, rose to get her coat. The others followed her to their feet and the ritual goodbyes began: Paul and Arturo shook hands warmly; Arturo and Rosa smiled and air-kissed; Francesca gave both her sister and her brother-in-law big hugs and then they went through the outer door onto the landing and began to make their way down the stairs towards the main door of the block.

When they were half way down the stairs and Paul was just about to shut the door, Francesca stopped and felt her pockets and then checked her bag. 'My lipstick,' she said, 'I must have left it in the living room after I'd shown Rosa the photos of Venice.'

'I'll go and look,' said Paul.

'I'll wait for you in the car,' said Arturo and carried on down, 'the sooner I get it started, the sooner the heater will start doing something', he called back over his shoulder.

Paul found the lipstick immediately and took it out to Francesca who had made her way back up to the door. 'Thanks,' she said, and smiled, slipping the lipstick into her pocket as she almost skipped down the stairs so that Arturo would not be kept waiting.

As she extended her arm towards the door, which Arturo had pulled to but not completely closed, there was a tremendous explosion outside and both halves of the door, including the half that had been bolted, flew inwards throwing Francesca back against the stairs and knocking Paul back a couple of steps from the doorway.

When his brain began to function again, and processed what had just happened, a couple of seconds later, he rushed down the stairs to where Francesca was lying, moaning. 'Franci.' he yelled desperately, as he knelt behind her and tried to be calm as he looked for any obvious injuries She moaned again and lifted her head. He put a hand to the side of her face and spoke to her in what he hoped was a calming voice. 'Just try and lie still, until we know that there's nothing broken.' Rosa arrived at a run and almost roughly pushed him to one side and took over. Paul stood, turned and moved to where the doors had been. A medium sized saloon, that he thought might once have been an Alfa Romeo GTV Coupé had been blown into the middle of the road where flames and black smoke poured out of where the roof and doors had, until recently, given the car its sleek elegant lines. Now, the roof had split open like an over-ripe tomato and the driver's door trailed on the floor by the side of the car, held only by the remnants of one hinge. The heat made it impossible to approach and Paul knew without any doubt that Arturo was dead. The car that had been parked behind the Alfa was also on fire and, pulling himself together, Paul raced back upstairs to get the fire blanket that Rosa insisted on keeping in the kitchen, so that he could try and douse the flames in the second car before they reached the fuel tank.

By the time he was back down again, the first police car had arrived and, despite the numerous nearby car alarms that had been set off by the blast, he could hear more sirens in the distance. 'Stay inside, Sir,' said a young, ashen-faced policeman. 'There's a major incident here.'

'Let me through,' said Paul, pushing past him, 'If we don't put the fire out in that second car the tank's going to blow.' He didn't wait for an answer, but began to beat the front of the car with the blanket, 'somebody get some water,' he called. The second policeman from the car, joined him with a fire-extinguisher, and together they managed to douse the flames before there was a second explosion.

Within minutes two ambulances, a fire-engine and three more police cars had arrived on the scene. Francesca did not seem to have any serious injuries but the doctor on board the first ambulance gently explained that it was better if she went to hospital to be checked over as a precautionary measure. She insisted, however, on walking to the ambulance, giving one arm to Paul, but ignoring the paramedic who tried to take her other arm. As he supported her up the steps into the back of the ambulance she leaned towards him, as though for extra support and said, 'Take my phone out of my pocket. Let Adriano know what's happened – and don't tell anyone anything that Arturo told you.'

As he helped her turn to lie down in the ambulance, he managed to slip one hand into her coat pocket and, without being observed, transferred her phone into his own pocket.

Rosa was allowed to travel with Francesca in the ambulance and Paul stepped back to watch it pull away. 'I'm afraid that we're going to have to ask you some questions, sir,' said the older of two plain-clothes policemen who had materialised alongside him, 'can we go upstairs?'

Paul showed them into the living room and then excused himself for a minute to go and clean his hands which had been blackened by the burning cars.

No sooner than the bathroom door had closed behind him, he took out Francesca's phone and pressed the key that said Address Book. Luckily, 'Adriano' was one of the first entries and, even more luckily, despite the time, he still had his phone turned on and picked up after the second ring.

'*Ciao, bella,*' Paul realised that Adriano thought that it was Francesca calling.

'Hello. You don't know me. I'm Francesca's brother-in-law, Paul Caddick.'

'OK,' there was a note of curiosity, maybe concern in the two letters.

'I'm afraid there's been an explosion.'

'Oh God. No! Artu'!' now there was a clear note of anguish in the voice.

'I'm sorry – If it's any consolation, he won't have suffered.' There was the sound of weeping now. 'Francesca, should be alright – they've taken her to Careggi to be checked over.' The weeping continued. 'I have to go now, the police are waiting to talk to me...' Still only weeping. After a few more seconds he hung up and finished washing his hands.

'So, Mr Caddick. Do you have any idea who the driver of the car was?' Paul looked at them, stunned.

'Shit!' he said, in English, and then reverting to Italian, 'You don't know, do you.'

Once he had told them the identity of the victim, the more senior of the two policemen was on the phone straight away. He then apologised to Paul saying that he had to await further orders. Paul shrugged resignedly and made espressos for all three while they waited. They tried to make small talk but it was desultory then, after little more than ten minutes, the phone rang. Paul picked up and almost immediately passed the phone over to the policeman.

'Vichi' …. '*Si*' …. 'Just over half an hour ago,' …. 'We only just found out,' ….. 'Outside friends' house,' ….. 'Two, man and wife – and his girlfriend,' …. 'Don't know yet,' …. 'Alright,' …. 'About twenty minutes.' He pressed the red button on the phone and passed it back to Paul. 'I'm afraid you'll have to give your statement at the station. Given the identity of the victim, there are far more important people than me who need to talk to you. Could you be ready to leave in ten minutes, please? I'll ring my colleague at the hospital and ask her to let your wife know where you are – although, I'm pretty sure that she will need to be seen as well.'

'OK. No problem. I just need a jacket and we can go straight away, if you like.'

'Take your time. You'll have to wait at the station anyway – I'm sure that the people who want to talk to you will take their time getting out of bed.'

Chapter 2

The policeman was right. Once they got to the Questura, Paul was led upstairs to a somewhat disorderly office with lots of unfinished paperwork on the large desk. He saw from the nameplate on the door that Vichi was a commissario but couldn't remember whether or not he'd already been told this. A large faux-leather swivel chair was behind the desk and facing it were two institutional looking chairs in moulded grey plastic bolted onto tubular metal frames. Instead of inviting Paul to take one of these, however, Vichi cleared the papers off one of a pair of more comfortable chairs that had been placed on either side of a small round wooden table near the only window to the room.

'I'll just straighten the papers up on my desk while we wait,' he said, 'it wouldn't do for the big boys to arrive and think I'd been out catching criminals when I should have been keeping on top of the paperwork.' Paul appreciated the commissario's attempt at lightening the mood, and nodded gratefully as he sat down. 'Can I get you a coffee, or something?' said Vichi as he tapped a pile of papers into a neat pile at one end of his desk.

'What I'd really like is a cup of tea, if that's at all possible.'

'I think it would cause a crisis in the officers' mess if I asked them to prepare a cup of tea for an Englishman – but I can send someone out to the bar across the road – just give me a minute.' He swept a handful of pens and paper-clips off the surface of his desk and into the top drawer and then straightened up the blotting pad in the middle. He stood back for a second and eyed the overall impression critically, 'That will do – I look like a conscientious policeman now.... Right,' he picked up the phone and tapped in three numbers and then, after about ten seconds, 'Mavaldi? .... Vichi here..... I need you to nip across the road and get me a pot of English Breakfast Tea, or as close as they can get … Yes …. I don't know; just a minute.' and then placing his hand over the speaker without thinking, and turning to Paul, 'How do you take your tea?'

'With a drop of cold milk – no sugar – and tell them to make sure that the teabag goes in while the water is still boiling.'

'OK, did you get that, Mavaldi? … Oh, sorry; a drop of cold milk – unsweetened – and the teabag must go in while the water's boiling.... Yes..... English…. in my office. Thanks,' and then to Paul, 'It should be here in less than ten minutes.'

'Thankyou.'

Unlike Vichi's superiors, the tea did arrive on time and, although it didn't compare with a pint-mug of freshly brewed builder's tea, in leaf form rather than bags, it wasn't too bad and made him feel a lot better. Vichi gave him a copy of the Police Federation Monthly, with an apologetic, 'I'm afraid it's the only reading matter we've got,' and this had the desirable, from Paul's point of view, effect of making him doze off after a few minutes.

He was awoken by the near contemporaneous sounds of the door opening and Vichi's chair scraping backwards as he rose to his feet. Three men and a woman entered. The one in front was a bull-necked, well-dressed man in his fifties who looked vaguely familiar. This man looked straight at the commissario, 'Ah, here you are, Vichi. We've been looking all over for you.'

'I thought we'd be better waiting in my office, Signor Questore. Signor Caddick is effectively one of the victims of tonight's explosion and is here to help us. So it didn't seem right to leave him to wait with our usual nightly clientele.'

'Thankyou, Commissario,' said the woman who had entered with him. 'You did well. Now, if you wouldn't mind, my colleagues and I would like to borrow your office for a while. We'll call down if we need anything.'

Vichi hesitated for a moment then said, 'Of course,' and turned towards the door. 'Thankyou,' said the woman to the Questore who, realising that he too was being dismissed, followed Vichi out of the door.

The woman, who was dressed in a pencil grey skirt and matching jacket over a high-collared white blouse, sat down in the chair opposite Paul and her two acolytes, as Paul thought of them, brought over the two plastic topped chairs from the desk and placed them so that, with the woman, they formed a semi-circle hemming Paul in.

Paul, still somewhat shaken by the evening's experience, expected some sort of preamble, at least a pretence of sympathy, but there was none. One of the two males placed a digital recorder on the small table and flicked a switch so that a red button appeared.

'How long have you known the Magistrate?'

'Arturo – the man who was blown up?'

She nodded briefly, 'Arturo dell'Omodarme, investigating Magistrate to the Tribunal of Florence.'

'I first met him sometime between half-past-eight and nine this evening.'

'And how did that come about, Mr Caddick?'

'We'd invited my sister-in-law round for dinner and she rang last weekend to ask if it would be OK if she brought a friend... that friend turned out to be Arturo.'

'When exactly, last weekend?'

'I'm afraid I don't remember. Francesca spoke to my wife when she phoned. My wife mentioned it to me at breakfast on Sunday, so it was probably Saturday evening.'

'And who did you tell about the visit?'

'Tell? The only people we told about the visit were my in-laws, as we knew they'd be pleased that Francesca was coming round, especially if it meant that her friend was a serious boyfriend.'

'She has problems with relationships, does she?' put in one of the two men while leaning his head slightly to one side and raising a sardonic eyebrow.

'Problems? No more than anyone else, as far as I'm aware – perhaps you should try one sometime,' replied Paul, who felt irritated by the expression on the other's face.

'I think that what my colleague was asking,' said the woman with a smile around her mouth that did not stretch to her eyes, 'was why your in-laws would be particularly pleased if the magistrate was her boyfriend,'

Paul shrugged, 'Francesca's thirty-three almost thirty-four, it's only natural for her parents to want to see her settled down – I think that to a large extent, who it was is irrelevant.'

'Did you invite your sister-in-law, or was she the one who suggested coming round?'

'I don't remember. She knows that she's welcome any time. It will have come up in a phone call between my wife and Francesca that she was free and tonight was a convenient night for us, but it could have been either of them who suggested it – it's not a big deal.'

'Who else did you tell?' interrupted the man again.

'That Francesca was coming round? It was no secret, but at the same time we didn't go round announcing it – it was just no big deal – I may have mentioned it in passing while chatting with work colleagues at the university over a coffee, but if I did, it was so insignificant that I don't remember.'

'We'll decide what is significant and what isn't. We'll need the names of any of you colleagues who you may have mentioned it to before you go home,' said the man. Paul rolled his eyes.

'When dell'Omodarme was at your house, what did you talk about?' said the woman, as if the other man had never spoken.

'We talked a bit about photography, a bit about archaeology, a bit about England, a bit about the children, and he told us how dull his job was, most of the time.'

'And how did the conversation get round to his job?'

'We were discussing various crime writers and someone, I can't remember if it was me or my wife, asked whether his job was like that of Tommaseo in the Montalbano series.'

'And?'

'And what?'

'Is it?'

Feeling on edge after the trauma of the explosion, Paul was unable to keep the sarcasm out of his reply, 'No. I'm sure you'll be pleased to know that he didn't see his job as being to develop sexual fantasies to provide motives for murder.'

The woman's expression did not change. 'Did he speak about any of his current cases?'

'No, he didn't.'

'None at all?'

'No. He didn't give me the impression as being the type of person who would be indiscreet with friends, let alone with people who he was meeting for the first time.'

'Talk us through the minutes that led up to the explosion. As accurately as possible, I want to know exactly where everyone was, exactly what everyone said, and the reasons for which people did what they did.'

To the best of his ability, Paul described the scene from the point where Arturo suggested that he and Francesca should be making a move. The woman and the aggressive man who had previously interrupted listened carefully while the other man, despite the presence of the digital recorder made his own notes. They were particularly interested when Paul explained why Francesca was still in the building, and not in the car with Arturo, when the bomb went off.'

'So your sister-in-law went far enough with dell'Omodarme to ensure that he got in the car on his own and then went back to where she knew she was safe,' said the man, thrusting his head forward from the neck in a Mussolini-like gesture.

'No,' said Paul with forced patience, 'She'd forgotten her lipstick and she waited a moment on the stairs while I went to find it and then, once she had it, she almost ran down the stairs to catch up with Arturo.'

'How lucky,' said the man, sarcastically. 'When the bomb went off, she was still on the safe side of a pair of thick wooden doors.'

Paul gripped the arm of his chair tightly as he resisted the temptation to punch the man.

'As I said, she ran down the stairs. If she'd been a quarter of a second quicker, the door would have hit her as it blew open, and may well have killed her. I take it that you're trying to suggest, for some reason, that Francesca knew that there was a bomb; if she did, then her behaviour in running down the stairs would make no sense whatsoever.'

'How long have you known Francesca Conte?' asked the woman, still with no sign of any emotion on her face.

'I first met her, briefly, on New Year's Eve 1985 but didn't really get to know her until the following spring when I was introduced to my wife's family.'

'And has your relationship ever developed beyond that of brother and sister-in-law?' interrupted the man again. Paul gave him a contemptuous look and then turned back to face the woman who calmly instructed him to answer her colleague's question.

Paul knew that his level of irritation was rising dangerously, and knew he should control it but failed to do so, 'No, I've never had an affair with my sister-in-law or my mother-in-law, or even my grandmother-in-law. Is there anyone I've missed out? Oh, I haven't had a relationship with my father-in-law or the family cat either!' There was no reaction from either the man or the woman, although Paul noticed the second man, who had not spoken, lift his head briefly and look at him before lowering it over his pad again.

'You said you talked about photography. What exactly did you talk about?'

'I'm a photographer. There are some of my photographs on the walls in the living room. In my view, they're quite good. Arturo was complimentary, as any normal person who's a guest in a house for the first time would be, and he asked a few general questions about how I'd taken them and how I'd learnt to photograph.'

'And how did you learn to take photographs?'

'I'm pretty much self-taught. I read lots of books and experimented with different techniques and gradually developed my own style.'

The questioning continued for well over an hour, going over and over the same ground; only the tone varied: sometimes it was aggressive and sometimes wheedling – but the outcome was always the same, although Paul became increasingly irritated.

'So when did you become a photographer?'

'Look – why don't you just check back in your notes? This is at least the fourth time you've asked that question, and the answer still hasn't changed,' he glared at the man who held his stare mockingly.

'Alright' the woman stood up, followed by her two assistants. 'That will be all for now. We'll be in touch – in the meantime – do not speak to anyone else about this matter – and do not attempt to leave the country,' and she led the other two out of the room. Paul wasn't quite sure what he was meant to do, so he waited a few minutes until Vichi reappeared, by which time he had fully regained his composure.

'Charming colleagues you've got. Who were they – leftovers from the Banda Caritá?'

'Vichi smiled, 'Almost. You've just been speaking to the regional director of SISMI. Come on, I'll get Mavaldi to run you home. Get some sleep.' Vichi offered his hand and Paul shook it.

Chapter 3

'So tell me again,' said Paul, 'What's the difference between SISMI and SISDI?'

'Both organisations were formed in 1977 when the previous overarching security service, SID, the Servizio Informazioni Difesa was broken up into Military and Internal sections, supposedly to ensure greater public accountability. OK so far? … Good. Right, now listen carefully... SISMI is the military security service; it is responsible for evaluating and reporting on external threats but also for anything that poses a threat to the integrity of the Italian State. SISDI is the internal security organisation dealing with internal threats to Italy, including organised crime.'

'OK, ' said Paul, 'I get that, but why is this being dealt with by SISMI, surely it should fall into the remit of SISDI?'

'That,' said Francesca giving a brief wan smile through the pain caused by the numerous bruises and abrasions that Paul knew covered most of her body, 'is a very good question. Someone, at a very high level, almost certainly a member of CESIS and or COPALCO, must have had a very good reason for allocating the case to them.'

Paul put his hands up in front of his chest, palms facing Francesca in a gesture of helplessness. 'I'm sorry, Franci – you forget that I'm not immersed in these acronyms everyday – if you don't explain them, you're going to lose me again.'

Francesca tossed her head back in frustration, then winced as she clearly regretted the brusque movement. 'Alright, sorry. CESIS is the body set up to link the two agencies to the Council of Ministers and to ensure that they talk to each other at a high level to avoid duplication; COPALCO is a parliamentary committee set up to oversee the work of the two agencies. Alright?' Paul nodded. 'COPALCO on its own is unlikely, although there is some crossover between the two bodies. For SISMI to be involved means that someone has determined that blowing up Arturo represents, or is linked to something that threatens the integrity of the state but... that doesn't really make sense, does it?'

'From the little bit that Arturo told me when we in the kitchen last night, he was very much on the side of the state – but I didn't get the impression that he was a key part of the state.' Paul looked somewhat guiltily at Francesca. 'Sorry, I'm not saying that he wasn't...'

'I know what you mean. Don't worry about it,' responded Francesca wiping a tear away from the corner of her eye.

'Would it be better if we put this discussion off until later, when you've had time to take it all in?' asked Paul gently. 'You must be feeling terrible.'

'No,' she said, taking hold of his wrist. 'We've got to go over it now while it's all still fresh in our minds. It might be several days before we get chance to discuss it again, and by then it might be too late.'

'OK,' said Paul, wanting to stop her getting worked up – even though he had no idea what she thought it might be too late for.

'What Arturo was trying to unravel, if it succeeds, could endanger the state as we know it... but only a handful of us know about the investigation and none of those who do have the influence to get SISMI involved so quickly.'

'I think,' said Rosa, who had sat quietly and listened since she had brought Francesca home from the hospital, 'that the only logical explanation for SISMI being involved so quickly, is that they were aware that this was going to happen.' They looked at her for a moment in stunned silence. Paul struggled to work out the implications but after a few seconds Francesca nodded.

'I think, you're probably right.'

'So you're saying that SISMI planted the bomb themselves!'

'They won't have planted the bomb themselves but, they will have arranged it while making sure that they were far enough removed from the bombers to prevent exposure if the bombers are caught. What they will have done will have been to make sure that when news of the explosion came through, they were well placed to take control of the investigation before anyone else got hold of it.'

'So what you need to know, ' said Paul thoughtfully, 'is who allocated the investigation to SISMI and then you've got one of the conspirators that Arturo was after.'

'Not quite,' corrected Rosa, 'You'll know the identity of one of the conspirators, but you won't have any actual proof, and the person you identify may not even be one of the most important of them.'

'I need to find an honest magistrate or policeman who's prepared to take over from Arturo, and I need to do it soon. I can't do anything without having some authority behind me.'

The doorbell rang, and Paul went over to the intercom by the door to the apartment.

'*Chi é?*' he asked, and then, as soon as he heard his mother-in-law's voice anxiously identify herself and ask if Francesca was there, '*Si...È aperta,*' as he pressed the button that unlocked the newly replaced street door.

A few seconds later she erupted into the apartment and rushed into the living-room in search of her younger daughter, to be followed in a more measured way by her husband.

'*Ciao*, Paul,' he said, peeling his gloves off and putting them in the pockets of his long camel-hair coat which he then carefully slipped off and hung on one of the hooks by the door. 'How is she?'

'*Ciao*, Guido. Cuts and bruises and fairly shaken up, but she'll be OK... Come through.'

As they entered the living room, Francesca, whose face was just visible over her mother's shoulder, smiled at her father and mouthed, '*Ciao*, Babbo,' then she said gently to her mother, 'I'm fine except for a few bruises – really – but it might be better if you don't squeeze me for a couple of days. 'Her mother quickly released her from her embrace and moved back while still holding her hands.

'I know you'll be OK physically, but it must be terrible losing your... losing a... losing him like that... and right in front of you too.'

'Yes, Mamma, it was horrible but I don't actually remember much about those few minutes and I was on the other side of the door, so it's not as though I saw anything. It was Rosa and Paul who had to deal with the mess.'

'I know that but... he meant a lot more to you.'

Francesca appeared lost in thought for a moment and then said, with a note of urgency in her voice, 'Listen, Mamma... in fact listen all of you. Arturo and I were not in a relationship. We were good friends and we worked together, but there wasn't, and never would have been any romantic ties between us.'

'But we thought...'

'I know, Mamma. And I'm sorry, but there was a reason why we let people think that there was something between us... and I think it's better that anyone outside this room who thought that, continues to believe it.'

'But I don't...'

'It's alright,' broke in her husband. 'If that's what you want, Franci, then that's how it will be. I'm sure that you've got very good reasons. Your mother and I won't ask any more questions about him

– will we Lia?' He smiled at his daughter and looked at his wife with a questioning raised eyebrow.

'*Va bene*,' she agreed with a sigh. 'I'm sure you know best – but if you do feel the need to talk about it, make sure you come and see me.'

Francesca smiled, lifted one of her mother's hands and kissed it. '*Grazie*, Mamma.'

An hour later, the Contes had insisted on taking their younger daughter back to stay with them, and the apartment seemed strangely quiet as the door clicked shut behind them.

'Tea?' said Rosa.

'Please,' he said, although they both knew that the answer was a foregone conclusion. He slipped the CD of Bolero into the hi-fi, replacing the Vivaldi that had been playing earlier, and pressed the 'on' button, before slumping down on the settee.

'It's not like you to put music on,' said Rosa, a couple of minutes later as she brought the mug of tea through and snuggled up alongside him.

He smiled, 'I think I've probably read too many spy stories, I suddenly thought it might be a good idea to put it on while we talk about this. It's all been so hectic, and we were both so shattered when we finally got in last night that I feel as if we haven't spoken to each other since the blast.'

'Franci told me that they weren't together while you and Arturo were in the kitchen last night, so at least that bit wasn't a surprise today.'

'Yes. I wasn't convinced by them and more or less challenged Arturo about it, and he said that they were just friends. He also said that it had been Franci's idea to let people think that there was more to it than that – but he didn't explain why.'

'Franci told me, ' said Rosa, and Paul looked up, 'Arturo was gay and had to find a way of not letting people know.'

'But that's ridiculous. I know he's a magistrate, but so long as he hasn't been a hypocrite and officially denounced homosexuality as evil, or something like that, who cares? There are even some politicians now who are openly gay.'

Rosa shook her head patiently and smiled at him sadly, 'It wasn't for Arturo, it was for his partner... He's a priest.'

'Aaah,' said Paul, 'I can see that that that might cause a few difficulties.'

'Just a few.'

'Adriano!' said Paul, suddenly, and got up and went to the coat-stand from where, after a few seconds rooting through pockets, he extracted the phone that Franci had given him the previous evening. Then, going back into the living room, he held it up to Rosa and explained. 'When Franci was getting into the ambulance last night, she slipped me her phone and asked me to tell "Adriano" what had happened. When I got chance to ring, this Adriano sounded heart-broken.'

'You didn't tell anyone else, did you?' said Rosa, anxiously, giving Paul an earnest look.

'Of course not. I rang from the bathroom while the police were waiting for me to get cleaned up... and I didn't tell SISMI that the reason why Arturo came last night was so that he could ask me to take some surreptitious photographs for him, to help him get the evidence he needed for a major investigation.'

'Wow! And you said...?'

'I said "Yes", of course – but, as he's now dead, you're the only person who knows that and, as he didn't tell me what it was he wanted me to photograph, there's not a lot I can do – unless Franci is able to continue without him.'

'Rosa sat up straight and looked at him with a serious look on her face, 'And you'd still be prepared to do it – even after last night?'

He took both her hands and looked her steadily in the eyes, 'If you tell me not to, I won't.'

'And what about the kids?'

'If I do it, it will be especially for the kids... Can you imagine in ten years' time when they want to know about the family history – what are you going to say? "Your great, great grandfather helped Mussolini into power and your father did nothing when he could have helped prevent another slide into dictatorship," or are you going to say, "Your great, great grandfather helped Mussolini into power but your father helped prevent Italy slipping back into right-wing dictatorship" - it's your decision.'

Rosa smiled and put her arms around him. 'Come on. We'd better make the most of the time we've got – but you'd better put some even louder music on first, if you think there might be people listening!'

Chapter 4

'Well, Signorina. Tell me why you particularly want to work for me, and give me some reasons why I should consider finding a place for you – you have ten minutes.'

'Firstly, let me thank you for seeing me at short notice. I know you're very busy and I know that you don't usually see people in this way... Judge dell'Omodarme told me that you were the only judge who he could be one hundred percent sure was not corrupt, and he said that if anything ever happened to him, then I should come to you and now...' Francesca paused and took a deep breath, 'and now, something has.'

'Signorina. I'm touched by the faith that Judge dell'Omodarme had in me and, it is because of my regard for him, and because I'm aware that you were his... that you were close to him... that I have made an exception to my usual rule in not seeing people who apply for jobs with me without going through the normal channels. However, while you have my deepest sympathy and I am happy to do anything I can to help you, within the regulations, I am unable to give you a position on my staff.'

Francesca gave a slight smile. 'That is pretty much what I expected you say, and I would have been disappointed in both you, and Arturo's judgement, if you had taken a different position, but, you said that I had ten minutes and, if I may, I would like to use the time I have left to tell you why Arturo dell'Omodarme was murdered and what he was working on – which in many ways amount to pretty much the same thing.' She looked Judge Ciancolini in the eye, and he nodded for her to continue. 'By training, I am a journalist, and my ambition was always to be an investigative journalist. Until eight months ago, I worked as a freelance, selling articles here and there and occasionally doing short term contracts with mainstream newspapers and magazines – mainly during the holiday season. A year ago, shortly after the Interior Minister had promised to tighten up the country's morality laws, I was doing an investigation for a piece that would have exposed him as a hypocrite and, in almost any other European country would have brought about his resignation, and possibly a vote of no-confidence in the whole government.'

She glanced at Ciancolini who was frowning, which she knew was because he assumed that she wanted him to take a political stance. 'Bear with me... While he was ostensibly on a skiing holiday in a small, very discreet resort in one of the side valleys of Val d'Aosta, he had several very interesting visitors. Leaving aside the rent-boys, who were the reason why I had followed him there, he also had visits from several very wealthy, very influential people, and also a certain Salvatore Stiappa who I believe is better known as 'Snuff'.' Ciancolini was now looking interested and, as she looked at him, motioned her to continue. 'Fortunately, I had done some research for an article on links between Mafia, Camorra and 'Ndrangheta for *Repubblica*, which they eventually decided not to publish, so I knew who Stiappa was.'

'I managed to persuade a maid in the hotel to allow me to place a microphone in the hotel's conference room which the minister had booked for the following morning. The quality of the recording was not brilliant, but what they seemed to be discussing were plans, firstly to ensure that the leaders of the left are discredited before the elections and, where necessary, to arrange accidents for senior members of the left who pose particular problems for them.'

Colour had been gradually draining from the judge's face as she spoke and now, the pencil which he had unconsciously been tightening his grip on, snapped in half between his fingers. He looked at it, as though amazed that it were there and then looked back at Francesca who was waiting to see how he responded.'

'So you took your information to Judge dell'Omodarme.'

'He had a reputation for honesty, for not being afraid to ruffle people's feathers, and for not being influenced by politicians of either side... fairly similar to your own reputation – it could have been you in that car on Saturday evening.'

'And now you want me to take over from where he left off?' He continued without giving her time to respond, as if the answer was a foregone conclusion. 'I'll need to have all the information that he had – both the initial evidence that you came up with, and any other information he had gathered since he started looking into it – I take it that he has managed to find more evidence and that we are not relying solely on a poor quality recording?'

'When I approached him it turned out that he already had concerns about Rossi's probity but, until he was sure that what I had was what it seemed to be and not just something that I had misinterpreted, he employed me on a casual basis to find more evidence, and then, when he was fully convinced, he took me on full-time, to enable us to work together without depleting his slush fund.'

'His slush fund?'

'Anything that Arturo earned other than his salary, money for writing articles, money for appearing on television discussions and things like that, he kept in a separate account, which he used to fund expenses that he felt it was more secure not to publicise; he called it his 'slush-fund.''

At that moment, the buzzer sounded on the phone on Ciancolini's desk and a red light began flashing. He looked at his watch and pressed the speaker-phone button. 'Yes, Daniela,'

'Advocate Scala is here to go through the notes for the Oddo case with you, Signor Giudice,' came a slightly tinny voice from the speaker on the phone.

'Could you please ask her to take a seat for a moment? I'll just be a couple of minutes.' and he turned the phone off. 'Signorina, I assume that as an investigative journalist you can find out where I live - ' Francesca nodded, 'Come to the back door of my house at nine-thirty this evening. There's a lot we need to talk about.'

He rose, as did she, and he accompanied her to the door. Then, so that his secretary and the waiting lawyer, who Francesca noticed was an attractive brunette with shapely calves protruding from a navy-blue skirt, could both clearly hear, 'And again, my condolences, Signorina – please let me know when the funeral is – Daniela will make sure that I get there.' He shook her hand and his eyes followed her as she left the office.

Chapter 5

Francesca broke off her account as the waiter approached and held out the bottle of wine for Paul to confirm that it was the right one.

'Estroverso' said the waiter, making sure that the brightly coloured label was tilted toward him. Paul nodded and then, as the waiter was about to pour a drop into his glass to be tasted, gestured with his hand that Rosa would do the tasting. The waiter smiled obligingly, poured two centimetres of the rosé into Rosa's glass and then took two steps back to wait while she tried. Paul watched as she took a large sip and held it in her mouth for a few seconds to fully savour the flavour, then she swallowed, smiled and nodded appreciatively to the waiter who stepped forward, half-filled Paul and Francesca's glasses and then added more to Rosa's to bring it to the same level.

'So what happened when you went round to his house?' asked Rosa, as soon as the waiter was out of earshot again.

'He'd obviously done quite a bit of checking up during the afternoon, not just on the Ministro dell'Interno and on Snuff but also on me and on Arturo. He started by asking me to write down everything that we'd discovered so far – a request that I refused of course – and I told him that I was quite happy to go through it verbally. He'd already checked the accommodation records for the Val d'Aosta, so he knew that I was telling the truth about Rossi being there when I said he was, and he's also discovered by cross-checking that several of the other guests in the hotel were using false names. I told him the names of the people I'd recognised and about most of the information that we've been able to put together since then.'

'Why only "most"?' asked Paul.

Francesca gave a smile that suggested genuine amusement, 'Of all the Judges in Tuscany, Ciancolini is probably the most inflexibly moral – that was one of the reasons why I originally went to Arturo, rather than him – For him, everything has to be open and above board whereas some of the ways in which we've gathered information involved illegal surveillance, breaking and entering and what the law would technically describe as 'acts intended to corrupt a public official'. At least for now, it's better that he isn't told exactly how we've gathered information. Obviously, he will need to be told eventually, and I'm sure he suspects that not all the methods we used were legitimate, but I'm banking on him taking the view that the end justifies the means for now, and being pragmatic enough to avoid asking awkward questions.'

There was another pause while the waiter brought out a large platter of *antipasti di mare* for them to start with, then Rosa asked how the judge had reacted to the information Francesca had given him.

'I don't know if you've ever seen him, but he has a fairly pale complexion all the time – well, last night, it just carried on getting whiter and whiter every time I gave him a new bit of information. He didn't say anything while I went through it, just made little noises occasionally to show that he was following. When I'd finished, he stood up, went over to the sideboard and got out what seemed like a very expensive bottle of whisky and two glasses which he filled with very generous measures. '

'But you don't like whisky!' said Rosa.

'No,' said Francesca, 'but if it looks as if the bottle probably cost a week's wages, I can force myself to make an exception – and it would have been rude to let him drink on his own!...Anyway, he asked what I suggested we did next and I told him that we needed more resources but that, especially in the light of what happened to Arturo, the problem would be to make sure that everyone involved was completely trustworthy. He came up with a few names, but some of those were impractical – there's no way that they could be used without having to explain their removal from their current duties – particularly because some of them work for people who, I believe, are involved in the conspiracy.

'So who do you have, who you can rely on?' asked Rosa.

'There's a senior police officer who was already helping Arturo; a brigadier in the National Cybercrime unit, several members of the specialist police bodyguard unit, a sec...'

'The what?' interrupted Paul.

'The specialist police bodyguard unit – it was set up after Borsellino and Falcone, so that escorts assigned to public figures who are considered to be at risk, are assigned highly trained specialists with anti-terror experience to babysit for them. Ciancolini is a long-time friend of the Assistant Head of the squad and when a credible threat to Ciancolini's life is received shortly, four officers who are completely above suspicion will be assigned – ostensibly to protect him, but actually, they'll be working for us, gathering information amongst other things. We should also be able to get someone assigned as part of the Ministro dell'Interno's security detail.' Paul nodded his approval. 'The secretary of a major financier who we know to be involved, a variety of other people who work for various ministries and businesses and...' Francesca looked at Paul, 'you! That is, if you're still happy to help even though you're seen what the consequences can be.'

'Paul's with you all the way,' said Rosa, before Paul could open his mouth, 'We've talked it through; we're clear about the consequences; we've taken the kids into account, and we're both a hundred percent with you.'

Francesca leaned over and hugged her sister, with a tear in her eye. 'Thankyou.'

The arrival of the first course, a large bowl of *linguini allo scoglio* which was placed in the centre of the table so that they could help themselves once they had finished the amounts that the waiter lifted into their plates, brought another halt to the conversation, which was not resumed until the two sisters had finished theirs and Paul was finishing off the contents of the serving dish.

'So will you be working directly for Ciancolini?' Rosa asked her sister.

'Yes... and no,' said Francesca, causing Rosa to raise her eyebrows quizzically and Paul to pause with a forkful of *linguini* poised in front of his mouth. 'Ciancolini thinks, and, once I was over the initial shock, I agree with him, that if I go from being the assistant of one judge who was seen as being a determined campaigner against corruption to being the assistant of the judge who most resembles him, it will not only flag up to those who killed Arturo that Ciancolini is going to take over, but it will also make me seem to be more important than the image of the brainless bimbo who only got the job because of her legs, that Arturo and I had cultivated.' She held up a hand to indicate to Rosa that she shouldn't interrupt. 'However, what Ciancolini has done is speak to Judge Graziadei. He's told Graziadei that I've been to see him to ask about a post and that obviously, while he's not prepared to take me on without my going through the official entrance exam route, he does feel a bit bad about not being able to help me even though I've just lost Arturo. As he expected, Graziadei said that he'd be able to find me a place in his office.'

'I don't get it,' said Paul, who had now cleaned the serving dish with a piece of bread. 'Surely, if Ciancolini can't employ you – and I get the reasons for that – then surely you're better off having free time than just any old job with another judge.'

Francesca gave a broad smile, 'Graziadei's in his seventies now; he should have taken his pension and ridden off into the sunset years ago. Everyone knows that he's lost it and, as a result he only gets assigned to very simple cases, and not very many of those. There are already three others who work for him and they have very little to do – at least one of them spends most of the day on Facebook and apparently they can pop out for a coffee or even to do their shopping whenever they like. They say that he's always liked having his office full of young women, and in the past, if you wanted to work there, you had to be prepared to do plenty of 'overtime', but apparently he can't manage it anymore, although he still likes to keep his office full of women, because he thinks it makes people think that he's still 'got it'.' Rosa pulled a face registering distaste but Francesca continued, 'the good thing is, that once I'm in there, I'll have access to all the computer systems, as well as having pretty much all the free time I need.'

'And I thought that we wanted to save this country from corruption!' said Paul with mock seriousness.

'Dream on!' said Francesca, as the main courses arrived.

Conversation was limited as they worked their way through the carefully prepared fish dishes they had ordered and, what there was, was almost exclusively about the way the fish had been prepared and how it was still not easily to find a restaurant in Florence that served good fish at affordable prices. 'Let's hope no-one waxes lyrical on TripAdvisor,' said Rosa, or we'll never be able to get a table.'

'No,' said Paul, 'it's too far from the centre; you won't get many tourists prepared to walk as far as Ponte della Vittoria. This is for locals and well informed food lovers only.'

'Let's hope you're right,' said Rosa.

Chapter 6

Paul put down his red pencil, leaned back from his improvised desk and felt his vertebrae creak back into position as he pushed his shoulders back after two hours of marking dictations. It was a good job that no more than half the class ever turned up, he thought; life would be unbearable if he had twice as much marking to do. Or probably, he thought, more than twice the marking, as the ones who did attend classes regularly tended to be the more able students who were far less likely to make stupid mistakes. No doubt, when the exam results came out, there would be a queue of disgruntled students waiting to see him, suggesting that he may have inadvertently under-marked them, or that he had been unduly harsh in his marking because he didn't like them. When he suggested that they may want to consider whether there might be some correlation between their level of lesson attendance and their performance in exams, the odd one would see the light, but the majority would see it as confirmation that he was biased against them because they had missed his lessons – it was the same every exam session, and probably always would be for as long as every student who had passed their *maturitá*, even if they had scraped through with the bare minimum of marks, was entitled to sign up to do a degree with the *Facoltá di Lettere* and attempt to do a language degree.

The university authorities had no interest in discouraging students, providing that they paid their annual fees, and the Professors, who should have been helping students, were more interested in ensuring that more students were signed up with them than with their colleagues or, as Paul considered would be a more appropriate term, rivals. He still remembered vividly an experience from the end of his first year as a *lettore*; some days after the exam results had been posted on the noticeboard, and after the students had had their official opportunity to queue to harangue the *lettori* who had marked the papers, he had been sheepishly approached by a student in a bar near the university. Unlike the majority of those who had failed, this was a girl who had attended most of the lessons; her work was always round about the pass mark, although it tended to be just below rather than just above. She could make herself understood easily while speaking English, despite a tendency to use Italian grammatical constructions rather than English ones – the problem was, that when she wrote, even when being dictated to, she did the same and had to be marked down for it. She was a pleasant girl, a few years older than most of the other students, if fact, a few years older than Paul himself. He played over the scene in his head: He had been lost in thought and she must have been standing next to him for a few seconds before she had timidly attracted his attention; *'Mi scusi, Professore.'*

'Oh, *ciao*, Giuliana. Can I get you a coffee?' She had declined with a smile and a shake of the head.

'I'm sorry I couldn't get to the feedback appointment session on Wednesday. I'm afraid I had to go and visit my grandmother in hospital.'

With many of the students, he would have only pretended to believe the excuse, but as Giuliana attended regularly, he had no doubt that she was telling the truth. 'Don't worry. I realise that some things in life are far more important than queuing for five minutes feedback from a *lettore* in English. What can I do for you? Let's sit down at this table.'

'I was wondering, if you could give me any tips about how to improve my performance in examinations – about how to improve my English.'

They had talked at length, and it emerged that while he had assumed that she had started university later than her peers, she had actually started at the same time but had taken eight years to get to the third year of the notionally four year course. It appeared that his colleagues and previous *lettori*, had always been very encouraging when she had been to see them, telling her that she had just been unlucky on the day and shouldn't be disheartened. Although he knew that it would be easy for him to do the same thing, tell her how encouraged he'd been by her improvement during the year, and how persistence would be rewarded in the end, he had decided to be honest. He had explained, as gently as possible, how some people, if they started learning languages fairly late, found it difficult to train their brains to automatically switch into the different type of thought patterns that were fundamental to different languages. He had told her honestly that, if she continued to resit the exams in every session, sooner or later she would get the minimum pass mark and would be able to move on until she was finally in a position to write her thesis and be awarded her degree. 'But,' he had said, 'you will pass with the minimum mark, or somewhere very close to that.

If you want to pass a degree for the satisfaction of being able to call yourself, *"Dottoressa"* then that's fine – but by the time you are awarded your degree, you'll be very close to, or maybe even over, the maximum age for sitting the public entrance exams for jobs which require a degree without specifying a high mark.'

Seemingly unaware of the tears that were running down her face, she had asked him what she should do, and he had pointed out that there were many businesses that did not require employees to have degrees, particularly in the hospitality sector, and that she had lots of qualities, not least the ability to communicate with clients in spoken English that would help her be successful. She had been silent for what had seemed like ages but had finally looked at him through the tears and said, 'Thankyou, *Professore...* but why has nobody ever explained this to me before?'

All he had been able to do was shake his head and say, 'I don't know, Giuliana. I'm very sorry,' he had never seen her again.

'Are you OK?' asked Rosa, putting her hands on his shoulders and bringing him out of his reverie.

He brought his left hand up, placed it on top of hers over his right shoulder and tilted his head to the right so that it rested momentarily on the hands. 'Yeah, just reflecting on the benefits of a university education.'

She laughed, 'I think I can rescue you from your boredom – Franci sent me a message.' He lifted his head and twisted round to look at her. 'The message said that they need you to take some pictures for a travel article in Rome.'

He gripped her hand more tightly. 'Did she say when?'

'No. It was just that simple message. For some reason, I think she's a bit wary of what she puts on her phone.' Paul inclined his head to show that he had understood.

'Can you find out what time she finishes work and tell her I'll be there to pick her up so she can tell me more about the client.'

She kissed him, 'Do what you need to do... but be careful.'

He would have liked to have used his motorbike but even though he could have taken a spare helmet in the back-box, it would be far too cold for Francesca to travel pillion wearing clothes suitable for a heated office, and so regretfully he took Rosa's tired old Panda instead. Although there were plenty of armed police around outside the *Tribunale di Firenze*, there were no traffic wardens to be seen and the police seemed to consider enforcing traffic regulations as beneath their dignity, so he was able to pull the Panda onto the narrow central reservation to wait for Francesca to come out. If anyone really wanted to destroy the justice system in Florence, placing a car-bomb here would be a simple matter, he thought with a shudder.

There was a steady flow of people entering and exiting the building but, as it approached six-thirty, there were less and less people going in and those exiting became a steady stream. Finally, he spotted Francesca and made his way across the road as she looked around for him. She saw him as he crossed, said a quick goodbye to two colleagues with whom she had exited the building and then joined him, air-kissing both sides of his face.

'Over there,' he said, nodding vaguely in the direction of the Panda and gently taking her arm to steer her through the traffic.'

'I take it, you got the message then... Where are we off to now?'

'Apparently you're expected at your parents', so I thought I'd give you a lift up there... or at least as far as the Piazzale... You can tell me all about my new book when we arrive, and I can take a couple of shots while I'm there... I've got a new lens to try out.'

They were both quiet on the journey: traffic was very heavy until after Porta Romana, and even if Paul had wanted to use the journey to talk, he wouldn't have been able to concentrate.

The sky was a slate grey and relatively few tourists had ventured up to Piazzale Michelangelo although there were still enough there to make them appear inconspicuous when Paul parked the Panda near the statue of David. Without bothering to lock the shabby car, they walked over towards the low wall around the Piazza, where Paul set up his tripod and carefully attached the body of his camera. Francesca watched silently as he took what appeared to her to be a ridiculously long lens out of his bag and carefully screwed it onto the front of the camera.

'What's that?'

'That is a one-fifty to five-hundred millimetre zoom lens. With this, I should be able to take sharp, high quality photographs, at a distance. Which may come in useful to photograph some of the buildings I'm going to see.'

She smiled, 'I hope that's not all you've got. There'll be times when you need to get in fairly close.. and hopefully, not be noticed... That one seems to be shouting out, "look at me and say cheese".'

'Don't worry. I can be discreet. I won't just be taking this... Now, tell me what I need to do in Rome.'

Francesca became serious. 'It's not just in Rome. The train you'll be getting will be the five to five from Florence on Wednesday; that gets into Chiusi just before half past six, where you'll need to change... Yes, I know... there are plenty of trains where you wouldn't need to change,' she said, holding up a hand to forestall his objections. 'But, the next train from Chiusi to Roma Termini is at five past seven, and we know that Girolomo Vercellese, the Under-secretary for Defence has booked a seat on that train, and we'd like you to be on the same train.'

'I take it that you believe he's one of the conspirators.'

She nodded, 'We have good information to suggest that his main reason for going to Rome is to meet up with some of the other conspirators and to have separate meetings with at least some of the hit-men who they intend to use. What we don't know is where any of these meetings are due to take place. We do have access to his work diary, which his secretary very helpfully keeps on a spreadsheet, and we know that these meetings will not be taking place while he is the ministry. It is possible that he may be meeting someone on the train, on the way to Rome, but it's more likely that meetings will take place in Rome, either in the evening or very early in the morning. What we need you to do is to be near enough to him on the train to be able to photograph anyone he speaks to, and then to keep an eye on him on the platform in Rome.'

'What about the rest of the evening?' asked Paul, 'surely the best time for a clandestine meeting would be in the evening when everywhere's dark.'

'We may be light on numbers, but we can scrape up a few people in the capital who we can rely on. If he requests an official car to meet him at the station, his request will go to one of our people inside the Specialist Police Bodyguard Unit, who will assign another of our people as his driver.'

'So I'm just there to possibly take pictures on the train?' asked Paul, who was surprised to feel a twinge of disappointment.

Francesca shook her head. 'No. On Thursday and Friday, you'll be taking artistic photographs to illustrate a book on significant post-renaissance buildings in Rome – which just happens to include most government departments. Someone will contact you in the morning to let you know which buildings to focus on, and in particular, which windows in those buildings require particular attention. Obviously, you'll need to do some general shots as well, just in-case you're challenged by anyone who needs to see proof that the pictures are for a book.'

'Obviously,' said Paul, drily. 'Do I get my own train tickets and arrange my own accommodation, or is there a Moneypenny involved?'

Francesca looked at him blankly and then repeated, 'Moneypenny?' but this time with a rising intonation at the end and a slightly furrowed brow.

'The name's Bond – James Bond,' said Paul in a terrible attempt to put on a Scottish accent. 'Did you never watch any Bond films? Moneypenny is Bond's boss's secretary; she usually sorts out transport and accommodation details – never mind, I'll get my own ticket and find some accommodation when I get there. I doubt many places will be full up at this time of year.'

Francesca pulled a small note-book out of her shoulder bag, wrote something in it and then pulled the page out and offered it to Paul. 'Here you are, Mr Bond. When you know where you're staying, call that number – and remember... you're married to my sister, so don't try and be too like Bond.

Paul laughed. 'Come on, I'll take you up to your parents' house. I'd better come in and say "Hello", or they'll be offended.

As Francesca turned her key in the door, Paul thought back to the first time he'd been invited to the house, nearly twenty years earlier; after plucking up the courage to ring the bell, he'd wanted to run before the door was opened – now, going into his in-laws' house felt almost as comfortable as walking into his own home. The last door on the right in the hallway was closed but, even though the door was a thick one, it did not stop the sound of loud classical music leaking into the rest of the house. Paul smiled, 'I take it Nonna's hearing continues to get worse.' Francesca half turned towards him and managed to shrug her shoulders, roll her eyes and shake her head all at the same time. She continued and went through the door at the end of the corridor, into the kitchen-diner where her mother was chopping vegetables. '*Ciao*, Mamma – I'm back.'

'*Ciao*, Franci. How was your day?' and Lia carefully put her knife down and turned to embrace her daughter, before catching sight of Paul. 'Paul! What a nice surprise. What are you doing here?'

'*Ciao*. I found that I'd got too many of your daughters, so I thought I'd better choose one and return the other.' He kissed his mother-in law on both cheeks. 'Actually, I was near the Tribunal and realised it was just about Franci's finishing time, so I thought I'd save her the trouble of having to take two buses to get home... What are you cooking?' he asked, looking over her shoulder.

'Nothing much tonight, just a vegetable soup and then some veal liver. Why, are you staying for tea?'

'No. Not tonight, thanks. Rosa's expecting me, and I know she bought a nice piece of salmon this morning. I wouldn't say no to a coffee though.'

'Can you make it yourself, while I get on with this.'

He turned to get the coffee maker and the coffee out of the cupboard. 'Do you want one?'

'No thanks, but you'd better ask Nonna. Her sense of smell is still very good, and she'll complain about being forgotten about, if you don't ask her.'

Paul laughed, 'I'll make the coffee first, and then ask her. If I go through now, she'll keep me talking for ages before I can make the coffee... How is she?' he asked as he spooned the coffee into the holder above the water.'

'Difficult... or to use one of your English words, cantankerous. She won't have a hearing-aid, so she just turns her music up higher and higher and then complains that we're all whispering, so she can't hear what we're saying. And until they agree to give her a hip replacement, she's more or less stuck in her chair – which she hates – and that means that she's generally in a bad mood.

Once the espresso had bubbled through into the top of the coffee-maker, he placed the coffee maker, two espresso cups and the sugar bowl onto a small tray and carried the tray through to the corridor. With his free hand he knocked twice, quite hard, on his grand-mother-in-law's door and then, without waiting for a reply, opened the door and entered, almost shouting, *'permesso'*. The old woman turned towards him in her chair and peered through the dark eyes that were now veiled by cataracts. He placed the tray on the small table in-front of her and took one of her hands in his. *'Buonasera*, Maddi. I've brought you a coffee.'

'I didn't ask for a coffee,' she said, somewhat petulantly while reaching out to the other side to lower the music.

'That's alright,' replied Paul, cheerfully. 'I don't mind drinking two. How's the hip? Any news?'

'No... I'm thinking of asking the hospital to take me off the waiting list.' She waited for his response, but he said nothing and just gave her hand a squeeze, so after a while she continued. 'I'm eighty-five. Even if they find me a new hip in six months, what am I going to do with it? I can't see properly, I can't hear properly – even if I tell Lia and Guido that I can. There must be lots of younger people on the waiting list whose lives would be transformed by the opportunity of having a new hip... it's far better that one of them gets moved higher up the waiting list.' She stopped again, and after a few seconds, when she realised that he wasn't going to going to argue with her, said, 'Well. What have you got to say about that?'

Paul said nothing until he'd poured the two coffees and placed one in her hand, then, 'What do you want me to say? Knowing you, it's probably what I would have expected – being prepared to sacrifice yourself to help others. Were you expecting me to try and change your mind?... Because I'm not. So long as they give you plenty of pain relief for the hip, and move you up the list for the cataract operation, then I'm happy. But,' and he made his tone of voice more solemn, 'you must do something about your hearing. It's not fair on Lia and Guido that you have to play your music so loud – you can almost hear it down in the Piazzale!'

'Alright,' she said, sulkily, 'I'll try,' and he smiled, confident that she would not be able to see the smile through her cataracts.

'And you can stop smirking. Even if I can't see you, I know what you're doing... Tell me about Rosa and the kids; how're they doing?'

'As usual, Rosa is wonderful: happy, healthy and wise. The kids got back from their skiing trip yesterday, and haven't stopped talking about it since – especially Alessio, with it being his first time. We've had to promise to take them up to Abetone for the day, as soon as we have a free Sunday.'

The old lady leaned back in her chair and closed her eyes for a moment. 'I remember when we were girls – your grandmother and I – up in the Val d'Aosta; I remember being terrified at first, but being determined not to get left behind. Chiara was very good – never afraid of anything but, once we came back to Tuscany, we never got the chance to go again.'

They chatted for a few more minutes; Paul was still always pleased when she reminisced about his own grandmother who had died after giving birth to his father. Finally, he kissed her again, replaced the Bolero CD, although at a slightly lower volume, and returned the coffee things to the kitchen.

'I'd better be going,' he said to Lia, 'Rosa will be wondering where I've got to. Say "Bye" to Franci for me, and say "Hello" to Guido when he gets in.'

She gave a little laugh. 'I will, if I'm still awake when he gets in. I thought we'd have lots of free time together when he retired from teaching but, since he got elected to the Council, he seems to have more work to do than ever. I'll have to tie him down on Sunday to make sure he's here when you all come round for your dinner.'

'You do that. Bye.'

'Bye, Paul. - Mwah, Mwah.'

Chapter 7

At half past four on the Wednesday, Paul joined the queue outside the ticket office in Florence's Santa Maria Novella station, ready to shuffle forwards each time the number over one of the windows of the Biglietteria flashed to indicate that they were ready for another customer. While in the queue, he used the time to observe his fellow passengers, trying to work out if anyone was keeping an eye on him. He wasn't quite sure what he was looking for; he knew that, unlike in films, anyone given the task of tailing him would probably be too professional to be spotted but, as far as he could ascertain, no-one behind him in the queue looked the least bit suspicious and, if they were in-front of him in the queue, then they would have fun buying their ticket, as they couldn't know where he was going.

Eventually he bought his ticket and went and stood on the platform next to the one he really wanted, where a train was leaving for Piombino, five minutes after his own train was due to leave. He waited until he heard the doors of his train slam closed and saw the guard start to raise his flag; he turned, darted across to the nearest door, wrenched it open and leapt in, closing the door behind him and immediately leaning out of the window to see if anyone else was following his example. No-one was. When his heartbeat slowed down again after the sudden burst of energy, he made his way along to a half-empty carriage, placed his large black rucksack onto the luggage rack, and sat down, giving a respectful nod to the elderly couple who sat opposite him.

The seat next to him was occupied from Figline onwards by a seminary student, who, when Paul entered, was just finishing explaining to the elderly couple that he was returning to Rome after visiting his family. Almost immediately, the student took out a breviary and began to read out loud, albeit in a low voice. The couple opposite looked on approvingly while Paul pretended to drop off to sleep, a pretence which soon turned into the real thing.

It was the tinny announcer's voice coming in from the platform at an intermediary stop, that woke him up again and, once he had assured himself that he had not dozed for too long, he determined to stay awake for the remaining stretch until Chiusi, although he leaned his head on the window and stared fixedly through it, to dissuade any of his fellow travellers from trying to draw him into conversation. Finally, after stopping with no explanation for five minutes in the middle of nowhere, just outside Chiusi, the train creaked into motion again and edged its way into the station.

Paul was one of only three people to descend from the train at the station and he watched the other two scurry off in different directions, before making his way to the toilets to give himself an excuse for having got off but not left the station. Once he had heard the train pull away, he rushed out of the toilets, swore at the tail lights that were disappearing into the distance, and, putting on his most concerned expression, asked the time of the next train for Rome.

'You're in luck,' said the porter to whom he had addressed the question, 'there's one at five past – gets into Rome at about twenty to nine. You didn't leave any of your things on the other train, did you?'

'No. Luckily. I took my bag with me when I went to the toilet... Oh. Is the station buffet open?'

The porter shook his head. ' 'Fraid not; there are problems with the roof. You've got time for a quick coffee over the road though.'

Paul thanked the porter and made his way across to the bar; it would give him the opportunity to see Vercellese arrive and also to see if he had any kind of escort. It also, of course, gave him the opportunity to grab a sandwich as, by the time he'd found somewhere to stay, it would probably be quite late to find somewhere to eat in Rome.

He saw Vercellese step out onto the platform just after the usual tinny distant voice erupted from the station's public address system; 'The next train to arrive at platform two will be the nineteen o five express to Roma Termini, calling at Orvieto, Orte and Settebagni. This train will terminate at Roma Termini. Please keep away from the edge of the platform.' The train clattered slowly into the station two minutes later and Vercellese stepped up to the door of the first first-class carriage as soon as the doors began to open. He stepped to one side to let a man get off and then entered the carriage and made his way along towards the far end where a double seat was free, placed his travelling bag down on one and sat down on the other. Paul waited until two other travellers had got into the carriage before getting on himself, and then made his way to a seat, two behind Vercellese. The advantage, he thought, of being close to the end of the carriage was that if Vercellese did meet anyone, by visiting the toilet, he would get the change to take photographs as he went past – so long as he were careful.

The seat next to Vercellese remained unoccupied. At Orte, a woman paused in the corridor by Vercellese and gave a pointed look at the bag that was occupying a seat, but he ignored her and, after a moment, she clearly decided that she didn't fancy an argument and moved on to the next carriage.

Paul had just switched off the small camera in his coat pocket when, Settebagni, the last stop before Rome was announced. To his surprise, Vercellese began to button up his coat and put his hand on his bag. Not wishing to risk losing him, Paul slipped out of his seat and made his way back down the carriage until he was by the door; if Vercellese got out at the front of the carriage, he would be able to follow him and, if he didn't get off, then neither would Paul. He tried to remember everything he knew about Settebagni, and realised that it amounted to more or less nothing. He had certainly never been in his twenty years in Italy, and didn't recall even having driven through it. This could be difficult.

To Paul's relief, Vercellese ignored the two taxis that were standing outside the station, a fug of smoke emerging from the partially opened window of the second car in line where the two drivers were sitting waiting for fares. He turned left and strode confidently along a pleasant tree-lined avenue with Paul following at a reasonable distance on the other side of the road. After about three hundred metres, Vercellese turned to the left along a smaller road which Paul realised must take them over to the other side of the railway line.

As Paul carefully turned the corner, he saw Vercellese disappear into a tunnel under the railway where he was silhouetted by a wall lamp at the far end, and from where the echo of his footsteps could clearly be heard. Paul kept as close to the side of the road as he could, reaching the start of the tunnel just as Vercellese emerged from the other end. Quickly he slipped his shoes off to avoid the echo alerting his quarry, and made his way through as quickly as possible, hoping that Vercellese didn't turn around while he passed under the bright light. Fortunately, he didn't.

Vercellese turned to the right after the tunnel and walked along a narrow road, parallel to the railway-line for over half a mile before turning up a lane to the left towards what appeared to be open countryside. After another two hundred yards he stopped by a large gate, leaned towards one of the gate-posts – talking into an intercom, Paul assumed – and then disappeared through the gates, which Paul heard clang shut behind him. Once he had been swallowed up by the trees, Paul made his way cautiously to the gates. As he had suspected, there was an intercom panel on one of the gate posts with a small video screen. He looked around and saw a video camera mounted on the other gate-post and noted with relief that the record indicator light was not illuminated; it must only be activated when the bell was pushed, or when some other sensor triggered it. The name plate below the intercom was blank.

Paul continued up the road for another hundred yards to see if he could see anything through the trees, but other than faint lights indicating that there was some kind of building, he could see nothing. Leaving the road on the opposite side to the house in the woods, he made his way back through the trees, which were much sparser on that side, until he was almost opposite the gates. There, he took out another camera, put in a thousand ASA film, the fastest he had, and attached it to a small tripod, which he clamped firmly to the tree trunk. He looked at his watch – just after nine. He would give it until ten-thirty and if he hadn't seen anything by then, make his way back to the station and hope to get into Rome to find some accommodation.

Just after ten he heard the sound of car engines and quickly extracted his hands from under his armpits where he had been keeping them in an attempt to stop them going numb with cold. A few seconds later, a yellow light began to flash on top of one of the gate-posts and there was a faint bleeping as the gates began to swing slowly back. The first car to emerge was a dark-blue or black Mercedes with heavily tinted glass so he couldn't see the occupants; the second car, however, had normal glass and he fired off a sequence of shots, hoping that Francesca, or the people she was working with, would be able to make something of them. After the cars sped off into the distance and the gates closed again, he waited five minutes until he was sure that no-one else was coming out and then packed his equipment up and made his way back to the station.

It was after midnight when he emerged from the station in Rome and not fancying either the cheap, open-all-hours, no-questions-asked, rooms-available-by-the-hour hotels very close to the station, or any of the upmarket hotels where people with money to burn could turn up at any time of day and receive five star service, he made his way over to the taxi rank.

'There's a twenty euro tip for you if you can find me a reasonably priced hotel in Trastevere, that doesn't have rats.'

The taxi-driver smiled. 'Hop in. I know just the place for you.'

Fifteen minutes later the taxi pulled up outside a fairly plain façade on Via Mameli in Trastevere. 'It doesn't seem very open,' said Paul doubtfully.

'Trust me,' said the driver cheerfully, 'I want that twenty euro tip, then I can knock-off early for the night.' He got out and walked up to the door. Paul watched from the car, still doubtful. The driver pressed the door-bell three times and then took a pace back as he waited for a reply. The next thirty seconds seemed interminable to Paul, but the driver seemed relaxed until finally he leaned forwards and spoke into the intercom. Then he stood up, half turned to face the car and beckoned to Paul, who got out of the car with his bag in his hand.

As he reached the taxi-driver and the door of the hotel, the door opened and a man who had obviously thrown some clothes on quickly stood at the door. 'Client for you, uncle,' said the taxi-driver, 'Any chance of a coffee.' The hotelier nodded to the driver and smiled at Paul.'

'*Buonasera*. If you'd like to follow me through into the reception, I'll take your details and sort a key out for you – Giuseppe. Make yourself a coffee, and make one for the *signore* as well, if he'd like one.'

Paul slipped thirty euros into the driver's hand and was about to refuse the coffee automatically but then changed his mind.

'That would be very nice – if you're sure it's no trouble.'

'He's making one anyway, so it's no trouble at all.'

Paul filled in the registration form and the hotelier took his ID card to photocopy it. 'I expected you to give me a passport,' said the man, conversationally, 'I didn't think you looked Italian.'

'I'm not,' said Paul, ' but I've lived here a long time now and I'm officially Resident.'

'And how many nights will you be staying with us for?'

'At the moment, just three nights. Although there's a chance I may need to come back to Rome again some time during the next few weeks, so I may be back if you're not full.'

'Just give me a ring first to check, but there shouldn't be any problem until we get closer to Easter.'

The taxi-driver came through from the back room and handed Paul a coffee with a smile. 'I'm off now. Glad to have been of assistance, *Signore – Ciao* Zio. See you soon.' And he was gone.

As the hotelier led Paul to his room, he pointed out a room to one side where breakfast would be available between six-thirty and ten, and another door which he said led out to the back, 'In Summer, most people breakfast out there, in the courtyard, but it's a bit cold for that at the moment.

The room was larger than he had expected with a high window, which he imagined must let a lot of light in. The decoration looked to have been done fairly recently and with a fair amount of taste and the furniture looked reasonably new. A desk under the window held a tray with drinks making facilities and a selection of biscuits. There were two cupboards under the desk and the hotelier explained that one was a mini-bar and the other a safe. Instructions for setting a combination for the safe were on the inside of the door, which was currently unlocked. There was a shower room to one side of the room where soap, shampoo, a disposable toothbrush and mini tube of toothpaste had been provided. Paul expressed his approval to the hotelier and wished him goodnight then, after waiting five minutes to ensure that the man was out of earshot, he picked up the phone and rang the number Francesca had given him. There was a bleep as the phone went straight to answer-phone mode without any preliminary message.

'Oh, hello,' said Paul, caught slightly off guard by the lack of a message, then he pulled himself together. He identified himself, gave the address of the hotel, and said that he had a film that needed developing as soon as possible, '...but don't come round too early, I've only just got here,' he ended and hung up.

Chapter 8

'Well, well! Look who's here,' said the tall man who opened the door. With his left hand still on the inner door handle, he leaned across and rested his muscular right forearm on the opposite door jamb, blocking the doorway. 'Three weeks without so much as a phone call and then you just turn up on the doorstep as though you only left this morning.'

'Give me a break, Marco. I've been busy – things have been a bit tough recently. I'm here now, and there's nowhere I'd rather be... I brought you this as a peace offering,' and Francesca held up a bottle of Brunello di Montalcino, '...but don't open it straight away... I'm desperately in need of a cuddle first.' She smiled and he released his hold on the door-handle and took his other arm off the door jamb, then he leaned forward and, putting his arms round her, lifted her onto tiptoe and kissed her. When they'd finished, he hooked his foot around her bag, pulled it through the door in to the apartment and then, turning, pushed the door shut with his other foot.

Fifty minutes later he managed to tear his gaze away from her breasts as they gently rose and fell with her breathing as she slept, slipped quietly out of bed, carefully pulled up a sheet to stop her getting cold and went through to the shower.

After a quarter of an hour, he placed two coffees on the bedside table next to Francesca and sat on the edge of the bed. Sliding his hand under the sheet, he gently caressed her and bent over to wake her with a kiss on the lips. Her eyes opened, initially with an alarmed, preoccupied look, then they focussed on his face and she smiled. 'I've made you a coffee... don't worry, it's decaf. Drink it, then cover yourself up while you talk to me – I want to be able to concentrate on what you're saying.'

'Talk about what?' the hand that had continued to caress her stopped and squeezed her flesh instead. 'Oww! What was that for?'

'Don't bullshit me. The Francesca Conte I know – My Francesca Conte – would never admit that things had "been a bit tough", unless things were really, really serious and you wouldn't have come here when you're worried, if you didn't think I could help.'

She turned her head away from him and appeared to study the Robert Doisneau on the opposite wall for a minute before turning round again. Finally she turned back, 'When I set off, I had decided to tell you everything, then the closer the train got to Rome, the more doubts I had, until you opened the door, and I thought it was better not to...' She stopped and he withdrew his hand and folded his arms in front of himself, clearly not satisfied with the explanation, if it could be called that, and waiting for her to continue. With a sigh, she recommenced, 'We always said that we wouldn't involve ourselves with each other's work – that work and pleasure had to be kept separate.'

He shook his head, 'Not quite. If I remember right, it was your idea because you said that if you ever wrote about anything where the information could be traced back to me, it would ruin my career. You were the one who justified that by saying that the same protection should be extended to your work. It was just a fiction to make me feel better about not giving you information – it didn't really make any difference to me whether I knew the details of your investigative journalism or not – so it might be a good idea if you trust me and tell me what the problem is.'

After a moment's thought, she sighed. 'Let me slip something on and we'll go and sit at the table.' and she sat up and slid a long, shapely leg over the side of the bed. He noticed that the sign of her bikini brief could still be seen quite clearly, despite it being February and his mind wondered idly whether she had been using a sun lamp. Her idea of "slipping something on" amounted to putting one of his cotton shirts on which hung down at the front and left very little to the imagination. Concentration would be hard, he thought.

He was wrong. Once he heard that she had come within seconds of being killed by the car bomb in Florence that he'd read about and that if she hadn't mislaid the lipstick that he'd given her as part of her Christmas present, she would have been in the car when it exploded, all thoughts of sex left his mind. It took two hours for Francesca to fill him in with all the details; every time she tried to summarise events and evidence, he stopped her and insisted that she went over every detail, pointing out that if he were going to help he needed all the information and, if she were ever going to be able to present her evidence in court, she needed to make sure there were no weak points.

'So that's where we are now. My brother-in-law is somewhere in Rome, ready to produce photographic evidence of any meetings that take place; we have a few policemen who we trust absolutely, assigned to protection duties to some of those we know are involved and Snuff is under surveillance.'

'But, even with all those, it will be difficult to get enough evidence that will stand up in court...' Francesca looked at him expectantly. 'So what you really need are recordings of meetings that take place in places that they think are secure... for which you really need a security consultant who has some experience of breaking and entering – even if, that security consultant is currently on parole, and will go to jail for ten years if he is found doing something illegal... like bugging government offices.'

She took his hand. 'Now do you realise why I decided that I couldn't ask you to help? The risk for you is too great.'

'And if I don't help, and you don't get your evidence, what happens then?' Francesca looked down and didn't reply. 'I'll tell you what happens then – Prodi and other centre-left leaders are assassinated, almost certainly with collateral damage, as the Americans would call it; the wishy-washy part of the current government looks too weak to do anything about it, and the right wing members of the coalition will use their power over the media to convince enough of the masses that the problems can only be solved by stronger government, even if that means sacrificing democracy. A majority of the senior ranks in the military would welcome martial law being imposed and would give their public support to a supposed government of technocrats... Does that sound about right to you?'

She gave a slight nod – an unhappy look on her face. He continued, 'And what's going to happen to outspoken opponents, and people like you and me who they would probably class as subversives? I like the Tuscan archipelago but I don't fancy spending the next twenty years on a prison colony there – even if you are able to wave at me a couple of times a year from the women's section.'

Chapter 9

Drnnng...drnnng...drnnng...drnnng...drnnng...   It took Paul nearly thirty seconds to wake up, work out what had woken him up and then to locate the telephone and press the right button.

'*Si*...' hoarsely, then he cleared his throat, 'err Paul Caddick.'

'*Buongiorno*, Signor Caddick,' came a fairly deep female voice with a distinct Roman accent, 'a gentleman from your office has arrived to see you.'

'Oh. O.K... What time is it?'

'It's five past eight, *Signore*.'

'Could you please tell him that I'll be down in ten minutes, and tell him I'd be delighted if he'd join me for breakfast.'

'Certainly, *Signore*.'

Paul showered quickly and then, after dressing hurriedly, slipped the film he'd taken out of his camera into his pocket and made his way down to reception. There was no-one behind the desk but he followed the smell of coffee through to the room that the hotelier had indicated was the breakfast room. He found himself in a luminous, cream coloured room with diaphanous white curtains framing a large window that gave onto a courtyard where several large plants had been wrapped in insulation to protect them from frost.

A woman, who he guessed to be in her mid-fifties and who he assumed to be the hotelier's wife, was busy at the coffee machine preparing a cappuccino and a handsome, strong looking man in his thirties was sitting looking relaxed at one of the tables looking at a copy of *Il Messaggero*, Rome's daily newspaper.

'*Buongiorno*,' said Paul, with a smile towards the woman, and then made his way over to the man at the table who started to rise. Paul stopped him with a gesture and then with a smile sat down opposite him.

'*Buongiorno*, Paul,' said the man, and Paul understood that, as the man was meant to be someone he worked with, that he was not going to get an introduction, at least while the woman was in the room. 'Did you sleep well?'

'Yes, thankyou. Very well... although I was very late getting here as I got delayed on the way,' he glanced at the woman who was still in the room. 'I'll just sort out some breakfast, then I'll have to tell you all about it.'

The woman brought the large *cappuccino* over and placed it in front of the man, who thanked her, then she looked at Paul and raised an eyebrow enquiringly. 'Could I have a coffee, please... but could you also make me some tea and... I'm sorry to be fussy, but could you put the water onto the teabag as it boils, rather than bringing me a pot of hot water and the tea-bag separately?' She nodded, clearly used to all kinds of strange requests from guests in the hotel.

As she went over to make the drinks, Paul excused himself for a moment and went over to fill a plate with Roman pastries, and a kiwi, so that he could tell Rosa with a clear conscience that he had had fruit for breakfast.

When he got back to the table, the man had taken an envelope out of his inner pocket and placed it by the side of his cup. Once Paul had sat down, he pushed the envelope over towards him. 'In here, there is a list of the buildings that the editor would like to be included in the book. I've prepared a rough itinerary for you, indicating which particular shots are most important, and also which ones must be taken at particular times to have the light in the right direction.' Paul nodded to show that he had understood the message.'

'I already have a film for you to develop, which I think may include some interesting shots. I thought that it might be interesting to have some night shots included.' He took the film out of his pocket and pushed it across the table. 'The sooner you can let me have some feedback the better, as some of them may well need some follow-up shots done.'

At that point, the woman brought across Paul's drinks and informed them that if they needed anything else, just to give her a shout as she'd be through in reception. Once she had left the room

Paul, in a low but urgent voice, recounted everything that had happened the previous evening at Settebagni, and was complimented on his quick thinking.

'We need to be able to contact you, possibly at short notice as there may be some changes to some of the targets' schedules.' He took a Motorola Razr phone out of his pocket and passed it over the table to Paul. 'Use this phone when you need to contact us, but remember not to use it for any other calls, especially not for calls to your home phone or any of your family's mobiles.' Paul nodded. 'There are four numbers already stored in the memory, but without names: the first one is mine, the second one is Francesca's and the third one is Judge Ciancolini's... Oh, and keep the phone switched to 'vibrate', you don't want it ringing at awkward times.'

'And the fourth number that's stored?'

The man hesitated. 'It's better that you don't know that at the moment. You should only use that if it's a real emergency and you can't get any response from the other three numbers.'

Paul shrugged and smiled. 'OK. That's fine... I take it that you're assuming that my own phone is unsafe.

Now it was the man's turn to smile, 'Actually, I think that it's very unlikely, but we just can't afford to take any chances – we don't know how they knew where dell'Omodarme would be on the night he was killed. Better to be safe than sorry, as they say in your country.' He rose, and placing one hand lightly on Paul's shoulder to indicate that there was no need for him to rise, took Paul's right hand and squeezed it briefly. 'My name's Marco, by the way... I'll be seeing you.' and he made his way towards the door. Paul heard him thank and say goodbye to the woman in reception and then for a few seconds heard the noises of the Roman street outside as the outer door was opened and then closed again. He slipped the Motorola into his pocket and slowly finished off his breakfast while thinking how cloak and dagger everything seemed to have become.

When he had finished, he thanked the woman in reception and made his way back up to his room. Before opening the envelope that Marco had given him, he took his own mobile out and dialled the number of the flat in Florence. After six rings the call was transferred to the answer-phone, ' I'm sorry, but the person you are calling is unable to take your call at the moment. If you'd like to le... Hello, I'm here,' broke in the slightly breathless voice of Rosa, over the end of the pre-recorded message.

'You sound out of breath. Have I caught you *in flagrante*?'

'Ha, ha, very funny. Someone's got to rush around trying to get the kids out of the house in time for school. It's alright for some, off on their holidays taking pretty pictures. Next time, I'll take the pictures and you can chase the kids.'

'I'm sure you're doing a wonderful job as usual, and just think, later on while you're sitting with your hands around a nice warm mug of hot chocolate, I'll be outside in the freezing cold hoping that my fingers don't drop off while I'm waiting for the perfect shot...' and then with a change of tone, 'Everything OK? I'm really missing you already.'

'Everything's fine; Alessio was a bit miffed that you weren't here to go through his English homework with him, but he eventually deigned to allow me to have a look through it; Mati has a new boyfriend, although she won't talk about him; and the hot-water bottle filled your place perfectly... How about you?'

'Oh, I had an interesting journey down. I felt I needed some air at one point and got off the train and finished the journey on a later one, so I got here quite late.'

'Where exactly is here? Are you near the main sites?'

'Not too far away, but I'm away from the main tourist sites, over in Trastevere, where it's a bit more peaceful. It's a nice little hotel on Via Mameli, not too expensive but clean and friendly. We could have a few days here sometime, either just us, if we can park the kids with your parents, or even all four of us so we can show them the sights.'

They chatted for another couple of minutes and then said goodbye agreeing that Paul would call in the evening, unless prevented by work commitments.

After the phone call, Paul emptied the contents of the envelope onto the small desk that was positioned under the window in his room. There was a map of central Rome with a number of ministry buildings clearly marked on, as well as a number of other locations that had been circled and from which pencil lines led to numbers that had been written in the margins. When he turned the map over, he found a key to the numbers showing that some were the homes of ministers and other politicians, three were bars and two were restaurants. A printed sheet held the itinerary that he had been promised with two times and locations highlighted, one in the late morning and another one at six-thirty in the evening. He checked the itinerary against the map and assumed that the order of the locations that had not been highlighted had been arranged to make the route he was to follow more convenient for him. There were also a further four A4 sheets on which had been printed a total of twenty-three portrait photographs; three of these he recognised as government ministers, four were in uniform and, from what he could see of their collars and shoulders, obviously very senior, while another three looked familiar although he couldn't put names to them.

Although he wasn't keen on walking around with the photographs, he decided that he had no choice and, having taken out his SLR camera and two biggest lenses, carefully eased the sheets with the photographs under the base of his camera bag. Once he had replaced the camera and lenses he put his coat on, clipped the strap of the camera bag under the flap on the shoulder of his thick padded jacket and made his way downstairs.

Handing his key in at reception, he asked politely what time the hotel doors were locked in the evening so that he wouldn't need to disturb anyone, and was told that the doors would be open until half past twelve and that, after that, he would need to ring the bell. He thanked the signora and said that he hoped he'd be back well before that.

Turning left out of the hotel, he made his way along to the junction with Viale Trastevere, glad to feel the sun on his face for a few minutes, despite the biting cold. When he reached the Tiber, instead of crossing over the Ponte Garibaldi, which would have been the shortest way, he decided to turn right so that he could take the next bridge along and pass over the Tibertine Island before reaching the centre. He remembered an excellent meal he'd had on the island with Rosa, shortly after they had married and wondered if the little trattoria was still there. He was pleased to find that it was and, as even at this early hour, the front of the restaurant was open for the sale of ice-creams, he couldn't resist treating himself to a small tub of lemon and coconut gelato.

On the far side of the bridge, he crossed the Lungotevere and made his way round the edge of the two thousand year old ruins of the Teatro Marcellum until he came out on the other side and made his way northwards towards the imposing white bulk of the Altare della Patria or, as most people derogatively referred to it, The Wedding Cake. A few early tourists were already posing for photographs in front of the pointless marble monument, erected in the enthusiasm of Rome becoming Italy's capital in the second half of the nineteenth century in an attempt to match up to the nearby Roman ruins. He wondered how many of the tourists knew anything about the history of the monument or were able to interpret its many sculptures and bas-reliefs. He realised that he'd never really had a good look round as the monument had only fully reopened in 1997 after being closed for nearly thirty years. Another thing to do when he came back to Rome with Rosa, he thought.

From Piazza Venezia he followed the Via dei Fori Antichi for a few minutes, before regretfully turning left, just as the Colosseum was beginning to become clearer in the distance. From there, twenty minutes fairly brisk walking took him steadily up until he was in front of Termini station, from where he knew that it was less than a quarter of a mile to the Ministry of Defence. As soon as he had passed the front of the station he turned right into the road running parallel to the station where, many years before, as student, he had passed four nights in a seedy hotel: very run down, but very, very cheap, which had been what mattered at the time. There were still several hotels and small *pensioni* on the street but none of them looked anything like as seedy as the one he remembered. Not just me who's made progress then, he thought, smiling to himself.

Soon, he found the left turn into Via del Castro Pretorio, where he knew that part of the Defence Ministry was situated at number 5. There were no police outside the main entrance in the granite façade of the four storey building where the flags of Italy and the European Union hung limply from flagpoles to either side of the first-floor balcony surmounting the main entrance. A CCTV camera attached to a pole five metres to the right of the entrance, and another seven or eight metres to the left were the only security measures he could spot, although he was sure that there must be others somewhere slightly less obvious.

Having checked his watch and found that he still had three-quarters of an hour to spare before his itinerary said that he must be there, he continued along the road and took the first right. This took him down to the far end of the station where an underpass allowed him to pass under the railway lines and then make his way up the far side of the station before cutting across by the heads of the platforms, to emerge again in the road parallel to the station. He quickly checked the section of the road after its junction with Via del Castro Pretorio and then, finally satisfied that other than a gate way to one side of the facade, there was no other vehicular access, he returned to the main entrance.

Once there, he confidently stepped through the main entrance, walked up to a large glass window marked 'Reception', and rang the bell next to a sign that said, 'All visitors must report to reception before continuing', and a smaller one that said 'Ring for attention'. A smartly dressed young man in a captain's uniform, came over to the window from a desk some metres behind and pressed a button that caused the window to slide upwards with a gentle whirring sound.

'*Desidera?*' asked the captain courteously but with an air of authority.

'*Buongiorno*. My name's Paul Caddick. I'm a photographer based in Florence, and I've been commissioned to take a series of photographs for an illustrated book looking at the architecture of public buildings in Italy. The project has been cleared with the Culture Ministry and, as I've just arrived in Rome, I thought I'd start by taking a few pictures of this building as it's so near to the station.'

He pushed over a piece of paper with the Culture Ministry's letterhead, and signed by a civil servant who was a friend of a friend of Judge Ciancolini.'

The captain gave a brief look at the paper and shook his head. 'I'm afraid that things will be pretty busy in here soon; you've come at a bad time. If you'd like to make an appointment, I can arrange for someone to show you around part of the building next week.'

Paul gave his pleasantest smile, 'That's fine. I'll make an appointment now, and then I'll just take a few photographs of the facade before I go, just in case the light is not suitable when I come back.' So long as the Captain didn't raise any objections to him photographing the outside, this was exactly what he'd been hoping for, as it would allow him to monitor arrivals at the building over the next half hour or so.

The captain shrugged his shoulder, evidently not particularly bothered when Paul photographed the outside, and opened a large diary on the desk in front of him. 'Would eight a.m. on Monday be alright?'

I'd prefer later in the week, if that's possible. I won't be in the city over the weekend and it will be much later on Monday when I get back.'

The Captain looked again and offered the same time but on Wednesday, which Paul accepted and thanked the Captain for his assistance.

Back on the road outside, Paul set up his tripod in the shelter of a tree on the opposite side of the road, from a point where he would have a clear view both of the main entrance and of the entrance to the carpark. Obviously, if the cars that arrived had tinted glass and their occupants entered the building directly from the carpark, his plan wouldn't work but, despite the experience of the previous evening, he felt it was unlikely that he would again find himself up against heavily tinted glass.

Over the forty minutes which was all he dared allow himself, seven cars turned into the carpark and three left. The three that left were almost certainly not relevant but he carefully photographed their occupants anyway, just as he did with everyone who passed through the main entrance whether going in or coming out. Of the seven cars that went in, four contained people who he did not recognise, two contained people who he thought were some of those on the photographs he'd been given but didn't recognise, and the last one, which was escorted by two police outriders contained the Minister himself and another man whom Paul did not recognise.

When he moved on, he found a bar in Via Marsala from where he could see the beginning of Via Castro Pretorio. He had noted down the numbers of the cars that had entered and, if they turned his way afterwards, he would be able to see if there had been any change in their occupancy. Two sandwiches, a coffee and a half litre of beer that he was making last as long as possible later, the minister's car emerged and he noted that the minister had lost his companion. Two of the other cars also came his way, as did four of the people who had arrived at the building on foot while he had been taking photographs before. Two of these people were now accompanied by others, while the remaining two were now together, suggesting that they could have been in the same meeting. When he was satisfied that there was nothing more to do there, he asked for his tab and pushed over a ten euro note to pay.

To make sure that he had pictures of other public buildings on his film if he ever had to hand it over, he made his way to the Treasury Building which was only ten minutes' walk away, and took a few shots, before making his way back to Termini and buying tickets for both the underground and the bus network. Then, after carefully checking that the line he wanted was A and that the correct direction was Anagnina, he took his place on the metro for the seven minute ride to Ottaviano. Once he had ascended from the underground, he quickly located the bus stop for the Number thirty two bus and, after waiting a few minutes, found that he had to stand all the way to the De Bossis Tennis Stadium, and so was unable to take in any of the sights on the way.

After he had walked a few minutes through the quickly darkening air, he found himself in front of Palazzo Farnesina, the seat of the Foreign Ministry and also of a renowned Gallery of

Modern Italian Art. He realised immediately that getting any useful photographs here would be far more difficult, if not impossible. Not only were there two car-parks but there were several possible entrances to the Palazzo itself – and it was going dark.

He wandered through the main entrance and, under the pretence of studying the museum opening hours, made a note of all the possible entrances to official parts of the building. He then went round to the side carpark and had a look at the cars parked there. With relief he noticed that many of the cars in this carpark had official Ministry permits and so he hoped that, if any persons of interest to Francesca's investigation arrived, they would come this way.

Although he felt somewhat exposed, and knew that he would find it difficult to explain his presence if challenged, he set up his tripod by the side of a large Fiat van, which he hoped would shelter him from most people's view. Placing an infra-red lens on his camera, he then spent the next hour, photographing everyone who entered or exited the building.

He was fairly sure that none of the people whose photographs he had been given had passed by, although there had been a few who had never turned their faces in his direction. However, there was one face that he was sure he knew, but couldn't place; because of the van that was sheltering him, he didn't see which car the distinguished looking man in his seventies came from, which meant that he wouldn't be able to identify him unless he remembered where he had seen him, or if his face was recognised by someone else.

Just after half past seven he saw two workmen come out of the side entrance of the building and head in his direction. Deciding that they were heading for the van, he quickly picked up his tripod and retreated behind the vehicle and cut across the carpark before stopping again four rows further along. As he was doing this, he almost missed the man he had seen previously coming out, accompanied by a middle aged woman with a fur collar turned up so that it covered a good part of her face. Grabbing his camera, he fired off several shots as the couple made their way to a taxi that had stopped a few metres further along. As the man opened the rear door of the taxi to let the woman in first, for a second he was facing directly towards Paul, although Paul was sure that as he was looking towards the darkness he would not be able to make him out. It gave Paul, however, the opportunity to firmly plant both elbows onto the roof of a nearby car so that he got a steady shot of the man's face.

Chapter 10

'The pictures you took last night were really interesting. Even though one of the cars had tinted glass and we can't know for definite who was in it, we've been able to identify it from the plate.' Marco stopped and slid a forkful of *penne all'amatriciana* into his mouth.

'And?' asked Paul, looking directly at him, while he swirled the Genazzano Rosso gently around his chalice with his right hand, having rested his fork on the edge of the steaming bowl of *spaghetti alla carbonara*.

The car is one of the so called, *auto-blu*, made available to government ministers, important public servants, and quite often their friends, at an enormous cost to the taxpayer.' He paused and with eyebrows slightly raised, met Paul's gaze directly. 'That particular one is available for the exclusive use of Loriana Cabrini-Pellé, Parliamentary Under-secretary at the Justice Ministry, and former television presenter.'

'...who appears regularly on television explaining unpopular government policies, as she's far more photogenic than the Justice Minister himself,' added Paul.

'Exactly. We've been trying to get someone reliable inside the ministry to keep an eye on her this afternoon, since we saw your photograph – but apparently, she hasn't been in to the ministry today.'

'Did you manage to identify any of those in the other car?'

'We identified three of them; one was your friend Vercellese, one was a Colonel in SISMI and the other was the Vice Questore of Frosinone – we assume that the driver was just an employee, probably of the Colonel, as the car is registered to his wife.'

'You've been working quickly – I'm impressed – Let's hope that some of today's photographs prove to be as useful. At the very end of the roll are some photographs of a man who I'm sure I recognise but I just can't place. If you could let me have a copy of that one as soon as possible, I'm sure that sooner or later It'll come back to me.'

They avoided talking about the conspiracy for the rest of the meal, concentrating all their efforts on enjoying the *abbacchio* that both had ordered as their main course.

'Do you come here regularly?' asked Paul as his companion put down his knife and fork having cleaned every last bit of food off his plate.

Marco nodded, 'It's unusual for a week to pass without me coming here at least once. The cook's an old friend of mine from when we did our military service together, and I've got to know the owners quite well over the years too. Usually, when I come in, I sit and eat in a corner of the kitchen, let Pietro, my friend, decide what I should eat and just trust him absolutely. It's mainly a trattoria for locals, good quality local produce without the fanciness that you pay extra for in any of the restaurants that are more likely to be visited by tourists.'

Paul smiled, 'That's the sort of place I like to eat too – the trouble is, it's getting more and more difficult in Florence, every year you seem to have to go further away from the centre to be sure of getting good food at a fair price – it's all these foreigners.'

Marco looked at him and realised that he was joking and laughed. 'Oh, don't worry, even foreigners come in useful sometimes.' He raised his glass towards Paul, who reciprocated. 'What do you think of this wine?'

After taking another sip, Paul nodded his head approvingly, 'I like it. I hadn't come across Genazzano before – I assume it's local.'

'Fairly local. It's from the Sacco valley, up in the hills between Rome and Frosinone. The owner of this place is from there originally and still owns a vineyard. Genazzano has to contain a minimum of eighty-five percent Ciliegiolo grapes, but this particular one varies between ninety-two and ninety-four, depending on how the grapes turn out each year. I suppose that you've got very used to Tuscan wines now.'

'I have, but I still appreciate other good wines as well, and wherever I go, I always try to find a good local wine.'

'Even when you go back to England?'

Paul smiled again, 'It's not as hard as it used to be – probably because of global warming. It's still almost impossible to find a good red, but there are some quite classy whites around now. They've even been winning awards at European wine festivals – so don't mock!'

The other held his hands up in submission. 'I'll make sure that I try an English white next time I go to England – the perfect accompaniment to my fish and chips.'

'What do you want me to do tomorrow? If possible, I'd like to get the twenty past six train back to Florence.'

'That shouldn't be a problem. The only meeting that we're aware of tomorrow is at the Communications Ministry down in the EUR Zone. If you take the Metro down to the EUR Fermi station, you'll be almost there. We know that Marelli is scheduled to have a meeting there with Capraia, the Communications minister at eleven o'clock. There is a chance that we may be able to get a microphone in there, which would tell us everything but, if they decide to change rooms, or if something interferes with the microphone, we'll be relying entirely on you to photograph people going into the building between ten-thirty and eleven, and people coming out between twelve and twelve thirty. Ring me when you've finished and I'll arrange to pick the film up from you.

Chapter 11

'It's only me,' shouted Marco as he entered his flat. There was no reply and after hanging his coat up on the rack, he made his way through into the lounge where he could hear the television.

'Hi,' he said, entering the room.

'Shhhh!' came the urgent command from Francesca who was sitting on the edge of chair, leaning forward towards the television and holding up a hand to reinforce her message.

He looked at the television as he moved forward to join her; it seemed to be a documentary about nature, but then he noticed the news feed ribbon rolling around the bottom of the screen. At the moment, the information was about Afghanistan – he looked at her quizzically. 'Cabrini-Pellé,' she said, and then pointed to the screen as the news flash came round again, "Parliamentary Under-Secretary, Loriana Cabrini-Pellé, found dead in car after hit and run accident -".

'How long has this been showing?' he asked grimly, picking up the remote control.

'I turned on about ten minutes ago and was channel-hopping when her name caught my eye – so I've no idea.'

'There's the "*telegiornale della notte*" on RAI 3 in a few minutes; hopefully, we'll get more details there,' and he changed channels to wait for the late night news.

'I'm sure we will,' said Francesca, but that doesn't mean they'll be accurate. What did you get from Paul? If it hadn't been for the pictures he took last night, we wouldn't have known that Cabrini-Pellé had anything to do with this, and it would have just looked like a normal accident.'

'He's given me a film from this morning that may have some useful shots on it, but he wasn't as hopeful about the one from the Foreign Ministry – although he did say that right at the end, there was someone he was sure he'd seen before, but just couldn't place. You never know; it could be useful.'

'Possibly, but there must be so many people going in and out that the chances of seeing someone you've seen before must be fairly high.'

'Here we are,' said Marco as the familiar signature music of the news bulletin announced the start of the programme. As usual, an attractive blond with very long legs and unseasonal clothing, leaned against a glass topped desk facing the camera, but this time, the 'hello-I'm-your-friend' smile that usually marked the start of news bulletins was absent, and the newsreader looked suitably serious.

'Good Evening. Our leading news item tonight is to announce the death of Parliamentary Under-Secretary for Justice, Loriana Cabrini-Pellé. Our correspondent, Giuliano Becchi has more on this story.'

The shot changed to a shot of one of station's leading reporters standing at the start of what appeared to be a motorway viaduct, on which numerous blue lights could be seen flashing, well beyond a police barrier that was blocking access to the bridge. 'According to Colonel Aurelio di Gennaro, who is leading the investigation, it appears that the Parliamentary Under-Secretary's car left the road and crashed through the barriers after an incident involving another vehicle. The car, an official ministry car, came to rest on its roof in thick undergrowth fifteen metres below the motorway. Both Cabrini-Pellé, and her driver are believed to have died on impact.'

The screen split into two, with the bottom left hand corner now showing the leading presenter in the studio. 'Giuliano. You say that the incident involved another vehicle. Do the police have any information about this vehicle?'

'I'm afraid not Barbara. At first it appears that police believed that no other vehicle was involved, and that Cabrini-Pellé's driver had fallen asleep at the wheel, or the car had suffered some catastrophic mechanical failure. However, the Captain of the fire-crew that was called to the scene, says that there is evidence of a side impact with another vehicle. At the moment, all that we know is that the other vehicle is believed to have been white, and must almost certainly be fairly substantial to cause this accident.'

'What time did the accident take place, Giuliano?'

'Again that's not clear at the moment. We know that she left her office at the ministry just after seven last night, but her whereabouts since then are unknown. She was due to have a meeting with representatives of the Supreme Court this morning, but her staff cancelled this, when they didn't see her arrive at work. The car was found shortly after nine o'clock this evening by a French lorry driver who had stopped on the bridge near the broken barrier and spotted the bottom of the car down below.'

'Thank you, Giuliano. We may well be back with you for an update later in the programme.' The presenter shuffled her papers and then, looking straight at the camera, and presumably the telecast, 'On the line we have Giacinto Marelli, the Secretary of State for Justice.' The screen split again and a photograph of a bald man, bearing a striking resemblance to a pit-bull appeared on the right hand side.

'*Buonasera, Ministro*. Thank you for coming on at such short notice, and may I begin by offering my condolences.'

'Thankyou. First and foremost, I'd like to offer my sincere condolences to Loriana's family; my thoughts are with them as they attempt to make sense of this tragedy. This is a very sad day for Italian politics, indeed for Italy as a whole. Loriana was what you journalists would term a rising star in the firmament of Italian politics and a loyal and generous colleague, who will be sadly missed.'

'I'm not sure if you heard my colleague's report from the scene, but it appears that another vehicle was involved in the accident. Obviously at the very least, the other driver is guilty of failing to stop after an accident, but do you think that it could be worse than that? - Do you have any reason to believe that this may have been more than just an ordinary hit and run accident?'

'What we mustn't do at the moment is come to any conclusions before all the evidence has been gathered. I have full confidence in the investigating officers to do a full and thorough job, and only then will we be able to take any action that may be necessary. However, because of the diligence with which Loriana carried out her job, she has made a lot of enemies, particularly on the extreme left, and if, and I repeat, if, it is shown to be necessary, we will have no hesitation in clamping down on any groups that are shown to be fundamentally opposed to the values of our country.'

'Thank you for your time, Minister.'

'Thank you.'

Francesca and Marco looked at each other, appalled by the significance of what they had just heard.

A picture of Cabrini-Pellé now filled the screen. 'Loriana Cabrini-Pellé first came to public notice as a hostess on a late night variety show on *Telé Sicula* in her native Sicily. From there she moved to RAI 1 when, under the previous government led by the current Prime Minister, the channel was controlled by Rocco Lesine, a long time business associate of the Prime Minister. While working for RAI 1, she established a reputation as a formidable interviewer with whom many politicians were reluctant to cross swords. In 1996, at the age of twenty-eight she was elected to Parliament as a representative for the Province of Agrigento and since then her rise has been meteoric, becoming the youngest minister in the current government when she was appointed as one of the Under-secretaries in the Justice Ministry at the start of the current legislature.' As the announcer went through the summary biography of the politician, the image on the screen changed to show her: presenting *Telé Sicula*, interviewing Massimo D'Alema for RAI 1, shaking hands with the Prime Minister and finally, standing alongside Giacinto Marelli.

At the end, the picture returned to the news-reader, 'Loriana Cabrini-Pellé leaves a husband and a five year old daughter... And now – In other news...' the usual smile was back, and Marco turned the volume right down.

'I don't get it,' said Marco, 'Why kill her? She's just the sort of person they need on their side, if they're planning a coup... and we know she was at a meeting with them last night.' He leaned forward on the chair and ran his fingers back through his hair. Francesca leaned right back on her chair, head thrown backwards, deep in thought while distractedly cracking her finger joints.

'We know why they would want Cabrini-Pellé on their side, but what if...' she paused, 'what if she's less opportunistic and more principled than we've given her credit for; we know that she's a determined right winger who doesn't mind whose fingers she treads on as she climbs the political ladder, but that doesn't necessarily mean that she'd effectively agree to overthrow the state. What if they tried to recruit her and she refused – maybe even threatened to expose them – perhaps working for the Ministry of Justice actually meant something to her.'

'I think you may be right,' he said, 'and if you think about it, handled carefully, she's almost as valuable to them dead as alive. Did you hear what Marelli said? "No hesitation in clamping down on groups shown to be fundamentally opposed to the values of our country". We know that they control the media, so it wouldn't take too much for them to be able to get the people to accept tougher new laws.'

'On the other hand,' she said thoughtfully, 'they're playing a very dangerous game, and it could all blow up in their faces.'

He looked at her, 'How do you work that one out?' he said with a puzzled expression.

She leaned forward and put an arm round him. 'They need to build up fear and anger in the public, so that the public will support tough new laws and a suspension of democracy, but... if the people are angry enough and we can give them proof that it's Marelli and his group who are behind the violence, the public will turn against them.'

'The problem then,' said Marco, 'would be in making sure that the reaction from the other side wasn't equally repressive.'

Francesca got up. 'I'm going to grab some sleep. There's a train for Florence at six-fifteen. I need to be sitting in front of Judge Graziadei's office to smile at him when he gets into work in the morning, and then I need to go and talk to Ciancolini. If you could develop those photographs before I go, it would be helpful.' She bent and kissed his forehead then went through into the bedroom.

Chapter 12

Following the absorption of three cups of double strength espresso, and the application of copious amounts of make-up to disguise the bags under her eyes, Francesca managed to be at her desk in time to smile demurely and cross her legs as the old judge walked in. He gave her a slightly lopsided smile and asked if she had managed to collect the papers from Rome, and when she replied in the affirmative and informed him that they were on his desk waiting for him, he proceeded into his inner office and left her in peace to play solitaire on her computer.

She had already sent a message to Ciancolini telling him that she needed to see him urgently and he had replied, asking her to meet him in a pizzeria on the Via Pistoiese at twenty past one. Making sure that, to her co-workers, she appeared to be absorbed in the game on her computer, she slid the pictures that Marco had printed out of her bag and studied them one by one. She was able to put names to a few of those who appeared, particularly from the pictures taken in the morning. One she found particularly interesting was of a bald, or shaven headed, young man, apparently in his late twenties, who had been photographed both walking into the building on Via del Castro Pretorio, and then another of the same man, with his collar turned up high, turning into Via Marsala later on. She was almost sure that she had come across his face before while researching an article on the Calabrian 'Ndrangheta, the previous year. As soon as she could get away, she'd be able to check against her files.

She had quickly discover that, providing she got all her work done, and providing that Graziadei had already left, it was quite acceptable – in fact, almost expected – for the girls who worked in his office to leave by twelve-thirty. Accordingly, soon after quarter past, she joined with the other two girls in using the screens of their monitors as mirrors to reapply lipstick and touch up her make-up. Once she had handed over the largely irrelevant file that she had picked up from Rome, and earned further gratitude from Graziadei by giving him a brief summary of its key points, she had followed as many links as possible relating to the photographs and other information to do with the case – a task which was greatly facilitated by Graziadei keeping his log-in to the classified system taped under his keyboard.

As well as finding more useful information about the faces in the photographs, she also managed to find out who had been on duty for CESIS when the task of looking into the explosion that had killed Arturo had been allocated. It was clear that the CESIS operative had been responsible for allocating the case to SISMI, but she was not convinced that the person concerned was senior enough to be a major player in the plot. She wasn't sure if she should press Ciancolini to lean on him, or whether, for the moment, they might be best just monitoring his movements and communications. He would probably be less well protected than his bosses and could well inadvertently lead them to the leaders of the plot.

At twelve thirty, making sure that she wasn't the first one to leave, she switched her computer off and put her coat and scarf on. Slipping out of the rear of the building, she made her way across to the inappropriately named Viale Toscania, which seemed more like the access road on a rundown industrial estate, than a road which should be dignified with the title Viale. Having walked most of the way down the Viale, thinking that it definitely wasn't a road she'd like to walk down after dusk, she turned right into another, only slightly more welcoming thoroughfare. Fortunately, when she emerged onto the next road, there were some residential blocks in the distance and it felt almost as if she were back in the real world. Turning left, then immediately right again allowed her to cut through to Via Baracca where she knew that she could get either the number thirty or thirty five bus to the Pizzeria from a bus stop opposite the public gardens.

Checking the information attached to the bus-stop sign, she saw that buses were meant to pass every twelve minutes so, even if she had just missed one, which she was fairly sure she hadn't, as she'd been able to see Via Baracca for at least three minutes before arriving there, she would be in good time to meet Ciancolini.

Once on the bus, she saw that she was in no danger of being overheard and took out her unregistered phone and rang Marco in Rome.

'Hi, it's me – any news?'

'Not really. There are plenty of police around the Justice Ministry, questioning anyone who goes anywhere near, but it seems to be more for show than anything else. One interesting bit of information I have got is that not long before she left the ministry the other night, Cabrini-Pellé was heard shouting on the telephone. Unfortunately, all we know is that there were quite a few strong negatives in there, but we don't know who she was shouting at, or what she was being negative about – but it does seem to lend weight to your theory that she was refusing to get involved. How about you?'

'I managed to stay awake all morning, smiling at Graziadei at appropriate times, and did as much as I could to check out some of the pictures in the photographs – I didn't learn much new there... but I did manage to find out who was on duty when the explosion that killed Arturo dell'Omodarme was allocated to SISMI. A Captain Bolano.'

'That's excellent... what are you going to do about it?'

'Good question. I still haven't decided... I'm on my way to meet Ciancolini now and, if I tell him, he'll want to go by the book and bring him in for questioning.'

'Whereas, you think that he could lead us to someone bigger.'

'Exactly... although it's yet another person to monitor.'

'I think, you're probably right.. but it's your call.'

'I know... Heard anything from Paul this morning?'

'No, not yet. I would think the chances of him turning anything new up this morning are fairly slim, but you never know.'

'OK Bye for now. Keep in touch.'

The small pizzeria they had chosen to be out of the way, turned out only to function as a bar at lunchtimes, becoming a pizzeria in the evenings. That didn't worry Francesca, who was feeling almost too tired to be hungry, and was happy just to order a *tramezzino* and a hot chocolate as she waited for Ciancolini to arrive. The judge arrived five minutes later and got himself a *birra piccola* and a cooked ham and mozzarella sandwich before joining her at the table she had taken furthest away from the door, which was also next to a small radiator.

It took half an hour for Francesca to summarise the developments from Rome, being careful not to reveal that she had been able to access confidential files using Graziadei's log-on, or that Marco would be using his contacts in security to bug a number of key offices in ministries. She had no doubt that Ciancolini was on their side, but in some ways he was too honest and she couldn't be sure how he would react if he knew about some of the unscrupulous methods that she felt were their only chance of averting catastrophe.

He was shocked at first to hear her theory that the conspirators had been responsible for the death of Cabrini-Pellé, but was convinced when he was shown the photographs of her official car – the car in which she had been killed – emerging from the gates of the villa outside Settebagni, the night before she died, and then told of the reported arguments she had had on the phone before leaving the ministry.

'Has time of death been established yet for Cabrini-Pellé?' he asked.

'I don't know,' she said. 'That may be something that's easier to find out from your position. Why?'

'Because, if the time of death were placed before she left the villa, then that would mean that other people in the villa knew about the death and, in all likelihood, were responsible for it... And that, would place our friend Vercellese, very much in the frame for murder.'

'But that doesn't help, does it?'

He raised an eyebrow, 'Go on. Explain.'

'If we arrest Vercellese it does two things: it removes from the game the only person who we have definitely identified as being a key player in the group and, it alerts the others involved that we're keeping an eye on them. What it doesn't do, is provide us with any direct link to the conspiracy.'

'So what do we have?'

'We have eight names of people who are definitely involved – although probably not all at the top level; we have the names of at least twenty others who may be involved and, most importantly, we still have the element of surprise. What we don't have is a clear idea of the power structure – and until we have that, I don't think we can risk making any move.'

Ciancolini leaned back on his chair, looking concerned. 'It goes against the grain, not to take action when we have clear evidence of involvement in a murder – and the death of Cabrini-Pellé definitely was murder, wasn't it?'

'It was, but to use the evidence we have that shows that Vercellese was involved, would alert the other conspirators that we've been watching him and would make it more difficult to gather further evidence... it would also, almost certainly, put Paul's life at risk. We've nothing to lose by waiting – it's not as if Vercellese's going to do a Craxi and escape to Tunisia.'

Ciancolini still looked worried but Francesca smiled reassuringly. 'I think we've probably got at least three months to try and pull this together. Prodi's fairly popular at the moment; the majority of people see him being President of the European Commission as being a mark of respect for Italy, and realise that it allows him to get the best deal for the country. If anything happened to him now, instead of being an excuse for a draconian security clampdown, which plays into the hands of the extreme right, he'd get a massive sympathy vote. They need to make people doubt him before they get rid of him.'

'I suppose you're right but, I want keeping up to date with all developments. Now, if I'm not going to issue an arrest warrant, what can I do that will help to move things along?'

Chapter 13

'And how did he react to your suggestion?'

Francesca smiled at her sister, 'I think he wasn't sure whether to be shocked at the thought of having the conversation, or flattered that I thought he was influential enough to get private audiences with both Romano Prodi and the President of the Republic. He went red first and then white.

'Will he... be able to?' asked Paul.

'There's a Belgian journalist who I know through the ICIJ who should be...'

'Just a minute' said Paul, interrupting her, 'What's the ICIJ?'

'ICIJ stands for the International Confederation of Investigative Journalists – journalists in lots of different countries who pool resources and work together, when necessary to look into cross-border issues – mainly, but not exclusively, financial and criminal.'

'And you're a member,' said Rosa, 'it sounds very important.'

'Not yet,' said Francesca with a smile. 'The only publication in Italy, whose journalists are regularly involved in ICIJ is "Espresso", but I got involved three years ago when I did an internship there and was working with a team of journalists who were looking at a labelling fraud involving meat from different EU countries... Anyway... One of the Belgian journalists we were working with was a girl called Marie, who was the lowest of the low, just like me – so we got on. Now, she's working as a political reporter for "La Libre Belgique". They regularly run interviews with different European Commissioners and, if she can get one with Prodi, we should be able to fix it so that Ciancolini is with her when she meets him.'

'So, your friend gets her interview, and Ciancolini gets to talk to Prodi... What's he going to tell him?'

'We think that at this stage, as the bodies are starting to accumulate..' Paul smiled inwardly at Francesca's exaggeration, 'we need to tell Prodi, so that he's aware of the danger he's in.'

'I thought you said – or maybe it was Arturo – that even if Prodi was warned, that he wouldn't do anything... that he'd think it made him look paranoid, reacting before there was any threat that the public were aware of.'

'I'm sure he won't like it, and I'm sure he won't make any significant changes to his routine, as a result but, what I hope it will do, is allow us to establish a channel of communication with him.'

'What about the President?' asked Rosa, is Ciancolini important enough to be able to get an appointment with him?'

'He might be able to get an appointment through official channels, although that would take time and be very public, but again we've got another way of getting in. A friend of his, Cecco Busoni, a successful surveyor with his own business, is the son of Giorgio Busoni who, so the story goes, saved the President's life when they were both partisans back in forty-four. Although the President was a Christian Democrat, until that party imploded, while Busoni was a convinced communist, and even served as an MP for seven years, the two remained close friends until Giorgio Busoni died three years ago at the grand old age of ninety eight. If the request to meet comes from Busoni, he'll agree.'

'Alright,' said Rosa, 'That part of your plan seems feasible. Now tell us why you're convinced that the conspirators won't make any significant moves in the next three months. If Prodi has public support now, how is that going to change over the next few months? I can't imagine the current government getting any more popular, so surely, Prodi's popularity won't change.'

'Mitrokhin.'

Rosa looked enquiringly at her sister but Paul's eyes narrowed. 'What? The Russian spy? You mean that Prodi's going to get drawn into that?'

Francesca nodded, then after glancing at her sister decided it was easiest to explain from the beginning. 'Vasili Mitrokhin was a Major in the KGB. In the first half of the nineteen fifties, he was one of their field officers, involved in a number of undercover operations around the world. In the mid-fifties, something went wrong during one of the operations he was involved in and he was removed from active operations and transferred to the KGB archives, where he remained until he retired in the mid-eighties. He claims that in 1956, after a speech by Khrushchev that criticised Stalin, he became disillusioned with the system and horrified by the nature of their undercover operations around the world. Now, as we all know, any good whistle-blower needs evidence so, when the archives were being transferred to a new site, he very diligently copied out by hand over a thousand documents and made detailed notes from a lot more.'

Paul looked at her, 'You're joking, aren't you? At a time when the KGB was being run by Andropov or Putin, or someone similar, with probably the most obsessive security controls the world has ever seen, you want us to believe that someone who worked there – even someone fairly high up, could just sit down and copy out by hand thousands of documents.' He shook his head in disbelief and Francesca just smiled and then continued.

'That's pretty much the conclusion that the CIA came to after he walked into the American embassy in Riga in 1991...'

This time it was Rosa's turn to interrupt. 'I don't get it. If it was the Soviet system he objected to, why wait until after the system had collapsed before contacting the Americans? What was his point? Surely, what he should have been doing was revealing the information inside Russia, giving Gorbachev more justification for having reformed the system.'

'A very good point, I think. Except that by 1991 it was Yeltsin in charge, but that just makes your point even more valid. Anyway, I'm just filling you in on the official details for now. It's probably better if you just accept it for now and then think about the inconsistencies and the implications when you know everything.' They both nodded their agreement and, after an approving smile from Francesca indicated that he should go ahead, Paul topped up their glasses with wine.

'Mitrokhin didn't give up after the Americans rejected him as a fantasist, he just walked across the city and offered his services to the British. Depending on how you view him, the British were either more astute, or more gullible, that the Americans. Straight away, they saw his defection as a major coup and despite Russia having an open access policy at that point, sent in their spooks, to retrieve Mitrokhin's archive from under the floor of his dacha. Back in Britain, the linguists employed by the security services began to transcribe and then translate the thousands of pages of Cyrillic writing into English.' She took a sip of her wine before continuing.

'The British, of course, passed on everything to their friends in America, and the FBI, always ready to get one over on the CIA, declared that it was the greatest intelligence coup ever. They also sent relevant extracts to security organisations in other friendly countries – including of course, Italy.'

'Why only extracts?' asked Paul.

Francesca ignored his interruption and continued, 'After SISMI had had them for some time, they requested a copy of the whole archive – a request that was granted. Now, there are those who think that when SISMI requested a copy of the whole archive, they suggested a few tweaks to some of the original extracts that had been sent to them – of course, conveniently, there's now no trace of the original extracts – No. Ask me afterwards, when you've heard everything – In 2002, our current government which, as you know, has quite a few friends who hold senior positions in SISMI, set up a parliamentary commission to establish what implications the revelations in the Mitrokhin archives have for the Italian state.'

'Yes,' said Rosa, 'Now that you've mentioned it, I vaguely remember reading about the Commission being set up, but I haven't heard much since,' and she gave Francesca a look to apologise for the interruption.

'The British, of course, were already carefully managing the release of the information,' allowing a Cambridge University professor, who some have accused of being effectively a propagandist for MI5 – or 6, I can't remember which – to publish a book, jointly with Mitrokhin, about the archive... but back to Italy; you're probably going to say that Parliamentary Commissions are made up of representatives from all the parties in parliament – and you're right – but, the representatives from the governing parties are in the majority and, more importantly, they also have the Chair, so they can decide which members of the commission are allocated to which sub-committee or working party. By doing this, they can make sure that they manage the interpretations that are put on the findings. Because the contents of the archives relate to security, the committee's findings are kept secret until the time comes for them to publish their official report. Now, those on the committee from the left take their roles very seriously and, as far as I'm aware, there have been no leaks from them, however, regular hints appear in the right wing press, suggesting that many of the leaders of the left, may well have had contacts with the KGB in the past. When challenged about where they get their information from, they usually claim that it has been taken from what's been published in England.' She looked at Paul.

He nodded and said resignedly, 'I'll have a look. I need some light bed-time reading.'

'Thankyou. Although I doubt you'll find anything; I've already read the book published in England and, I know my English is nothing like as good as yours, but I couldn't see anything, apart from a few allusions.'

'By "leaders of the left", I take it you mean current leaders,' said Rosa.

'Not just current leaders; the archive goes back to the thirties, so there are obviously plenty of references to people like Bordiga, Togliatti and Gramsci, but that's hardly surprising – they were fleeing from Fascist persecution, so the obvious place to find safe haven was Moscow, where they were treated like heroes. I don't think anyone would condemn them for wanting Russian help against Mussolini. It starts to become damaging when it implies that people who are still remembered by many people here were co-operating with the Russians during the Cold War.'

'Berlinguer?'

Francesca nodded, 'Berlinguer, Amendola – and obviously that brings into play people who knew them and who are still active now: Napolitano, D'Alema – and Prodi.'

'But surely, allegations about people like these are easy to disprove.'

'Not as easy as you'd think; Berlinguer, as head of the PCI, one of the largest national communist parties in Europe, regularly attended international conferences of the different national Communist parties. When he was there, he obviously spoke with lots of people, some in public and some in smaller, private meetings – if Mitrokhin's documents say that certain matters were discussed in those meetings, then it's difficult to refute them. Berlinguer can't do it – he's dead, so's Amendola... and if you think about it, the translation supplied by the British, almost certainly with the approval of their American friends, is not likely to be helpful to anyone who's ever been associated with the PCI... And think about Prodi... when he's not a politician he's an Economics professor, and Economics professors go to a lot of international conferences over the years. With a tame Parliamentary Commission, it becomes fairly easy to smear people.' She leaned back again and distractedly ran her fingers back through her dark hair.

'I can see that,' said Paul, ' but given what you said earlier about everything having been copied by hand by Mitrokhin, I can't see that there's anything to prove that the contents aren't complete fantasy. Why is he being taken seriously when it could easily be a work of his imagination?'

'Do you know anything about auditing?' asked Francesca with a wry smile, to which Paul shook his head and adopted a puzzled expression.

'No? I assumed not... Well, if you can imagine checking the books of a large company, you obviously can't check every piece of paper, and in the ones you do check, there will certainly be some small errors given that they're produced by humans. To decide whether or not the company's accounts give a "true and fair" view, auditors have to work on what are called "confidence levels" which are worked out by mathematical formulae. Usually they work on a ninety-five percent confidence level to establish whether there is a "true and fair" view. Now think of all the things that have happened in the west since the nineteen-thirties... most of them are of little relevance anymore, are they?... So imagine taking nine hundred and fifty documents that can be verified as being correct, but which, while they may be of interest, are of no current strategic value, and then slip in amongst them, twenty of thirty other documents that cannot be verified, but which tell a plausible story, and there you go, you have an archive which provides a statistically "true and fair" view... the archive contains lots of material that seems to confirm things that the British and Americans were worried about during the Cold War and that makes them more likely to believe the other things as well.'

'What is Mitrokhin's motivation for revealing all this information meant to have been – surely, if he wanted to expose what was happening, he needed to do so well before 1991? Surely it all came too late,' asked Paul.

'If you just look at Mitrokhin, then you can argue that his primary motivation was money. Since 1991 he's been well looked after in London by the British Taxpayer as well as earnings from the book with the university professor. If we accept that we're living in a capitalist society based on free-market economics then we can't be surprised if people do things for money.' She paused.

'But?' said Rosa, 'I can feel a "but" coming."

Francesca smiled and gave a slight nod to her sister, 'You're right. Three countries have set up commissions to look at the Mitrokhin Archive: Britain, Italy and... India. Now the British not only have their investment to protect but they also invented Capitalism, so they're fine with the idea that anyone – except a valorous Brit, of course – would do anything for money; here in Italy, the commission seems to have its own secret agenda which appears to be to smear left wing politicians; in India, where despite recent modernisation programmes that are glorifying capitalism, there has always been a much more...' she struggled to find the right word, 'I suppose you could say "spiritual" approach to life – they came to the conclusion that neither Mitrokhin's motives nor the contents of his archive could be trusted.'

'So, what you're suggesting,' said Paul, 'is that Mitrokhin used those two years between eighty-nine and ninety-one to assemble his archive, with the support and assistance of the KGB – or other bodies in Russia who had a reason for letting the West have a lot of accurate but irrelevant information, carefully seeded with some that was misleading. The wall may have come down but the Russians, or at least some influential Russian elements, were ready to take down some of the West with them...' He paused, 'But as an explanation there's a flaw in that line of reasoning... from what you said earlier, it sounds as if the Westerners most likely to be damaged by this, at least here in Italy, are those on the left like D'Alema and Prodi... It doesn't really make sense.'

'It does in a sort of twisted way,' said Rosa quietly. They both looked at her. 'Think back to Moro. Although he was a Christian Democrat, everyone knew that he was on the left of the party; the right was worried about how far he would go in looking for common ground, and the majority of those on the left were hoping that, at last, there was some chance of social justice for all, even those who weren't Christians. Unfortunately, the Brigate Rosse weren't prepared to accept the limited amount of reforms that were on offer, and thought that Moro had betrayed them… And we all know what happened then... It's possible that the hard-liners in Russia saw the failure of left-wingers in the West to make their case sufficiently strongly to win the democratic argument, as a betrayal that needed punishing.'

'But that would lead to the right wingers taking complete control in the West – surely that can't be their objective,' objected Paul.

'We've never been very effective on the left, because we can't usually agree amongst ourselves, so it wouldn't be sacrificing much from their point of view... And remember, Marx said that the eventual overthrow of Capitalist society is inevitable, so maybe... helping it to reach its peak sooner, will also hasten its decline.' She slipped an arm through Paul's and rested her head on his shoulder.

'So where does that leave us?' asked Paul.

'Well... Prodi's not due to give evidence to the commission until the beginning of May so we've probably got until Easter before they start to increase the level of little hints and malicious smears in the press. If we can get the evidence we need by then, and can convince the President to use his executive powers to authorise the necessary arrests without going through the normal unwieldy procedures to get warrants, then public sympathy for Prodi and D'Alema will make them Mitrokhin proof.'

There was a brief moment of silence as each reflected on the situation, then Paul stirred, *'Caffè?'*

'Limoncello?' added Rosa.

There was common assent to both questions, and Paul went into the kitchen to sort the drinks out.

When he came back through, five minutes later with a tray holding three espresso cups, three glasses of *limoncello* and a bowl of homemade chocolate truffles, he saw that Francesca had taken a big pile of photographs out of her bag and placed them on the table.

'I've got the photographs you took at the Foreign Ministry and the ones you took on Friday morning down in the EUR district. We've identified quite a few people in them, but there are a lot of unknowns – I thought it might be worth having a quick look through together to see if we can identify any more.'

The look through wasn't very fruitful, although none of them had really expected that it would be. Most of the relevant people had already been identified. Rosa smiled as she saw the PalaEUR in the background of one of the shots. 'I remember taking Mati there back in March ninety-nine to see the *Spice Girls* as part of their *Spiceworld Tour*... you refused to come for some reason!... Oh! 'she exclaimed,' dropping the photograph with the PalaEUR and picking up one of the last photographs Paul had taken outside the Foreign Ministry, 'What's he doing there?'

'Ah! He's the one I said that I was sure I'd seen before, but I couldn't remember where.'

'Siena. That's where we saw him. Don't you remember, back in that first winter we were together? We went to see Avvocato Guerrini at his legal practice in Siena – foul, repulsive man – was really horrible about Nonna.'

'Of course! I knew I'd seen him before, but just couldn't place him. You're right... even though he's aged a bit over the last twenty years.' He looked at Rosa, and took her hand reassuringly, 'I remember you were more upset by him than I was.'

'Don't mind me. But if one of you would like to explain at some point, it might be helpful,' said Francesca.

'Paul and Rosa looked at each other. Paul nodded and Rosa turned and took her sister's hand. 'You remember that when Paul and I first met, he was trying to find out about his grandmother – Nonna's sister's relatives – relatives who we'd never been told anything about – and about whom, Nonna still doesn't like to speak?' Francesca nodded. 'Well, while Paul was still not welcome at home, we went to see the son of Nonna's older sister, who's a lawyer in Siena. It was awful. He treated us with contempt, was offensive about Nonna, and made it very clear that he wanted nothing to do with us.'

'And,' added Paul, 'not only is he a lawyer who does a lot of his work for people on the extreme right, but we're also pretty sure that he's a Freemason.'

'Charming! Is there anything else I don't know about my family?'

Chapter 14

It was almost two in the morning before Rosa and Paul had finished filling in Francesca on what they had discovered years earlier about the family background. She was a little hurt at first that she hadn't been told about everything before, but she gradually accepted that, for as long as their grandmother was alive, and wanted everything kept secret, that Rosa and Paul hadn't really had a choice, especially as there hadn't seemed to be anything that affected anyone still alive except Nonna.

'But this could change everything. As we're descended from a long line of shady political operators, most of whom make Machiavelli seem like a choir-boy, and given what you said about Guerrini's client base, he could well be at the hub of everything. Even the Freemasonry... they always thought that the list they found of the P2 membership was incomplete – this could quite easily be its direct descendent.'

'Guerrini's not going to be the figurehead of the coup. If he's true to the family's modus operandi, he'll be pulling the strings in the background, letting others expose themselves... but if we keep a close eye on him and find out who he sees and who he gets in touch with, we may well find that we're a lot closer to the centre of the conspiracy than we thought we were.'

'Don't forget that even twenty years ago, he kept files on all the family, so all three of us will need to move very circumspectly when we're anywhere near him,' said Rosa.

'Is there any chance of a phone-tap?'

Francesca gave a wry smile. 'Officially, no chance – unless Ciancolini can get the President to agree to give him the authority to take whatever measures he deems necessary – but... a friend of mine... has the technical know-how to arrange something illegal... I'll give him a call first thing in the morning and get him up to Florence. I'll have to talk to Ciancolini as well; he can go through official channels and he might just have a contact who can infiltrate the Freemasons.'

'As an Investigating Magistrate, he must know loads of them. Isn't Italian public life full of them?' asked Rosa rhetorically.

'Not just Italian public life,' said Paul darkly,' I think you'll find them over most of Europe.'

'Right,' said Rosa, 'I'm going to bed. We've got to make sure the kids get off to school in the morning. Franci, I'll bring some sheets through; you can crash on the sofa in the study.'

'OK. That sounds like a good idea. If I'm up first, I'll make the coffee.'

'*Buongiorno, Mamma; buongiorno Zia.*' said a bleary eyed Mati, easing herself onto the chair at the end of the table, 'Pass the Nutella, Alessio.'

'*Ciao*, Mati. How's it going?'

Mati rolled her eyes in a way that can only be achieved by a fourteen year old girl but Francesca, who could never resist teasing her niece continued with a sweet look on her face, 'And how's the latest boyfriend?'

Mati glanced her way for a moment and then said archly, 'I'm resting at the moment; boys can wait.'

'Very wise.' said Francesca, sounding serious, 'Give it a couple of years and we can go out on a manhunt together.' This earned her a dirty look from her sister, and a quickly smothered look of horror from her niece at the thought of going out clubbing with her ancient aunt, who'd be in her mid-thirties in a couple of years.'

'That would be really nice,' said Mati, with a transparent lack of enthusiasm that caused all the others to smile.

'Tell you what; if you get a move on, I'll give you a lift to school; it's more or less on my way.'

'It might be quicker on the bus,' said Mati, doubtfully, 'there'll be loads of traffic.'

'Doesn't matter, I've got a new bike; we'll be through the traffic in no time.'

'OK. That's cool,' said Mati, withdrawing a biscuit from her caffé latte just in time and pushing it into her mouth before it broke.

'What bike is it?' asked Alessio, looking up from his Gameboy.

'Ducati 800SS,' said Francesca, and Paul could tell that she'd been dying for someone to ask her.

'Wow! That's brilliant; much better than Dad's old Honda. When do I get to go on it?'

'I'll tell you what,' said Francesca, reaching out a hand to ruffle his hair, 'One Sunday when Fiorentina are playing at home, I'll pick you up and we'll go to the Stadium; I know someone who can get us good seats.'

'Gee, thanks. That'll be really good. Can we go when they play one of the big teams? I'd like to see them beat Lazio. That's a fascist team isn't it?'

'I think that's a bit of an exaggeration.' said Paul. 'In the past they had the backing of the Fascist regime, and because of that, they tend to attract right wing supporters even now but, like most of the others, they try and get the best players they can afford and I doubt if, as part of the recruitment process, they ask players about their political affiliations. It's not that long since Paul Gascoigne was playing for them, and I doubt very much that he was a Fascist... but, yes,' he admitted, 'I'd quite like to see them stuff Lazio too.'

When Mati was ready, Francesca slipped on her thick leather jacket and picked up her keys. 'There are a couple of helmets and two pairs of gloves in the box on the back; the helmet will probably be a bit big, but it will keep you legal – I need to avoid picking up fines now I'm working at the *Tribunale*.'

Alessio came down with them to look at the new bike which was black and silver. 'I expected it to be yellow, or red,' he said with a slight note of disappointment, 'most big Ducatis are in those colours; they look really good.'

'Yeah, well, maybe I'm not an attention seeker like you, or maybe it's because I'm middle aged – that's what your sister thinks, isn't it Mati?' There was no reply from Mati, whose head had disappeared into a plain black helmet with tinted visor.

Francesca gave Alessio a brief hug and then mounted the bike and put her own helmet on. Mati climbed up behind her as she worked the choke and pressed the starter. She nodded to her nephew, and then having glanced over her shoulder slipped the bike carefully out into the flow of traffic, checking in her mirrors as she did so to see if any other vehicles pulled out behind her. She was fairly sure that no-one was trying to follow her but, just to make sure, as soon as the traffic flow thickened, she pulled to the left and began to thread her way forwards between the two lanes of traffic.

When they set off, she could feel Mati's thighs clamped tightly to her and was conscious of her jacket being gripped tightly but, as Mati began to have more confidence in Francesca's ability to handle the big bike and thread it through the traffic, she relaxed and began to enjoy the ride more although she did unconsciously tense her leg muscles again as Francesca opened the throttle to make sure she beat the lights on the Via Circondaria. She would have to carry on working hard at school to make sure that Rosa and Paul had to maintain their promise to get her a scooter if she passed the school year with good marks in all subjects.

A group of her friends were already near the gates of the *liceo* in Via Puccinotti, leaning casually against the wall, several of them pulling on cigarettes as they relaxed before going into school. Francesca dropped Mati off about ten metres beyond them and passed her the keys to open the top-box and replace the helmet and gloves. As Francesca still had her helmet on, instead of kissing as they parted, they exchanged a quick high five before Mati joined the watching teenagers and her aunt, knowing that Mati would want her to put on a show, revved the engine more than was strictly necessary and roared off into the distance. 'My aunt,' said Mati, 'She's alright.'

There were a number of reasons why Francesca had treated herself to the bike; what she told everyone was that it was something she'd always wanted, and now she could afford it, so why not and, to a certain extent, that was true – but she knew that it wasn't the real reason. If it hadn't been for Arturo's murder she would never have got round to buying a big bike. Although, at times, she felt a little apprehensive while threading through traffic, this was far outweighed by the knowledge that the bike gave her far more independence and made her much more difficult to follow. It would also, she hoped, mean that, if necessary, she was able to follow other people without being noticed – that had been why she had avoided the classic Ducati colours of yellow and red, preferring instead the more sober black and silver that had disappointed Alessio. She smiled in her helmet as she thought about her reply to her nephew – she knew that, if she hadn't had to think about practical concerns, that she would have gone for the yellow, and that those who knew her best, like Rosa, would consider her to have always been the biggest attention seeker in the family.

At twelve-thirty she emerged from the *Tribunale* after another morning of pointless work tasks and Solitaire and, after a careful check to make sure that it had not been tampered with, got on the bike again. After a few hundred metres, she turned off the road and cut down a narrow alleyway that was comfortably wide enough for a bike, but not wide enough for a car to follow. When she came out onto the road at the other end, she almost immediately pulled into the side between two parked cars, and watched the entrance to the alleyway for over a minute just to make sure that no-one on two wheels was following her.

When she was satisfied, she turned the bike round and headed towards the Ponte dell'Indiano to cross the Arno. Once she reached the end of the *viadotto*, she turned right onto the Fi-Pi-Li superstrada for a short while before joining the motorway at the Firenze-Scandicci junction, opening up the throttle and heading in the direction of Rome.

Just over an hour and a quarter later, she pulled her glove back on, having paid the motorway toll and made her way carefully up the hill from the Orvieto motorway exit, past the bottom end of the historic Pozzo di San Patrizio and into the centre of the town. Leaving the bike near the ornate Cathedral, she made her way down to a somewhat expensive looking trattoria in a cobbled street nearby and pushed the door open. Marco was sitting at a table set for two, situated just by the window, reading the *Gazzetta dello Sport*. She went over and kissed him on the cheek before easing her leather jacket off and settling into the chair opposite him.

'This looks a bit expensive,' she said, looking around her at the rustic brick archways, terracotta floor tiles and immaculately laid tables.

'Nothing but the best is good enough for you,' he said with a smile, then after a pause, 'and anyway, the owner is a distant relative of mine, so we'll be treated well. We can also stay the night, if you don't have to get back.'

'Alright. I'll have to buy a couple of things as I wasn't expecting to stay, but so long as I can get away by quarter to seven in the morning, it shouldn't be a problem... I talked to Rosa and Paul last night...'

He reached out a hand and laid it on top of hers, 'Let's eat first – just for once, the rest can wait.' He glanced over at one of the waiters and the young man, who had clearly been keeping an eye on them as they settled down, came over immediately, note pad at the ready.

'May I get you some drinks before I take your orders?'

'Yes please. I'll have a Campari and soda... Franci?'

'For now could I just have a lemon juice, please – I need something refreshing.'

'Certainly, I'll get them straight away and... could I just say that as well as what's on the menu, today we also have *Pici al coniglio e tartuffo* and, as main courses, *stufato d'istrice and trippa alla romana*.' The waiter gave a little bow and moved away to get the drinks.

'Mmmm. Interesting specials. I like the idea of rabbit and truffles as a pasta sauce, but I've never been keen on *pici* – it's impossible to eat them without getting some of the sauce down your front.' As she said it she watched his eyes lower to where the swell of her breasts was accentuated by the sheen of her silk blouse. 'Don't even think it,' she said, waving an admonitory finger at him.'

'I can't imagine what you mean, ' he replied with a smile and an exaggerated sigh, 'I'm a perfect gentleman and my thoughts are entirely honourable.'

She leaned forward, 'That's a shame – I was thinking of accepting your invitation to stay the night... but if you only have honourable intentions, I may as well go back to Florence.'

'I may be corruptible. You'd better put me to the test before you make your mind up.'

Chapter 15

After, Marco lay on the bed, watching the equally naked Francesca brushing her hair, as she sat in-front of the dressing-table mirror. 'Have you been to New York?' he asked.

'No. Why?'

'There's a picture there by Degas called 'Nude brushing her hair,' or something like that – can't think what brought it to mind at the moment.'

She laughed, 'Bear in mind that there are lots of pictures of mythological scenes showing what happens to voyeurs.'

He got off the bed and went and put his arms around her. As she finished brushing, she put the brush down and gently removed his arms, kissing one of his forearms as she moved them away. 'Put some clothes on; we need to talk, and I need to go out and buy a new pair of knickers and a toothbrush.'

'So you want me to find out as much as I can about this lawyer, Guerrini... the Freemason angle could be an interesting one, although it could make things even more complicated... I don't suppose Ciancolini is a member of any lodge, is he?'

'She smiled, imagining the Judge with his trousers rolled up to knees, wearing a leather apron and holding a trowel. 'I'd like to see it if he was,' then becoming more serious, 'I'd be amazed if he was, but I'll ask him... I'll also ask Dad if he knows of any honest masons who might be prepared to talk to us, off the record.'

He looked at her with curiosity, head tilted slightly to one side, 'Why would your father know any?'

'When he was a teacher, you can't imagine how often he came moaning, saying that such and such could only have been appointed to their teaching posts because both they and some of those in the Education Department at the *Regione* must be masons... and now he's a City Councillor, he's even more convinced.'

'And do you think anyone's likely to talk to him?'

She shrugged, 'It's worth a try. I know that originally the masonic lodges were set up not just to protect their members, but also to do good deeds – so of all the masons he's come across, there must be some good ones who'd be prepared to put their loyalty to the State ahead of their loyalty to their Lodge.'

'*Ma,*' he said, indicating that he hadn't much faith in the success of this idea, then he stopped suddenly in front of the window of a lingerie shop. 'How about those?' he said, pointing at a pair of very skimpy thongs with a raised faux-fur heart on the front.'

She giggled, 'Mum always used to say, "make sure you've got clean knickers on in case you get knocked down and have to go to hospital", but I think she'd probably prefer me to arrive at the hospital knickerless than wearing those – and anyway, I'm at least twenty years too old to wear something like that.'

He put an arm round her, 'You can wear those for as long as you've got a good figure, and there aren't many eighteen year olds who can compete with your figure.'

Francesca kissed him, 'Flattery will get you everywhere, you know that, but I still don't think I'd feel particularly comfortable riding the bike or sitting at my desk tomorrow morning. I'll tell you what – if you get a pair of the ones you can buy with an elephant's trunk on the front, I'll get those to wear when we're together, but I need to buy some more practical ones as well.'

When she had bought a change of underwear, a toothbrush and a top she could wear for work the following morning, they continued to walk around the town. 'It's not at its best at the moment,' said Marco, 'everything's pretty drab here during January; people are getting over New Year and the *Befana* and are recharging their batteries so they're ready to come to life again for Carnevale.'

'What about the ministers and others we're watching down in Rome – are they recharging their batteries at the moment?'

'Most of them seem to be keeping a fairly low profile at the moment. Except for Marelli, of course. He's appeared on every news-channel, at least once, talking up the terrorist threat, and arguing that the only way to protect the citizens is to tighten up some of the "overly liberal laws that have been allowed to creep onto the statute book", although he never gets challenged on how far he intends to tighten them up. Caprai, the Minister for Communications has supported him, insisting that in future there needs to be a greater level of editorial control, to ensure that young people are not radicalised and turned against the State by extreme left-wing propaganda.'

'How about the Mitrokhin Commission – has that met since last week? D'Alema was meant to be appearing before it again, wasn't he.'

Marco clapped his hand to his forehead, 'I forgot to tell you. Mitrokhin died, last weekend, in London, so even though it doesn't really make a difference, as they have his archive anyway, they've suspended the hearings for a week, as a mark of respect. It probably won't make much difference, it just means that if anything is unclear, they can't go back to the original source, to verify it.'

They walked to the end of the street where a large tree filled Piazza was dominated by a large *Caserma*, sat down on one of the many benches in the square in front of the barracks, and Francesca snuggled up to him to keep out the cold. 'Ciancolini should be on his way to Brussels now; I spoke to Marie yesterday, to confirm that she can get an interview with Prodi – Ciancolini will accompany her, ostensibly as her technician.'

'Let's just hope that their security isn't too tight in Brussels. We don't really want Ciancolini to be arrested – that really would draw attention to the investigation.'

'He'll be alright. I think he's more resourceful than he looks.'

'Let's hope so... What about the President of the Republic?'

'I'm going to see Cecco Busoni the day after tomorrow, He's got a study in Tavarnelle, and he's also the Deputy Mayor for the *Comune*, apparently he's pretty popular and has been pushed to stand for the provincial or regional councils on a number of occasions, but has always refused.'

'That's unusual: a politician who lacks ambition.'

'I hear that he's a very reluctant politician who only agreed to stand locally to please his father before he died.'

'And you're sure he can be trusted.. and if he can, that he can get Ciancolini in to see the President.'

'That's what Ciancolini says... Did you manage to get the bugs into the offices in the various ministries?'

'It wasn't easy, but we've managed to get them into most of the offices. Surprisingly, the biggest problem has turned out to be the Communications Ministry, down in EUR; we got the bugs in, but there's so much technical equipment in the building that something is interfering with our signal; we're working on it.'

She shot him a sharp glance, 'When you say "we", who else is involved?'

'Don't worry, 'Raffaello and Nico are as honest as they come. I met them when I was in prison; I'd trust them with my life.'

She shook her head in disbelief, 'So what were they inside for... a holiday?'

He met the doubt in her voice with equanimity, 'Raffaello, saw two policemen giving a tramp a kicking in a doorway one morning, and decided that he ought to make the sides a bit more even. Unfortunately, a squad car just happened to pass by as he was laying in, and the judge gave him two years. As for Nico, he was convinced that his employers were involved in dodgy financial practices and used his computer skills to set about proving it. He found evidence that incorrect financial figures had been signed off by the company's auditors and thought he was doing the right thing by going to the authorities. The owner of the company he worked for had friends in high places and Nico was prosecuted as a hacker. Ironically, five years later, his ex-boss is under arrest, several officials at the banks they dealt with and two accountancy firms they used, are all under judicial investigation. Not a word of an apology, let alone a pardon and compensation for Nico of course.'

Francesca laughed, 'It sounds as if our prisons are more efficient recruitment agencies than the labour exchanges.'

'You can laugh, but you'd be surprised. You obviously get some genuine thugs and amoral characters, but a lot of the people in there are people who just happen to have developed their own moral code that doesn't fit in with the ideas of some people in influential positions. Now, of course, we're starting to see quite a few more people in there who've previously held important positions and then come unstuck.'

'Mmmm. I can think of quite a few more who I'd like to see join them.'

He put an arm round her, 'Well, give it another few weeks, or maybe months, and either they'll be in there, or we will.'

Francesca woke half an hour before the alarm and hearing the rain outside decided that she'd better make an early start for what was going to be an unpleasant journey up the motorway on the bike.

She picked up her clothes and slipped quietly into the bathroom, hoping to let Marco sleep a bit longer, but when she came out of the bathroom she saw that he had also got out of bed and disappeared.

A couple of minutes later he reappeared carrying a small tray with two espresso cups on it. He smiled, 'When I heard the rain, I realised you'd want to get away as soon as possible, so I went down to the restaurant kitchen and made some coffee; I'm sure they won't mind.'

'You're a treasure,' she said taking one of the small cups and disposing of its contents in one mouthful. 'If I go now, and the rain doesn't slow me down too much, I might just have time to get changed before I go into work.'

'Go on,' he said, taking the empty cup from her. 'the quicker you get away, the less risks you'll have to take to get there on time. I want you to get there safely... Here, let me hold the jacket while you slip in to it... OK?... Here are your gloves.... Be careful... and send me a message to let me know you've arrived safely.' She gave him a quick kiss and then slipped out of the door quietly.

Chapter 16

Cecco Busoni's study was down a side-street less than a hundred metres away from the central piazza. As the street was one-way, she left the Ducati in the piazza and completed the journey on foot. There was no longer any sign of the previous day's rain and, despite it only being early February, it felt quite warm in the square where the surrounding buildings kept out the cold northerly wind but allowed in the late winter sun. The surveyor's study, stood out from the rest of the buildings in the street, not because there was any great architectural difference, but because it was the only building not to have shutters on its downstairs windows.

The wide glazed door was set back about a metre from the front of the building in an entrance way which had one wall at a right angle to the door and the facade, and the other sloping away from the door at an angle of about one hundred and twenty degrees, almost as if Busoni expected all his clients to arrive from that direction and then to leave the same way. A white plastic plaque on the sloping wall, confirmed in red letters that this was indeed the study of 'Geometra Francesco Busoni', although a smaller plaque that had been glued onto the bottom of the other, informed her that Sara and Susanna Busoni were also qualified surveyors and were working out of the same study.

There was no bell, and Francesca found that the door opened to her touch, and made her way inside. A woman of about her own age, with fairly plain, but friendly looking features, looked up from a large drawing board that was propped up at an angle, casting a quick look at the wall-mounted clock as she did so. 'Hello,' she said, in a rich friendly voice, 'You must be Francesca Conte, here to see my father... I'm Susanna... pleased to meet you.'

Francesca took the hand that was offered to her, noting that the grip was surprisingly firm, and confirming that she was indeed the expected visitor. 'I'll take you through to see him, then I'll make you both a coffee... or would you prefer tea?'

Francesca raised an eyebrow in surprise, 'I think that a tea would be nice on a day like this, although I'm not used to being offered tea when I go somewhere new.'

Susanna smiled, 'My father spent three years working at the Cafe Royal, in London, in the mid-fifties, before he came back here and studied to become a surveyor. He acquired a taste for tea while he was there, and it's never left him.' She opened a door at the back of the room, poked her head in and said, 'Babbo, Signorina Conte is here to see you... I'll make some tea.'

A jovial looking man with white hair and beard, probably well into his seventies, came towards the door with a hand outstretched, towards which she raised her own. To her surprise, he raised her hand to his lips and kissed it as a greeting. 'Welcome, signorina. Please come in and take a seat... Judge Ciancolini said that you were coming to ask a very important, and very sensitive, favour, but wouldn't go into any more detail on the phone. I'm intrigued. Please tell me how I can help.'

She had been going over this conversation in her head, on the bike on the way over, but now, everything she had mentally rehearsed seemed artificial and, deciding that she was going to go with Ciancolini's judgement, she decided to go straight in. 'Over the last few months, we have become aware of a group of right-wing conspirators who are well advanced in their plans to mount a *coup d'état*. We believe that it is possible to thwart the plotters but, as a significant number of them hold influential positions, including in the security forces, we're unable to follow the usual procedures in trying to avert this threat.' She looked at Busoni, who looked grave but motioned that she should continue.

'Before Judge Ciancolini became involved, the covert operation to expose the conspirators was being led by Judge Arturo dell'Omodarme – does that name ring any bells?' She glanced at him and he nodded to show that he knew who she was referring to. We also have good reason to believe that Loriana Cabrini-Pellé was under pressure to throw in her lot with the conspirators but refused – and paid for that refusal with her life. '

'Just a minute; Cabrini-Pellé died in a road traffic accident, didn't she?'

Francesca gave a mirthless smile. 'That's what we're all meant to believe, but we have conclusive evidence to show that the events of that night did not play out in the way that the authorities have claimed. Cabrini-Pellé was murdered, and her former friends have tried to make the best of it by using it to suggest that tougher laws may be needed – to help guarantee the Public's safety, of course.'

He looked perplexed, 'This is a very bad situation, but I'm not sure how I can really help you, other than by wishing you luck.'

Francesca leaned forwards towards him. 'Signor Busoni; there is a way in which you can be of great assistance, but before I ask for your help, I want to make sure that you fully understand how serious this situation is,' and she proceeded to outline for him what they knew about the plot, including the threat to assassinate Prodi and other key leaders of the left, after having first used information from the Mitrokhin Commission to turn the people against them.

It took over an hour to explain the complexities of the situation to Busoni and why they were hoping he could use his late father's old friendship with the President to get access. When she had finished, he didn't say anything but went over to the window and looked out, clearly deep in thought. Francesca sat silently, until he turned having made his decision, when she looked at him expectantly.

'My father always said that we'd won the battle against the right; that Marx was right, and that once the bourgeois Christian Democratic Party had been exposed and swept aside, the triumph of the proletariat would be inevitable... I never really believed him – although it was a beautiful dream – and he was always disappointed that I didn't get more involved in politics... Now I think he was right – about getting involved in politics, I mean. People like me have just stood back and let others get on with it, and that's one of the reasons why the country's in such a mess... But if there's anything I can do that will help democracy, then I will.'

Francesca was about to speak but he silenced her with a motion, ' You probably don't know, but my grandfather and my little sister were both killed by the fascists, and I'm sure they took years off my mother's life... When my father went to join the partisans, he thought that we'd be safe, back in our little house in Bargino, but he was wrong; they kept coming, hoping to find my father and making life as difficult as possible for my mother. Then one day, they arrested her. My little sister didn't understand what was happening and tried to hold on to her. They just threw her on the floor and she banged her head.'

'Bargino!' said Francesca with a note of surprise.

'Yes. It's a little village just a few kilometres along the Cassia, half way to San Casciano... It's where I grew up... Blink and you'd miss it.'

'Sorry, Yes... I know where it is. I was just surprised, although I suppose there's no real reason why I should be... My grandmother lived there for a few years before the war... but you'd be too young to remember her.'

He gave her a warm smile, 'I always like being flattered, it's good for my ego, but I'm afraid I was already eight years old by the time Italy joined the war... what was your grandmother's name... the village wasn't really big enough for people not to at least be aware of everyone else.'

'Maddi, or Maddalena Campolargo. She was born in 1918, but I think that until she was fourteen, she spent almost all her time in the Val d'Aosta.' She smiled at him but was surprised to see that, although his mouth still seemed friendly, something seemed to have hardened around his eyes.

They were both silent for a few seconds, then he sighed and began to speak. 'How much do you know about your family's history, signorina?'

'Very little, I'm afraid. My grandmother cut off all contact with the rest of the family after the war and has always refused to discuss them. What little I do know, is what I've been told by my older sister and my brother-in-law who, odd as it may seem, is the grandson of my grandmother's sister. There was quite a fuss at home when they met.'

Busoni's eyes seemed to have relaxed again and warmth returned to his voice when he spoke again. 'The Campolargo family lived in a big house up on the hill between Bargino and Santa Cristina in Salivolpe – there's nothing left of it now, except the foundations, and they're covered with grass and brambles. The house was badly damaged when the Allies came down the valley in forty-four and people helped themselves to most of the stonework to rebuild other properties, hoping that that would dissuade the Campolargos from ever coming back.' He smiled at her half apologetically. 'Your family were the effective lords of the local area for well over two-hundred years until the Second World War, but your great-grandfather and most of your grandmother's older brothers and sisters threw in their lot with Mussolini and most of them shared in his downfall. I didn't really know anything about it at the time but later on, my father used to sit for hours and talk about the past, and what we needed to learn from it. The Campolargos were such important players that they had quite a big influence on our family.'

'So,' Francesca asked hesitantly, 'do you remember my grandmother?'

He shook his head, 'I'm afraid that little boys only really take any notice of grown up women, if they're particularly pleasant or unpleasant towards them. I must have seen her at some point, but I have no recollection of her. I remember what must have been one of her brothers, because everyone was scared of him, and all us kids tried to keep well out of the way if we saw him coming into the village. Someone who I do remember quite well though is the Englishman who ran away with your grandmother's sister. He knew my father and my father helped them to get away... but I don't remember that, my father told me about it, years later.... But he came back... the Englishman... he came back late one night, not long before the end of the war. My mother told me a little bit about him the next day, and then my father told me the whole story later on.'

'What an amazing coincidence. I must tell Paul – my brother-in-law – I'm sure he'd really like to talk to you about what you remember. He never knew his grandfather because he was killed just after the Allies took Florence. He's buried in the military cemetery at Compiobbi.'

Now it was Busoni's turn to look surprised. 'I wish my father had known. He'd have wanted to go and pay his respects.'

'Did... did your father tell you anything about my grandmother?' asked Francesca, trying her hardest not to seem too desperate for information.

'Most of what he told me was about the older brothers and sisters – almost all things that were unpleasant as far as regarded the brothers and the oldest sister, and then positive about Chiara, who I think he saw as having been very brave. All I can remember him saying about your grandmother is that he thought she'd been forced into an unfortunate marriage with someone influential in the regime – I'm sorry if that's upsetting to hear about your grandfather.'

'Don't worry,' she gave a reassuring smile, 'like Paul's grandfather, ours was killed when Florence was liberated, and he's someone else who my grandmother has always avoided talking about. I get the impression that he wasn't a great loss to her.'

'Now... we could talk about the past for a long time, couldn't we? But that's not going to affect the future, and I think we both realise that that's what's important at the moment... Susanna!' he called.

Seconds later the door opened and Susanna Busoni put her head around, '*Si*, Babbo?'

Busoni smiled at her, 'Susi, could you possibly find me the number of the Quirinale; I need to make a call.'

Susanna nodded and withdrew, managing to hide any surprise she may have felt.

Within a minute she was back with a number written on a post-it note. 'Here you are. This is the general number for the public; I hope that's the right one.'

'That's great. Oh, by the way, you must have a chat with Signorina Conte here – we've discovered that our families knew each other in the dim and distant past.'

'I'd be delighted to. Is there anything else you need just now? I've got a client coming in soon to talk about possible designs for a roof-terrace on his house.'

Busoni grinned at her, 'Go on. I'm sure you'll be able to persuade him to choose the design that you think is best.' She withdrew, pretending to look hurt at the suggestion that she would manipulate her client.

He tapped the number she had given him into the phone on his desk and pressed the speaker-phone button. They heard the phone ring three times and then a serious female voice said, 'Thank you for ringing the Quirinale, official residence of the President of the Republic. If you know the extension you require, please dial one followed by the extension; if you are ringing regarding a petition, please dial two; if you are ringing about the President's official schedule, please dial three; if your call relates to a specific ministry, please dial four and make your selection from the following menu; if you are calling about any other matter, please wait for the next available operator.' Busoni waited and after ten seconds, which was presumably considered long enough for all callers to decide how to proceed, they were regaled with the rousing sound of the National Anthem, *Fratelli d'Italia*.

As the last notes of the anthem were abruptly cut off, the female voice was heard again, 'We're sorry, but all of our operators are busy at the moment due to an exceptional volume of traffic; your call is important to us and someone will be with you as soon as possible. Alternatively you may wish to consider going to our website, www.quirinale.it and clicking on Frequently Asked Questions,' and then *Fratelli d'Italia* started up again.

Busoni gave a resigned shrug of his shoulders and leaned back on his chair, elbows resting on the arm rests and hands steepled with the tips of his index fingers resting on his lips. Francesca rolled her eyes and shook her head.

Suddenly, just before the anthem reached its climax, a different, younger sounding female voice cut in, in place of the music, '*Buonasera*. My name is Nadia from the Information Office of the President of the Republic; how may I help you?'

'Ah... *Buonasera*, Signorina. My name is Francesco Busoni; I'm a surveyor from the Val di Pesa in Tuscany, and I've known the president for over fifty years. I need to speak to the president urgently regarding a private matter, and would be grateful if you could put me through to his office, where I'm sure they will need to verify my identity before putting me through to him personally.'

The voice of the receptionist at the Quirinale sounded slightly less confident as she said, 'Would you mind just holding the line please, while I see what I can do?'

'Of course, Signorina... Oh, and if it's at all possible, could I listen to something other than *Fratelli d'Italia* while I wait.'

Francesca heard the receptionist laugh and admired how Busoni seemed to have the knack of putting people at ease. 'I think we may be able to manage a bit of Verdi, if that's OK.'

'That will be lovely, thankyou,' said Busoni, and winked at Francesca as the receptionist's voice was replaced by the first notes of the overture to *La Forza del Destino*. 'She'll be asking her line manager what to do when someone calls claiming to be an old friend of the President – I suppose that they must get plenty of calls from people claiming to know him.'

Francesca nodded, 'The first stage will be checking your phone to make sure that it's registered to the person you claim to be and then to see if your name appears on their list of undesirables – it's a bit like passport control.'

They obviously had efficient systems for checking people out, for in little more than a minute the music was interrupted and the receptionist was back again, '*Pronto* – Signor Busoni?'

'Yes, I'm still here, enjoying the music.'

'I'm sorry to interrupt it, but I'm putting you through to Laura Foggini, one of the President's personal assistants.'

'Thank you, Signorina, that's very kind of you, have a good day.'

'And you, Sir, it's been a pleasure speaking to you.' There were a few seconds of indistinct metallic noises and then another, this time very business-like, female voice came on the line. '*Buongiorno*, Signor Busoni, I understand that you wish to speak to the President; may I ask what about?'

'I'm afraid it's regarding a very private matter, and one on which I'm only able to speak to the President directly.'

'I'll need to run a few security checks and then, if everything is alright, the President will call you back when his schedule allows. May I just ask for some basic information to speed up the verification process?'

'Of course. Ask away.'

The PA took down all Busoni's personal details and then asked how he'd made the acquaintance of the President, and what level of contact they'd had in the past. Busoni explained how his father and the President had fought together with the partisans in the last months of the war, and how their shared experiences had created a lasting bond. After the war, the President had visited the Busoni home on many occasions before he became famous and they had had sporadic contact since. In recent years that had amounted to little more than exchanging greetings on family birthdays or at

Christmas, but the President had always told Busoni that if there was ever anything really important, he shouldn't hesitate to call.

'We'll have to double check this information, but we should be able to get back to you within half an hour to give you an idea of when the President may be able to call.'

'That's excellent; I look forward to your call.' Busoni put the phone back in its cradle and smiled apologetically at Francesca. 'I hope you weren't in a hurry,' she shook her head and he continued, 'Let me show you round the office while we wait, so that you appreciate the type of work that we do... but first I'd better make some more coffee... It's my turn!'

After he'd made the coffee, he showed her the different rooms in the building, explaining who worked in them and what their particular areas of expertise were, talking her through some of the plans on the walls, which she found intriguing.

They had just got back into Busoni's office when the phone rang. Busoni picked up almost immediately.

'*Pronto*. Studio Busoni.' …... 'Ah.. *Buonasera*, Signor President. I didn't expect to be speaking to you so soon; your charming assistant said she'd ring to let me know when you'd be available,' …. (Busoni laughed), 'OK. OK. Alé; I promise I won't call you Signor President again – unless we meet in public.' …. 'They're fine, thankyou. You know that Sara has had the baby, don't you?' …. 'Yes, yes. Of course. I will.' … 'And how about yours? How's your charming wife?' …. 'Oh. I'm sorry to hear that. You must be taking her to too many boring receptions now you're a VIP.' … 'Give my love to all of them, won't you. And make sure you make enough time to play with the grandkids won't you.' … 'Listen, I know you're busy, and probably have a queue of Ministers and Ambassadors waiting to see you, so I'll get to the point.' … 'Yes, of course. Listen; there's something that I need to discuss with you urgently, but it's something I can't really discuss over the phone.' … 'Yes, it's serious. You know I've never asked for anything before,' … 'No. Don't worry; I'm not in trouble, and I don't want any favours for myself or my family – it's all above board – just very sensitive.' …. 'I'd rather not wait until next week; I can get down there if you can find an hour to fit me in anytime on Saturday or Sunday.' …. 'Yes. I'm sure, and yes, it is that important.' … 'OK. That would be great; just one thing; I won't be alone, there'll be someone else with me.' … 'No, I'd rather not – you'll understand why later,' … 'Yes, I can vouch for this person absolutely.' … 'No problem. Thank you, Alé; we'll see you on Sunday morning,' … '*Ciao*. Same to you.' and he replaced the phone. Francesca looked at him, leaning forward slightly in eager anticipation to hear what he had to say.

'Your end of the conversation sounded very promising,' she said, fishing for further information.

'So was his. The only slight complication is that he's scheduled to travel down to Naples tomorrow morning. Some visiting dignitaries who are dangling a big trade deal, have expressed a wish to see Pompeii and Herculaneum, so instead of hosting them in Rome, he'll be using Villa Rosebery, his official residence in Naples. It means we've got more travelling to do, but I thought that the sooner I could get you, or Judge Ciancolini, in to see him, the better.'

'I'd love to go with you, but it might carry more weight if the Judge goes with you so, provided he's back from Brussels and willing to go away again straight away, then I'm afraid it will be him.'

'Ah well. Never mind. I've got a lot of catching up to do with Bettino, although I think that I might have enjoyed your company more.'

Chapter 17

'Well done, Franci. It could hardly have gone better.'

'Yeah. He was a lovely old man, still sharp as a knife and full of enthusiasm. I think he was half hoping I'd suggest taking him down to Naples on the back of the bike.'

'Should I be jealous?'

'I've got to keep you on your toes, Marco; I don't want you taking me for granted.'

'Not much chance of that!'

'Alright. I need to get some sleep now... speak to you tomorrow... Be careful!'

'Don't worry about me. Sleep well. Bye.'

'Ciao, ciao. Buonanotte.'

Francesca didn't put the phone down immediately after the communication ended, but waited a few seconds before giving it a little kiss and gently putting it down on the bedside-table. She turned the light off, pulled the duvet up to her chin so that her shoulders were covered and slowly pushed her feet down towards the end of the bed knowing that, despite feeling tired, she wouldn't be able to get to sleep until her cold feet had warmed up so that they matched the rest of her body.

As she lay, waiting, she tried to collect together and organise the different strands of their investigation into the conspiracy, but her mind kept drifting back to Marco. She wondered why she had waited until he had rung off before sending the kiss, surely he deserved more from her. Thinking of how she had said, "I don't want you taking me for granted," she felt guilty, knowing that, if anything, it was she who sometimes took him for granted. He was loyal, intelligent, handsome and a considerate lover with a good sense of humour – so why didn't she tell him what she felt? He made no secret of his own feelings for her, and yet she'd always held back from fully committing. Why?

She imagined him playing with small children, and in the picture she imagined, he didn't look out of place... but there was something missing... what was it?... that was it... she was missing... her imagination didn't stretch to showing herself visions of herself as a mother, looking after little children. But, why not? She liked children... she'd doted on Mati and Alessio when they'd been young – still did, in fact – and Rosa had never had any problem in finding a willing baby sitter. Rosa; she thought about her elder sister with affection. She'd always looked up to her as the person she most wanted to be like while she'd been growing up; she'd never wanted to be a princess, or a singer, she'd just wanted to be pretty, clever, athletic and praised by everyone, like her sister was. But Rosa had changed after Mati was born; she'd become gentler, less ambitious, channelling her energy and her hopes in to her children, less driven... less selfish. No – she shook her head – Rosa had never been selfish; she'd always done everything she could for her younger sister – it was more some sort of desire to be as successful as you could be, that she had lost.

Was that what she, Franci, was afraid of? Was she afraid that by committing herself definitively to sharing her life with someone else, with all that that entailed, that she would be giving up on other things – the things that she thought of as defining who she was. Yes, she thought – that was probably it; she was afraid that by committing herself to Marco and then having a child, or children, she would no longer be the Francesca she'd worked so hard to become. Under the duvet, she let her fingers glide over the smooth, taut skin of her belly and abdomen and tried to imagine how it must feel to be distended by pregnancy and how hard it would be to get back in shape afterwards. As she did so, she realised that what was really stopping her taking the next step with Marco was fear – not fear of Marco, but fear of change, fear of having to definitively grow up – and she knew that it was a fear she would have to overcome.

She opened her eyes wide, determined to focus on the realisation that had just come to her, knowing that otherwise, the thoughts she'd had while half asleep would be indistinct, or even completely forgotten, when she woke up in the morning. When she allowed herself to relax again, she thought about Rosa, how happy and contented she was, and how she'd carved out a successful career for herself as a researcher at the university, and with her glass paintings. Then she thought of Donatella Curci, the immaculately turned out Head of HR at the *Tribunale* – when she wasn't within earshot, the other girls who worked there gossiped about how she'd been driven to succeed and how, in the past, she'd turned down several proposals from one of the most eligible judges, because she thought that marriage at that time would interfere with her career –

now she was successful, but in her early fifties and alone. She'd achieved what she'd set out to achieve, and now what? Was she really happy? Did she have someone to share her success with? Did she even have friends rather than acquaintances? Francesca doubted it. She realised that she felt sorry for Curci, and that she didn't want her life to end up like that, with people feeling sorry for her. She leaned over and groped on the bedside table until she found her mobile. Opening the cover, she tapped in, "Ti amo", found Marco's number in the "Address Book", pressed send, then turned the phone to silent and closed the cover.

When the alarm went off in the morning, memories of the previous night's thinking seeped back into her consciousness as she gradually became more awake. She leaned over and picked up her phone. There was one message and she felt her heart-beat increase as she clicked on the icon. The message just said, "Of course ;-))", and she felt a surge of warmth spread through her; he hadn't just replied with 'I love you too,' or something similar, as she'd expected, he'd realised that there was no need; she already knew that he loved her, and he knew she knew – there was no need to tell her again, as if it were a revelation – everything was as it should be.

After a *caffé latte* and a handful of biscuits, she rang the number of Rosa and Paul, remembering that she needed to tell Paul what she had learned about his grandfather the previous day. It was Alessio who answered and they chatted for a minute before he saluted her and passed the phone to Rosa. Again there was friendly sisterly chat for a couple of minutes before Francesca said, 'Actually, Rosa, I was hoping to grab a quick word with Paul; is he about?'

'No. Someone rang him last night and asked him if he could go down to Rome and take some more pictures for the book project. He got the train at six fifty and doesn't get back into Florence until twenty past nine tonight. I can't see him getting here before ten.... Is it something I can help you with?'

'It's not really help I need; it's just that I was talking to someone yesterday who met Paul's grandfather during the war. I thought he'd be interested.'

'Oh, he will. When can you come round and tell us about it?' said Rosa enthusiastically. Almost forgetting that Francesca didn't know their grandmother's secret, that Paul's grandfather was actually theirs as well.

'Not this evening; maybe Thursday afternoon, if you're both free. We could meet for a coffee in The Giubbe Rosse... I'm buying.'

'It's fine with me. I'll ask Paul tonight and let you know. I think he's got to meet some students whose theses he's supervising, but he should be done by four and he'll already be in the centre.'

'Alright. Provisionally four thirty then, and if there are no free tables in the Giubbe Rosse we can always go across to Paszkowski.'

'OK I'll let you know. *Bacioni. Ciao, ciao.*

'*Ciao* Rosa – Big hug!'

After she had ended the call, before she had even had time to slip the phone into the pocket of her jacket, the opening bars of the theme tune to Benigni's *"La Vita é Bella"* vibrated through it. She flipped it open again and clicked on 'Messages' and then 'Inbox'; the screen told her that there was a message from "Ciancolini" and she pressed to read the message – 'Arrive Peretola 14.20 Coffee my house 18.00'. She tapped in, 'Everything OK?'. pressed "Send" and waited.

After five minutes, she decided she couldn't wait any longer or she'd be late for work, slipped the phone in her pocket, double locked the door, and left.

The morning passed a little more quickly than some of the others had, as she was given a file relating to a child abuse case, to read through and prepare notes on for Graziadei to consider. Although she did a thorough job with the file, preparing comprehensive notes for the judge and inserting numbered markers to make it clear what the evidence was that would support each stage of his developing argument, she had completed the task before eleven.

After carefully checking that no-one else could see her screen, she used Graziadei's login to access the Ministry of Justice database and looked up Busoni. As she had expected there was very little on Busoni and his daughters: Busoni had been arrested and locked up overnight while still a teenager, for throwing a brick through the window of the ex-Casa del Fascio – he had been warned for Causing Damage to Public Property, but things had not gone beyond the warning. Francesca could imagine that in the immediate aftermath of the war, when most Italians were keen to claim that they had never supported fascism, throwing a brick through the window of a building that had previously been the home of the fascist administration was hardly likely to have been considered a serious crime. One of the daughters had been fined for Possession of Cannabis, a few years before, but that was the full extent of their criminal records.

Cecco Busoni's father, however, Giorgio Busoni, had a much more colourful history. In the post war period, he had been arrested several times during demonstrations, but none of these had led to criminal charges. Before that, however, he seemed to have been almost constantly in trouble with the Fascist regime. Francesca was glad that the process of digitising the ministry's archives had recently been completed, even if, as yet, it wasn't available to the general public. Many of the smaller charges, which had led to fines, or confiscation of goods, were clearly the result of petty harassment by the regime, but on several occasions he had been arrested for 'Disturbing the Peace' or 'Using offensive language to a public official', charges which had each time earned him stays of between four days and a month in the old Murate prison. Most interesting of all, however, were two entries from during the war years: In December nineteen forty he had been one of fourteen men from the Province of Florence who had been charged with desertion and sentenced to death, in absentia; he had obviously not been caught and the sentence had not been carried out, but later, in October nineteen forty-three he had again been given a summary trial in absentia, accused of sabotage and acts injurious to the good of the state; again he had been sentenced to death, and again they had, apparently, been unable to capture him.

Delving deeper in to the classified files of the Ministry, she found that in nineteen sixty-two he had also appeared as a character witness in the trial of a low level Mafia boss. In his statement, a copy of which was held in the file, Busoni said that, yes, he was aware of the accused's Mafia background but that after the Allied invasion, he had joined the allied troops and regularly risked his life as an advanced scout - unlike several of those now sitting in judgement over him, who had made sure that they were well out of harm's way during the fighting, while not being reluctant to take plaudits afterwards. While there could be no doubt, he had said, that the modern Mafia with its links to international crime syndicates and propensity to violence, was an abomination, the Judges would do well to remember that it had originally started because the nobles and absentee landlords had ignored the needs of the people they claimed to protect and the Italian State had been unable to protect the Sicilian people after the island had been annexed in eighteen sixty. If the accused was involved in the wider 'Mafia' crime movement, then he deserved no sympathy, he said; but if, he was, as he believed, only a low level local operator, then the Judges needed to ask themselves before passing sentence, what real differences there were between the old style Mafia and the more idealistic forms of Freemasonry.

Busoni had recently been elected to parliament and was, to a certain extent, protected by Parliamentary Immunity at the time, but the lead judge had ordered that while a record of his character reference should be held on the court's files, it must be redacted from the version made available to the public. Francesca smiled as she imagined the fiery communist MP lecturing the middle class judges about how they should do their job.

Chapter 18

Having left the bike at home, she caught the bus into the centre after leaving the Tribunale at quarter to one, determined to push all her concerns to one side for a couple of hours and to buy something nice to wear for next time she saw Marco. From the end of the bus-line, outside the station, she began to make her way up the road toward the Duomo but, seeing a large crowd of tourists on a guided tour in front of her, changed her mind and cut across to her right until she emerged in Piazza Santa Maria Novella.

Despite being one of the most attractive and historic piazzas of the city, the square, which was bathed in winter sunlight was as close to being deserted as one could ever hope to find it during the day. She was tempted to enter the Basilica itself and refresh her acquaintance with the frescos of Masaccio, realising that it must be at least fifteen years since she had last found the time to admire them. Tempted - but the glow of the sun on her face helped her resist the temptation, and instead she made her way to one of her favourite *gelaterie*, where the proprietor already had a few tables placed optimistically on the paving outside.

She chose a table just outside the door where she would get the maximum benefit from the sun as well as a convection effect from the wall behind her. When the smiling waiter came out, as soon as she'd settled at the table, she asked for a large cone with balls of *gianduia, stracciatella* and fig ice-cream, with a cup of hot chocolate to follow a few minutes later. Recognising that she was a local and not a tourist, the waiter asked if he could bring her the newspaper out to be browsing while she was at the table, and she thanked him with a smile.

As in most of the bars and *gelaterie* in the city, the newspapers made available to the customers were *La Nazione* and the *Gazzetta dello Sport*. Clearly passing a judgement on her, which a few years before she was sure that she would have protested about, the waiter only bought her *La Nazione*, which amused her – perhaps middle-age was creeping up on her faster than she had realised. She casually skimmed the first three pages as she began to eat her ice-cream, but stopped when she turned over to the fourth page and saw a heading two thirds of the way down the page: "Attempt against Guzzanti thwarted". Mechanically, she continued to eat spoonfuls of ice-cream in her mouth, but without paying any conscious awareness of what she was doing or how it tasted – all her attention was now focussed on the article and its implications.

Senatore Paolo Guzzanti was a former journalist who had been elected to the Senate in two thousand and two as a member of the governing block and appointed as head of the Mitrokhin Committee when that body had been set up later in the year. She knew that he was an excellent communicator, being familiar with his journalistic articles, but couldn't be sure whether he was responsible for the direction the Commission was taking, or whether he had been put in place as a convenient figurehead, to ward off accusations of bias. But why would anyone want to kill him?

According to the article, Mario Scaramella, a lawyer who was working as an intelligence analyst and investigator for the Commission had discovered a plot to assassinate Paolo Guzzanti. A Ukrainian former KGB defector, Dimitri Malik, and a number of other Eastern Europeans had been arrested by the Italian security forces, acting on information supplied by Scaramella. Malik's group had been found to be in possession of a significant arms cache, including high-tech grenades, corroborating the information supplied by Scaramella, the hero of the day. The article praised the security forces for the rapidity and effectiveness of their intervention and lauded Scaramella for his effectiveness as an investigator.

As a trained journalist, Francesca could see that the article had been built on limited, probably patchy, information, and probably wouldn't have given it a second thought at that stage, had it not been for its link to the Commission. She looked at the by-line on the report and it wasn't one she recognised, so it must have either been written by a very junior reporter or have been submitted by a freelance. If the former, then the information would need to be treated with a pinch of salt until something more definite emerged;

if the latter, however, then that raised interesting questions about who was behind the story, how extensively had it been disseminated and, who stood to gain from the story. Putting to one side for the moment all thoughts of buying new clothes to please Marco, she took out her phone and dialled an acquaintance who worked for *La Nazione*.

'*Pronto. Chi parla?*'

'Gian-Marco, ciao. It's Francesca here, Francesca Conte. How are you?'

'Hi, Franci. The quick answer to your question is "busy – very busy" and, as I'm sure that you didn't ring me out of a sudden concern for my health and welfare, you'll need to get straight to the point – lovely as it is to speak to you.'

'Am I really so predictable?' she teased.

'Yes. You are. Now what do you want? - I really am very busy.'

'OK. Page four, today; who wrote the article on Guzzanti – was it one of yours, or an external?'

'Guzzanti – just bear with me a minute, I'll check.' Francesca heard the sound of rapid clicks on a keyboard, then his voice came again, 'Hello,'

'Yes, I'm still here.'

'It was written by an external – sent in by an agency that's given us a good steer on a number of breaking stories previously. Why do you ask?'

'Oh, just curious. I was flicking through while I had a coffee and it caught my eye. There was something that didn't seem quite right to me.'

'In what way?' she smiled as she could tell he was trying to make his question sound casual, while she could feel a genuine journalistic curiosity seeping through his voice.

Usually, she would have taken pleasure in keeping him guessing, but this time she knew that she couldn't afford to be precious and that they weren't in competition for a story; having him onside and prepared to pass on any information he found, was the most important thing. 'Well,' she said, 'If SISMI or SISDI have really prevented the assassination of the chair of a Parliamentary

Commission, why is it tucked away on page four, rather than on the front, and why do I get the impression that the information in it has not been cross-checked – and why does it strike me as a bit too much of a coincidence that Scaramella, who's working as an investigating lawyer for the Commission, should just happen to be the one who discovers that there's a plot to assassinate the Commission's president – information that allows the security services to turn up just at the right time – or is it now standard procedure for terrorists to keep their arms caches in their own homes at all times now?'

There was a silence. She could imagine him sitting back in his chair, chewing the end of his pencil as he thought about the article.

Finally, 'Not a bad set of questions for a retired journalist who's got a cushy job at the *Tribunale* now. I'll look into it.'

'Thanks, Gian-Marco – and let me know what you find out, won't you?'

'Don't worry. I will – even when I know I'm being used. *Ciao*,' and he rung off.

Before making her way inside to pay for her ice-cream and hot chocolate, Francesca worked her way through the address book on her phone again, looking for other contacts that she had made in the past who could be useful to her now. Finally, she found what she was looking for and pressed "Select" and then "Call".

The phone rang several times and then, just as she expected it to go to voice-mail – 'Capuano.'

'Hello, Rita. My name's Francesca Conte. I'm not sure if you'll remember me. I was a junior reporter working with 'Espresso", a few years ago. We met while I was doing some research on links between the Camorra and some of our senators. I came to see...'

'Florentine, lots of dark hair, fairly tall, and doggedly persistent?'

Francesca smiled. 'Certainly the first three of those.'

'Alright. Yes – of course I remember you. What can I do for you?'

'First of all; are you still based in Naples?'

'I am. For some reason, my genius appears to go unappreciated anywhere else.'

'A travesty! Still, at least it means you don't have to try very hard either to find a good pizza, or material for crime reporting.'

'Hah! I can't think what you mean; I'm not overweight and Naples is the most idyllic city in Europe – no-one has been murdered on my street for at least two months.'

'I know, Naples is a true utopia but, talking of murder, what can you tell me about Dimitri Malik?'

There was a long pause, then Capuano said, 'I'm afraid I've never heard of Dimitri Malik.' Francesca was surprised; Rita Capuano was a successful freelance journalist because she had a network of contacts throughout the Neapolitan underworld – it was hardly conceivable that she wasn't aware of what was in the papers that morning. Just as she was about to give her a nudge in the right direction, Capuano continued. 'Listen, Francesca. It's been ages since I last saw you and we've got a lot of catching up to do. Why don't you come down at the weekend, and I'll make an exception and force myself to eat one of those pizzas that you were talking about?'

Francesca realised that Capuano had got important things to tell her – things that she wanted to tell her as soon as possible – but things that it wasn't wise to discuss on the phone. She would have to go, she thought. 'That would be lovely. I've been waiting for my first trip to the sea of the year – just one thing – I may have my boyfriend in tow – if I do, you'll like him – you share similar interests,' she added, hoping that Capuano would understand that, as well as being a boyfriend, Marco was also involved in her reason for going to Naples.'

'That's good. I'm fairly sure that you can get one of the new super-fast trains from Florence at about six, and be in Naples by nine – not like a few years ago, when it used to take over five hours. I'll be in the station bar, sitting under the clock – you've got no chance of finding my place on your own, and the taxi-drivers will fleece you.'

'That's really good of you. I'll see you then.'

After paying, she took her other, unregistered, phone out of her bag and rang Marco as she walked. He didn't answer immediately, but rang back a few minutes later. She was not surprised to hear that he had heard about the reports and had been making enquiries of his contacts. He too had come to the conclusion that someone was carefully orchestrating the release of information. No official confirmation had yet been given, and only those papers who had been sent the article had printed it, although none, as yet, in prominent positions due to the lack of corroborating evidence. Other newspapers had begun to make reference to the arrests on their websites, but as yet they were only reporting the report, rather than the arrest itself. He had received confirmation from one of his contacts that the arrests had taken place, but his contact had been unable to tell him where the Ukrainians had been taken, only that they had not been taken to Naples' infamous and overcrowded Poggioreale prison.

What Marco had been able to discover was that the by-line on the report was a pseudonym. There was no record of any journalist of that name belonging to the professional association, or of having been employed as a junior trainee by any publication. He had been able to track down several previous articles by the journalist, each of which had broken potentially sensitive stories in vague terms. Interestingly, each story, when developed had resulted in items which damaged the reputations of left-wing politicians, although only ever by inference, not by producing verifiable facts.

He was keen to accompany her at the weekend and said he would book a ticket and join her on the train, if nothing urgent came up to prevent him travelling. She reminded him that there was still a possibility that she would have to leave him for part of one of the days if Ciancolini was unable to accompany Busoni to meet the President. Neither of them however, really thought that this scenario was likely, as opportunities for a private audience with the President in Villa Rosebery, did not come along very often.

The call with Marco was a fairly short one as he was testing out some new surveillance equipment that he had managed to install in the Communications Ministry, and which he hoped would get around the interference problems that had afflicted his standard 'took-kit'. By the time they hung up, however, she had almost reached the Arno and, after checking her watch, she turned left into a road where she knew she would find some small boutiques, which hopefully would provide her with the lingerie she was looking for. If she didn't, she thought, she could always really splash out and buy something in one of the designer boutiques on Via dei Tornabuoni.

As it turned out, there weren't as many boutiques in the street as she'd remembered and, having been disappointed by what was on offer at the home stores of the major fashion labels on Via dei Tornabuoni, she made her way to Piazza della Repubblica where she remembered having seen a dedicated lingerie store with an unusual Japanese sounding name. Here she finally found something that she thought wouldn't be too uncomfortable but which would appeal to Marco's baser instincts. Neither the quality of the workmanship, nor that of the material, was comparable with those she had seen in the designer stores, but she was fairly sure that Marco wouldn't notice that.

When she had done her shopping, it was till only a quarter to four and she decided that rather than continuing to kill time in the centre, she would go up to her parents' house, change, and then ride over to see Ciancolini on the Ducati. She felt she had ample time to cross the river and make her way up the steep steps from Via del Monte alle Croci and even have a chat with her grandmother, before she needed to go out again and, being on the bike, would make getting home again later, much simpler.

When she got in, her mother was already back and beginning to prepare things in the kitchen. She went in and gave her a kiss on the cheek; her mother smiled.

'You should eat out more often, instead of spending three hours every day in the kitchen.'

Lia Conte shrugged. 'I think I probably enjoy cooking as much as I do eating – maybe more! So don't you go worrying about me... Oh, by the way...You had a visitor.'

'A visitor! Who?'

'Commissario Vichi, from the Questura. He was the officer in charge after the explosion. He wants you to ring him when you can... I wrote his number on the pad next to the phone.'

'Ah... Good afternoon, Signorina. Thankyou for ringing. May I ask how you're coping in the aftermath of what happened?' She couldn't tell whether or not there was a touch of irony in Vichi's voice, and she felt a little pang of guilt as she realised that, she'd been so wrapped up in the investigation, that she had hardly thought about Arturo.

'I'm alright, thankyou. I've been trying to keep as busy as possible so I don't have too much time to think about it.'

'That sounds like a very sensible approach to take; get on with your own life while you've got the chance. Very sensible.'

'I suppose so, yes... Is there any news about the killers? Are you any nearer to solving the case?'

Vichi ignored the questions and instead told her that he thought that they ought to meet, and asked if there was any time the next day that would be convenient. Francesca said that she was sure that if he came over to the *Tribunale* in the morning, she could be freed up for however long was necessary, otherwise she could call in to the Questura in the afternoon, before she went home. He said that unfortunately he would be tied up in lots of boring meetings during the morning but suggested that they meet in one of the bars in the centre, on her way home. She suggested that they meet at the Enoteca Fuori Porta at one-thirty, so that she could get a bite to eat as well. He agreed, and they left it at that.

Maddi, her grandmother was in considerable pain from her arthritic hips and in one of her more abrasive moods as a result. She did not seem particularly pleased to see Francesca, and didn't have much to say while she was there, but she still complained and made her grand-daughter feel guilty when she stood up to leave. She wondered whether to mention her conversation with Busoni to her grandmother, but decided that it would be better to wait until she was in a better mood.

Telling Lia that she wasn't sure whether or not she'd be back to eat, she left on the bike and made her way down the Viali to the Ponte San Niccolò and then threaded her way through the traffic until she had passed Piazza le Cure and could enjoy the relative freedom of the viale.

Ciancolini buzzed her in as soon as she pressed the buzzer just before six and, closing the door firmly behind her, she made her way along a short corridor to where an open door gave onto a well-lit room. Looking up from some papers on a large, very expensive looking desk, the Judge looked up, smiled and waved her into a comfortable armchair to the side, then looked down again and quickly signed three more pieces of paper before giving her his full attention.

'So, how was Brussels?' she asked, as he looked up.

'Grey and damp, but I've brought you some Belgian chocolates.'

'That wasn't what I meant.'

'I know. I know. Give me a second.' He opened a drawer on his desk and pulled out a CD. 'There's a copy of Marie's interview with Prodi, on here... it's in a mixture of English and Italian, with a few bits of French thrown in every now and again, ' he handed her the disc, 'listen to it at your leisure... Marie was very good. She'd been given a thirty minute slot with Prodi and she managed to get everything she needed for her piece in just over five minutes. I had been allowed in with her as her technical assistant, and while she explained who I really was, she took the photos for the interview that officially, I was meant to be taking. Once she'd done that, Prodi let his receptionist know that Marie had had to rush away to deal with a family emergency, but that he would be with the photographer for another fifteen minutes or so.'

'Neatly done,' said Francesca.

'Prodi listened very carefully to all I had to say, without interrupting, and then asked a few pertinent questions at the end to clarify a few points. He's extremely intelligent and could see the various implications straight away. As expected he wants everything kept as quiet as possible for as long as possible... otherwise, if he starts to demand greater protection when he's in Italy, on the grounds that he's in danger from right wing plotters, it makes him look weak in the eyes of the electorate – at least until we've got proof that will stand up in court if necessary... He understands that our job is made much more difficult because we can't be sure who we can trust, and he is aware that the main function of the Mitrokhin Commission seems to be to throw as much mud as possible at left wing politicians, hoping that some of it will stick. Unfortunately, he just seems to see that as an unfortunate and inevitable facet of Italian public life. With regard to the Security Services there are, apparently, already secret plans for a root and branch reorganisation to take place within a year of a change of government. The hope is that by removing most of the cancer, the rest will be suffocated by the reliable elements in the service.'

'Mmmm. I hope that the reality is more effective than the metaphor, because I'm not quite sure that that's how you definitively eradicate cancer.'

'Even in the best organisations, you're always going to get the odd bad apple but hopefully they won't dare to raise their heads again. He seemed fairly confident that it would all go OK.'

'Anything else?'

'He has agreed that security should be tightened every time he comes back into Italy, although he insists that this must be unobtrusive... He also insists that he will appear in front of the Commission as requested. Even though he knows that nothing he says is likely to make much difference, in his view the consequences of refusing to appear by relying on his immunity as a European Commissioner, would be much more damaging in the short term.... That was it really... there wasn't time for much more... although he did give me a secure private number that I can reach him on... Now it's your turn to bring me up to speed on developments here.'

She gave a wan smile, 'I hope you're not tired of travelling, ' he raised an eyebrow, 'because you've got an appointment with the President of the Republic, in Naples, on Sunday morning.' The eyebrow seemed to go up further, if that was possible. I went to see your old acquaintance Busoni yesterday, and while I was there, he managed to get through to the President and arrange an appointment for the pair of you. Unfortunately, he has to go to Naples for a few days – to Villa Rosebery – on official business, so to avoid delay, that's where you need to go.'

'Villa Rosebery – that's an odd name.'

'Apparently, at one time it belonged to a former British Prime Minister; he donated it to the British government and, after a few years, when they realised how much it was costing them to maintain it, they generously passed it on to the Italian Royal family. It was used as an Airforce headquarters for a few years after the abolition of the monarchy, but it's now been done up and is used by the President to host foreign dignitaries who don't need to see too many politicians during their visit. I believe it has a lovely view over the Bay of Naples from Posillipo towards Vesuvius.'

'And how much does the President know already?'

She shook her head, 'The President knows nothing. Busoni knows pretty much everything but, because the President trusts him, he agreed to see you both on the strength of Busoni insisting that it was vitally important... Oh, he knows there will be someone with Busoni, but we decided not to give your name just in case you couldn't go.'

'OK. I'll talk to Busoni tomorrow about the travel arrangements... Anything else?'

'Yes. It's a bit of a coincidence, but you won't be the only ones going to Naples this weekend...' and she explained about the article that had appeared in several papers that morning and about the results of the enquiries that she and Marco had so far been able to make.

He leaned back in his chair, biting the tip of the index finger on his right hand as he reflected, gazing vacantly towards a large old oil-painting in the style of Claude Lorraine, which hung on the wall to one side. Francesca waited while he sorted through the implications in his head. 'This is serious.' he said finally. Francesca gave a small nod. 'If you were just any Tom, Dick or Harriet, who didn't know what you know about this case, what logical conclusions would you draw? In whose interest would it be to kill Guzzanti?'

'It would be in the interests of someone who has a lot to fear from the Commission's findings – someone who wanted to warn the Commission off.'

'Exactly. And who appears to have the most to lose from the Commission.'

'Romano Prodi.'

Ciancolini gave a grim smile, 'So without actually assassinating Guzzanti, who, from their point of view, has been doing a pretty good job, they have sacrificed a few pawns to make it look as if Prodi was behind an assassination plot. Very clever.'

'That's more or less what I thought; there's a lot of clever planning going into this plot; they seem to be gradually building up the pressure and making sure that the public has no way of really telling who are the good guys and who are the bad guys. We're playing for very high stakes here.'

He raised his hands to his face and sat for a moment, eyes covered and deep in thought. Then, sliding his hands down and clasping them below his chin, he said, 'This makes it even more important that I can convince the President on Sunday. If he doesn't use his executive power to give me full authority to make swift arrests at the appropriate time, over-riding Parliamentary Immunity, then the plot will succeed... the only flaw I can see in their planning is that they may just have been over-ambitious,' he stopped and looked at her.

Francesca shook her head, 'I was with you until near the end but, what do you mean, "over-ambitious"?'

'Think about it... they have a Parliamentary Commission which they will use to discredit Prodi and other leaders of the left under a veneer of respectability; they have foiled a plot by a Ukrainian former KGB man to assassinate the Chair of the Commission; the murder of Cabrini-Pellé gives them an excuse for a clamp down and makes it easy for them to blame the left – pretty much all they need to ensure that a right-wing authoritarian government can be elected... and yet, we know that they're also considering taking out the leaders of the left. Provided that we can establish the links between the leaders of the coup and the hit-men, then we have a way of exposing them and subjecting them to the appropriate legal processes.'

She nodded, 'It may be that the person I'm going to see this weekend to get more information on Malik, may also be able to help us with the hit-men – if the Camorra are involved at all, she'll have the contacts to find out what's going on.'

Ciancolini raised his eyebrows in surprise. 'You seem to know some very interesting people, Francesca. Are you sure that this person, with all his contacts is entirely trustworthy.'

'Absolutely,' said Francesca, deliberately not correcting the judge's gender assumption. 'We'll have to follow up the leads to get the evidence to stand up in court, as it wouldn't do for my source to become known as a grass, but this person has my complete trust.'

'Alright,' sighed the judge, 'I suppose I'll just have to be satisfied with that, won't I,' Francesca gave him her most captivating smile in gratitude.

Chapter 19

Commissario Vichi was already seated at a corner table when she arrived at the enoteca just a few minutes late. When he saw her appear in the doorway and look around, as her pupils adjusted to the interior light, he stood up and waved to catch her eye. He remained standing as she made her way over to his corner and pulled out a chair for her. She slipped her coat off and draped it over the back of the chair and then sat down, an action which he copied a moment later.

'*Buonasera*, Commissario. How can I help you?'

He seemed to make an effort to smile – an effort that wasn't entirely successful. '*Buonasera*, Signorina. Thank you for coming. There are a few things I'd like to talk to you about but, as I assume

you must be hungry at this time, it may be better if we order first.'
He raised a hand to attract the attention of one of the waitresses and
beckoned her over.

'*Prego*. Are you ready to order?'

'Just a glass of warm milk for me, but I believe that my
companion would like some food.'

The waitress scribbled something on her pad and turned to
Francesca who said, 'I'd like the cheese platter and a glass of
Nipozzano, please.'

'Certainly, madam. Would that be small, medium or large?'

'Medium please... thankyou.'

As soon as the waitress was out of earshot, Vichi looked at her.
'I understand from the conversation that I had with your brother-in-
law, on the night of the explosion, that one of the topics of
conversation had been crime writers...' He paused to make sure that
he had her attention and she looked at him wondering where this
was going. 'I enjoy a good crime novel myself, although sometimes
I despair at how we are portrayed. However, one thing which I see
quite often in the novels and which unfortunately, sometimes
reflects the truth, is that there is quite often unreasonable pressure
from above, and equally unfortunately, not all branches of the
services whose primary aim is to ensure public safety and respect
for the law, are always singing from the same hymn-sheet.' Again
Francesca said nothing; although she thought she knew where Vichi
was going, she felt that she needed to be on her guard.

'From your reading of Camilleri, I'm sure that you will have
noticed that his Commissario often carries out parallel
investigations, even when he's been officially told to stay away
from a case.' Francesca nodded to show that she was following him.
'Now. This conversation has never taken place... I'm sure that you
with your background as an investigative journalist can understand
that.' again she nodded, and then they both sat back for a few
seconds as the waitress returned with their drinks and with
Francesca's food. She watched Vichi take two pills out of his top-
pocket, place them in his mouth and swallow them with a mouthful
of the milk. He grimaced before recommencing.

'Judge dell'Omodarme was an important person, and I have no problem with the investigation being taken over by a body with more technical expertise and possibly more experience of dealing with sensitive cases... What I do have a problem with is when that "superior" body, in this case SISMI, takes on a case, throws almost no resources at it, and then moves very quickly towards archivisation. It's when things like this happen that my natural curiosity gets the better of my discretion.'

Francesca dipped a wedge shaped slice of *pecorino di Pienza*, into the little dish of honey that accompanied the cheeses, and popped it into her mouth, determined to remain impassive. Vichi, realising that, at least for the moment, she wasn't going to give him any help, continued: 'Now, I think it would be fair to say that the information that you, your sister and your brother-in-law gave us at the time was not complete... For example, you allowed us to believe that there was a personal relationship between yourself and dell'Omodarme, when in fact, that wasn't the case, was it?... Because he was in a stable relationship with someone else who needed to keep that relationship secret.' She cut the rind off a piece of well-seasoned pecorino and cut herself a slice. 'Don't worry, Don Adriano's secret is safe with me.'

Francesca looked him in the eye, 'What is it you want to know, Commissario?'

He met her eyes without blinking. 'Why don't you tell me why he was killed, and then we can move onto who killed him – I assume that the two are closely linked.' She reflected for a moment and then decided that, as he had already found out some things for himself, it was probably wisest to place at least some trust in him.

She put her fork down. 'I'm sorry that we misled you about the nature of my relationship with the judge. Until that evening, even my sister and Paul had been under the impression that Arturo and I were lovers. It was, as you have correctly guessed, partly to keep his real love secret, and partly to provide a reason for the presence on his staff of a reformed investigative journalist.'

'A change of career that I assume is as much a sham as the pretence that there was a deeper relationship between the two of you.'

'To be fair, we did become very good friends – just not lovers.'

He acknowledged the point with a slight nod of the head and then continued, 'Presumably, it would also be fair to say that dell'Omodarme was killed because of whatever it was that he was investigating – What was that?'

Again, she wondered how much it was safe to tell him. As he was clearly not working with SISMI and had been briefly involved just because he happened to be the Commissario on duty that night, she decided that, so long as what he was told didn't expose anyone else, she was prepared to let him have some information – he could turn out to be a useful ally later on. 'Judge dell'Omodarme was investigating a suspected plot, in which several members of the current government are involved, to discredit leading opposition politicians, suspend democratically elected institutions and impose martial law. Fortunately, the investigation has been able to be carried on by others, since the explosion.'

'So, the logical conclusion is that the bomb was planted with the intention of bringing the investigation to a premature end and, as it was only a lucky chance that prevented you being in the car when the bomb went off, the assumption must be that it was aimed for you as well, which means that your life must still be in danger.'

She opened her eyes wide and gave him her most demure look, 'Not me, I'm just a simple secretary now. If I'd been involved with the investigation, I wouldn't now be working for a semi-retired judge who now only deals with fairly minor civil cases. I'd be working for one of the judges specialising in criminal investigations.'

'I see... working for Judge Graziadei, clearly keeps you fully occupied all the time, doesn't it?' She smiled at him, seeing that he understood how convenient her present position at the Tribunale was. 'Given the dilatory way in which SISMI carried out their investigation into the explosion, would it be reasonable of me to assume, that some of the important people involved in the plot hold fairly senior posts in that organisation?'

She smiled, 'As you know, I'm just an insignificant secretary. I wouldn't dream of questioning the assumptions of an experienced police officer like yourself.'

Now it was his turn to smile. 'Remember, that I'm on your side, Signorina – for as long as that is compatible with being on the side of law, order and social-justice.' He pushed his chair back and stood up, extending his hand towards her. As she took it and he gave it a brief shake he added, 'I've taken up enough of your time. Enjoy the rest of your meal.' and he turned and walked away, pausing only to speak briefly to the waitress who had served them and press a twenty euro note into her hand.

The following afternoon, the sky was grey and overcast, and a fine cold drizzle reminded her of a visit to England as winter seemed to be making one last effort to dampen everyone's spirit. Paszkowski's outside tables were enclosed by an enormous gazebo-like structure that had been attached to the front of the elegant old café, ensuring that customers were not put off by the weather, and the structure was illuminated by temporary lighting.

Rosa was seated at a table on the left hand side as Francesca walked in and pulled down the hood on her coat and looked around. Making her way over to the table that had a good view of the colonnades along the west side of Piazza della Repubblica, she noticed that there were two shopping bags on the floor by her chair, and understood why she had not arrived together with her husband.

'*Ciao*, Franci. Paul should be here soon, he didn't fancy meeting me in the ladies-wear section of Rinascimento, so we agreed to meet here.' Francesca kissed her sister on both cheeks and sat down. 'Never marry an Englishman, if you want someone to go shopping with you and give you advice... They're useless; they haven't got the patience to wait while you try things on and if you ask them what they think, everything is "alright". The only clothing they really have any opinions on is underwear, and even then, the things they think you should buy are usually the most impractical and uncomfortable things in the shop,' she laughed, and Francesca blushed slightly, glad that her sister couldn't see the lingerie she'd bought the previous day for Marco's benefit.

'You should have told me... I could have come a bit earlier and gone with you. We haven't been out clothes-shopping together for ages. Let me know next time – or, I'll tell you when I need to go.' She looked down at the bags, ' What did you get?'

While Rosa was showing her the things she had bought, a smartly dressed waiter came across and hovered discreetly by their table. They explained that they would shortly be joined by a third person and would prefer to order then, if that wasn't a problem.' The waiter gave a little bow of his head and moved across to another table.

After five minutes of clothes-talk, Paul arrived, and shortly after, they ordered a large pot of peppermint tea and a dozen *bignolini*.

He waited until their order had been delivered to the table before turning to the reason they were meeting. 'Rosa said that you've been talking to someone who knew my grandfather?'

Francesca smiled, ' "knew" might be overstating it slightly. He remembers meeting your grandfather during the war, when he was a child – and later on, his father told him more about him. He seemed to know quite a bit about our Campolargo ancestors too,' she said, looking at Rosa, '… a lot more than Nonna has ever told me.' She noticed her sister dart a glance at Paul and thought he gave an almost imperceptible shake of the head in return.

'Tell me more about this man you were talking to,' said Paul, keeping his voice steady.

'He's the mayor of Tavarnelle,' she said, 'someone who Ciancolini has known for a long time, and whose father was a Communist member of parliament for a few years... I went to see him because, at some point during the war, his father saved the life of our current President and, despite not always seeing eye-to-eye politically, they remained in contact until the old-man died a few years ago. Ciancolini thought, rightly as it turned out, that this man... Cecco Busoni, he's called... might be able to get him a private meeting with the President, without going through the official channels.'

'OK,' said Paul, 'tell us about that first, then tell us what he knows about my grandfather.'

Francesca nodded, and explained to them how Ciancolini and Busoni would be seeing the President on the Sunday morning and how, hopefully, Ciancolini would be given extraordinary powers, enabling him to over-ride Parliamentary Immunity and move swiftly to make arrests when there was sufficient evidence. Then she moved on to tell them what Busoni had told her about Paul's grandfather.

Paul was excited by the news; 'That's amazing. It was really difficult to find out any details about him, and in all these years, I've only ever come across one person who met him – I need to go and see him, and talk with him, when this other business is sorted out.'

'I told him, you'd probably want to meet him... But, how much do you two know about the background of Nonna's family? He didn't seem too keen to tell me about them, and I didn't want to press him, because the most important thing was obviously getting his help in seeing the President.'

Rosa reached out and placed a hand over her sister's. 'It's complicated... very complicated.'

'Try me.'

Rosa sighed. 'Alright. I'll tell you what I can... but there's a lot I can't tell you because we promised Nonna that it was something we wouldn't talk to anyone about while she was still alive... You remember when Paul and I first met... how Nonna and Mamma refused to have anything to do with him, and did everything they could to try and put Paul off?' Francesca nodded. 'Well, a big part of that was because, after the war, Nonna was so disgusted at the roles various members of the family had played in the Fascist regime, that she'd cut off all contact with them... Even though it was absolutely nothing to do with Paul and his grandmother: Nonna's sister, had run away from home and the family, Paul was just lumped in with the rest of them...'

Paul took up the story, 'When I first came over, I was determined to find out something about this mysterious Italian grandmother who'd died fifty years before, and whom no-one seemed to know anything about. Everywhere I asked, at first, I seemed to be banging my head against a brick wall, but I gradually found out more and more about the family, until I found out that a sister of hers was still living in Florence. I was surprised at the unfriendly reception I got, but I found out that someone I knew who was studying at the University knew Rosa... and once I'd met her, there was no way anyone was going to get rid of me.' He gave a warm smile to Rosa. Eventually, Nonna told us more secrets about the past, that she thought, and still thinks, were really shocking, and that she thought would mean that we would decide that it wasn't a good idea to stay together.'

'In some ways it was a relief for her to tell us her secrets, that she'd been jealously guarding for forty years, but it was very painful for her to do it, and we promised never to say anything to anyone while she was still alive – not even to Mamma,' added Rosa.

'Or to me!'

'Franci; you were only fifteen at the time... I'm not sure how you would have taken it, and then... once we'd promised Nonna to keep her secret, we couldn't tell you... could we?'

Francesca looked at them and sighed, 'I suppose not.'

There isn't time now, but I don't really see any reason why you shouldn't know everything about the family history – except for Nonna's secret,' said Paul. 'In fact, now that it appears that Guerrini is involved in this planned coup d'état, it's probably a good idea that you do know.... It would take ages to tell you everything but to sum it up briefly, you could probably say that for every regime change in Tuscany, and then Italy, for about seven hundred years until the Second World War, there was probably a Campolargo involved behind the scenes,' said Paul.

'And the worst of them,' added Rosa, was probably Nonna's father, our great-grandfather, who played a big part in helping Mussolini come to power.'

Francesca was incredulous and Paul had to explain to her how Domenico Campolargo had introduced Filippo Marinetti, the founder of Futurism to the radical French philosopher, Georges Sorel whose influence led Marinetti to glorify violence as an instrument of change. Campolargo had later convinced Marinetti to merge his fairly peripheral Futurist Political Party with Mussolini's *Fasci Italiani di Combattimento* to create the Italian Fascist Party in 1919. After that he had always been behind the scenes, helping to develop the movement's apparent philosophical and intellectual foundations. 'If it hadn't been for his eldest son – our grandmothers' brother – becoming too closely identified with the excesses of the regime, no doubt the Campolargos would have continued to be important players, even after the fall of Fascism.'

'I suppose,' said Rosa, picking up the thread, 'that Guerrini, as the son of Nonna's other sister, is just carrying on the family tradition... as, I suppose, are we by trying to expose the conspirators and defend the democratic institutions.'

Francesca laughed, 'Rosa, do you realise how pompous you sound at the moment. I'll start to believe that we're really important if you carry on like that.' They all relaxed, glad that the tension had been broken.

Chapter 20

Francesca's seat on the train was in the last carriage and, when the train drew smoothly into Naples station, she had a long walk from her carriage to the ticket barriers along the dimly lit, slightly curving platform, one of eighteen that appeared to stretch out for ever. Marco had joined the train at Rome but, as he'd bought his ticket at the last moment, his seat was ten carriages further forward and, as the train was almost full, neither of them had attempted to change seats during the journey – consequently, she found him sitting on a bench a few metres before the barrier, looking relaxed.

He stood up and they embraced. She declined his offer to carry her bag, which wasn't particularly heavy and, after looking round to get her bearings, led him over towards the station bar to one side of the busy new McDonald's. There was a crowd of people milling around near the counter: some waiting to pay at the till: some holding out their receipts hoping to attract the attention of any one of the three baristas who were flitting between the customers, the coffee machine, and the sandwich grills, and others, who had managed to get served, eating sandwiches from paper napkins and sipping coffees or glasses of strong red wine.

To one end of the room at a table by a stand of magazines and newspapers, sat a woman who appeared to almost blend into the background; she was neither ugly nor beautiful and all her features seemed to be instantly forgettable. Even her clothes appeared to have been chosen as if to help her blend into the background; they were neat and tidy, but in no way eye-catching. If anyone who had seen her, had been asked to describe her five minutes later, they would have found it very difficult except possibly for the bi-focal glasses which, when she took them off, hung on a chain around her neck.

Although she appeared to be engrossed in her paper until they were almost at her table, she was clearly fully aware of everything that was happening around her as she folded the paper and put it down, without looking up as they approached her. Only when Francesca stretched out a hand to pull back one of the free chairs did she look up and meet their eyes. Marco, who had not met her before, was struck by the intensity of the look she gave them, and gave a slight shudder as he had the unaccountable feeling that she was able to look right into their minds.

'Ciao, Rita. This is Marco, a friend and colleague... from Rome,' said Francesca, looking from Capuano to Marco and back again.

'*Piacere.* Don't bother sitting down – we'll go and find something to eat somewhere where we can rely on privacy; I take it that neither of you have eaten yet.' She pushed her chair back and slipping on a dull brownish jacket, made for the door as they followed her. Outside the bar, she turned to the right and made her way to the tobacconists where she turned to them and instructed them to each buy a block of ten tickets for the urban transport network.

Once they had done this, she led them towards the old Circumvesuviana station in Piazza Cavour, which had recently been converted into a station for the constantly evolving Metro, past several groups of young men who appeared to be using the station as a meeting place. Francesca noticed that most of the men appeared to be of either African or Middle Eastern descent and none of them gave the impression that they were doing any more than just surviving in the city. One group of six young Africans, was sitting cross-legged on the floor playing cards, a pile of large Adidas sports bags piled up alongside them.

'Street vendors?' asked Marco.

'They'll have been working the streets round the station all day, selling fake handbags, belts and wallets by Gucci, Prada, Dolce and Gabbana and almost anyone else you can name. There are always groups of them here at this time, waiting for the collectors to come round and pick up ninety-five percent of the day's takings from them. Then, when they get too tired to stay here any longer, or when the police kick them out, on the rare occasions they feel they need to make it look as if they're doing something, they'll be back off to the filthy, overcrowded hovels that they're charged a fortune for in rent,' explained Capuano, without any trace of emotion in her voice.

'Why do they live like that?' said Francesca, half rhetorically.

'For some of them, even this is better than what they've left behind. But for most, they've handed over their life savings to be brought over here and yet still owe more money to the traffickers. Until they've worked off their debt, they're effectively slaves, and they can't do anything about it because they're all illegal.'

'And the police do nothing?'

Capuano shrugged. 'The Camorra are far better funded than the police, so either the police go to war knowing that they're fighting a losing battle or they turn a blind eye and allow the Camorra to regulate the labour market. They understand the principles of supply and demand as well as any economist; have a big enough pool of labour so that they have to compete against each other for the jobs, even if the money on offer is only enough to allow them to survive and not to improve themselves. Because they have links with the people traffickers in North Africa, they control the flow of immigration – with a little help from the Mediterranean – and, if they need to reduce numbers, the police are only too glad to help. Everyone's happy: the North Africans escape the war-zones; the Camorra makes lots of money; and the police are praised for the round-ups and deportations.'

Marco looked at her, 'Isn't that a slightly cynical summary?'

'Cynical, but unfortunately not far from the truth,' she replied.

They walked in silence for a while, past hoardings keeping people out of the excavations for the latest Metro extension and past an eclectic mixture of imposing old buildings with an air of terminal decline, and drab post-war blocks which, while matching the older buildings in size, seemed purely functional and lacking in the sense of faded grandeur to be expected in a former capital. They passed the large renaissance church of Santa Caterina a Formiello, the white walls and cupola of which rose majestically above the poorly rendered front wall of a building that had been placed apparently thoughtlessly in front of the church, obscuring part of its facade. The exterior walls of the church between its granite columns and above its granite base, appeared to have been recently re-rendered and the gleaming whiteness made the surrounding buildings with their graffiti appear even more squalid than usual.

Beyond the Piazza, they continued along a road where no two consecutive buildings seemed to be of the same height. Most of the blocks seemed to be of post-war construction, although the occasional impressive archway suggested that there had been buildings on the site before the present ones.

'I suppose,' said Francesca, 'that much of this area had to be redeveloped after the war.'

'Partly because of the war and partly because of the various earthquakes over the years. Later on, when we get into the vicoli, you'll see that there are still buildings reinforced with props that were put up after the big earthquake in nineteen eighty.'

As they approached the far end of the road, the buildings began to seem more uniformly substantial again, and balconies full of plant pots became more frequent than balconies with washing lines. The ground floors of most of the buildings were mainly given over to commercial uses and most of the openings were covered with heavy metal shutters for the night. Both the shutters and the walls between regularly supported political posters for a bewildering array of parties and causes, and there were signs that many more had been removed or peeled off. Some of the posters and many smooth areas of wall had been graffitied, with fans of Napoli declaring their undying loyalty to the *Curva Sud*, various declarations of affection: "*Ti amo Titti*", "*Gennaro per Bruna*" and others offering more explicit suggestions of what lay in store for their objects of desire; one declared undying faith in Maradona, despite his having left Napoli thirteen years earlier.

Finally they emerged on the busy Via Forio and turned left past what appeared to be a collection of semi-permanent stalls to complete the last three hundred metres to the station. Inside, they had to negotiate the minor building works that were part of transforming the station from a stop on the historic Circumvesuviana line into a stop on the new Metro system, although as far as Francesca could tell, the changes in the station appeared to be mainly cosmetic. The rolling stock certainly hadn't been upgraded since her last visit to the city, some years before, and she was glad they were only in the tunnels for a few minutes before emerging at Toledo, from where it was only a five minute walk to the Funiculare Centrale.

For Francesca, using the funicular railway, was always one of the first things that came to mind when she remembered previous visits to the city, and it was with a slight feeling of disappointment that she followed Capuano and Marco out of the door on the other side of the carriage when they slid open at the first interim stop on Corso Vittorio Emanuele.

Compared to the busy streets below with their crowds of talking, laughing, shouting people, the Corso seemed almost deserted at that time in the evening as it snaked its way around the hillside, separating the upper and lower parts of the city. Almost immediately, however, Capuano turned to the right and began to descend into the narrow alleyways that criss-crossed the hillside. At one point Francesca noticed a faded sign for the San Carlo Opera House pointing down an alley way to their right, but very soon she had no idea where they were.

After a few minutes they approached an archway linking the two sides of the alley together, beyond which the way became stepped and dropped away towards the lower part of the city. Just before the archway a bedraggled looking black cat with a white nose glared at them balefully from its resting point on top of a stub of wall jutting out from their left. It turned its head slowly, following their movements and hissing as Capuano turned left, immediately after the cat's wall, and mounted two steps to insert a key into a plain door with weathered and flaking grey paint.

Inside the door, three doorways led off a dingy entrance, one of which stood ajar revealing a room with a tatty old table with two chairs, a number of cupboards and an old-fashioned cooking range. Half of the table-top was occupied by a word processor that must have been at least fifteen years old and several disorderly piles of paper. Capuano ignored that door and led them through the door at the end of the corridor.

Francesca came to a sudden halt, her mouth opening soundlessly until Marco bumped into the back of her, as she drank in the sight in-front of her. The room was a complete contrast to the one they had glimpsed from the hallway. As the property was built just above the sleep slope down to the city, its view was only partially obscured by other buildings and a large picture window had been installed to make the most of a view that, she could tell from the lights stretching in to the distance, must extend as far as Vesuvius. The furniture was tasteful, modern and minimalist, and extensive bookshelves covered the two end walls while a large work-desk holding a state-of-the-art, top-spec computer and printer was placed against the wall opposite the window.

'I need to live and work in the middle of the community, so I have to have a room where people can just pop in off the streets and see me without seeing me as one of the establishment – but at the same time, I don't see any reason why I shouldn't live comfortably since I can afford it. Really, I'd like slightly more solid furniture, but to get things in here, they have to be available in flat-packs.'

'I think it works really well,' said Marco, 'I don't think that more traditional furniture would be anything like as effective in this room. Which way are we facing... East?'

'South-East,' said Capuano, and, waving her arm vaguely towards the window, 'You can see all the way round the bay to the Bay of Sorrento and, if you stand on that side, you can see Capri as well... Anyway, you'll get a good view in the morning. For now, just drop your bags off and we'll go out and eat in five minutes or so... The bathroom's through that door there, if you need it, and your bedroom's just beyond it.'

Shortly after, they were back in the steep streets and alleyways that criss-crossed the hillside, following Capuano as she made her way confidently towards her destination. Marco tried to keep track of their route, but Francesca, realising the futility of this, just drank in the sights, sounds and smells that surrounded them.

It was the sort of area that no tourist guide would ever mention: the sort of area that no ambassador for the city would draw attention to. There was a wide range of graffiti and peeling posters of uncertain vintage on the walls; they passed several piles of rubbish bags, left haphazardly against walls; despite it being night time, washing still hung from some of the washing-lines that extended across the street; animated voices speaking the almost impenetrable dialect and fragments of televised drama floated out of houses; twice they passed groups of teenagers sitting chatting, playing cards, exchanging contraband cigarettes, or other, even less-legal substances, all while perched astride Vespas and other mopeds, which gave the impression that they had seen better days; there was no regular architectural pattern and buildings seemed to have been crammed together, not quite in line, wherever they would fit. Despite all this, however, she found the area fascinating, and could imagine that any artist who took the trouble to look at the area with an unprejudiced eye, could see it as picturesque – even the piles of rubbish.

While she was still drinking in their surroundings they arrived at a point where two alleyways met creating a wider space which someone – in a spirit of optimism, or humour – had designated as a piazza, a fact proudly displayed by a rough notice attached to one of the walls. Above a door, on one of the corners, a dimly lit sign informed them that they were outside *'Trattoria Alvaro'*, and it was towards that door that Capuano led them.

Other than the sign above the door, there was nothing to distinguish the outside of the small restaurant from the surrounding properties; there was no menu displayed outside, and the windows were no larger than any of the others.

Inside, two rooms had clearly been knocked together to make space for six tables, each of which could seat four people prepared to sit closely together, although it seemed inconceivable that there would be room for a waiter to pass between them if all the tables were occupied at the same time. The tables were formica-topped and the chairs were made of steel-tubes and hard plastic; all the furniture looked as if it hadn't been updated for at least thirty years. Plainly framed photographs of Napoli footballers, some of whom Francesca recognised and some she didn't, were the only decorations on the walls apart from one sumptuous painting of a reclining nude that seemed totally out of place in the dingy little restaurant.

'That's pretty impressive,' said Marco, looking at the painting and unable to mask the surprise in his voice.

'It's an early Gianni Strino,' said a smiling middle aged man with a cook's apron, who had emerged from a door to one side of the room. 'It was a present from one of my regular customers. Strino's making a big name for himself now, they say he's the best living Neapolitan Artist – Which table would you like, Rita?'

'That one there, I think,' said Capuano,' indicating the table furthest away from the painting,' then my friends will have the best view as we're eating.' The restauranteur removed the fourth chair from the table and pulled the other three out for them, and then disappeared through the door again. They sat down – Capuano sitting so that the painting was behind her, allowing Marco to face it.

'Can we have music?' said Capuano as Alvaro appeared again carrying an unlabelled litre and a large bottle of loosely corked red wine and three tumblers, which he placed on the table in front of them. He nodded his assent to her request.

'What is there to eat tonight?'

'*Pasta e ceci, pasta e fagioli* or *pasta e piselli* – then I can do you some *cicenielli.*'

'*Cicenielli?*' asked Francesca.

'Little fish, steamed and dressed with lemon and oil, or deep fried in a light batter – however you prefer,' explained Alvaro.

They all chose the *pasta e ceci* and a large dish of *cicenielli* to share afterwards.

As soon as Alvaro had retreated to the kitchen, Francesca looked at Capuano with an air of urgency, 'So, what can you tell us about Malik?'

'Malik is a very unpleasant piece of work. He was born in Sevastopol and talent spotted very early on while doing his military service. He claims to have been a fairly low-grade admin man in the KGB, who became surplus to requirements after the break-up of the Soviet Union... Like a number of others he traded some low-grade secrets for a new life and state pension in the west and, according to him, has lived quietly here in Naples ever since. Officially, he does some translation work for a cultural institute...'

'And unofficially?'

Capuano, gave a quick glance towards the door to the kitchen, pursing her lips, then, 'Unofficially – Malik was not an admin assistant at all – from what I can gather, his main role was to give a helping hand to racketeers in the west, providing finance and international contacts for the Camorra here in Naples and the 'Ndrangheta down in Calabria. That's why, when *glasnost* and *perestroika* meant that he was no longer needed by the Russians, it was natural for him to end up here. He still has plenty of contacts and he's very useful to the Camorra bosses. From what I can gather, he specialises in sourcing weapons from the mothballed stocks in the ex-Soviet Union, and either supplying them directly to the Camorra or selling them on to the Libyans.'

'And,' said Marco, thoughtfully, 'if he was in danger of being exposed by the Mitrokhin Commission, he would have had a motive for wanting to disrupt their work, and assassinating Guzzanti would have delayed the commission's work so much that it would have become meaningless.'

Capuano gave a half smile as she shook her head. 'That, I assume, is the conclusion that people are meant to come to. I don't believe that Malik has any concerns about the Commission; their work doesn't really affect his business and, I'm fairly sure that, if it did pose any sort of threat to him, there would be enough money moving about to buy himself protection. Assassinating Guzzanti would only draw attention to him and put his whole operation at risk and there are plenty of people in important positions who would lose a significant source of income if that were to happen. Italy has always had an ambiguous relationship with Libya – some of our governments – particularly the more right-wing ones, still haven't really accepted that it's no longer our colony... there's a reason why one of Ghedaffi's sons was signed up to play football in Serie A!'

'Not that he was a great success,' said Marco, 'but I take your point.'

At that point, Alvaro returned with a large serving dish full of steaming pasta and crushed chick peas, and a pasta dish for each of them.

'This is fantastic,' said Francesca, as she savoured her first mouthful, 'when we have *pasta e ceci* up in Tuscany, the chick peas are turned more into a smooth paste and we use smaller pasta, so it's more like *pastina in brodo*; this is much more filling with extra chilli to give it more of a kick.'

The, for Marco and Francesca, unexpected quality of the food, given the unprepossessing nature of the small restaurant, served to put their discussion on hold until after the serving dish had been emptied and, like their individual plates, wiped clean with bread.'

'How was it?' asked Alvaro as he cleared the plates.

'Terrible,' said Marco, with a smile as he indicated the completely empty dishes, and then, 'Compliments to the chef.' Alvaro smiled and bowed his head in a modest acceptance of the praise.

'Thankyou, Alvaro,' added Capuano, 'It's about time some of our Northern friends started to appreciate what Naples is really about. Make sure you tell Nunzia, how much my guests are enjoying her cooking.'   Alvaro smiled and bowed his head again before withdrawing to the kitchen with the empty plates.

'So, arresting Malik and his associates is not about stopping a plot against Guzzanti and the Commission, it's about getting the Commission noticed by the public and making it seem far more important than it really is,' said Francesca hesitantly.

'And lots of people will instinctively support a national institution that's under threat from foreigners, and be far less objective when they look at any information that comes out of the Commission later,' added Marco, shaking his head. 'But what about Malik? If important people are making money from his arms deals, surely he's too big a pawn to be sacrificed.'

'In a few days' time, Malik, and most of those arrested with him, will be transferred to precautionary house arrest while the investigation is ongoing. The charge of plotting to assassinate Guzzanti won't hold up and, when Malik has dropped out of the news, those charges will be dropped...'

At this point the appearance of the *cicenielli* caused another break in the conversation, and it was only when these had been despatched in the same manner as the pasta e ceci, that Capuano continued from where she had left off. 'One or two of Malik's men, who are considered expendable, will be convicted of illegal possession of weapons for unknown purposes. The time they've spent on remand will be taken into account and, in the worst case scenario, they may have a few more months to spend inside. They will, of course, be well compensated for any inconvenience caused them.'

'So, you think it's likely that Malik has been in on this from the start, and knew that he was going to be arrested?' asked Francesca.

'It would fit with their strategy of managing the flow of information, so that everything is seen how they want it to be seen,' said Marco.

'Given Malik's links with the Camorra, and the links that the Camorra have with some elements in the local police, it's inconceivable that Malik would not have been pre-warned. The weapons that were seized when he and the others were arrested, will be limited in number and no great loss to the organisation.'

'What would be interesting to know, would be who Malik's contacts are in the police, and which politicians they're linked to,' mused Francesca.

'I thought you might be interested in that,' said Capuano, looking at her watch, 'if we take our time over coffee and *digestivi*, there should be someone along soon who can help us.'

Along with the espressos, Alvaro brought out a bottle of grappa and a chilled bottle of *limoncello* – both clearly homemade. Capuano asked him to bring an extra glass as she was expecting someone else to join them. She then put thirty euros on the table which Alvaro took and then withdrew.

'Thirty euros!' exclaimed Francesca as the door to the kitchen closed behind him, 'It can't be only thirty euros... it would cost that much just for one of us in Florence!'

'And maybe for one and a half of us in Rome,' added Marco.

'Whereas here, it includes a decent tip, to let Alvaro know that we don't want to be disturbed.'

Shortly after, a swarthy man, with short-cropped black hair, in his early thirties slipped in through the door of the small trattoria and looked around suspiciously, as though there might have been someone hiding under one of the other tables, before pulling a chair up to their table. Having taken in Francesca and Marco with searching glances, he fixed his eyes on Capuano who had placed a twenty euro note on the table. The man looked at the note and shook his head.

Capuano placed another twenty on the table.

'Cento.'

'After... if your information is worth it... and maybe a bonus if I'm very pleased with you.'

He looked from the money on the table to Capuano and, evidently deciding that she was not going to put any more money down to start with, asked in what Marco initially though was a sulky tone, what she wanted.

'To start with, I want to know whether Malik was planning to kill the Senator in Rome.'

'Malik?' said the man, with a fairly unsuccessful attempt to appear as if he had never heard the name.

Capuano's hand moved rapidly so that it covered the forty euro's that were already on the table. 'Don't even think about messing me about, Leon.'

She held his gaze until his eyes dropped towards the money and he seemed to sag slightly in the chair. 'No,' he said eventually.

'So who set him up... and why?'

He was silent for a moment, head bowed towards the table, while Capuano sat with a patience that neither of the others felt. Then, he raised his head and a torrent of thick Neapolitan dialect which appeared to be liberally sprinkled with words and short phrases which seemed to be eastern European, poured out.

Francesca and Marco soon gave up trying to follow what he was saying, only getting a rough gist of what was going on from the occasional interjections that Capuano made.

Eventually, he came to an end and looked expectantly at Capuano. She extracted three further twenty euro notes from her pocket and pushed them over the table towards the man, but didn't take her hand off them. He reached out, picked up the initial forty euros and moved his hand towards the other sixty which were still under the control of Capuano, and stopped a few millimetres short of the edge of the notes. 'One last question,' she said without smiling.

He looked at her, head tilted slightly to one side, eyes narrowed. 'Who tells Malik what to do?'

Francesca saw a look of fear momentarily escape from his eyes. *'Iu nun saccio cchiu' niente,'* he said, shaking his head.

'Oh, I think you do, Leon. I think that you know a lot more than you're telling us... even though you've already told me enough to get you into big trouble if anyone found out.'

If the light had been better, Francesca felt sure that she would have seen the colour drain from his face then, after a few seconds, he began to talk again and, while it was till in dialect, and spoken in a very low voice, this time it was much slower, and they managed to follow most of what was being said. He explained that, at least once a week, Malik was visited by a Captain from the Municipal Police, and that, for the duration of these visits, the two men were closeted inside a room with two armed guards outside the doors. After the Captain had left each week, Malik issued orders to his lieutenants about what they were to do over the following few days.

Marco interrupted here, 'But this Captain will only be a go-between; what we need to know is who sends him – a go-between is not much use to us.'

Capuano now spoke to the man, this time herself adopting Neapolitan to speak to him and Francesca noticed that her hand and arm movements became much freer and more eloquent as she did so. The man replied, also in dialect and speaking even more quickly than before.

When he had finished, Capuano smiled for the first time since the man had entered, and released her hand from the money, which he took quickly. She nodded at Marco and Francesca, and Marco pushed a further fifty euros across the table. The man took it, stood up, gave them a curious little bow and retreated quickly from the restaurant.

'Beneventano,' said Capuano, the smile no longer on her face.

'Beneventano?' asked Francesca, and then, as realisation struck her, 'Dino Beneventano, the president of the Campanian Region?'

'And brother of the Under-Secretary of State for Reform, Devolution and Public Functions,' added Marco.

'Which is based in Palazzo Chigi, right at the heart of government,' completed Francesca.

'Let's go back to my apartment,' said Capuano. 'I need to fill you in on the rest of the things he told me – and you need to give me more detail about what is going on.'

Chapter 21

'What I don't understand, ' said Marco, 'is why he was prepared to give us this information for what is effectively not a great deal of money. Surely, his life must be at risk if he's passing over information like this.'

'As I told you, Leon has been in Naples for nearly twenty years now; he was a Russian sailor who jumped ship while the tanker he was on docked after developing engine problems. He's been working, doing little jobs for the Camorra ever since and, since the ex-soviets muscled, or bought their way, into parts of the Camorra's traditional businesses, he's acted as a sort of unofficial go-between. As far as the Camorra are concerned, one Russian's pretty much the same as another – the distinctions between Russians, Ukrainians, Bielorussians and all the rest, are pretty meaningless to them... but Leon can't stand the Ukrainians, which is why he's a useful source of information.'

'So what he said, pretty much confirmed your theory about what was going on with Malik, which means that, as far as we're concerned, Malik is of no real significance.'

'No. But what we have got is a line on another of the main players up in Rome and the knowledge that at least one of the larger regions is already under the conspirators' control. Don't forget... as well as being President of the *Regione,* Beneventano also owns Tele Campania. We know that the Ministry of Communications in Rome is headed by one of theirs and, if they can control some of the major regional channels as well, they're well on the way to winning the media battle.'

'How much hard evidence do you actually have?' asked Capuano leaning back in her chair. 'Because... it seems to me... that if you try and make a move too soon, without evidence that would stand up in a court... the appearance will be that, instead of the conspirators having planned a very clever coup d'état, what is actually happening is a left wing smear campaign to discredit the right.'

Francesca sighed. 'You're right, of course... We have a lot of evidence about parts of the plot; there are some things... some crimes... we could prove against some of the people involved but, what we don't have... at least not yet... is something that enables us to prove that all these things are linked and form part of a plan... I suppose that part of the problem is that, because we Italians have got used to regular stories about corrupt politicians, most people have come to almost expect it and would just shrug their shoulders rather than seeing what's happening as part of a bigger plan.'

'I think,' added Marco, 'that quite a lot depends on how well Ciancolini's meeting with the President goes tomorrow. If he'll agree to give Ciancolini the authority to take rapid action at the right time, without having to go through the usual bureaucratic channels, and is then prepared to publicly condemn the conspirators, then we may stand a chance of convincing the public.'

'Providing that we can find the proof that links all the conspirators together... Have we picked anything useful up from the bugging devices?'

Capuano looked at her quizzically and she looked at Marco.

'I run a small business in Rome, specialising in security equipment, including some work that's contracted out to us by the Ministry of Public Works. That's enabled us to install a limited number of bugging devices in the offices of some of those who we know are involved in the conspiracy... So far, the devices have allowed us to know when some meetings have taken place between conspirators, and have also provided information that links a couple of people very closely to the murder of Cabrini-Pellé... but we're still waiting for the big breakthrough.'

'If that big break through doesn't come fairly soon, you could be in big trouble. Remember, history is always written by the winners, and when they've already got a lot of the media on their side, it won't take much for them to portray you as the bad guys – whatever the reality is. The Italian people like to back winners; we don't have the cult of the underdog as the British do.'

Francesca shrugged her shoulders, 'It's a risk we've got to take. I don't think I could live with myself if I just sat back and let the right wing just trample over all the democratic reforms and institutions that we've managed to build over the last sixty years.' Capuano, tried to interrupt, but Francesca continued, 'Oh, I know it's not perfect..'

'Far from it!' interjected Marco with a shake of the head.

'...but what we've got, we've had to fight hard for, and we've got to keep on fighting hard, or we could find ourselves back under a fascist dictatorship before anyone realises what's happening.'

'There are still some people around who would like nothing better than to go back to having a strong ruler like Mussolini,' said Capuano provocatively.

'Oh, I'm not worried about them – the ones who're stuck in the past, wallowing in a false nostalgia. It's the more modern, clever, more media-savvy ones who worry me. It's ironic that when Gramsci developed his theory of hegemony, it was meant to act as a warning by showing how the ruling elites maintain their dominance over the masses – instead, it seems to have been adopted almost as a manual by those same ruling elites that it was meant to expose.'

'Franci's got all the passion to fight for the cause – as you can see,' said Marco, speaking to Capuano but looking at Francesca with adoring eyes.

'Well, just make sure you don't end up as a martyr to the cause,' observed Capuano dryly, 'the one thing everyone knows about martyrs, is that they're dead – and once you're dead, you're no good to anyone anymore.... Now, tell me how you managed to arrange this meeting with the President, and how, exactly, you hope to proceed from there.'

Chapter 22

'Pronto. Chi parla?'

'Ciao, Rosa It's me, Papa.'

'Hi, Dad. This is an honour; it's usually Mum who rings – she's OK, isn't she.'

'Yes, of course she is – and I do ring occasionally.'

'I know. I was only teasing. How are you, everything OK?'

'Oh, I'm fine. I thought I'd have lots of free time after I gave up teaching, and wondered how I'd fill it, but since I've been on the Council, I seem to be busier than ever – that's probably why you think I don't ring as much as I should.'

'Of course, Dad, because you were on the phone every day when you were teaching, weren't you. Now, I know you don't do small-talk on the phone, so why are you ringing – there must be a reason?'

'Well, I'm deeply hurt by the thought that my first born child doesn't think I'd ring her up just for a chat but, since you ask... I need a word with Paul, if he's in.'

'There you are you see – I knew it! Paul's not in at the moment and I don't know what time he'll be back – is there anything I can do? Or do want me to get him to ring you?'

'Maybe. Did he tell you that Francesca had asked me to see if I could put them in touch with a friendly mason?'

'Yes, I know all about it.'

'OK. Well, Professore Davide Magni, who taught Philosophy at the school where I taught, until he retired three years ago, was always quite open about being a mason, and we were fairly good friends so I decided it was worth asking him. Obviously, as the masonic lodges are male only, the obvious person to talk to him is Paul. I managed to speak to him this morning, and he agreed that Paul can go over and have a chat tomorrow or the day after.'

'That's great. Have you got the address and phone number handy?'

'I have, but this is where it starts to get a bit complicated. You see, Davide doesn't live in Florence anymore; he always complained about the traffic and the air quality in the city, so as soon as he and Veronica were both retired, they sold the house in Florence and moved into an old house up in the hills near Pescia, that Veronica's parents had left her when they died. He's shown me on a map and explained how to get there but it's probably easiest if I explain it directly to Paul, rather than introduce another link in the chain.'

'You're probably right. If he rings, I'll ask him to call in and see you on his way home, and if he doesn't, I'll get him to give you a ring as soon as possible. Thanks a lot, Dad – it's really important.'

'Don't mention it. Oh... and Rosa.. you come round sometime soon as well. We'll go for a long walk together and have a father-daughter chat without any of these impersonal mechanical devices getting in the way.'

'I will. Look after yourself and give Mum and Nonna a kiss. *Ciao, ciao!*

'*A presto. Ciao.*'

Paul raised an eyebrow and glanced up from the map to his father-in-law, 'So what exactly did you tell him to make him agree to talk to me?'

'I told him that Francesca is a freelance investigative journalist and that you've been helping her. I also told him that, during an investigation, names have come up of people who are certainly masons, and you need to make sure that they are only involved in crime as individuals and are not acting on behalf of the masons.'

'And that satisfied him? He didn't want more information before agreeing to meet?'

Guido smiled. 'I told him that I knew nothing more: no names, no idea what the crime was – nothing.'

Paul nodded, approvingly, 'So he can't warn anyone, and the only way he can find out any information is by talking to me. Clever.'

'I hope, in fact I'm sure, that Davide will turn out to be one of the good guys. He's not one of those who's in it to advance his career: he could quite easily have had a headship if he'd wanted, purely on his own merits. But power never interested him at all. Whenever decisions were being taken in the school, he always just went along with whatever the majority decided, unless he felt that it wasn't in the best interests of the kids. And, unlike some of my other colleagues, I never once heard a rumour that the children of wealthy or influential parents had their marks inflated in his class.'

'Alright. I'm happy to take your word for it. Now, how do I find him; I've been to Pescia a few times, but I don't know any of the surrounding villages except Vellano, where we went for a pizza once – I can't remember why.'

When Paul reached the village the following day, he could see Vellano, the largest of the ten castellated villages in Pescia's hinterland – or the Swiss Pesciatina as the local tourist board signs denominated it - on what, at first glance, appeared to be the opposite side of the steep valley, although a closed look revealed that there were actually two valleys in-between, separated by a steep ridge. He left his bike parked by a loggia under the apse of the village church, a loggia that had been dedicated the men of the village who had lost their lives in the First World War.

Rounding the corner of the church he found himself in what had been described to him as the village square, a description which he felt stretched the meaning of the word square to its limits. The church dominated almost all of one side; the side facing the church had a block of either two, or three, houses (he couldn't be sure where the division was); one of the short sides was mainly open except for a covered fountain and a tree which had been heavily cut back, while at the far end was the start of what seemed to be one of the outer walls of the castellated village. The house on the ground floor had a rustic pergola separating it from the square and, the way the stones on the upper floor had been sandblasted, indicated that it was part of a separate dwelling. A rusty sign indicated that parking was not allowed in the square although this appeared to have been completely ignored by an old Citroen Saxo, and an even older Lancia Thema.

There was no sign of life in the square, although somewhere in the distance he could hear at least two chainsaws at work in the woods. Once he had admired the view he went over to the second of two green wooden doors to the left of the square, a door which had a curious antler shaped piece of wood fastened to the wall above it. There was no bell so he gave two sharp knocks and then took a step back.

Almost immediately he heard the sound of the bolt being drawn back and then he found himself face to face with a smiling, lithe woman with short dark hair, whose age he found difficult to judge – she could have been anywhere between her late forties and her early sixties. 'Hello,' she said, with a smile that placed wrinkles around her eyes, 'you must be Paul,' and she held out a hand. Almost before he could reply in the affirmative, she insisted he should go in and take off as much as possible of his biker gear. 'My husband is down in the *campo*,' she said, 'I'll take you down there in a minute, but let me get you a glass of water first,' and she disappeared down some stairs to what he guessed must have been an underground kitchen.

The room was sparsely although comfortably furnished with an armchair and a small but comfortable looking two-seater settee and two highly polished tables in olive-wood. A pot-bellied wood-burner stood in one corner and a few photographs were spaced tastefully on the wall. One of these was an old one of a family group - probably from the early twentieth century; one was a less formal family group taken in the square outside, probably about thirty years before; one was a picture of a boat, and the largest was a modern family portrait where a handsome dark haired man in his thirties stood behind and to the left of a strikingly beautiful blond in a wheelchair. The woman was holding a baby, while a boy of five or six years old stood to her right.

'A hundred years of my family,' said Signora Magni, who had returned with the glass of water, unheard by Paul. These are my grandparents, and this little boy is my father; this is us with our children back in the early seventies, and this is Dino, our son, with his Swedish wife and our grandchildren.'

'And is this your boat?'

She shook her head, ' It's Greta's boat. She used to swim competitively until she damaged her back in a diving accident; now she's taken up sailing and hopes to make the team for the

Paralympics – she says it stops her feeling sorry for herself and keeps her sane.'

'They live in Sweden?'

She nodded, 'They have a beautiful house on one of the islands in Stockholm's inner archipelago. It's about fifteen minutes' boat ride to the city centre.'

'You've been?'

'Many times. It's beautiful, although a bit cold for me in spring and autumn.'

'Not Winter?'

She smiled and shook her head. 'Winters are meant to be cold. I put a big coat on and thick gloves, and I love it. Sometimes you can even skate on the ice in the centre of Stockholm, and quite regularly around their island. Dino's been there for nearly twenty years now and every year, he rings me up sometime in winter and says "the forecast says that next week will be cold and bright." As soon as I get that call, I get the first flight I can.... Anyway, you didn't come here to listen to me chattering away. I need to take you down to see Davide. This way.'

He followed her down the steep steps into what he'd assumed was the basement and saw that, as the ground fell away sharply from the square, the houses on that side had rooms below the square that still had windows facing the other way. The door from the kitchen opened onto a steep stone-flagged road that must have originally been a mule track. She must have guessed what he was thinking, as she said, 'The road up from the valley wasn't built until the fifties; until then, everything that arrived in the village was brought up on the back of mules. That's why the road finishes at the square; the original roads inside the village were all built before anyone ever dreamed of motor cars.'

She led him along the narrow streets between houses, half of which had been painstakingly restored and half of which appeared abandoned, until the houses ended and the street became a paved path dropping down towards olive groves and mixed woodland. 'This is the old road down to the valley – it's not far now.'

Paul noticed that strong but fairly low wire fences had been erected to separate the different areas of land. 'I suppose that now that a large proportion of the landowners don't live here anymore, they need the fences to remind each other where the boundaries are.' To his surprise, she laughed and shook her head.

'Trust me, even the landowners who live far away and only come here a couple of times a year to look after the olives, know exactly where the boundaries are. No, the fences are for the *cinghiali*.'

'Wild boar, so close to the village. I thought they were supposed to be shy, unless you disturb a mother with her young.'

'A hundred years ago, there were nearly a hundred and fifty people in the village -fifty years ago there were still over sixty, now there are twenty eight most of the time, and the majority of us are old and don't spend most of our time working in the fields. When the village was full, the animals kept well away – now they see the area round the village as a good source of food. A few years ago, someone decided to put a fence round his property to keep the animals out, and it worked, but that just made the problem worse for everyone else, so gradually everyone has put a fence round their property... Here we are.' she said stopping at a small wooden gate in the fence, flanked by bushes with white and intense red roses, but where the dominant perfume came from the adjacent rosemary bushes. 'Davide,' she called, 'your guest's here.'

'*Arrivo*,' came a voice from lower down the hillside.

'Have a seat here,' she said, indicating a wooden bench table, 'he'll be here in a minute,' and she smiled again and turned back up the path.

Paul didn't sit, but stood by the table taken aback by the beauty of his surroundings. Like most of the surrounding hillsides, the one on which he was standing had been carved into narrow, farmable terraces centuries ago, and until fairly recently had provided a precarious means of subsistence for the population of each of the ancient villages. The coming of motorised transport and the gradual development of better roads after the Second World War had changed all that, with villagers able to access more regular paid employment down in the valleys, which had led to an inevitable depopulation of the villages. Now, most of the hillsides were overgrown with just a few patches still cultivated and kept in pristine condition by old men who had felt the pull of their roots after retirement from the mills and plant nurseries in the valley.

Even to Paul's unpractised eye, it was clear that the area of hillside he found himself on, had not been continuously cultivated; he could see that, at its lower end edge, elder and chestnut trees had encroached on the olives, depriving them of the necessary light and there were signs that some areas had been dug out to tidy up after the original terraces had crumbled. The olive trees in most of the area seemed to be lower than those he was used to seeing in other groves, but the benefit of this was that the views were spectacular. Where he was standing, an area or terrace had been widened and a rustic pergola erected to shade the table which had been placed so that a tree-stump made an extra seat at one end. A few yards from the table, against the rear edge of the terrace was a masonry barbecue and a stone sink surmounted by a tap which had obviously been linked to a supply in the village. Rosemary and sage bushes had been planted nearby and their sweet smell added to the atmosphere.

A couple of terraces below the barbecue area he could glimpse blue and white patches through the olives and, as he stepped to the edge of the terrace he realised that a small pool had cleverly been created below a natural spring. Decking had been carefully placed around the pool and the whole was enclosed by a rustic wooden fence. The olive trees on the terrace immediately below the pool had been cleared giving anyone in it a clear view over the valley.

'You like my little piece of Paradise, do you?' said a deep rich voice to his left.

Paul turned and smiled, to find that a large man, upright but holding a walking stick in one hand, stood watching him from a sunken path he hadn't noticed before that ran down the side of the property just inside the boundary. 'I do. Very much.' He moved towards the man and held out his hand, 'I'm Paul; you must be Professor Magni. It's a pleasure to meet you.'

The man met his smile and accepted his handshake. Paul wasn't sure if it was because it was what he expected but he had the impression that there was something slightly different about the way the Professor shook his hand, but even though he was unable to show that he belonged, he felt that there was genuine warmth and intelligence in the other's look.

'Hello, Paul. It's a pleasure to meet you. Guido mentioned you many times over the years we were working together. I feel as if I already know you – so we'll forget about the 'Professor'; call me Davide.'

'Thank you. I will.'

'Now, Paul, before we sit down to talk, let me show you around. I know that Pride is a sin but when it comes to this little bit of land, I'm afraid I can't help it.'

Paul indicated his pleasure at the suggestion and his host turned round.

'I'm afraid I have to go fairly slowly these days, I have a touch of Parkinson's and I'm not quite as steady on my feet as I was a few years ago... This is the pool. There was originally just a muddy area below our little spring, but a little bit of enlarging has made all the difference. The decking around it makes it appears to be in the ground.'

'Stunning,' said Paul. 'And the way you've shaped the trees around it mean that it's hardly visible from outside the property.'

'Yes, although I'm afraid that my neighbour, who's passionate about his olives can't bear to look at them. Those four plants there...' and he waved his stick to show which he meant, '… haven't been pruned in the middle, so that they form more of a hedge but, like most of the other trees, they've been cut fairly low so that there's no need to go climbing up ladders when it's time for the olive harvest.'

'You harvest them yourself, then?'

'Oh yes. The olive harvest is one of the best times of the year in the village. Everyone seems to come alive and be happy. People who only return to the village occasionally find time to come back and join in. All through November, there isn't a moment when you can hear people singing as they work. Sometimes it seems that even people you thought had died reappear to harvest their olives. Both Marusa and I are at it from dawn until dusk and usually our son manages to get down from Sweden for at least a couple of days.'

'It must be a good boost to your pension. Genuine, artisan produced olive oil is really expensive.'

Magni laughed and shook his head. 'Armando, my neighbour, says that if I looked after my plants properly and harvested them all, I should be able to get over three thousand kilos of olives in a good year – but that would be really hard work and not really why we retired here. This had been in my wife's family for as long as anyone can remember but until about fifteen years ago, it had been allowed to grow wild. When we first started coming and I started to clean it up, we were lucky if we got fifty kilos a year. Now, even though we've cut them low, so we don't have to climb ladders, and don't bother with the more inaccessible ones, we get about five hundred kilos, enough to supply us and all our friends with extra virgin olive oil for the year.'

As he talked, Magni had led Paul lower down still and, to his surprise, he found that they had come to another area where the collapse of one of the original terraces had allowed the clearing of a wider area which had been shaded by a pergola of vines to provide a pleasant seating area. Magni unlocked the door of a storage box at the rear of the area which was full of the tools necessary to look after the olives as well as a pair of folding chairs and a small camping table. 'All mod cons,' he said with a smile, 'I used to come here when I had exams to mark and didn't want to be disturbed – although I sometimes got distracted and just sat and looked at the view – especially if I had a flask of red with me!'

'I don't know what to say – except that I can see why you referred to it as Paradise.'

Magni's eyes smiled at the compliment. 'If you don't mind, we won't go any further down – I can point out the other things from the terrace here – of course, if you want to go further down on your own, feel free to do so.'

From the edge of the area Magni pointed out a pile of stones lower down which, he informed Paul had once been a shepherd's hut and which was marked on the official cadastral map. When he saw that this last bit of information hadn't made much of an impression on Paul, he explained that it being marked on the map meant that it was possible to build another building there, if he were minded to do so.

'Idyllic.'

The tour over, Magni invited Paul to take a seat in one of the chairs on the area under the pergola and, having retrieved two bottles of Birra Moretti from a cool-box he'd carried down with him, sat down facing him.

'OK, Paul. Guido said that you needed to ask some questions about Freemasonry.' Paul nodded. 'Now, I'm sure you've heard lots of information about Freemasonry, and I can say fairly confidently that most of it will be nonsense.'

'I realise that, and I suppose really that that's why I need to talk to you, so that I can sort out the nonsense from the rest,' he looked at Magni expectantly.

'Alright. Perhaps it's better if you tell me why you want to know and that will help me decide what I can tell you.' He stretched out his hand to prevent Paul interrupting. 'There are certain bonds and duties of secrecy that I am bound by and you will have to accept those. I cannot reveal what another mason may have told me under a seal of masonic secrecy, and I will do nothing that may harm another member who has been faithful to the charitable objectives and code of honour of his, or her, lodge, but, one thing I will promise you is that I will not lie; if you have a question that I can't answer, I will say so.'

Paul nodded and smiled, 'That sounds fair enough. One thing that puzzles me already though is that you said, "his or her", I thought that one of the consistent features of masonic lodges was that they were male only.'

'Ah. I see that you know a little bit about Freemasonry but not a lot; should I start by giving you an overview, so that whatever specific information you ask about later can be put into its correct context?'

'That sounds like an excellent idea, if you can spare the time.'

'Paul, you forget that I'm a historian by training -there's nothing I like better than being able to explain aspects of history that interest me to a captive audience.'

'In that case, I'm all yours,' and Paul settled back in his chair.

'OK. You'll know of course that back in the medieval period, most trades were regulated by official trade bodies that set out the terms of apprenticeships, minimum standards and common terms of trade. Because there was a lot of building going on at the time and, as you'll have noticed, the civic buildings in particular were built to such a high standard that many of them have survived until the present day, the levels of competence required of masons was very high. That was how it all started back in the fourteenth century, although it didn't become masonry as we now know it until early in the eighteenth century when several masonic brotherhoods in London met together and agreed that there should be an over-riding organisation known as a Grand Lodge. From London, the organisation expanded rapidly so that it soon covered most of England and at pretty much the same time parallel organisations were being established in Scotland and Ireland.'

'Parallel but not the same?'

'That's right. Parallel but not the same. Each country has its own organisation which to some extent reflects different national customs but, in practice, the organisations have the same guiding principles, what is best described as a peculiar form of morality, veiled in allegory and illustrated by symbols. A fundamental tenet of all lodges, however, under whatever national jurisdiction they fall is that there should be no discussion of religion or politics in lodge meetings.'

Paul gave a slightly doubtful smile, 'And P2?'

Magni noted Paul's look and responded with another little smile, 'Bear with me: I'll come to P2 later – if I jump ahead now, it will be more difficult to understand.

'Sorry-'

'No problem... I won't take you through the whole history of the English or Scottish lodges, fascinating as it is, as what I assume really concerns you is Freemasonry in this country.'

Paul nodded.

'So I'll try and limit myself to essential background knowledge.... Well, after the failed uprising in 1715, many leading Scots went into exile on the continent and by that time, the masonic lodges had expanded beyond people who engaged in the profession to people who shared the over-riding objectives of Freemasonry, the so-called 'Landmarks of Freemasonry'. In 1720 James Anderson produced a written constitution for the Grand Lodge in London, which as the oldest governing lodge is generally recognised as having primacy over all others, and that constitution specifically excluded women from membership. You could say that the Masonic lodges in London were a precursor of the Gentlemen's clubs that were established later in the eighteenth century, and provided a more sober alternative to the coffee shops which were thriving at the time and which were viewed with distrust by the governing classes as they were used as meeting places by Jacobins and other undesirables – and you might be surprised to know that women were also banned by law from the coffee shops in England – so their exclusion from masonic lodges was not particularly unusual at the time. Over here on the continent, however, the exiled masons couldn't afford to be so picky about their members so women were allowed in very early on and then, when the French, and after them other European countries, began to set up their own lodges, it wasn't uncommon for women to be admitted, until eventually we got to the position where, although most lodges are all male, some are mixed, and there are even a few that are all female. Hopefully, that explains why I said "his or her" earlier.'

'It does. I understand now. Typical of my home country not to move with the times and cling doggedly to tradition.'

Magni gave a polite laugh at this and then continued. 'Wherever lodges are set up, and whoever belongs to them, they all follow the same basic principles: they can only be authorised by an existing Grand Lodge or three ordinary lodges; each member has an obligation to provide relief to those in need; to support and protect their families and other brethren, provided they haven't broken the law...' and here Magni gave Paul a piercing glance as if to gage his reaction, but Paul's countenance didn't change, 'and to tell the truth. Each Grand Lodge has complete control over the first three degrees of membership...'

'Which are?' said Paul, looking up.

'The three degrees are direct descendants of the original medieval levels of membership: entered apprentice, fellow craft and master mason; some will tell you that some jurisdictions have expanded these to thirty three which is, however, only partially true; fortunately this does not regard the lodges that come under the authority of the Grand Orient of Italy.'

'And may I ask which degree you have achieved?'

'Magni smiled again, 'Despite what you may have heard about the secrececy of masonic lodges, there is very little that I am prevented from telling you; I have achieved the level of Master Mason.'

'And... are you able to tell me what difference there is between the three degrees?'

'Does it have any particular bearing on your enquiry?'

Paul hesitated for a moment and then smiled, 'No, I must admit it doesn't... I was just curious.'

Magni seemed to have expected this answer, 'All you really need to know is that those initiated as apprentices are entrusted only with secrets of the order that are appropriate to their brief period of service; the reason for this is so that when they visit other lodges they are immediately recognisable as apprentices. When the leading members of the order deem that an apprentice is ready to become a Fellow Craft, they are invited to participate in another ceremony in which further secrets are revealed to them and they take an oath not to reveal those secrets to anyone outside the order or to those who are undergoing their apprenticeships. The process for passing from being a Fellow Craft to a Master Mason is very similar.'

'And are these secrets so terrible that they need to be kept as secrets?'

Here Magni laughed out loud. When he had recovered, he looked directly at Paul and said, 'I think, Paul, that if you knew what our secrets were you would be very disappointed. They're not really very exciting; think of an Accountant or a Doctor – they have a duty of professional secrecy regarding their clients, even when, most of the time, those clients are extremely dull. For as long as we have records, we know that men – and it is usually men – have felt the need to belong to a clearly defined group – being a Freemason meets that atavistic need, and the secrecy involved makes it feel special because it makes it exclusive. Being a Freemason for most people is just being part of a social group; there isn't really much difference between being a mason and being a Rotarian, or a member of the Lion's Club – in fact, it may surprise you to know that in the founding convention of Hamas they claim that both Freemasonry and Rotarianism are agents of Zionism and operate in accordance with its direct instructions.'

'And to what extent are the Grand Lodges linked? Who is it who has overall responsibility?'

'An interesting question, but one where I think you're going to be disappointed by the answer. I mentioned before that the English and Scottish Grand Lodges developed in parallel but separately, giving mutual recognition when they were in amity but remaining separate organisations and the same pretty much applies throughout the world. The United Grand Lodge of England is both the oldest and the largest lodge in the world – it is also the most traditional and conservative. It recognises as equals only those Grand Lodges which adopt almost exactly the same rules and regulations and withholds recognition from other Grand Lodges. The English strand of Masonry is one of three, and in most of continental Europe, all three co-exist peaceably. There is a European body called CLIPSAS which aims to promote harmony between the three strands and provide a forum where representatives can meet; it even recognises the legitimacy of mixed and female lodges. Ninety Grand Lodges in most countries and regions belong to this body – except the English, of course who, as the oldest Grand Lodge are reluctant to compromise, while supporting the aims of CLIPSAS in principle.'

'Of course.' said Paul, with a rueful shake of his head, 'A currency that pre-dates the Magna Carta, different dates for Mother's Day, World Book Day, even May Day, unless it happens to fall on the first of the month. It seems to be a badge of honour to be different, or awkward as most sensible people see it.'

'I couldn't possibly comment on that – it sounds as though I'd be intruding on private grief,' said Magni with a smile which Paul reciprocated.

'Now, you said you'd tell me about P2.'

'Ah yes, so I did... Right. The lodge that became known as P2, or Propaganda Due, was originally established in 1877 as a place where visiting masons from other countries, who were not affiliated to any established Italian lodge could meet. Gradually, however, its original function became less relevant and it became effectively a clandestine lodge for the friends and associates of Licio Gelli – I take it you know all about Gelli?'

'I'm not sure I know everything, but I've read up on him so I know quite a lot.'

'On the surface, charming and urbane, but underneath, calculating, determined and very, very dangerous. Even now, in his eighties, he's still capable of almost anything – even if he and his lodge hadn't been expelled by the Grand Orient of Italy for incompatible activities, his criminal activities would free me from any obligation I may have towards him as a fellow mason.... I met him, you know, years ago... He's from Pistoia originally and he was a Master Mason when I was an apprentice – even then, the order was a means to an end for him. I think the only principle he really agreed with was secrecy.'

'So at the time of Sindona, Calvi and the Banco Ambrosiano, Gelli and P2 were actually outside the mainstream of Freemasonry?'

'Not just the mainstream. The activities of his lodge that we know about, were completely incompatible with any type of Freemasonry.'

'What about the other nine hundred and sixty one members of P2? How do they stand in relation to Freemasonry?'

Magni stood up and walked over to the rail around the edge of the decking, where his stood silently, with his back to Paul for almost two minutes before he turned and faced him,

'Why don't you tell me what all this is about, then I can try to give you the answers you need?'

'That sounds fair enough,' said Paul, and for the next hour he slowly and carefully took his host through the evidence they had, what definite conclusions they had already been able to draw, and what was, for the moment unproven supposition, all without mentioning others by name, except Francesca, who Magni already knew about, and dell'Omodarme, who was dead.

'So you see,' he said finally, we may only have a limited amount of time if we're to stop this conspiracy and bring its architects to justice. So anything you can tell us about P2 and how it links in with the mainstream masonic organisations in Italy, is likely to be vital.'

Magni topped both their glasses up with water, reflected for a minute and then said, 'At the time the list of names was discovered in Gelli's villa, most of the members claimed to be entirely in ignorance of the fact that Propaganda Two was not approved by the Grand Orient of Italy. As the aim of the group was said to be to create a better and more stable society, they claimed that as far as they were concerned this was entirely reconcilable with the obligation to contribute to charity which bears on all members of all lodges. One thing that it's safe to say is that all members of Propaganda Two had in common is arrogance, and I'm sure you'll agree that for an arrogant person it's not difficult to see helping to reshape society as a form of charitable work and as, in their opinion, the most valuable thing they have to give is their time, it was easy for them to convince themselves that they were being charitable.'

Paul snorted.

'I'm not saying that I agree with them; I'm just telling you how they justified themselves. Well, apart from Gelli, and others who'd been part of the lodge when it was expelled, the vast majority of the others were allowed to remain members of their original Grand Lodges on the grounds that they hadn't done anything criminal or detrimental to the interests of other masons – a matter of opinion, of course. However, in my view, the three hundred plus who had been masons at the time of the expulsions, really had no excuse for not knowing that Propaganda Two was outside the Grand Orient. I think that, what you should really be interested to find out is who were the members of Propaganda Two but whose names didn't appear on the list found in Gelli's villa in Arezzo.

'I'm sure you'll already have done your own research into what's happened to the nine hundred and sixty-two on the list. Three of them, as you know, are in very senior positions within the government and others now hold very senior positions in the judiciary, the military and the security services. The problem you have really lies in identifying people who were members but whose names were not on the list, and probably younger members who have been recruited and groomed over the last twenty years.'

'If the majority of those involved were not charged with any criminal activities and were allowed to remain within their existing Lodges, what advantage would there have been for people not to have admitted to being members of P2 back in the eighties?'

Magni gave a slight shake of his head, 'Think about it, Paul. Reluctant though I am to admit it, not everyone within the masonic movement joins because they believe in what should be humane and altruistic ideals – some of them – I'm afraid to say – see the Lodges as an opportunity for networking and advancing their careers. Of this group of people, some will be people with real talent who would be of great value to an organisation like Propaganda Two. How better to recruit them than by having people within the movement who can make them feel like the chosen ones?'

'And do you have any ideas about who these people are – both the ones who weren't identified at the time and those who might have been recruited since?'

'I have plenty of ideas, Paul, but it would be against my masonic vows to tell you about most of them.' He smiled at the disappointment that Paul didn't manage to mask. 'However, what I can do, is tell you about things I have observed or heard, and which have helped me form my ideas – then it will be up to you to draw your own conclusions.'

Paul, who hadn't realised that shoulders had tensed up, felt them relax again.

'In my own lodge, in Pistoia, at the time Propaganda Two was expelled from the Grand Orient of Italy, there were four self-professed members; two of them chose to leave our lodge – as they are no longer members, I can give you their names if you like, but I'm sure they are of no significance – if the coup is relying on people like them, it's destined to fail anyway. The other two said that they would have no more connection with Propaganda Two; one of them died a few years ago and the other is a retired bank manager who is very unlikely to be involved in anything nefarious. There were, however, at least five more members of the lodge, who logic would say ought to have been recruited by Propaganda Two as exactly the sort of people who could be useful to them. Of the five, one is now dead, two are retired and presumably harmless, but the others occupy important roles in the Regional Administration.'

Paul gave a short low whistle. 'Interesting. I assume you're not able to tell me who they are though,' and he looked Magni in the eye.

'I'm afraid not,' said Magni, 'until such time as they can be shown to be involved in anything illegal, they're covered by my masonic oaths – whatever my personal feelings are about them.'

'You're not prepared to make an exception if you suspect them of being involved in a plot against the state?'

'I'm afraid not. If we're not rigid about the need for proof then we'll soon find that personal feelings about people become more important than truth. I can ask them outright. They don't have to answer but as masons, they are not allowed to lie to other masons. However, I assume that you would prefer me not to alert them to your suspicions.'

'That's right,' said Paul, 'You may even put your own life in danger by doing so.'

'There are some names that I can give you though, without breaching any masonic secrets,' said Magni with a smile. '

'Go on.'

'My father-in-law was a mason in the Pistoia lodge when Gelli was active there, and presumably at the time that he first became involved in Propaganda Two. There were two other masons to whom Gelli was particularly close and who, like him, moved away from Pistoia. One of them was a barrister, Ottaviano Corrazino and the other was an actuary, Roberto Cioni. Now, when Gelli was exposed, my father-in-law said that it was inconceivable that Gelli was involved but not the other two, and yet neither of their names appeared on the list. From what you told me earlier I think that both of these will be of particular interest to you; Cioni died five years ago, but his son, Silvio is currently Minister for Public Works – yes – I thought that would please you... Corrazino, although he's in his eighties is still alive and, apparently, flourishing. Whereas Gelli moved to Arezzo, Corrazino moved to Siena and, the last I heard, he was still active as Honorary Life President of the Sienese Law Society.'

'Yesss!' said Paul, unable to contain himself. They now had definite links between Gelli, P2 or whatever clandestine organisation had taken its place, the government and, what he had a feeling might turn out to be critical, a link to Guerrini in Siena. If Corrazino was Life President of the Sienese Law Society and Guerrini was senior partner in a firm of Sienese lawyers, they had to know each other.

'Davide! Davide!' Signora Magni's voice floated down the hillside.

'Davide!'

'*Si?*'

'You haven't forgotten that we're expected at the Lazzari's at eight have you, Davide?'

'Of course not, dear. I'll be up to get cleaned up and changed in a few minutes...' and then in a lower voice, ' I had forgotten. I'm sorry.'

'That's alright,' said Paul, 'I've learnt a lot and don't know how to thank you enough... Can I give you an arm to lean on, on the way back up?'

Magni gave him a warm smile, 'It's very kind of you to offer Paul, and it would probably get me there a lot quicker, but I've promised myself that for as long as I'm physically capable I'm going to get up and down this hill by myself. The day I can't manage it, will be the day when we put everything up for sale.... No, Paul, you be getting on with you. You've got a fair way to go. Remember to say your goodbyes to my wife on your way. If you think of anything else you need, feel free to come back another day. Just remember, that much of what you have heard about Freemasonry previously is untrue; as far as I, and I believe most other masons are concerned, the main objective of Freemasonry is to do good. Please remember that.'

'I will. And thank you again for all your help.'

As Paul rode carefully down the steep, narrow, twisting road that led down to the valley, he realised that, as he hadn't been sure what time he'd be back, he'd told Rosa not to worry about him and she'd said that she'd take the kids over to her parents for the evening. He'd have to get something to eat on the way back but didn't fancy the motorway services so he'd have to look for somewhere before then.

Luckily, soon after he got down into the main valley he saw a Trattoria-Pizzeria on the right, opposite a builder's merchant. He slowed down to make sure it was open and then pulled into the car-park that seemed to serve both businesses.

Entering the main door, he found himself in a fairly large modern room enclosed by curtained windows on three sides, with roughly sixteen tables carefully laid. Through gaps in the curtains covering the windows at the back, he could see that pots of flowers had been carefully arranged between the windows and the start of the steep hillside, while a glass door in the long windowed side-wall showed him a few steps leading to a large terrace; he assumed that when the good weather finally arrived, most clients would prefer to sit out there to eat. All the tables were unoccupied and he wondered if he were the first to arrive that evening but then a smiling waiter appeared and after giving him a friendly greeting, ushered him through another door and down a few steps into another, more intimate room where eight tables were set. Three of the tables were already occupied: one with a pair of what seemed to be commercial travellers, and the other two with families, one with a bored looking teenage daughter and the other with a pair of young children eating slices of pizza with their hands.

The smiling waiter pulled a chair out for him and, as he sat down, asked, *'Acqua?'*

'Si. Grazie... Naturale.'

The waiter inclined his head slightly in acknowledgement of the order and withdrew to the kitchen,

A minute later a waitress with long dark hair tied back in a ponytail arrived with the bottle of water, a menu and a wine-list. 'As well as what's written on the menu, we've got: *panzanella, funghi fritti* and *trippa* this evening.' She smiled and withdrew.

Paul poured himself a glass a water and opened the menu, ignoring the wine list.

'Are you ready to order?' asked the girl, returning with pen and pad in hand a couple of minutes later.

'I think so,' he replied, returning her smile. 'I usually like to try things that are unusual or house specialities. Can you tell me what the *"festonati da nerone"* are please?'

'Of course, *festonati* is a form of pasta a bit like a flat *rigatoni* but the size of small *ravioli*. The sauce is one of our specialities; it's made of sausage meat, mushrooms, cream and with a touch of tomato.'

'Mmmm. I'll definitely start with that then. How about the *"pizza da nerone"*?'

' *"Pizza da nerone"* is a red based pizza with very thinly sliced onion and thin slices of *coppa di cinghiale* – that's similar to *salami* but made of the neck and upper shoulder of the wild-boar.'

'Again, that sounds great. So I'll have the *festonati* and then the *pizza nerone* and, I may as well tell you now, I'll have the *tiramisu* afterwards – I never have any other sweet when I go to a new restaurant – it's the best way of telling how good a restaurant is.'

She laughed. 'I hope we can meet up to your expectations... To drink?'

He shook his head, 'I'd love to, but I don't when I'm riding the bike – another time,'

'If our *tiramisu* meets up to expectations,' she said with a smile, and took his order through to the kitchen.

While he waited for his food, he reflected on the information he'd gathered from Magni and tried to work out how it could be put to use and what the next steps needed to be. They could link together, the remnants of P2, a cabinet minister whose father had almost certainly been an undisclosed member of P2 and his first cousin once removed - the Sienese lawyer Guerrini. He knew that the new information was important but was struggling to work out how they could use it; although never usually spoken of, it was a matter of public record that several of the current government ministers had been on the list of P2 members and, given what he knew of Guerrini and the disturbing history of the Italian side of his own family, there had never really been any doubt about Guerrini's involvement since Rosa had first recognised him in the photo taken outside the Foreign Ministry. He'd have to sit down and talk it through with Francesca and maybe Ciancolini and Francesca's friend Marco as well.

He leaned back as the waitress approached with his pasta and placed it down in front of him. It was only when he took his first mouthful that he realised how hungry he really was, having only had time to grab a quick sandwich before leaving Florence, and... he had to admit, that the pasta sauce was very good. So good, that as he ate it, he managed to push all thoughts of the conspiracy to the back of his mind. The pasta itself was an unusual form that he didn't remember ever having seen on sale in the supermarkets. Luckily, although he was having pizza afterwards, the waitress had still brought him a bowl of bread and he was able to get every last drop of sauce off the plate before she returned to remove it.

'Everything OK?'

'He indicated the perfectly clean plate with a smile, 'I just about managed to get it all down.' The waitress smiled, took his plate and disappeared again.

While he waited for his pizza, he caught the Prime Minister's name in the conversation between the two commercial travellers and tuned into what they were saying. They were having a friendly argument in the way that work colleagues do to fill up the time, when they get on but don't know each other well enough to talk about families or common friends.

'… going to vote for him again – know he's been involved in some dodgy dealing in the past but you get nowhere in politics if you're honest.'

'That might be true but, if you're not honest, sooner or later it's going to catch up with you and then everything you've built up around you is going to come crashing down.'

'What does it matter if he's made sure his family are set up for life and his friends are doing OK? At least people take notice of Italy now – he's a major figure on the world stage – everybody knows who the Prime Minister of Italy is.'

'They do, but have you read what they say about him. He's a laughing stock and he makes us a laughing stock too. In other countries, if a public figure is even suspected of messing around with under-age girls his career would be over. In Italy, half the people who vote admire him for still "having what it takes" at his age. They don't stop to think that what it takes is to be a billionaire.'

'So what are you going to do then, vote for the socialists? We'll end up as part of the Soviet Union if what they're saying is true. Apparently there's proof that most of the Socialist leaders were secretly working for the Russians before the Russians discovered capitalism.'

'Yeah. That's a worry. If it's true I'll probably end up not voting at all.'

'What about Europe then – they say that prices are going up because we're in the Euro – it's all a German plot, finishing off what Hitler started but couldn't finish...'

Paul tuned out; the rabid right winger didn't really worry him. He wasn't sure if he really meant what he was saying or if it was just intended to gently wind his work colleague up – in either case, the man was clearly an idiot and there were always going to be some of those about. What worried him was what the other man had been saying; his heart was clearly in the right place but the insidious propaganda of the right, and the steady drip-drip of slurs against Prodi and the other leaders of the left was clearly doing its job. Somehow or other, they had to succeed in exposing what was happening and making sure that when it came to the election that the people were able to make an informed choice.

His pizza was equally good; the thin slices of *coppa di cinghiale* that covered the pizza blended in well with the sweetness of the onions, to make the experience of eating the pizza far removed from that of eating a standard *pizza al salame* that was often the easy option provided by pizzerias aiming mainly to exploit the tourist market. When he had emptied his plate, it was the original waiter, who seemed to be the one in charge, who came to take the plate away and ask if he'd like his *tiramisù* straight away, or if he'd prefer to wait a few minutes, and would he like a dessert wine to accompany it.

Paul said that he'd be happy to have the *tiramisù* in a couple of minutes and that he'd like a coffee to follow it. 'Do you get much passing trade - or is it mainly locals who come here?' he asked.

'That depends on the time of year... in Winter it's mainly locals although this is one the roads that leads up to Abetone – the ski resort,' he added, just in case Paul wasn't aware of Abetone, 'there's some passing trade due to that, both in Winter and during the Summer season when people go up there to get away from the heat. The villages in the hills around here also get fairly busy in the Summer, and because we've got the *giardino estivo*,' he gestured vaguely at the windows to the side, ' and a lot of people prefer to eat out when they're on holiday, we're pretty busy from mid-June through to the end of September.'

'Well. I'm glad to hear you're doing well... the food certainly merits it. I'll be calling again, next time I come this way.'

The waiter thanked him and went off to get the *tiramisù* which, as he had hoped, was excellent, made with just the right amount of *Marsala*.

After his coffee, which came accompanied with a small glass of grappa, he paid and got back on the bike for the ride back to Florence.

He was surprised to see as he rode through the outskirts of genteel Montecatini Terme on his way to the motorway, that for a two kilometre stretch after the horse racing track, the road was lined with scantily clad prostitutes every forty or fifty metres, mainly alone but occasionally in pairs. There had been a time, twenty years before, when similar sights had been common around certain roads in Florence, but the city authorities had made a concerted effort and driven them out - or more likely underground. At one point a carabiniere vehicle was parked fairly obviously but the two officers with it seemed to be paying little attention to the girls, and their presence didn't seem to bother the girls in any way. It obviously wasn't just the pimps in Montecatini who were making money he thought. Rosa had told him that a significant proportion of the 'girls' who plied their trade by the side of the road were actually transvestites, and he wondered how true that was, as he accelerated after the last roundabout towards where he could see the motorway lights in the distance.

Chapter 23

On the Sunday morning, wearing a plain headscarf and a fairly shapeless dun-coloured old coat of Capuano's, Francesca made her way down through the *vicoli* until she reached the long narrow Vico Lungo del Gelso which ran parallel to the elegant Via Toledo, separated from it by thirty metres and an abyss in social class. Here she made her way northwards past small shops, groups of women gesticulating and chattering away in the pure Neapolitan that she, as a northerner, found virtually impenetrable, past scantily clad street children playing football using rubbish bags for goals, or sitting preening on mopeds and scooters of various vintages with not a helmet in sight. She kept up a steady pace, not dawdling but not appearing rushed so as not to attract any attention, occasionally pausing to allow a scooter to pass.

The further she went, the more frequent became her glances from side to side until finally she reached a junction where a small grocer's shop had the 'r' missing from the sign above the window. Seeing this, she turned to her left and started to climb up an apparently nameless alleyway to her left, until she reached the second intersection, where she turned to her right, counted four doors along, and then knocked decisively.

Immediately, there was a loud barking inside and there was a thud as though something had been hurled at the other side of the door. Francesca felt terrified; she could feel the sweat running down between her breasts and she hoped her knees wouldn't give way – but she was determined not to show fear. There was a shout inside, presumably the dog's name, and the barking gave way to a growl.

The door opened a few centimetres and she could see two sets of eyes boring into her out of the gloom. The lower set, just below waist height, seemed to have a red tinge and glared at her just above a set of yellowed teeth from which the gums were drawn back, and which seemed to be the source of the menacing growl. The other set, which were slightly below her own were set in a swarthy face below a scarred shaven cranium.

'*Cchi vulé?*' asked a surprisingly high pitched voice.

Francesca, gathered herself, hoping that her voice wouldn't betray how scared she was feeling. 'I need to see Don Adolfo.'

'Never heard of him,' said the man.

'Rita Capuano told me I'd find him here,' said Francesca calmly, despite her heart hammering away in her chest.

'And what do you want with him?' the man said.

'That's my business and his,' said Francesca, trying to convey a sense of confidence.

'*Attènneti!*' said the man and the door was pushed closed. Francesca leaned a moment on the doorframe to steady herself.

The dog barked again and then there was a curse and a yelp. After a minute, she heard the sound of at least one chain being taken off the inside of the door which was then partially opened for her to enter. The shaven headed man replaced the chains, looked at her with evident dislike mingled with curiosity and beckoned for her to follow him down a corridor which involved walking past the dog that crouched on one side, growling softly and looking at her malevolently. She noticed that the man had a revolver tucked into the waistband of his trousers.

She was led through one door into a brighter room where four young men sat playing *briscola*. Again, she saw that they were armed and, as she entered the room, one of them stood up and, in a surprisingly polite voice and using standard Italian, asked her to take off her coat. Once she had complied she was quickly frisked in a very professional way and then the frisker nodded to the man who had let her in. 'Clean,' he said. The shaven headed one then knocked twice at a door on the other side of the room, waited five seconds, then opened it and showed her in.

A tall muscular man in his mid-forties with a disarming smile on a ruggedly handsome face with a scar along the right hand side of his jaw stood up to meet her. He wore a pair of mid-weight brown trousers and a well-cut, pale blue shirt that was open at the neck, revealing a large gold medallion perched on top of a mat of black hair. 'Take a seat please, Miss...' and he looked at her, waiting for her to fill in the gap.

'Francesca,' she said, pointedly not giving her surname. He nodded and smiled as if he understood.

She looked round the room which could easily have been the office of the chairman of a medium-sized company and saw that, in one corner, a two seater settee and two small armchairs were set around a coffee table. She avoided the settee and settled herself down in one of the armchairs, maintaining as upright a position as possible. 'Now, Miss... Francesca,' what can I do for you, or for Rita Capuano?'

She gathered all her courage and looked him in the eye as she spoke, 'I need to know who Salvatore Stiappa, commonly known as 'Snuff' is associating with. If possible, I'd like to know who he's working for at the moment, and better still, where I can find him.

The man was obviously an experienced poker player as he didn't show any sign of surprise at her demand but asked courteously, 'And why might a respectable young lady like you want to associate with a lowlife like Stiappa... if I may ask?'

'Because,' she said, 'I have good reason to suppose that he was responsible for the death of a very good friend of mine, and may well be plotting the deaths of other people who matter to me - I intend to stop that.'

He leaned back on the settee and looked her up and down. 'I'm not sure why you think I might know anything about Stiappa or why, if I did, you think I should tell you and...,' he looked down at her legs, ' what would be in it for me, if I were able to help you?'

Francesca gathered up the last remnants of her courage and replied, apparently calmly, 'Don Adolfo, you are a "man of honour" and you have a code of conduct to live up to. This is a purely business transaction... You believe, but have no proof, that Stiappa's cell was responsible for the deaths of Enzo and Toto Jacono, who I believe were business associates of yours... If you had proof of this, your code of conduct would mean that Stiappa has to pay for these deaths. Now my interest is mainly in the people who employ Stiappa – what happens to him is only a secondary concern to me. If you can give me information that helps me get his employers, I will get you proof about who killed the Jaconos – whether that be Stiappa or someone else.'

He looked her in the eye now, unable to hide a hint of admiration in his own, then he stood up and went over to the one small window in the room. He stood looking out for a few minutes, clearly thinking through all the possible ramifications, before finally turning to face her again. Francesca hoped that the rivulets of sweat she could feel, weren't showing through her clothes.

'And how do I know I can trust you? How do I know that you will deliver the killers of Enzo and Toto?'

'Capuano is my guarantor,' she said, 'Unless I'm killed before I get home, the first thing I'll do will be to prepare all the information you need and leave instructions that it is to be sent to Capuano on May 31st.'

'Why wait until May 31st?'

'That's my business. You've got the offer, now take it or leave it.'

Her heart was in her mouth as he looked at her coolly, and she wondered if the dog might be getting extra fresh meat later, but then he smiled and held out his hand. 'You've got balls, Signorina Francesca, and you've got yourself a deal.'

After he had provided her with all the information he could on Stiappa and his known associates, he stood up, indicating that the meeting was over. She also stood up and held out her hand again, which he took and gave a brief shake.

He did not release her hand immediately but looked at a photograph on the wall. She followed his eyes with hers and he said, 'Do you recognise the woman in that photograph?' Francesca shook her head.

He smiled, 'Barbara Lercaro... ask your friend Rita about her... and Signorina, are you familiar with English Literature?'

'Some of it,' she said, feeling confused.

'Well, I'd recommend you read a poem by Robert Browning called *"My Last Duchess"* - written in Florence, I believe – I'm sure you'll find it thought provoking.'

She nodded, unable to say any more, and he called, 'Cerbero!' and immediately the shaven headed man appeared and ushered her out without another word being spoken.

Outside, she maintained her dignity until she was round the first corner and then leaned against the wall and was sick.

'Barbara was a friend of mine – a very brave investigative journalist, who wrote about some of the Camorra who'd given her inside information, in a way that made it easy for their enemies to identify them. There was a bloodbath between various clans and soon after it had settled down, Barbara was gunned down as she went to meet her younger brother at the airport,' said Capuano.

'And the poem is about a Gonzaga Duke showing an ambassador who's come to arrange the Duke's next marriage, a portrait of the previous Duchess. It's very clear in the poem that the Duke is giving a subtle warning about what happens to women who give any hint of betraying him,' said Francesca, 'I've always thought it's one of the creepiest poems I've ever read.'

'I wish you hadn't talked me into letting you do this,' said Marco, and Francesca leaned over and kissed his forehead.

'Why did you tell him that it would be you getting the information about the Jaconos? If we gave them the information now, you'd be safe.'

Francesca shook her head, 'If they had it now, they might kill Stiappa before we get to him and, if they knew that you already had the information, Rita, they might not be too happy that you hadn't already passed it on.'

Chapter 24

Although they travelled back on the same train as Ciancolini and Busoni they were very careful to keep well away from them. Francesca wanted to ring the Judge to find out how the meeting had gone, but Marco, who was an expert in electronic surveillance techniques insisted that they should not even use the unregistered mobiles while they were in Naples or on the train.

'But I thought that the point of having unregistered mobiles was that they couldn't be traced,' she said, puzzled.

'If they're being monitored – which, although it's unlikely, we can't discount – although they don't know who's using the phones, they would know the approximate locations of those using the phones. Telling them that more than one of us is on this train, or has suddenly appeared in Naples, may allow them to tie us together. If they monitor the CCTV at the stations where the train stops closely enough, they are likely to spot both you and Ciancolini, which may enable them to put two and two together.'

'It's a bit far-fetched,' she commented with a pout of disappointment.

'You're right, ' he said, putting his hand over hers, 'it's far-fetched but not beyond the realms of possibility and you really don't want to be looking back in a few years and pairing together Ciancolini and dell'Omodarme in the same way as people now associate Borsellino and Falcone.'

She sighed, 'Alright, I'll be patient. Just as well, I've got you to look after me,' and she leaned over and rested her head on his shoulder and closed her eyes.

Francesca was soon asleep and managed to sleep on and off for most of the way to Rome where Marco said a reluctant goodbye to her as the train stopped at Roma Tiburtina Station.

'Remember – no calls until you're clear of the station in Florence. I'll speak to you tonight and I'll be up on Tuesday evening for a full debriefing. I need to spend the next couple of days going through all the latest phone taps and trying to see if we have any more pieces of the jigsaw.'

She kissed him and then watched through the window as he walked away along the platform, before settling back in her seat and gazing fixedly through the window as the train moved off again, although without registering any of the scenery they passed through.

Marco considered taking a taxi but decided that after the time spent sitting still in the train, he'd prefer to walk. Thirty five minutes later, as he turned the corner into Via Topino he paused as something struck him as unusual. What was it? Everything seemed quiet and there were just a few people on the street who were going about their normal everyday business, but his subconscious told him that something wasn't right.

He crouched down as if to tie his shoelace and, as he did so, used his practised eye to study the street in more detail. Three businessmen talking and waving their hands decisively as they walked along the pavement; a teenage girl walking along with headphones; two neighbours, whom he vaguely recognised, chatting together as one leaned on a red Fiat Punto; a few bags of litter outside doorways; the usual rows of parked cars, crammed together, with a Lancia Musa double parked near the tobacconists with its hazards flashing – No! It wasn't quite the usual row of parked cars – opposite the entrance to his building were two identical, silver grey Alfa 156s, not crammed in like all the other cars, but parked neatly, each with sufficient space to get out quickly. He though there was someone in at least one of the cars but couldn't be sure from where he was.

He shuffled back slightly, so that he was pretty well covered from view by the occupants of the cars. He was sure that, if they were waiting for him, they may well have been there for sometime and, as they could have no idea of when he would arrive, would not be fully alert. He took the unregistered phone from his pocket and formed a text to Francesca – "Probable visitors outside flat. Disposing of phone. Don't ring".

Two cars back from where he crouched, was a white Fiat Uno that he knew was parked there most of the time and which, if he were lucky, wouldn't be moved for a day or two. Easing back to the Uno, he reached underneath and placed the unregistered phone on top of the cross-member under the engine. If he were lucky, he'd be able to retrieve the phone later – alternatively, the phone would fall under the wheel of the Fiat if it moved before he could get back to it.

After edging into the shadow at the side of the street, he stood up and began to walk confidently towards the door of the building, not looking at either of the two Alfa's. Inserting the key into the outer door and turning, he stepped into the vestibule and over to the letter boxes that lined one wall.

As he placed his key into the lock of his own mail-box, he heard the outer door open again behind him. He reached into the box, pulled out a handful of letters, relocked the box and then turned. Two men, wearing near identical dark grey suits and white shirts stood within two yards of him, facing him. A third man stood outside the main door. The man to Marco's right had clearly strong hands hanging loosely by his side while the man eyed him carefully; the man to Marco's left had his right hand in his jacket pocket while with his left hand he held up an identity badge.

Marco looked at the badge and then at the man's face, trying to display an air of intrigued innocence.

'Signor Antognoni,' said the man, in a tone that made it clear that while he was aware that, a question was the expected way of beginning the conversation, he was only paying lip-service to convention by making a slight effort to imply that there could be more than one possible answer.

'*Si* – that's me. What can I do to help you?'

While retaining his dead-pan expression the man replied, 'We need to ask you a few questions, Signor Antognoni. If you wouldn't mind leading the way to your apartment.'

'Of course,' said Marco, 'I usually use the stairs, if that's OK with you.'

The man nodded and gestured toward the stairs with his ID card. Marco led the way up the two flights of stairs to the landing where his was one of three doors.

As the house key was on the same ring as the mail-box key, the keys were still in Marco's hand as he approached the door. He could feel the eyes of the two men watching every move attentively as he unlocked first the security lock and then the standard Yale.

As surreptitiously as possible, he scanned the room to see whether there were any signs that the security forces had been in his flat while he'd been away. He knew that if he was dealing with SISMI that they would be good but, as a security consultant himself, he was confident that if he'd had visitors, he'd be able to tell. Everything appeared to be in place but, as he sat down on one of the chairs by the table he saw that the small coffee cup on its saucer, perched on top of his filing cabinet was sitting completely centrally on the saucer, as one would expect it to be – only that he'd deliberately left it slightly off-centre, in such a way that only someone who expected it would be aware. It would have been necessary to move the cup and saucer to open the cabinet, and he could see that the saucer had been replaced exactly where it had been, with the cup facing in exactly the right direction – only a couple of millimetres more centrally on the saucer.

That was probably good news, he thought. Although it was possible that they'd been in his flat to plant some incriminating evidence on him, it was more likely that they had wanted to carry out a detailed search of his flat but didn't have the evidence to justify a search warrant. If that were the case then they obviously didn't have anything on him that would convince a judge to authorise a search warrant.

He gestured to the other chairs around the table. The man who had spoken previously sat down facing him; the other remained standing, in a position which made it impossible for Marco to see both their faces at the same time. 'What can I do for you?'

'Firstly, we need to know where you've been for the last two days.'

'I've been staying with a friend.'

'Which friend and where?'

'I'm sorry, but I'm not prepared to disclose that. It was a romantic weekend and I can assure you that neither I nor my partner committed any illegal act during the weekend.'

'We'll pass over that for the moment, but I must warn you that it may become necessary for you to provide this information if we are to be satisfied that you are not involved in our investigation... otherwise, your attitude could be construed as obstructive.'

'I'm sorry, that's not my intention, but it's a question of privacy... and not only my own. … What's this all about, anyway?'

'Nicola Petrini,' said the other man, speaking for the first time, 'How well do you know Nicola Petrini?'

'Nico?' said Marco, genuinely surprised.

'Nicola Petrini,' repeated the man, 'known to his friends' – and he stressed the word "friends" - 'as Nico.'

'I met Nico while I was spending a month as a guest of the state in Rebibbia.'

'Serving part of a sentence, the rest of which was suspended, and which means that, should you be guilty of the slightest transgression during the next four years, we can lock you up and throw away the key – and that includes consorting with people involved in criminal acts.'

'Which,' said the man who had so far done most of the talking, 'would almost certainly include Nico Petrini.'

'As far as I'm aware, Nico has been doing his best to earn an honest living as a Private Investigator since his release from prison, so I'm not sure what you're getting at.'

'Petrini was arrested on Saturday, using faked ID, inside the Ministry of Regional Development, and with his pockets full of mini cameras, microphones and transmitters. Are you able to explain that?' He fixed a steady gaze on Marco.

Marco shrugged his shoulders, 'I can't do any more than make an educated guess, and I'm sure you're perfectly capable of doing that yourselves – so why ask me?'

'And what would your educated guess be?'

'It seems quite obvious to me… As far as I know, most of Nico's cases so far have been marital infidelity cases… so there's obviously a wife or husband of someone working in the ministry who suspects their partner of doing unauthorised overtime and has asked Nico to get proof.'

The second man dropped one of Marco's business cards on the table, and the first man said, 'This was in amongst the fake ID papers that Petrini was carrying when he was arrested… how do you explain that?'

Marco shrugged, 'There are two answers to that question: the first is quite simple – carelessness – the second is that, as I often need to install security devices in my business, I buy the devices in bulk which makes it a lot cheaper; Nico has had a few devices off me, as it makes more sense than him just ordering a small number from the suppliers.'

'When did you last see Petrini?'

'I don't remember exactly. I bumped into him on Via del Corso a couple of weeks ago and we popped into a bar for a *ponce al mandarino* to warm us up. I can't remember exactly which day it was but I can remember it was bitterly cold.'

'You have a contract to maintain security equipment for some government departments...'

'I do.'

'So you would know how to gain access to locations that are off-limits to others, wouldn't you?'

'I suppose so, yes. But I think you'll find that all the departments I've worked for are one hundred percent satisfied with the work I've done, and with my professionalism.'

'So you would have been able to tell Petrini how the security systems worked and how they could be breached, couldn't you?'

'In theory. I suppose, but not all of them... and I'd hardly be likely to say, "here, take my card, so if you have any problems breaking-in, you can give me a ring," am I?'

The man who was sitting, stood up, 'We'll need you to come in at some time over the next two days to identify the equipment we found on Petrini... When you do come in, we expect you to bring your business purchase records with you, so that we can match the serial numbers on the equipment purchased by Petrini to those purchased by you. In the meantime you mustn't leave the city without notifying us first. You can reach us on this number,' and he dropped a card on the table, then turned towards the door. His companion followed him, then paused as he turned to close the door and stared at Marco.

'I've taken a dislike to you, Antognoni... I have an instinctive distrust of ex-cons who go into the security business. You'll see me again,' then he closed the door and disappeared.'

Nico arrested – that would complicate matters. He was confident that Nico wouldn't drop anyone else in it but, the fact that they'd been able to link Nico to him, meant that he would have to be even more careful than before – and it also meant that he was now shorthanded – there was no-one he knew who he trusted enough to replace Nico. Nico having been discovered in a Government Building also meant that his case would be dealt with by the security services rather than the state police or carabinieri, and they didn't play by the same rules. As he knew that they'd been through his apartment with a fine toothcomb, he was fairly sure that, even if it hadn't been bugged before, it would be now. The obvious thing for him to do would be to hunt through the apartment and remove all the bugs but that would only mean that SISMI would be back at some point to plant some more. No – he thought – best to take the initiative back from them. He checked his watch and rang Francesca's normal mobile.

'Pronto.'

'Hi Francesca. It's me Marco,' and he metaphorically crossed his fingers hoping that the use of her full name and his having identified himself, would alert her to the probability that the call was being monitored.

'Oh; hi Marco. I wasn't expecting a call from you.'

'I hope I'm not disturbing, but I thought I'd better tell you about an odd thing that's just happened.'

'Go on… I'm intrigued.'

'Well. I'd just got back home after a couple of days away and a couple of policemen turned up on the doorstep.'

'Not back in trouble again, are you? I thought you'd been sticking entirely to the rules since they let you out.'

'I have. I'm a model citizen now – apart from my association with seedy journalists like you…'

'Charming!'

'Only joking… No, the reason they wanted to talk to me was that an old friend of mine, a PI, has been arrested in one of the ministries, and they found one of my business cards in his pocket.'

'OK A bit silly of him, but what's that got to do with me?'

'Nothing directly, I just wondered if, with your journalistic contacts, you might be able to find out anything about my friend.'

'It's unlikely – I'm working as a legal secretary now, to bring in a regular income – but I can ring a couple of old contacts and see if they can find anything out for you – I can't promise anything though – and if I do find anything, it may take some time.

'That's alright. Anything you can do, I'd be grateful. I don't know him that well, but he always seemed like one of the good-guys... Nicola Petrini's the name

'Any other details that might help?'

'He's about twenty-eight and lives somewhere in the Prati area, north of the Vatican – with his parents, I think.'

'Alright, I'll try ringing a few friends – but it's not much to go on.'

'You're a treasure. Has anyone ever told you that?'

'Regularly... Was there anything else, or can I get back to washing my hair?'

'OK I'll let you go now. I'll speak to you soon.'

'*Ciao*, Marco. *Ciao, ciao*.'

'*Ciao*, Francesca,' and then as he heard her close her phone he added under his breath, 'and *ciao* to anyone else who may be listening.'

He leaned back in his computer chair, elbows on the arm-rests, hands steepled with the index-fingers pressed against his chin while he softly drummed the tips of the other fingers together while he thought.

The first thing he needed to do was to retrieve his phone from the underside of the Fiat Uno, but he needed to be very careful how he went about it; as the security services had undoubtedly searched his flat, and were almost certainly now bugging him, it was inconceivable that they wouldn't be watching him when he left the flat. In the meantime, he thought, he could do with a coffee and made his way over to the small kitchen in the corner of the flat. As he did so, he absentmindedly pulled a handkerchief out of his pocket to wipe his nose, and this caused a two euro coin to come out with it and fall to the floor.

The idea came to him as he bent down to pick up the coin, which had rolled to one side; if he could inadvertently drop a coin when pulling his handkerchief out, then why not something else – he dismissed the idea of repeating the incident with a coin, as it could well roll in the wrong direction – but something else – his keys, for example – they would be much easier to control. Smiling, he put the coffee on and then placed first his handkerchief in his pocket and then his keys.

It took a few tries, but after about ten minutes, he was confident that he could get the keys to fall pretty much where he wanted them to, which would allow him to retrieve the phone without arousing suspicion. Glancing out of the window, he was pleased to see that it was fairly dull outside; by six o'clock the light would be starting to go which would be the ideal time for his purpose: light enough for any watcher to see him drop his keys, but not light enough for them to see exactly what he did when he bent down to retrieve them.

Half an hour to go. He knew from experience that the best way to make the time pass quickly was to focus on something completely different so, when he'd drunk his coffee, he pulled his copy of Michael Dibdin's latest novel, Medusa, down off the shelf, and sat down to read for a while.

At five past six, he finished a chapter, put the book reluctantly on one side and reached across for his thick black leather jacket. Glancing briefly out of the window, he saw that the light was sufficiently dim for his purposes and, after quickly setting up a couple of innocent looking indicators that would tell him if he'd had uninvited guests again, he went out and made his way down to the street.

Sure that he would be followed but with no wish to lose his shadow, he didn't look round but just set off purposefully down the street slipping his gloves on as he went. Just as he came level with the back of the Uno, he pulled his handkerchief out of his right hand pocket and raised it towards his nose. As he did so, his keys, which appeared to have caught on the cotton of the handkerchief, fell down to his right and bounced off the kerb underneath the car, Marco making a show of trying to catch them as they fell.

He quickly wiped his nose and pushed the handkerchief back in to his pocket, then crouched down and ran his hand along the ground to find the keys. As he brought his hand out again, in one fluid movement he succeeded in grasping the phone as well. Standing up, he threw the bunch of keys up with one hand, a movement which allowed him to let the phone slip inside his sleeve, and then caught them with his left hand and slipped them into his pocket.

Now with a hand in each jacket pocket, he continued down the street before turning right at the end.

It was too early to eat, but he couldn't go back yet without arousing suspicion so, over the next twenty minutes, he walked across to the Borghesi Gardens and then spent an hour walking round the park. Anyone who was following him, wouldn't learn anything but would get plenty of exercise. Eventually, after exiting the park at its western extremity, he followed the road around the edge of the park in the general direction of home until he came to a pizzeria that didn't give the impression that its main clientele were tourists. Once inside, glad to be in the warmth, he ordered a *quattro stagioni* and a *birra media*. A couple of minutes later, another lone male – presumably his shadow – entered and sat at a table at the far end of the pizzeria.

As Marco had no personal grudge against his shadow, he took his time over his pizza, and then coffee and grappa, to make sure that the man also had time to eat properly before having to set off and follow him home.

Chapter 25

Having left the Ducati in the car-park below Piazza della Stazione, Francesca got away quickly from the station and was able to thread her way through the traffic on the Viali much faster than the taxi that Ciancolini used to get home. Consequently, when he unlocked his front door and made his way in, he was not surprised to find her sitting waiting for him in the kitchen.

'I'm going to have to start putting the alarm on when I go out, if it's so easy for anyone to just wander in.'

She smiled at him sweetly, although blinking as her eyes became accustomed to the light, 'You'd better ask Marco to provide you with an efficient security system – I'm sure he'd do it at a discount for you... Although, of course, anyone who happened to be familiar with the system would still be able to get in.'

'Actually,' she said, the smile disappearing completely from her face, to be replaced by a worried look, 'we have what could be a massive problem,' and as Ciancolini looked at her enquiringly, she continued, 'I had this message from him, just after the train passed Arezzo,' and she passed her mobile over to the judge.

'… "outside flat…. don't ring"… from Marco?'

'Yes.. What can we do? She said, with the hint of a tremor in her voice.' casting a look of appeal at Ciancolini.'

'He stood up and walked over to the sink to get a glass of water before replying.'

'We can't do anything… for now… No,' he forestalled her, 'it's not been much more than an hour. If we haven't heard anything by ten this evening, I'll start to make some discreet enquiries but, until he's been missing for twenty-four hours we can't declare him missing … and even then, how are we going to prove that it's been twenty-four hours? Are you planning on telling the authorities about the unregistered phones? That would drop everyone right in it – including Marco. He's a resourceful person; give him the chance to talk his way out of it – whatever "it" is, before going blundering in and making everything worse!'

Francesca sighed, 'I suppose you're right,' but she didn't look happy.

'Now,' said Ciancolini, 'I imagine that we each have a lot to talk about. – You go first.'

Still worrying about Marco, Francesca was hesitant at first until she became immersed in the details of her encounter with the Camorra boss.

Ciancolini raised his eyebrows when she reached the deal she had offered Don Adolfo.

'I don't think I can go along with the idea of handing someone over to a Camorra boss to be executed. We're supposed to be the ones upholding the rule of law, not making human sacrifices to achieve our ends.'

She shrugged, 'We're not sacrificing anyone; I didn't say we'd hand him over, only that we'd provide them with the information – and by that time, hopefully, Stiappa will be safely under lock and key... I'm sure that the state's prisons are quite capable of keeping a prisoner alive if they put their minds to it.'

Ciancolini shook his head, 'I'm not happy about this, Francesca. If ever anything...' He was interrupted by the ring of Francesca's phone.

"*Pronto*.' .... 'Oh, hi Marco. I wasn't expecting a call from you.' .... 'Go on... I'm intrigued.' .... 'Not back in trouble again, are you? I thought you'd been sticking entirely to the rules since they let you out.' .... 'Charming!' .... 'OK A bit silly of him, but what's that got to do with me?' ....'It's unlikely – I'm working as a legal secretary now, to bring in a regular income – but I can ring a couple of old contacts and see if they can find anything out for you – I can't promise anything though – and if I do find anything, it may take some time....... 'Any other details that might help' .... 'Alright, I'll try ringing a few friends – but it's not much to go on.'........ 'Regularly... Was there anything else, or can I get back to washing my hair?'.... '*Ciao*, Marco. *Ciao, ciao*.'

She leaned back on her chair and rolled her head around to relax her neck muscles, before turning back to Ciancolini, who was observing her attentively.'

'Well?'

'He obviously hasn't been arrested but, from the way he was guiding the conversation, I'd say that he's fairly sure he's under observation and has to be careful what he says.'

'For example?'

'For example, he said he'd been away for a couple of days; I assume he was telling me that they don't know that we were together, on the other hand...' (she thought)... by ringing me, he's not just letting me know that he's been released, but also letting me know that the police already know that we're at least friends – otherwise he wouldn't have informed the police by ringing me on an open line.'

'And how would they know that?'

'I've no idea.'

'OK He seemed to be asking for a favour; what was it?'

'Right. It's probably more something that you can help with than me – although obviously, I now need to be seen to be at least trying to help… One of his two collaborators has been arrested on the premises of the Ministry of Regional Development in possession of sophisticated surveillance equipment, and with one of Marco's business cards in his pocket.'

Ciancolini closed his eyes and shaking his head, sighed almost theatrically. 'Conspiracy to commit murder, espionage, breaking and entering – is there anything else in this vortex of criminality that you've dragged me into? I used to be a respectable judge with a reputation for probity.'

The sweet smile was now back on Francesca's face, 'Nothing you need to know about,' and the judge groaned.

'I suppose that you want me to find out how strong the case is against Marco's associate, and what stage the case against him has got to. Write down all the details you've got, and I'll see what I can do later.' She did so and passed a post-it note over to Ciancolini who pushed it to one side of the table.

'Right. Let me hear what you propose to do with the information you've got on Stiappa – I suppose things can't get any worse.'

'We talked about this last night, and I was going over it again on the train, before I got Marco's message… We need to bring Stiappa in, on a trumped up charge for some serious crime that took place on the weekend when we know he was in the Val d'Aosta with Rossi.'

'Do you have any particular crime in mind?'

She smiled, 'I'm sure that our friends in the National Cyber Crime Unit can come up with something and…' she looked at the Judge,' that would make it necessary to seize and examine all his electronic communications devices – and who knows what that might throw up… I know from when I was working as an investigative journalist that if you can get hold of someone's computer' you'll almost always find something – no-one is as careful as they think they are.'

He looked at her with grudging admiration, 'You're wasted investigating other people – you should have gone in for a life of crime yourself!'

'You never know. I might one day, if I get bored.'

'Alright. So what then? What do we do with Stiappa once we've arrested him under false pretences?'

'We charge him. We refuse bail… and then we offer him a deal. The more he tells us, the less time he spends locked up. If he doesn't help us then we throw away the key.'

'OK Go and see the Brigadier tomorrow, as soon as you can after you've finished with Graziadei. Tell him to do whatever he needs to do.'

'Now,' said Francesca, 'tell me all about the President and Villa Rosebery – How did it go?'

'It went,' said Ciancolini, 'as well as could have been expected. Busoni introduced me as an old friend, then after a quarter of an hour or so when they mainly chatted about their families – catching up on news like that, Busoni told him that I had something very important to discuss with him. He's a very astute politician and, although he's a very good listener, he's quick to interrupt if he sees any weakness or contradiction in what you say.'

'And did he find any?'

'Only on a couple of occasions when I'd tried to abbreviate things to save a bit of time, but fortunately, on each occasion, I was able to expand what I'd previously said and clarify the point.'

'I take it he was suitably shocked.'

'Yes and no… I got the impression that he's not over fond of the current regime and wouldn't put anything past them, but he was shocked and horrified that their conspiracy was so far advanced.'

'So he agreed to our request?'

'Pretty much in its entirety. He insists that the evidence we get has to be one hundred percent certain to lead to convictions in court. If we can back up what we say, to the satisfaction of the lawyers, we have his one hundred percent backing and… and this is probably even more important… anyone who has helped us will be granted retrospective immunity in respect of any laws broken during the investigation – although I assume that that wasn't meant to include assisting the Camorra to gain revenge for earlier incidents! We would probably have needed Andreotti to be President to get that one through!'

The judge continued to give Francesca a more detailed description of the meeting and of the guided tour which one of the President's personal assistants had given to him and Busoni. Francesca, however, only half paid attention to his description of the villa, her mind having drifted back to thoughts of Marco, wondering how he was spending the evening and whether or not they would be able to meet again before events came to a head.

It was ten to three in the morning when a noise she couldn't initially place woke her. Given the time, it took her slightly longer than usual to become sufficiently aware to identify that the noise was the vibration of a phone. She stretched out her arm, in the dark, towards the bedside table, where she succeeded only in knocking her phone off the edge and onto the floor.

More aware now, she pressed the switch for the bedside light and looked down to where the phone lay slightly to one side of its back and battery. The noise continued. Francesca sat up and looked around more attentively, until she realised that it was the unregistered Motorola vibrating on the dressing table. She slipped her legs out of the side of the bed and placed her feet on the cold hard tiles.

She pressed the green button on the phone and waited to see what would happen.'

'About time! I thought you were never going to answer,' came Marco's cheerful voice.

'Marco – what are you doing? Have you any idea what time it is?' she asked, realising as she did so that she herself hadn't the faintest idea. It could be half past one or half past seven - she had no idea.

He ignored the question. I can't stay long, I need to get back to the flat without being spotted.'

'Why? Where are you?'

'Don't worry, I haven't gone far. The old couple on the top floor have gone to Mauritius for two weeks, and they don't have a very effective lock; I decided that as my apartment is probably bugged, it would be better to come up here and borrow theirs for a few minutes. They'll never know, and I'm sure that they'd approve anyway, if they knew that it was all for the benefit of the state.'

'What happened this afternoon? And how worried should I be?'

'I think that they were fishing, more than anything else. I'm sure that Nico won't give anything away and, providing that he sticks to the agreed line that he was checking out a case of marital infidelity, then he should be alright. It's the story that the three of us have agreed between us if ever we get caught out. That way, we always have a good idea of what the others will have said and there's no risk of anyone contradicting the others.'

'But you think they've bugged your flat?'

'I am… but I think that that's because they caught him in one of the ministries, rather than because they know about our investigation. There's supposed to be a red alert over possible terrorist attacks throughout Europe at the moment. Unfortunately, it means that I'm not going to be as useful as I'd like to be, until this is sorted…. How did Ciancolini's meeting with the President go?'

'As well as we'd dared hope. Ciancolini now has the power to over-ride parliamentary immunity and make whatever arrests he sees fit, as soon as he has evidence that will stand up in court.'

Marco whistled softly, 'He must be feeling really pleased.'

'He was, until I told him about the agreement I'd made with Don Adolfo. He seemed to think that I was deliberately putting Stiappa's life in danger.'

'And aren't you?'

'Of course I am. I've still got a continuous ringing in my ears from the bomb blast that killed Arturo. If Stiappa was involved in planting that bomb, then he deserves whatever he gets!'

'OK But I assume that you didn't make that case to Ciancolini.'

'Not quite, although I think my views about Stiappa were fairly obvious.'

'So what now?'

'Now? We arrest Stiappa for something else and put him under lots of pressure, making it clear that the only way he's going to avoid a very long prison sentence is to tell us everything he knows about the conspirators. I doubt very much that he's one of them for idealistic reasons, so it shouldn't be too difficult for him to turn against them if he thinks it will save his own skin.'

'What about *omertà*?'

'It shouldn't be a problem here; as far as we know, the rest of the conspirators aren't *mafiosi* so the only people he'll protect are other members of the 'Ndrangheta and, as he seems to be the main man, the others will just be fairly insignificant foot soldiers, and I don't care about them.'

'What can I do?'

'I don't know. The judge is going to ask about Nico tomorrow, and I'll make a few phone calls as well – it may be worth your trying to get to see him; it would be useful to know how he got caught. Oh, by the way, the President's promised us all immunity for any minor lawbreaking we need to do while we're trying to get to the bottom of this – although I'm not sure how you'll be able to tell him that if you're surrounded by prison guards when you speak to him.'

'Don't worry. I'll find a way to reassure him. I'd better go now and let you get to sleep too. Look after yourself.'

'I will. And I can't wait till I can see you again.'

He made a kissing sound with his lips and hung up.'

'Love you,' she said quietly before closing her own phone.

Her initial thoughts were slightly less benevolent when Marco rang her again soon after five, but she soon became alert as he gave her a brief message.

'I've just had an important message. We may have found a weak link. Take the bus home after work today,' and then he rang off.

In her half-awake state she felt a mixture of irritation at having been woken again, disappointment that he had only been on the phone for a few seconds and a growing sense of excitement as she realised the importance of the message.

Knowing that she had no chance of going back to sleep again, she eased out of bed and quickly wrapped a thick dressing-gown around her and went to put the bathroom heater on.

While she waited for the bathroom to warm up, she made herself a coffee, choosing the two-cup *macchinetta* rather than the single cup version she usually used in the morning. When the coffee bubbled through, she poured half the *macchinetta*'s contents into a *tazzina* and drank it immediately before pouring her second cup, which she sat down to savour as she began to think through the implications of Marco's message.

He'd told her that he had two people working with him; one of them, obviously, was now in Police custody, so he must have heard something from the other one; that was the only possible way he could have known something at five that he hadn't know a couple of hours earlier. She tried to remember his associate's name but it wouldn't come to her – never mind – she was sure she'd remember it later.

After the second cup of coffee, she showered, turning the power to maximum and making the most of the extra time she had that morning as she liberally spread the shower -gel over her body wishing that Marco were there to spread it over her back and then to join her in the shower.

Since having the Ducati, she'd become used to the greater freedom it gave her and the amount of travelling time it saved her, particularly at busy times, so instead of doing the whole journey by bus, she took out the bike and placing a pair of shoes that were suitable for the office, in the back-box, put on a medium-weight leather jacket and set off towards a point where she knew that she could easily get the number five bus and also be able to park the bike safely nearby. Although the journey only took ten minutes and she wasn't travelling particularly fast she felt very cold by the time she pulled off Via Canova and having entered the residential area to her left, chained the bike to railings separating the characterless but functional six-storey blocks of flats from the main road.

'You're early this morning, signorina,' said the security guard at the entrance to the Palace of Justice, as she waved her *Tribunale di Firenze* ID card vaguely in his direction.

'Couldn't sleep,' she said with a smile, 'How are you this morning?'

'Mustn't grumble. Only another half an hour then I can go home. I like doing the night shift in winter. It means I get to see a bit of daylight before I go to work.'

'Well, make the most of it. I'll see you next week, when you're back on days... I don't suppose Judge Graziadei's in yet is he?'

He laughed, 'Best joke I've heard for a long time... No, the only judge you ever see at this time of the morning as Ciancolini. He's usually in well before the others.'

'Surely not this early?'

'Not everyday, but most days. In fact, he's in the building now – got here about ten minutes ago; grumpy as ever; never has time to stop for a chat. I'd keep out of his way if I were you.'

'Thanks for the advice, Beppe. See you later,' and she made her way over to the lifts feeling pleased. She'd hoped that Ciancolini would be in, and had managed to get confirmation without having to attract attention by asking.'

'Confident that, if Ciancolini was in the habit of arriving early, there would certainly be at least some of the secretaries in his office who would make sure that they were also there, she rang his office as soon as she had taken off her jacket and tidied up her hair in her own office.'

'*Buongiorno*. Public Prosecutor's Office. How may I help you?'

'*Ciao*, Daniela. It's Francesca Conte here, from Judge Graziadei's office. I've got a file here that Graziadei had asked Ciancolini to give a second opinion on. Is he in yet?'

'OK. Do you want to bring it along, or should I send the office junior along to get it in a bit?'

'Actually, for some reason, Graziadei was very specific about me delivering it into Ciancolini's hands personally. You know what he's like when he gets a bee in his bonnet.' She knew perfectly well that Ciancolini's PA had very little to do with Graziadei and would have no idea what he was like, other than his reputation as someone who was well past his sell by date. She heard her sigh.

'Judge Ciancolini's on the phone at the moment. I'll speak to him when he's free, but he's very busy so you might have to wait a while before you can see him.'

'That's OK. Thanks,' and she put the phone down with a smile, quite sure that Ciancolini would be able to see her as soon as he was aware of the request.

'Thankyou, Daniela. Signorina Conte may as well wait while I have a quick look at this file; it should only take a few minutes.' Daniela left Ciancolini's office, shutting the door behind her, and Francesca sat down across the desk from him, pushing the case file that she had picked up at random to one side.'

'I heard from Marco during the night,' she began without preamble. 'The message was very brief as he had to ring from outside the apartment, but I got the impression that he thinks we may have made a major breakthrough.' Ciancolini raised his eyebrows questioningly. 'You know that one of his associates was caught with surveillance equipment in his possession... well, he actually has two people working for him and, I assume, that the other one must have found something important.'

'So how are we going to get hold of this information if Marco is likely to be under surveillance?'

'I was told to use the bus today, so I assume that Marco's associate will be passing me the information on the bus after work. I'll need to see you as soon as possible after that.'

He shook his head, 'I'm at a meeting in Pisa all afternoon – not something I can get out of. I'll be back home about half past nine.'

'I'll be there waiting for you.'

He rolled his eyes. 'As soon as I get time, I'm going to get in an independent home security consultant to give me my privacy back.... Don't forget to take your file back with you.'

If Raffaello Mecocci was as good at collecting information as he was at delivering it, then Francesca could understand why Marco put so much trust in him. She was expecting to be approached on the bus which, as usual, was crowded with a mixture of commuters, children and South American and Philippine, but other than the usual appraising glances from some of the males – young and old – to which she had become inured over the years, no-one seemed to pay her any attention. Certainly, no-one made an approach to her, or even made eye contact; she even wondered whether to miss her stop and stay on the bus until its terminus at Filarete. Fortunately, she decided that it would be pointless; surely, if anyone was going to make contact, they would have done so in the first ten minutes of her journey as that was the only time they could know she was on the bus. Maybe something had happened to delay the messenger – it wasn't unheard of for Italian trains to be late, especially on the main line between Rome and Florence.

As she was putting her helmet on, she felt her phone vibrate and, glad that she hadn't got as ar as slipping her gloves on, pulled it out of her pocket. It must be Marco apologising or explaining why the information hadn't reached her. She flipped open the Motorola and an icon informed her that one message had been received from an unknown number. Left click. Left click. OK.

'Jeans back left', that was it – just that.

She felt in her back pocket and halfway down found something small and hard. A SIM card! Yes. She'd got the information – but how did she go about reading it? Presumably, if it was a SIM card, she must be supposed to read it with her phone. She prised off the back of the Motorola, breaking the end of a fingernail as she did so, levered the battery out, removed the phone's SIM and replaced it with the one from her pocket. Eagerly she reassembled the phone: battery, back, turn on, wait, press menu, press... she stopped – press what? She'd never done anything more than the basics with her phones and hadn't the faintest idea what most of the options meant. She toyed with the idea of trying each option in turn, but the thought of accidentally deleting, or corrupting the data on the card, stopped her. 'Rosa,' she said aloud. Her sister always seemed to have been good with technology and – if she were in – it would be quicker to go to her house than to go home.

'Hi, Franci. Joining us for lunch? I've just picked Alessio up from school.'

'That'd be great – although it wasn't why I dropped in. I was hoping you'd be able to help me with a technological problem.'

'I'll do my best. Tell me about it while I start to make some food,' and she pulled out a large pan and began to fill it with water.

While the water in the pan was heating up on the hob and Rosa finely chopped some onions and whisked some eggs with a few flakes of chili, Franci explained her problem. '… Normally, I'd just pick up the phone and Marco would make it all seem really simple, but I can't do that at the moment, and you're the most tech savvy person I know.'

'No, I'm not,' said her sister, 'There's someone who knows far more than I do. Don't forget I'm even older than you are... Alessio!' she called... 'Alessio!'

There was an indistinct grunt from the other end of the corridor, in response. 'Alessio.. Come here a minute, please, your aunt needs your help.' There was another grunt, although this time Francesca thought she detected a more positive note to it and, shortly after, her nephew stood in the doorway looking at them.

'*Ciao*, Alessio. *Come va?*'

He shrugged his shoulders and looked tragic, 'Maths homework... and Greek!'

Francesca smiled at him, 'Tell you what: if you can have a go at helping me, I'll give you a hand with the Greek. 'Fraid I can't really help you with the Maths – I've forgotten all the boring bits.'

'Deal... what's the problem?'

'I've been sent some information on a SIM card, but I haven't a clue how to access it. Would you have any idea how to do it?'

He put his hand out, 'Easy peasy. Pass it here and I'll go and get the Greek for you.'

'Let's eat first,' said Rosa, who was now tipping half a kilo of pasta into the boiling water, 'It'll be ready in ten minutes. There's no point starting then having to stop straight away.'

Francesca had been surprised at her sister using a whole bag of pasta, but when she saw the avidity with which Alessio devoured the over-sized portion that was placed in front of him, she understood Rosa's logic.

When they had finished the pasta with its egg, cheese and onion sauce, Alessio went straight back to his room, Rosa tidied up and Francesca sat down with Alessio's Greek exercise book. The homework was partly translating a few fairly straightforward phrases and then to complete some grammar and vocabulary exercises. She quickly translated the sentences for him but decided it was best to talk him through the exercises to help him understand.

After she had translated the sentences, she had just started to flick through the book, thinking back to her own time as a first year student at the *Liceo Classico* when Alessio came into the room with a grin on his face. She looked at him expectantly.

'If you're thinking of writing an article that'll blow the church out of the water, you've got everything you need here. This is brilliant!'

Francesca breathed in deeply and spoke while holding her breath, 'Come on... What's on there? Don't keep me in suspense.'

Alessio glanced across the room at his mother, suddenly aware that what he had to say wasn't really the sort of thing he'd ever imagined discussing in front of his mother.'

Rosa saw the look and nodded at him encouragingly, 'Go on. I promise not to be shocked.'

'I think you might be,' said Alessio. 'This is a recording of a telephone conversation between Maria-Grazia Fogazzini, a junior minister in the government, and her brother Andrea, who just happens to be not only a bishop but also the second most important person in the *Grand Equestrian Order of the Holy Sepulchre of Jerusalem*.' He paused for effect, but both were waiting for more so he continued, 'In the phone call, la Fogazzini is telling her brother that she's arranged for him to have the exclusive use of a secluded villa on the Argentaria for the whole of July... and that there will be fresh supplies of girls and boys for him each night. There's a lot more detail about what the girls and boys are prepared to do and how they can be assured of their silence afterwards – but you can listen to all that yourself. There's also a second conversation recorded which is between la Fogazzini and her boss, Silvio Cioni, where she asks him if everything has been tidied up after Cabrini-Pellé, and he assures her that all the loose ends have been tied up, and she doesn't need to worry.'

Rosa looked a little red in face, not sure whether or not she regretted having exposed her "little boy" to this information.

Francesca jumped up, 'That's fantastic. Thankyou... Can you show me how to access the data? There are other people I need to share this with,' then she paused, 'you do realise that you mustn't mention this to anyone, don't you? These are powerful people on the tape and, if the wrong people find out what you know, it could be very dangerous.'

'Promise me that you won't say anything to anyone,' said Rosa.

'I promise,' said Alessio, 'but I'd better get full marks for that homework!'

'You will... I'll go through it with you when you've shown me how to access this data.'

He smiled and pulled a memory stick from his pocket, 'It's all on here. All you need to do is to plug it into the USB slot on any computer and then, when the dialogue box pops up on the screen, click on, "Open to view files", then on "Conversation One" and "Conversation Two". '

'So how exactly did you get this data?'

'You really don't want to know,' said Francesca, 'Just be grateful we've got it; if we use it properly, it could give us the way in that we need... and if what we get from Stiappa corroborates the information, you'll have all the proof you need to make the arrests and satisfy the President.'

Ciancolini ran his fingers backwards through his hair from his forehead and then with his hands on the back of his head looked up at the ceiling for a few seconds before speaking.

'You do realise, don't you, how strong the opposition to this is going to be? It's one thing to demonstrate that priests in Ireland or America have committed abuses, but touch the church in Italy and there'll be massive opposition – and not just from those on the right.

A lot of people who may normally be perfectly rational and who would usually claim not to believe in God, become irrational when it comes to criticising the Church.'

'You're right up to a point but, with all the fuss there's been in America, I think that people here would be less reluctant to believe it than they would have been even two years ago – and the Church must know that. OK, we know that they'll find a way to protect Fogazzini, but they'll be desperate to avoid the public scandal as will Fogazzini himself. Much as I'd like to see Fogazzini ruined, the most we'll probably achieve there is an assurance that he'll never be let near young people again... But... as far as we're concerned, the key factor is that a government minister has been facilitating what he's been doing.'

'So what are you proposing?'

'I'm proposing that we use what we have to convince la Fogazzini that it would be in her best interests to tell us everything she knows about her fellow conspirators and their plans.'

'But why should she? Her career's over anyway when this comes out – and it's got to come out when her brother steps down, or is dismissed from his post as Bishop.'

Francesca smiled, albeit a humourless smile. 'It doesn't have to come out in public; I'm sure the church would be delighted if the Bishop retires to a life of contemplation in an isolated trappist monastery and as far as I'm concerned the only differences between him spending the rest of his life in a monastic cell, or two or three years in a prison cell and then a comfortable retirement, is that the former is for life and at the church's expense and the second is short term and at the taxpayer's expense. And remember, part of the conspirators' justification will be that they're ensuring public safety and the rule of law and order; so she can expect no help from her friends.'

Again there was a long pause before the judge spoke, and then there was a querulous tone to his voice. 'I'm not happy with this. My role is to uphold law and order and the dignity of the state, not to completely bypass all legal methods – laws are drawn up with safeguards for a reason.'

'Yes,' said Francesca, and in many cases, those safeguards are there to protect the people who've written the laws, not the majority of the people in the country – sometimes, you've got to take an overview and decide what's the right thing to do – even if that isn't always the same as what the law said.'

Ciancolini shook his head but Francesca gave him no respite. 'So, let's hear your alternative plan. If it's feasible then we'll go with it, but if it isn't then I don't see that we have any choice.'

Chapter 26

At four fifty-three a.m., the very small amount of light that managed to filter through or around the heavy wooden shutters and light curtains that covered the windows was just sufficient for Serena Cavani to pick out where the old mahogany wardrobe was, but not quite enough for her to see the profile of the hirsute man who lay snoring lightly beside her. She would have liked to have slipped out of the bed and make her way first to the bathroom and then, having cleaned herself up, back to her own room – but she didn't dare. She was afraid that if she moved, she might wake him, and if he woke he would expect her to do everything all over again. Refusing was impossible, not only because she had no doubt that he could be violent, but also because her father had made it very clear what her duty was – and the consequences of failing to do her duty, did not bear thinking about.

She heard a floorboard creak and then silence again. It must be one of her parents going to the bathroom and she thought how careful they were being not to make any noise that might disturb their visitor. She obviously wasn't the only one who was scared of him. Tentatively, she tried to ease the duvet towards her side of the three-quarter width bed but gave up the attempt as he stirred slightly; she would rather suffer the cold than risk waking him up or press herself closer to him for warmth.

There was another creak from the floorboards in the corridor. She shivered. She hated then all: her father, her braggart brothers, the special guests who turned up unannounced and who she had to satisfy, and most of all her mother for not doing anything to protect her. Well, as soon as she was seventeen, she was going – she'd heard that there were restaurants in some of the big European capitals – particularly London – where you could easily get a job in the kitchens or waiting on tables. She'd been saving up for nearly a year now and had already managed to hide away over four hundred euros; she should have nearly six hundred by the time she was ready.

At four fifty-five a.m. there were several contemporaneous loud crashes as police battering rams burst open each of the five doors that led off the central corridor and voices yelled *'Polizia! Fermatevi!'* and the helmet-torches of heavily armed officers quickly raked each room.

One of the beams shone directly into her eyes and instinctively she raised an arm toward her face only to find it knocked heavily to one side before it reached its destination. *'Ferma!'* She did as she was told, too terrified to realise that most of her goose-pimpled body was exposed to the glare of the torches. There were four officers in the room: two pulled the man off the bed and onto the floor, rolling him and slipping handcuffs on in what seemed to be a single fluid movement, illuminated by the torch of a third officer, while the fourth kept his gun and torch trained on her. Only when they were satisfied that the man was securely bound hand and foot, did the officer who had his gun trained on her, take a step back and, without taking his eyes off her, reach out with one hand for the dressing gown that was draped over the back of a chair. He threw it to her and said, 'Get out of bed and cover yourself, *puttana.*' Finally, she began to cry.

'Your Eminence. I'm sorry to disturb you but Don Adriano dei Sisti from Prato is here with a young lady who he says must see you urgently.'

The balding prelate looked up from the paperwork on his antique desk and frowned at the Deacon who stood before him.

'From Prato... What's he doing here? Didn't you tell him that he should be speaking to Bishop Simoni? That's the whole point of His Holiness appointing Bishops to dioceses, so that the parish priests have someone local they can turn to.'

'I did make that point to Don Adriano, but he insisted that this was a very particular case and that is was imperative that the young lady spoke to you, and to you alone.' The Deacon folded his hands in front of his cassock and stood, head bowed slightly, awaiting the Bishop's response.

'Alright. Bring them through in ten minutes, but please tell them that I am very busy with the affairs of my own Diocese and can only give them a few minutes.'

The Deacon bowed his head further in acknowledgement of the instructions and retreated out of the room.

'So, Signorina Cavani, apart from confirming your name, you are not prepared to give any response to our questions, other than shaking your head. I must warn you that your companion will be going to jail for a very long time, and the longer you remain silent in an attempt to protect the two of you, and possibly others, the more seriously the judge is likely to view your role as his accomplice.'

Serena made an indistinct sound as she tried to stifle a sob, which turned into '...not my companion.'

'Sorry. What was that again?' But she just shook her head and let her head sink forward. 'Think it over, signorina – but don't take too long about it,' said the inspector who was facing her across the table, 'I'll be back soon.' He got up, scraping his chair back noisily over the bare concrete floor and left the room, followed by the agent who had been standing impassively just inside the door.

'Poor kid,' he said quietly to the agent, as the door was locked again. 'Tell Palazzi to come up to my office.'

Ten minutes later, Serena heard the cell door being unlocked again and quickly tried to wipe her tears away with her sleeve before the inspector started on her again. To her surprise, a hand was placed gently on her shoulder and another, well-manicured hand came round and placed a small tray with a cup of hot chocolate, a cream brioche and a pack of tissues in front of her.

The small gesture of kindness broke her resistance and her sobbing became uncontrollable. She was only vaguely aware of the hand on her shoulder moving across her back to hold her tight and allow her to rest her head on a soft cotton blouse, gently perfumed with jasmine.

After a couple of minutes, she managed to get a degree of control over herself and pulled away feeling confused and embarrassed. 'It's alright,' said the female agent in a surprisingly gentle accent which she knew was from somewhere in the north. 'Drink the chocolate before it goes cold, and get some food inside you.' Too exhausted by her experience to resist, Serena did as she was told.

'Well?' said Bishop Fogazzini, with scarcely disguised impatience, as he pushed the papers on his desk to one side and looked across at the tired looking priest and the attractive dark-haired woman who the Deacon had shown into the seats facing his desk. His Deacon had called her a young woman, but he guessed that despite still having good skin, she must be well into her thirties, and this disappointment only increased his irritation at the unexpected visit. This would be a very short interview he thought.

It was not the priest who spoke, as the Bishop had expected it would be, but the woman who looked him directly in the eye and without any preamble delivered a hammer-blow, 'We have evidence that your sister is not only abusing her position as a minister and a parliamentarian, but also that she has been helping you with your holiday arrangements.'

Fogazzini looked at the woman, trying to collect his thoughts. He rotated his episcopal ring with his thumb and, with his other hand, absent-mindedly gripped his pectoral cross.

'I have absolutely no idea what you are talking about, my child – and I must ask you both to leave – I'll be writing to your Bishop,' he said, directing the latter part of his response at the priest.

'I don't think so,' said the woman, taking a digital recorder out of her pocket, placing it on the desk between them and pressing 'play'. Fogazzini, heard his own voice, telling his sister what services he required from the young people who were to be brought for him, and his sister's voice calmly promising to make all the necessary arrangements and to ensure secrecy.

When she judged that he'd heard enough, Rosa pressed the 'stop' button and waited for his reaction wondering whether he would at least have the dignity to admit his faults and show some degree of penitence. She was to be disappointed, although not really surprised. After a few seconds, he looked her in the eye and began, 'It's very easy to take things that are said on the telephone, out of context. What you don't understand...'

'Enough!' interrupted Don Adriano, surprising both of them. 'You're a disgrace to the holy office you hold. How dare you try to justify what you do?' He glared at the bishop.

'I... I... What is it you want? How much do you want?'

'You disgust me,' said Don Adriano, and Rosa reached out and placed a hand on his arm.

'We are not here for money. There are two things that must happen,' said Rosa: 'firstly, you must resign your post as Bishop and confess your sins to your superiors in the church. It will be up to the church to decide how you should be punished… and I'm not talking about a confession in the confessional and a punishment of three Hail Marys and seven days of fasting'

'But,' interrupted Don Adriano again, 'if you are placed in any other role where you will ever have any contact with young people, all the evidence will be passed to the state police,' and I will make sure that you are not only publicly humiliated but also locked away for a very long time.'

The bishop bowed his head for a moment, then raised it again and looked at Rosa, 'And secondly?'

'Secondly, you will pick up that telephone now and let your sister know that she will be visited by someone coming from you on urgent business and it is important that they are seen as soon as they arrive.' Rosa watched him hesitate before answering, knowing that he was calculating the chances of getting out of this, just as Francesca had predicted he would. '… And you will not contact your sister, or anyone who you know to be in contact with her, for at least twenty-four hours.'

He hesitated again before answering, and this time she was sure that the pause was only for effect, aimed at giving them the impression that he was giving in completely.

'All right. I'll make the call... but what if she's in a meeting this morning and can't take the call.'

'She isn't,' said Rosa, with a smile that chilled him, 'we checked.'

He made the call.

'… No. I'm afraid I can't tell you why over the phone... I'll be in touch …. *Ciao bella*.' He put the phone down; 'I've done what you asked.'

Rosa and Don Adriano leaned back in their chairs without saying anything. He watched them, perplexed.'

'What more do you want? I can't just ring up The Holy Father out of the blue... I have to prepare for that.'

'Don't let us stop your preparations' said Don Adriano, 'We're not ready to leave just yet.'

For almost twelve minutes, Don Adriano and Rosa sat calmly in their chairs without speaking and the bishop sat watching them, getting more and more nervous, sweaty and fidgety.

Eventually when the wait had become almost unbearable and the Bishop felt on the verge of screaming, Rosa's phone rang. She pressed the reply button and put the phone to her ear and listened. After only a few seconds, she said, 'OK. That's great.' and hung up. Turning towards Don Adriano, she said, 'We can go now: our colleagues are with the minister. Out of the corner of her eye, but without looking at him, she registered the disappointment on the bishop's face, smiled, stood up and, followed by Don Adriano, headed for the door.

On the other side of the door she said quietly, 'I'm sure he was thinking just what Franci said he would be thinking. He was just waiting for us to leave to let his sister know what was really happening. If he had the chance to do that before Franci and Ciancolini got to his sister, we may well have had a nasty accident before we got very far.' Keeping her head down to avoid offering too much of herself to the security cameras and feeling pleased that she had been able to play a key part in bringing about the downfall of the conspirators, Rosa led Don Adriano across the vestibule towards the outer door but, as she did so, she failed to notice the refined looking elderly man in the elegant camel-hair coat who looked at her with a frown on his face from across the room.

'I'm sure that it will all work out OK in the end,' said Palazzi gently, the inspector can be a little judgemental at times but, when things have been explained to him properly, he's actually very reasonable... when you feel ready, if you tell me all about it then I'll make sure it's presented to him the right way.'

Serena shook her head causing some loose tears to roll down her cheeks, 'I can't,' she said, I can't.'

'Don't worry. Just tell us what you know – even if it doesn't all make sense to you – it might mean something to us. The more I know, the more I can help you.' Again the girl was silent although she cast a look at Palazzi as if asking for guidance. 'Tell me everything you can about Salvatore Stiappa – that would be a good start.'

Serena looked up, clearly confused, 'Who?'

'I suppose he may have been using a false name, but the man you took home last night – his real name is Salvatore Stiappa.'

'What!... But you can't... But I didn't... It's not true...' and she attempted to rise out of the seat but, Palazzi, calmly put her hand on the girl's arm and applied gentle pressure to keep her down.'

'Shhhh. It's alright... no-one's judging you... you'd be surprised how many girls we see who end up falling into prostitution almost by accident, and don't know how to get out of it again... I can help.'

Serena cried quietly. Palazzi continued, 'Your father explained how guilty they feel because neither he nor your mother have been able to get a job. They understand that you need money so that you can have some of things other girls of your age have.'

Serena's face and neck suddenly reddened as though she'd been slapped hard, 'No!' she cried with sudden anger, 'No. It's not true! … I hate him. I hate him, and I hate her as well for not doing anything about it!' And then the whole story came out. Now that she knew that her parents were prepared to sacrifice her to save themselves, any last vestige of family loyalty she may have felt disappeared, and her anger was stronger than the fear she felt at the inevitable consequence or her talking to the police. '… and now they'll kill me for having told you this.'

Ashen faced with horror at what she had heard, Agent Palazzi got out of her seat, went round the table to the girl and put her arms round her for a few seconds. 'Listen, Serena. You mustn't worry about anything. I need to go away and explain your story to the inspector, but the first thing I'm going to do is to get you moved to somewhere more comfortable. I'll be back to talk to you again in an hour or so and I'll probably have someone with me – but you mustn't be afraid. I promise that everything's going to be alright.'

'You've been sent by my brother?' she said, extending her hand towards Ciancolini with a practised smile. Ciancolini ignored the proffered hand and gestured towards the chairs around the desk.

'Sit down, Minister; we have important things to discuss.' And he sat down in the visitor's chair closest to the minister's desk. Fogazzini looked as if she were about to protest but then thought better of it, gathered her dignity and sat down. When she was settled, Ciancolini continued, 'Information has come into my possession, as Investigating Magistrate, that while in post as a Minister of State, and Minister for a party that argues for the primacy of traditional moral and religious values, you have used your power and influence to provide sexual companions for your brother, the Bishop of Todi. Furthermore, some of these companions have been below the legal age of consent.'

The watching Francesca felt as if she could almost see the confidence draining away from Fogazzini. 'Not below the legal age of consent,' said Fogazzini weakly.

'If I may remind you of the law, Minister... while the legal age of consent is fourteen, different criteria apply if one party is over eighteen, there is more than a three year age gap and the older party holds a position of responsibility where they can reasonably be expected to be able to influence the younger person... I think, Minister, that it would be very easy to argue in court that both you and your brother hold positions which enable you to exert influence over others... Furthermore, ' he added as the minister remained silent, 'it is also a serious crime for an adult to pay for sex with an under eighteen... and although we do not have evidence of this, I have no doubt that we will have shortly. It stretches the bounds of credibility to expect us to believe that a group of adolescents would willingly provide sexual favours for a middle-aged, slightly overweight Bishop, if there were no money changing hands.'

'So you've come to arrest me – just like that,' said the minister, crestfallen.

'Actually, and against my personal instincts, which are influenced by a significant amount of contempt, I'm here to offer you a deal.'

'No, Stiappa. We have evidence available linking you to an attempted hack of CIA files last November. We raided two of your other regular hideouts at the same time as the one in Viterbo and, amongst other things we seized was a laptop.... Our computer experts have already had a go at the machine and have recovered files that you thought you'd deleted.'

Stiappa looked up from his manacled hands where he'd been nonchalantly picking at the nails of his left hand with the index finger of his right. He gave a smile intended to irritate the officer facing him, 'You won't find anything on my computer – not only because I'm innocent but also because, even if I had done something, I wouldn't be so stupid as to use a computer.'

The Brigadier smiled back, unruffled, 'I'm glad to hear that you're not stupid, because that should make it easier for you to see sense and do what's best for yourself.'

'I want my lawyer... You can't hold me for more than an hour without giving me access to my lawyer.'

'Bravo! ... I see you've been brushing up on the law – you weren't expecting to find yourself in any trouble were you? ... No? ... What a shame you must have stopped reading before you got to the section on anti-terrorism... If you'd got that far, you would have known that where terrorism is involved, we have special powers that over-ride the normal regulations.'

'What's terrorism got to do with anything? You can't hold me under anti-terrorism measures!'

'Oh, I think we can, Signor Stiappa. Our American friends are pushing us very hard to uncover the Italian end of this hacking operation, and they'll be delighted if we deliver them a suspect with all the necessary evidence. I assume that then, after a little bit of extraordinary rendition, they'll do whatever they have to do to find out everything you know.'

Stiappa shook his head and snorted, but again the Brigadier was unperturbed. When he began speaking again, it was as though he were talking to himself at the beginning. Very impressive, the range of methods the CIA have available for getting information... shame really that we're not allowed to use some of them here...' Then after a pause he looked directly at Stiappa and continued, 'Waterboarding! Did you ever see anyone waterboarded? ... No? ... Pity ... Very impressive you know... they say that they can make anyone talk in the end... it's a really horrific experience... But that won't affect you, will it Signor Stiappa because I'm sure you're intelligent enough to realise that you're better off telling them everything they want to know before it gets unpleasant.'

'I can't tell them anything because I've never been involved in anything to do with terrorism.'

The brigadier threw back his head and laughed out loud for a few seconds 'Oh, Signor Stiappa, if only you knew how many people start off by saying something like that... some of them can even fool lie detectors... but they don't last too long with the waterboard... You'll talk alright!'

Despite the fact that the bare-walled interview room was unheated, beads of sweat were appearing on Stiappa's forehead. The brigadier stood up abruptly, 'I'll leave you to think over it... I'm going for a coffee and a cigarette. My colleague will bring you a bottle of water,' and he left the room.

The Maresciallo who had left the room with him said solicitously, 'I'll get Botta to make you a coffee.'

The Brigadier shook his head and smiled, 'I'm going to stretch my legs and get one from the bar down the road. The longer Stiappa has to think things over, the more malleable he's likely to be later... I'll give you a shout when I'm back.'

Once he'd turned the corner and was out of sight of the Caserma, he took his mobile out of his pocket and scrolled down the list of contacts.

'*Ciao* Bernardo. News.'

'Not yet. I haven't tackled him about the conspiracy yet. I've just left him thinking over what the CIA might do to get information out of him, if they know he's involved in cyber-terrorism.'

'You sound as if you're almost enjoying it.'

'I think I am, really. He's an extremely unpleasant piece of work and deserves everything he gets... although I think the CIA might be offended if they'd heard what I just told Stiappa would happen to him.'

'So what next?'

'I'm going for a coffee then, when I get back, I'll explain to him just how strong our evidence of cyber-terrorism is. We'll let him panic a bit, then we'll offer him a possible way out.'

'OK Keep me informed – what about the others you took in?'

'Phbbbt! Waste of time. The father's a small time local gangster who we've been keeping an eye on for a bit. He's claimed no knowledge of Stiappa – said that his daughter picked him up last night and brought him home, but the daughter, who seems to be pretty much a victim in all this, is now singing like a canary. The mother's just a waste of space.'

'*Ciao. Ci sentiamo.*'

'We know that over at least the past six months, you and other public officials have been involved in a conspiracy intended to subvert the lawful democratic processes of the State... We have evidence that clearly demonstrates the involvement of some, if not all the conspirators in the murder of Loriana Cabrini-Pellé...'

'B..but I...'

'Don't interrupt, please. You'll get the opportunity to have your say later. For now, I just want you to listen – We know that the Mitrokhin Commission is being used as a vehicle to discredit prominent left-wing and centre-left politicians with the public and...' Ciancolini paused for effect,   'we know that the plan also involves the possible assassination of Romano Prodi either before or after the next elections at a time when leaks from Mitrokhin have removed any sympathy that the majority of the public may have for him. - We know the identity of many of your fellow conspirators – enough to obtain convictions – but we don't know all of them.'

'And that's where you're going to help us,' added Francesca.

Fogazzini shook her head, 'I can't... I don't know what you're talking about... You must have got it wrong or been misinformed... I can't believe that there is any such conspiracy... If I could help you, I would – believe me.'

'The trouble, Minister,' said Ciancolini, eyes fixed on the minister, ' is that I don't believe you – and the reason I don't believe you is that there is incontrovertible evidence to back up what Ive just said.'

Fogazzini shook her head again, although it was clear from the way her skin had puckeded around her eyes that she was worried. 'That's impossible!'

Francesca sighed theatrically and rolled her eyes. 'Let me ring around a few of my journalist friends and spread the news about how the minister has been procuring under-age sexual victims for her charming and very pious brother, the Bishop of Todi.... It seems as though we're wasting our time here. Have her locked up somewhere secure – her brother with her, if she wants.'

'You can't do that!' said Fogazzini, the pitch of her voice rising.

'I think you'll find that I can,' said Ciancolini, placing the authorisation from the President on the desk between them. Fogazzini appeared deflated. 'Let's not be too hasty,' he continued smoothly, turning towards Francesca. 'I'm sure that the Minister will see the sense in co-operating without making a fuss. '

'Why should I co-operate? And how do I know I can trust you to keep your word?'

'You can't, but you don't really have any choice, do you?... Whatever you choose to do, your career in public life is over. If you don't co-operate, both you and your brother will be arrested amidst a wave of publicity. You will be kept in solitary confinement in view of the risk of your being able to influence witnesses and tamper with evidence. You'll stay there until such time as we are ready to arrest the other conspirators... I think it's highly likely that at least one of the others will turn state evidence, in an attempt to save their own skin, and at that point you will be tried both as a conspirator and for what you have done for your brother. Your lack of co-operation when offered the opportunity, will serve as an aggravating feature.'

Francesca, who was watching the minister's face intently, saw her swallow and then run the tip of her tongue around her lips which appeared very dry.

'And if I were able to help you in some way?'

'If... If we were confident that you had given us all the relevant information that you know, then there would be no leak to the media; your brother would be able to retire to a monastery – provided that certain conditions are met; you would resign from your post on health grounds and be charged with only lesser offences when the whole conspiracy is unmasked.'

'Not just your post as a minister,' added Francesca, 'but also your position as a deputy.'

'I'll have to think about it carefully.'

'No.' said Ciancolini calmly. 'We need to know your decision now. Either you agree to co-operate, or I arrest you now and you leave this building with us.'

Fogazzini sat still, gazing fixedly out of the window. Francesca was aware of the ticking of the wall-clock that she had not noticed previously. The air in the room seemed charged with tension as the two principal actors in the drama sat immobile.

Suddenly, Fogazzini turned to face Ciancolini again. He looked at her expectantly and watched as her hand stretched out to the telephone unit. Without picking up the receiver she put a gently trembling finger on one of the buttons.

Immediately, an efficient sounding female voice came out of the unit. 'Yes, Minister,'

'Mara... Cancel all my appointments, please.'

'Just for the morning?'

'No, Mara... Cancel ALL my appointments, and get me the Prime Minister on the phone.'

'But, Minister...' then the secretary evidently thought better of it, 'Yes, Minister. Of course, Minister. Right away Minister.' Fogazzini and Ciancolini remained sitting silently, facing each other for nearly five minutes until the phone rang and a red light lit up.

'Yes, Mara...'

'I have the Prime Minister's Office for you, Madam Minister.'

'Thank you, Mara.'

'Pronto,'

'Pronto, Minister Fogazzini,'

'Yes, I'm on the line.'

'One moment please...'

Then the room was filled with the well-known sound of the Prime-Minister's voice, 'Maria-Grazia, this is an unexpected pleasure. What can I do for you?' Fogazzini tapped the speakerphone button to off and picked up the receiver instead so that Francesca and Ciancolini could only hear her half of the conversation.

Francesca moved towards the phone to put the speakerphone back on, but Ciancolini stopped her with a shake of the head.

'Prime Minister, I'm afraid I've just had some very bad news about my health. I'm going to have to step down from my post immediately,' …….. 'Yes, Prime-Minister,' …... 'Very bad, I'm afraid,' …... 'No. Nothing, I'm afraid,' …. 'A complete withdrawal from public life,' …….. 'No... Complete and permanent I'm afraid.' …….. 'Yes, I'm very sorry.' …... 'Thankyou, Sir. That's very kind of you.' ….. 'I will,' …... 'No, not yet. He's in a meeting with ministers Marelli and Rossi this morning, and can't be disturbed – I'll have to speak with him later.' At this point Ciancolini shook his head decidedly and wagged his finger at her, to indicate that there was to be no direct communication between her and the Secretary of State she worked for. She nodded to show that she understood. 'Of course, Sir, if you could possibly inform him for me, that would be a great weight of my mind.. I really wouldn't want to break down in front of him,' ….. 'Of course, Sir. And thankyou, Sir; it's been an honour to serve you and the country.'…. 'Arrivederci,' and she hung up. Ciancolini nodded his approval.

'Now,' said Francesca, 'You need to start talking.'

Marco entered the Metro at the station under the main concourse at Termini and, without rushing, headed for the barriers. He was pleased to see that today he'd been assigned his usual shadow as it saved him having to take the trouble of identifying the new one. Since his return from Naples and his questioning by the security services, he had ensured that while varying his routine as much as possible, he had done nothing particularly interesting and had made no attempt to lose his shadow. Today, however, would be different, and he intended to engineer it so that he would seem to have 'accidentally' lost his shadow.

He used his monthly travel-card to pass the barriers, picked up a copy of the free newspaper and headed for the southbound platform on Line B. One minute to wait for the train – he looked briefly at the front page – all things he had already heard on the radio and then flicked through to find the sports pages where he could catch up with the latest football rumours.

As he stepped through the door of the nearest carriage, he watched his shadow casually enter the door at the opposite end. Both men sat down with their newspapers open and Marco paid the other man no more attention during the fifteen minutes or so it took for the train to reach the EUR Palasport station where he left the carriage slowly enough to ensure that there was no risk of losing his shadow too soon. Outside the station, he crossed the road to the busy bar overlooking the lake and beyond that the hill with the Palasport at its summit, and ordered a latte macchiato and a brioche. His eyes followed the attractive barmaid with the shortish blond hair with a little pony tail on top and he smiled as he imagined the elbow in the ribs he would have received from Francesca if she'd been there. Following the barmaid's movements, however, allowed him to scan the mirror behind the coffee machine and the rows of bottles to make sure that he knew exactly where his shadow was.

His shadow was quite good at his job, and it had taken Marco a while to identify him on the first day, but now he was fairly sure that the other man was aware that Marco knew he was there, and hoped that this would lead him to lower his guard.

Finishing his drink, he placed a two Euro coin on the counter and with a general '*Arrivederci,*' turned and made his way to the door and then across the street. He didn't even glance at the Ministry of Economic Development but instead made his way along Viale America and then turned left by the side of the large building shared by the Communications Ministry and the headquarters of the Italian Post Office. He couldn't help grinning as he imagined how his shadow must think that finally his luck was changing as he was in an area surrounded by several ministries.

After less than four hundred metres where the broad tree-lined road widened out even further to create an elongated roundabout around the Marconi obelisk, he turned right into a large grassy piazza with museums on each side and a marble colonnade at the far end. Keeping to the right, he headed for the entrance of the National Museum of Prehistory and Ethnology. Even if his shadow was ultimately to have a disappointing day, at least he'd have a chance to pick up a bit of culture along the way.

Marco spent the next hour and a half meandering around the museum, which he knew well, admiring his favourite exhibits. Occasionally he caught a glimpse of the other man in the distance, pretending to be deeply engrossed in a study of the ancient artefacts. Eventually, after ostentatiously checking his watch, he doubled back slightly to make sure his shadow didn't lose him and headed for the exit at a leisurely pace. Back on the other side of the road, he made his way to the upmarket White Gallery which, despite its exterior being almost as discreet as it was possible to be in the EUR district, was the fashion store of choice for Rome's wealthiest residents. It also happened to provide him with one of his most lucrative security contracts.

At the entrance he lifted his arms slightly so that the concierge, who was actually a highly trained security guard, could see he wasn't carrying anything he shouldn't be, smiled at the man, who allowed no sign of recognition to show on his face, despite having been trained by Marco, and then passed through the discretely placed security scanners. Politely declining the offer of a personal shopping assistant for the duration of his visit, he made his way past the displays of, Jimmy Choos, Stella McCartney, Alexander McQueen, Salvatore Ferragamo and others to the escalator.

On the third floor, he nodded to the security guard and headed towards the manager's office. An hour later, after reviewing and upgrading one of the two servers that controlled the system, he emerged from the office with the manager and walked round the third floor with her, ensuring that all the hidden cameras were working appropriately and speaking to a couple of newer members of staff to check that they were completely comfortable with their part in maintaining the security protocols.

Finally, he shook hands with the manager and kissed her on both cheeks before taking the escalator downwards. The manager watched him go, watched the other man follow him at a suitable distance and then, when both had left the building, called over a young woman who appeared to be unable to decide between Dior and Givenchy, but who was actually an undercover store detective.

At the bottom of the road, Marco made his way casually along Viale America back towards the Metro station. When he was less than sixty metres from the entrance, a silver Fiat Uno that had just turned out of Via Colombo passed him, braked and then reversed up to him. The driver, the undercover store detective from the store, leaned across and spoke to Marco through the window. He nodded, smiled and got in. The Uno pulled out into the light traffic and headed northwards towards Central Rome.

'No taxis around?' he asked.

She shook her head, 'They all wait by the lower entrance to the Metro – it's easier to park there.'

'Excellent,' he said, 'I told the new trainee that he wouldn't be able to track me successfully. He'll have learnt a lesson today.'

She laughed, 'Where do you want me to drop you?'

'Just in case he's better than I thought and has somehow managed to stay behind me, I'd better just make doubly sure. If you turn left at the third junction, you pass under a viaduct almost immediately. I'll jump out there and, if he is still behind me, you'll be gone well before he turns the corner.'

'OK No problem. It's better than spending all day trying on clothes and shoes that I'll never be able to afford.'

In reality, Marco was sure that he'd lost his shadow already but he was aware that, as he'd been picked up very close to the Ministry of Economic Development, it was possible that the security cameras had picked it up and – although it was very unlikely – that the car was being tracked from other cameras along the route. He knew that they would be invisible under the viaduct, and intended to make completely sure that he was free to go wherever he wanted.

Slipping quickly out of the Uno under the viaduct, he quickly stepped into the shadows and then reversed his jacket so that it changed from red to brown, slipped on a pair of photoreactive sunglasses and then walked confidently along the pavement.

'Friday the twenty-eighth to Sunday the thirtieth of November. The hard-disk on your computer tells us that you were using the dark net and attempting to hack the CIA's files over in America. Our records show that your computer was being used in Benevento that weekend and, our forensic linguistic experts have analysed other examples of your writing and are statistically certain that it was you using the computer.'

'But that's impossible... I wasn't in Benevento at the end of November.'

'The judges at the extradition hearing aren't going to believe that Stiappa, are they? It would take a considerable amount of effort to create such a sophisticated computer trail if it wasn't there already, and why would anyone want to do that? No, Stiappa, you are, to put it in common terms *fottuto*.... unless, that is,... unless you can demonstrate that you were somewhere else that weekend.... Think about it Stiappa.... I'll be back later,' said the Brigadier.

Two hours later, the Brigadier re-entered the cell accompanied by two other officers in plain clothes. The Brigadier sat down facing Stiappa and the other two sat at each end of the desk so that the gangster couldn't see them all clearly at the same time.

'Well, Stiappa; have you thought it over? Are you going to be able to come up with an alibi that has a chance of convincing us?'

Stiappa looked back at him, 'What do you want me to say? You've set me up and you obviously want something, so why not just tell me what you want me to say, and I'll decide if I'm prepared to say it.'

The Brigadier put on a pained expression, 'Signor Stiappa, or maybe I should call you Snuff, as your friends do... you need to be careful not to hurt my feelings. All I want you to do is to tell the truth. All of us here,' and he made a sweeping gesture to take in the other two, are only interested in upholding the rule of law and the values of the constitution. Tell us the truth about where you were and what you were doing that weekend, and you'll find that we get on much better.' His face returned to its previous expressionless mask. Stiappa studied him.

'What's in it for me if I co-operate?'

'If you can prove that you were somewhere else that weekend, then you don't get a one way ticket to America... or Guantanamo Bay.'

'I didn't want anything to do with it at first. When Cioni first spoke to me about it, I thought he was just testing me out; I didn't think he was serious; it sounded so incredible. I just laughed and said that it would be wonderful to stop the reds from ever forming a government again... Then I gave him a wave and went home.'

'What happened then?' asked Ciancolini.

'I got a call just after five the next morning: It was Cioni. He told me that we were both needed for a meeting with Rossi at six-thirty. He was sending a car for me,' she paused.

'Go on, Minister,' she was prompted. 'You went to the meeting with Cioni and the Interior Minister; we need to know where it was, who was there and what was said – preferably by whom.'

'Cioni, Rossi, Vercellese, Nicola Maroni the Vice-Questore of Frosinone, and Lesine.'

'How active a role did Lesine play?' asked Ciancolini, trying to hide his elation at the linking of the media magnate to the conspiracy.

'He didn't say a lot,' answered Fogazzini, he just confirmed that all his media outlets would be fully supportive of the group's actions and that, in the meantime, they would do as much as they could to damage the reputation of Prodi, D'Alema and other leading left-wing politicians. He also guaranteed to underwrite any necessary costs.'

'So, four elected members of Parliament, two of them Secretaries of State and the others Ministers of State, decided to subvert the democratic processes of the state, for you own interests...'

'No!' she interrupted, 'it isn't... it wasn't like that. There weren't just the three of us; there were other ministers involved... we more or less had a democratic mandate.'

Ciancolini raised a sceptical eyebrow. 'So who else was part of this democratically elected group of political vigilantes?' asked Francesca, making no attempt to veil the sarcasm in the question.

'Marelli, Caprai, Beneventano and Cabrini-Pellé – but then she was killed in the accident.'

'Accident.'

'Yes, of course. Cioni rang me to let me know just before the news was made public.'

'And you believed him!' said Francesca, shaking her head.'

'Yes, of course... what... do you mean you...'

'No, Minister,' broke in Ciancolini with calm authority, 'We didn't have anything to do with Cabrini-Pellé's death but, we were keeping Vercellese under observation and we know that after Cabrini-Pellé left her office for the last time, she went to a meeting with Vercellese and others – a meeting from which she didn't emerge alive.'

'But that's not...'

'We believe,' continued Ciancolini, ignoring Fogazzini's attempted interruption, that like you, she was asked to join the conspiracy, but that, unlike you, she had the integrity to turn it down – although unfortunately, that refusal cost both her, and her driver, their lives.'

Fogazzini leaned back in her chair for a moment, as if stunned, then she shook her head and looked at Ciancolini as if expecting him to contradict himself: 'But that's not possible, Loredana believed in all the values that we were fighting for – she was a natural fit who was destined for great things.'

'She may have shared many of your values but it appears that she held one other belief that the rest of you didn't.' Fogazzini looked at him with a puzzled expression on her face, frown lines appearing between her eyebrows. 'The belief,' continued Ciancolini, 'that you had to win the argument with the people and take power through the ballot-box.'

'I don't believe it!'

'We have evidence, Minister. Vercellese would have been arrested some time ago, if that wouldn't have alerted the rest of your group to that fact that he was being followed.'

Fogazzini shook her head but said nothing. She got slowly out to her seat and made her way over to the window. Ciancolini gave a quick glance at Francesca who nodded to show that she had understood and followed the Minister to the window. Although the window was only on the first floor and a fall would probably not kill Fogazzini, they were both aware of the possibility of her making a dramatic gesture which could seriously delay their interrogation.

'Don't worry,' said Fogazzini bitterly, as though reading their minds, 'I'm not going to jump... not yet, anyway... I have to see my brother.'

'You can see your brother when we've got a detailed statement from you – you have my word,' said Ciancolini.

'And then?'

'And then it depends on exactly what is in your statement and on how willing the President is to grant clemency or a pardon.'

'And my brother?'

'If you co-operate fully, and make no attempt to contact your fellow conspirators, then the Italian State will take no action against your brother – providing that the Vatican agrees to his redeployment to a calling where he will no longer have any contact with young people.'

Fogazzini bowed her head and leaned it against the wall for a while, then she turned and said, 'Alright, but you must let me speak with my brother first.'

'Agreed,' said Ciancolini, on one condition.

She tilted her head and looked at him, 'you must keep the phone on speaker-phone while you talk to him and you must not say anything that could cause him to warn any of your fellow conspirators. As far as he's concerned we are only speaking to you because we became aware of his sexual proclivities.'

'OK. Agreed.'

'So, how did it go?' asked Paul, as soon as he heard Rosa walk through the door and throw her keys down on the shelf in the hall.

'Everything went just as planned... Give me a minute to nip to the loo and I'll tell you all about it.'

'OK I'll mix you a G and T!'

When Rosa came back into the room she flopped down on the settee next to Paul, pulled her feet up and leaned against his shoulder as she reached out for the gin and tonic.

'Well?' he asked as she put the glass down again after taking a long sip.

She smiled, 'It feels wrong to say it, but it feels really exciting to be actually involved, doing something useful rather than leaving it all to you and Franci… I thought I'd be nervous, but as soon as Don Adriano told the Bishop's secretary that we needed to see him on an urgent matter that couldn't wait, it was as if nothing else existed – I was totally focussed and everything was really clear – it was just like it used to be when I was competing in gymnastics and feeling confident.'

Paul gave her thigh a little squeeze and she continued to fill him in on the details of the meeting with the Bishop, making him laugh when she described the increasingly panic stricken look on his face as his bluster and attempted threats failed to have any effect. 'While we waited for Franci to let us know that they'd managed to get in to see his sister I was worried he might have some sort of seizure – I don't think I've ever seen anyone look so red in the face.'

'I think you did brilliantly, but I always knew you would – still it's a shame I couldn't get out of invigilating the written exams at the university, I'd rather have kept you out of it if I could. They've already killed at least twice and I'm sure they won't hesitate to do so again if they think their little game is in danger of unravelling.'

'How sweet that you still want to protect me after all these years; my very own caveman.'

Paul ignored the provocation. 'I'm serious. The closer this gets to the end, the higher the stakes and the more dangerous it's going to be – this is not really the best time for you to be getting involved. If this goes wrong, they'll have no hesitation in taking out those who have opposed them.'

Rosa took another sip of her drink and tilted her face up towards his, 'Don't worry – It won't go wrong – I've got a good feeling about this now that I've been able to do something.'

'Mmmm – are you sure that the good feeling doesn't come from the gin?'

Marco reached the top of the Spanish steps and turned and leant on the parapet, scanning the steps behind him to make absolutely certain that he hadn't picked up another tail. Several families, a handful of back-packers or inter-railers and that was about it. He took his mobile out and tapped in a number.

'Raffa – *sono io* ….. The Sculpture Gallery in Villa Borghese – forty minutes …. OK.' Then he closed the phone, slipped it back into his pocket and, after giving another careful look around, slipped into the shadows on the southern side of the Piazza below the "Spanish Steps" and made his way northwards until he reached the Villa Medici museum where he left the road and cut through the park to a wide viale where he was able to cross into the large park surrounding the Villa Borghese.

It took a quarter of an hour to make his way through the park to the Borghese Gallery but that still left him ten minutes to spare before his appointment. He considered taking a detour to use up the time and avoid the security cameras in the villa but decided that the chances of anyone who was looking for him monitoring every security camera in Rome were so infinitesimally small that he would purchase his ticket straight away and use the time revisiting some of his favourite Bernini sculptures.

As usual he found that wandering amongst the sensual marble sculptures made him feel immediately calmer and the corners of his mouth turned up slightly as a serene smile took over his face. He was lost in contemplation of The Rape of Prosperina when a voice behind him said, 'looking at the how the flesh seems to be giving under Pluto's hand, you wouldn't believe it was stone would you?'

Marco shook his head slowly then turned his mind back to the matter in hand.

'*Ciao*, Raffaele. If we move over to the other side of the sculpture of Apollo and Daphne, we'll be out of view of the security cameras – you really don't want to be seen with me.'

'I was getting worried when neither you nor Nico had been in touch for two days.'

Marco explained as succinctly as possible what had happened to Nico and how he'd been drawn in to it because of the piece of paper in Nico's pocket.

Raffaele shook his head disgustedly, 'That was careless; Nico should have known better…. Anyway, I think I've got something that might interest you; - he wasn't smiling.

Marco raised his eyebrows and Raffaele continued, 'Last night, Marelli received a short call from a mobile that I was able to triangulate to San Basile in Calabria… When I was inside, I spent a week sharing a cell with someone from San Basile… he was telling me that it was ironic that he'd been arrested for misdeclaring expenses as he was probably the only person in San Basile who wasn't involved with the 'Ndrangheta…. The message said, "Firework party on Saturday. All set." and that was it…. Saturday's tomorrow.'

'Nothing else?'

'No. that was it. I've checked back through all the records we have and there are no other calls to or from that number, so they're obviously being very careful.'

'Does Marelli have any known links to Calabria?'

Raffaele spread his hands out wide, with upturned palms to indicate that he had no idea. 'You'll have to ask some of ones you're working with if they can help you there.'

'OK, I'll get on to it. Who else has Marelli been talking to, particularly direct calls to other ministers and senior police officers?'

Raffaele pulled a plastic wallet out of the inside pocket of his jacket and passed it over to Marco, who slipped it into his own pocket.

'Alright. It's best if we split up now. Don't ring me, as at some point they'll manage to get a tail back on me again and may even pull me in for more questioning. I'll ring you when it's safe to do so. In the meantime see what you can find out about Nico.'

Raffaele gave him a brief wink and moved casually across to admire another of Bernini's masterpieces while Marco moved into the next room where he paid homage to a reclining nude by Canova before making his way to the exit.

Once outside, force of habit made him automatically check around himself again but he was sure he was still at complete liberty; knowing how understaffed the city police were with all recruitment having been suspended for two years, he thought that the chances of his being located were minimal. Considering his options he decided that walking to Castro Pretorio, the nearest Metro station on Line B, would not take him much longer than waiting for a taxi to pass and flag it down, so he set off through the mainly residential streets around the park.

In Piazza Fiume he picked up a copy of the day's newspaper and just gave the front cover a brief glance before rolling it up and slipping it under his arm to browse later on while on the metro.

It was only after the first stop, when a seat was freed up that he unrolled the paper and folded back the front page to look inside that he spotted the article: "Leading politicians may have KGB links.

"A member of the Parliamentary Commission set up to investigate the allegations made by Soviet defector Vasili Mitrokhin, last night expressed concern that currently active politicians almost certainly had ties to the KGB. The source indicated that an interim report which is due to be released shortly will suggest that not only former leaders of the Italian Communist Party, Enrico Berlinguer and Giorgio Amendola, had ties with the oppressive security organisation but also others who have now risen to prominence such as Massimo D'Alema and President of the European Commission, Romano Prodi. It is believed that Prodi will shortly make an announcement that he is to return to domestic policies and will almost certainly be chosen to lead the rag-tag collection of parties that will form the left-wing block for the next general election.

"Although no details have yet been released of the extent to which Prodi was able to pass sensitive details about national security to his Russian paymasters, the implication was that they were significant.

"Doubts have already been raised over Romano Prodi's integrity with calls for investigations into his business dealings before entering politics. Although nothing was ever proved, strong suspicions remain that, as president of IRI, Prodi benefitted greatly from a number of deals brokered by the state owned agency, particularly the merger of Italdel and Siemens and the sale of SME to international conglomerate Unilever. It has also been claimed that as President of the Council of Ministers between 1996 and 1998 he used his influence to have investigations into his previous business deals dropped.

"Prodi has long been suspected of having links with far left groups including the Red Brigade. It will be recalled that in 1978 Prodi and a group of left-wing colleagues from Bologna University were able to give police a tip-off about the safe-house in which Aldo Moro was being held, following information received during a séance. There have long been those who believe that the séance was just a cover story and that the tip-off was really the result of a difference of opinion amongst the Red Brigade strategists.

"Despite his avuncular appearance which has, in this newspaper's opinion, led to him being underestimated by right-minded Italians, it is clear that the day of reckoning is fast approaching for President of the European Commission."

Marco noticed that the article was uncredited, despite its prominent positioning in the paper. He also noticed that it had been strategically positioned next to articles about the Mafia expanding their field of influence into Emilia-Romagna – Prodi's own region - and the growing threat posed to Italy's tourist industry by environmental pollution, accompanied by a picture of corroding barrels of waste, clearly marked "Toxic" and with a caption stating "Italy faces her greatest threat" - a caption which was placed, very conveniently between the image and the article about Prodi. You didn't need to be an expert in Media Studies and Communications to understand the insidious effect that articles such as this would have. He looked around; he could see at least eight other copies of the same newspaper in the crowded carriage, and who knew what they'd managed to plant in other newspapers.

Judging that he still had at least five minutes before reaching his destination, he flicked through the rest of the paper, trying not to be distracted by the football, to see whether he could find any clue about where the fireworks planned for the weekend could be. Unable to spot anything, he left the paper on the seat and squeezed his way towards the nearest exit as the train approached Jonio station.

Five minutes later he tapped a code into a discreet key-pad below a panel of names and doorbells set to the right hand side of an innocuous looking doorway in Via Favino.

Inside the entrance hall, instead of heading for the main lift or the stairway, he opened a door which blended into the panelling on the side-wall so well that the casual visitor wouldn't notice it, flicked the timer-light switch on and made his way down the bare concrete steps into a long dingy corridor that ran the whole length of the building with eight regularly spaced steel doors on either side. When he reached the third door, he rotated the five dials on the sturdy combination lock that secured it, lifted the lock off the hasp, pushed the door forwards and reached for the light-switch.

'Fogazzini has given us some useful information, but I get the impression that she's fairly peripheral to the central core of plotters – there to make up the numbers and give them more credibility – almost a democratic mandate, I think she called it herself.'

'And Stiappa seems to be torn between his image of himself as a *"uomo d'onore"*, with all that that entails, and a desire to save his own skin. He won't sell-out any of his own men but as for the politicians he's working for.... I think if the price is right that he'll play ball.'

'And what is his price?' asked Paul, 'surely, almost anything is worth paying if it helps us to tidy up this mess.'

'He wants full immunity from prosecution for himself and for all his men and he also wants fifteen million Euros transferred to a bank account in The British Virgin Islands before he'll say anything… the immunity isn't a problem – I think that the signed piece of paper I have from the President allows me to do that, but I have no idea where I can get hold of fifteen million Euros… even the President can't just get hold of that sort of money.'

'There just might be a way,' said Francesca slowly, with a look at Ciancolini.

There was an uncomfortable pause and then the judge said, with an air of resignation, 'Go on… I'm sure I've already broken almost every guideline in the professional code of conduct… unless you're planning an armed robbery, I don't imagine things can get any worse.'

Well,' she said, with a look at Paul and her sister, 'Do you remember the year before last when I spent a couple of weeks in Sweden, following up links for a corruption story I was working on?' Rosa nodded. 'While I was there, I was introduced to a journalist called Larsson who's been working on corruption stories within Sweden… It seems that Larsson is writing a series of novels at the moment and has been researching a number of things outside his normal area of interest.' She paused again and the others looked at her expectantly while she took a sip of wine. 'Camilla, the friend I was staying with, made a comment about how securely things could be encrypted on the Dark Web, and Larsson laughed and said that while he'd been researching his novels he'd come across people who could break any encryption in a matter of minutes and do all sorts of amazing things. When we asked him for examples, he said it was possible to fit some sort of 'collar' around part of a server that would divert all internet traffic through a duplicate mirrored server.'

Paul and Ciancolini both looked at her with confused looks on their faces, but Rosa nodded in understanding, 'You mean so that when they think they're going online, everything they do is diverted through a system controlled by someone else, so that anything of interest can be filtered out or dealt with appropriately?'

'Brava,' said Francesca with a smile, 'that's it exactly.'

'I still don't get it,' grumbled Paul.

Rosa took his hand, 'If someone – let's say Stiappa – sends an e-mail to his mother saying "Happy Birthday", we, who will have control of the duplicate system, just let it go straight through, and the same with any reply. On the other hand, if we're expecting him to contact his bank then, as soon as he's entered his password, his online communication gets transferred to a mock-up of the bank's site… Once he's on there, the mock-up will behave in exactly the same way as the bank's own site would.'

'I've got it,' said Ciancolini, 'so when he's expecting fifteen million to appear in his account, fifteen million will appear in his account – but it won't really be his account,' he laughed *with relief.*

'Geniale,' said Paul, 'But what happens when he tries to spend the money?'

'He won't get the chance – or at least not until it's too late. He'll only have access to a computer to check that the transaction has gone through. I'm sure his account will be in some offshore bank that's beyond Italian jurisdiction, so once he knows that it's in there, he'll be sure that we can't take it back,' explained Francesca. She looked at Ciancolini, 'will the Brigadier be able to sort all this out?'

Ciancolini pulled a face and shrugged his shoulders to indicate that he had no idea, but then reached for his phone.

'Bernardo. It's me. Listen. I may have to pass you onto someone else who's somewhat more technically adept than I am, but I'll do my best to explain first.….. You know that Stiappa is demanding fifteen million…. Yes…. Before he's prepared to tell us anything…. Well; one of our colleagues has just mentioned something she was told about in Sweden a couple of years ago…. Yes, Sweden. Bear with me…. I know…. Apparently, it's possible to route all communications from a computer through a duplicate server, without the user being able to tell the difference…' He paused, partly to allow the Brigadier to ask for clarification if it wasn't clear, and partly so he could glance at Francesca for reassurance. She gave him an encouraging nod accompanied by a small smile. 'OK. The idea is this: at the appropriate time we tell Stiappa that the money has been transferred to the bank of his choice – obviously it will be a bank beyond Italian jurisdiction – OK so far? …. Good. Right. We then give Stiappa access to a computer so that he can log on to his bank, check his balance and do anything else he has been granted permission to do. Now, the clever bit is that when he logs into his bank, he will actually be logging into a fake duplicate bank site which, after taking him through all the appropriate security stages, will confirm that his money is sitting there, ready and waiting for him, or an associate of his, to spend it or do whatever else they wish to do with it. Once he's happy that the money is there we take the computer off him again for as long as he remains in custody. Well, what do you think? Can it be done?' Ciancolini leaned back in his chair and brushed a trace of sweat away from his forehead with his free hand while he waited for the Brigadier's response… 'OK Call me back.'

He looked at the others who looked back at him with eager anticipation, Francesca literally on the edge of her seat. 'He thinks so, but he needs to run it past one of his geeks. He thinks that setting up the fake bank site could be fairly complicated as we need to understand exactly how it works first before we can create a clone. He thinks he'll be able to give me answer in about ten minutes.'

The four wall-mounted monitors lit-up and cast a greenish hue over the desk where the PC gradually came to life. Marco minimised the Windows on the screen so that only a flashing cursor remained and then typed in the control string to access the Tor encryption programme. He smiled as he thought about the benefit he had gained from a spell in prison; if he'd been locked up with some mindless thug or opportunist thief, life would have been dull and unproductive, but making him share a cell with a computer fraudster had enabled him to learn all sorts of skills and tricks that he'd since been able to put to good use. Before his spell in prison, he'd vaguely heard of 'the dark web' but knew absolutely nothing about it; he'd been amazed to learn that contrary to public perception, the vast majority of what was on there was benign and there for legitimate reasons – it was only a small part that was used for criminal activities. There were all sorts of reasons for networks to be set up that couldn't be accessed from the surface of the web or found on any search engine. When he'd initially expressed scepticism. His cell-mate had explained it in simple terms by pointing out that institutions such as banks had to have a secure place to store passwords and PINs, that could be accessed by those with a legitimate reason but which would not be accessed by any outsiders. Marco now had two networks of his own: one which he used to store the security details of clients and their security systems, allowing him to carry out checks, upgrades or, if necessary, upgrades, and the other which he used for his own communications with Nico and Raffa, and where he stored information and links to areas which he was able to access using the hacking skills that he had also been taught in prison.

Another series of keystrokes brought up grainy, but adequate images on the wall-mounted monitors from the mini-security cameras that his two assistants had managed to install in various ministries. He watched them for five minutes, until he was fairly certain that he was unlikely to see anything of interest, and then turned his attention to the official electronic diaries of the various ministers who were suspected of involvement in the plot.

As before, he found nothing in any of the diaries that gave any clue as to possible targets for the "fireworks" mentioned in the communication that Raffaele had intercepted. All the ministers and under-secretaries seemed to be going about their normal business: Marelli had a series of fairly standard meetings programmed in Rome; Caprai was due to be guest of honour at the annual dinner and award presentations of his local football club; Vercellese had a meeting with a group of local government representatives in his office in Rome in the morning and then had tickets for the opera with his wife in the evening; Rossi had cancelled a planned meeting with union leaders in Livorno due to a family illness and

Beneventano would be on an official visit to meet his Croatian counterpart. Nothing!

Accessing the hidden sites of each of the main newspapers, to ensure that he didn't miss any stories that had not made the editorial cut, he skimmed through them to see if there was anything there that stood out as a potential target for a terrorist attack. A couple of the right-wing newspapers had short pieces about Mussolini's former right-hand man and son-in-law, Galeazzo Ciano, as it would have been his birthday, which Marco, as a keen student of history, dwelt on briefly, but there were no events in the country that he thought he would have picked if he had been a terrorist looking to make an impression.

Just over an hour later, feeling particularly frustrated by his lack of success, he closed down the system and made his way out of the building. Once outside, he gave careful looks in each direction before stepping out of the shelter of the doorway and, keeping in the shadows until he had passed three more doorways, made his way down the street.

'I've been cleared to make a transfer of ten million, but not a Euro more. Take it or leave it.'

Stiappa shook his head and looked the Brigadier directly in the eye, narrowing his eyes slightly and momentarily clenching his jaw, *'Quindici,'* he said flatly.

The Brigadier leaned back in his seat, rested his elbows on the armrests and joined his fingertips together so that his hands formed a cage like shape in front of him.

'I can't go to fifteen but I've got a bit of flexibility, although I'm sure you expected that.' He leaned down and extracted a laptop from a bag he'd placed on the floor by his feet when he'd entered the room.

'I need the account details in the Virgin Islands,' said the Brigadier, pushing over a sheet of paper and a pen.

'Phone,' said Stiappa, holding out a hand.

The Brigadier glanced at one of the two officers who stood on either side of the door and nodded. The officer slipped out of the door and the room returned to silence as they waited for his return. The Brigadier looked relaxed and, from the expression on his face, one would have thought that he was miles away, sitting on his balcony without a care in the world. Stiappa, on the other hand, looked tense and constantly made little adjustments to his position on his seat. The other officer by the door, remained motionless, apparently uninterested in the two protagonists in front of him, although since his colleague had left the room, his right hand had shifted so that it was closer to the shoulder-holster he wore on his left.

When the first officer returned, he silently handed a mobile phone over to the Brigadier who, without looking at it, slid it across the table, 'Be my guest – but don't talk about anything other than the account.'

Stiappa nodded and punched numbers into the phone.

'Gigi?….. *Totò sugno* ….. So, so. Listen; I need the BVI co-ordinates….. Yes, now….. OK I'll call you back in five minutes.' The Brigadier made a cutting motion with his left hand and Stiappa pressed the button to end the call and placed the phone down on the table in front of him.

'I need to…'

'I understood,' the Brigadier interrupted him, and then leaned back in his chair again apparently still completely relaxed. Stiappa tried to match the Brigadier's demeanour without quite managing it.

Finally, without looking at his watch, but precisely five minutes after Stiappa had put the phone down, the Brigadier nodded towards the phone. 'Make the call.'

Once again, the number was entered into the phone which was answered on the fourth ring.

'You got them?….. OK. Read them out slowly…………..' Stiappa began to jot down a long sequence of letters and numbers on the paper in front of him. 'Was that "*tre, sei*" or "*sei, tre*"?… Got it – Carry on……………… Now read it through again, slowly................. Alright. That's all...... No, not now.' and he brought the call to an end.

The Brigadier held out his right hand and Stiappa pushed both the phone and the sheet of paper back across the table.

With the sheet of paper to one side, the Brigadier began to type onto the laptop while Stiappa watched nervously. Finally, he turned the laptop round so that the screen was facing the other man.

'All you need to do is drag the pointer to the box on the bottom right hand side of the screen and click where it says "authorise" and the money should be in your account in minutes.'

The Brigadier kept his eyes fixed firmly on Stiappa's face as his eyes first scanned the screen and then moved carefully from left to right and from top to bottom. Despite his attempts to disguise his emotions, the trained eye of the Brigadier detected first surprise and then relief in the other man's face which he then tried to mask with feigned anger.

'It's only thirteen, I asked for fifteen. You'll have to increase it, or I won't do it.'

'You disappoint me, Stiappa. I told you that I had some room for manoeuvre and I've done you the courtesy of not haggling as if we were in the Grand Bazaar in Istanbul. I know that you're going to press that button and so do you, so do everyone a favour and press it now.'

'What happens if I press authorise and then don't have any useful information for you?'

'Scroll down to the next page, Stiappa.'

Stiappa looked puzzled but did as he was told and looked at the page in front of him, 'Only two million immediately?'

'That's right. You get two million now, as a gesture of good faith, and you start talking. In two hours' time, if we think we're getting our money's worth, you reconfirm and a further five million magically appears in your bank account. You then open up your heart for a further four hours and, if you've been a good boy, you reconfirm again and get the rest.'

'How do I know you won't go back on the deal when I've told you everything?'

The Brigadier smiled at him, 'You don't. You'll just have to hope that my word is as good as that of any *"uomo d'onore"* won't you.'

Stiappa sat, glowering at the Brigadier, who appeared totally unconcerned while the former clearly underwent an internal struggle before finally reaching forward and, after brusquely moving the mouse so that the pointer was over 'authorise', jabbed his finger down on the left hand button with a force that risked pushing it through the top of the table. 'Let's get on with it.'

'Don't sit down,' said fellow PA Maria-Carla Giustini as Francesca came through the door of the office they shared with two others. 'Ciancolini rang down; he wants the file he was looking at the other day. Said it was urgent and that you'd know what file he was talking about. He didn't sound in a very good mood – I said that if he told me the name of the file, I could take it up for him straight away as you weren't in yet. He put the phone down on me.'

Francesca gave a resigned sigh for the benefit of Maria-Carla, dropped her bag on her chair and draped her jacket across its back and then went over to the racks of shelves to retrieve the file that had served as a cover for their previous meeting in his office. 'I'll make a coffee as soon as I get back,' she said, and Maria-Carla nodded, her attention almost entirely focussed on finishing her nail-varnish.

'Have you seen the papers? … No… I assume not from the look of surprise on your face.' Ciancolini brusquely pushed a pile of the day's papers across the desk to her. With her right hand she spread the pile out so that most of each front page was exposed: "Return of the Red Brigade", "The ugly face of Socialism", "Bomb Blasts wreck ceremonies", "Child killed in politically motivated attack", and so on. 'What the hell is going on? At a delicate time like this, how can anyone on the left even conceive of doing something so stupid? This makes everything we're trying to achieve so much more difficult…'

Francesca did her best to shut out Ciancolini's nervous tirade as she read through the report in one of the less biased of the newspapers, trying to make sense of the information. When he realised she was paying no attention to him, he subsided into silence although he had unthinkingly picked up a pen which he tormented in his hand as he waited impatiently for her to speak. Finally she looked up with a furrowed brow, 'I don't understand. It says here that the six blasts all had significant elements in common, but I don't see what the logic is behind the choice of targets and why the right wing press have jumped to the conclusion that this is left-wing terrorism'.

'Look at that one,' he said, jabbing a finger towards the paper headed, "The ugly face of Socialism", and then continued without giving her time to follow his instruction. "Yesterday was – or would have been – the birthday of Count Galeazzo Ciano – Mussolini's son-in-law. Each of the six bombs was in a location with strong links to his life. For a long time he was seen as Mussolini's likely successor, so, according to *"Il Giornale"* today's extreme left-wingers have used the anniversary of his birth to warn that those who wish to move the country to the right are under threat. They've planted bombs near: his birthplace in Livorno; Venice and Genoa, the two places where he went to school; two locations in Rome where he lived at different times, and Verona where he was sentenced to death and executed – As a warning, it could hardly be more eloquent.'

Francesca sat down heavily on the chair facing Ciancolini across his desk. 'I still don't get it.'

'Look, Francesca; I'm a judge; I've always tried to keep out of politics because I believe that the judiciary should be above party politics. You got me involved in this because you brought me evidence that important people had been, and still were, breaking the law – putting the very principles on which the state is founded at risk. Now it's starting to look as if I've been drawn into one side of a battle where both sides are in the wrong, and I'm not sure I can carry on working like this. I think I need to present all my findings to the Ministry of Justice and let them take it on from there.' He looked desperately unhappy.

Francesca sat back in her chair for a minute, stunned by Ciancolini's change of heart then she suddenly exclaimed, *'Cazzo!'*

'Look, Francesca, I'm….'

'No! Listen. Think about it… those bombs weren't planted by the left at all. They were planted by the right, and they're having exactly the effect they were intended to have by stirring up feelings of revulsion against the left. Who's going to vote for parties that have supporters they can't control – who desecrate the memory of the dead and who are prepared to put children at risk.'

Ciancolini shook his head sadly.

'Think,' she said, now leaning forward urgently over the desk, 'Most Italians know very little about the Fascist period; it gets skimmed over in our schools, because, as a nation, we're still ashamed of our past. Because of that, most people only know very sketchy details. I bet that there's a majority of people in Italy now who haven't got a clue who Ciano was. Mussolini's descendants have always been allowed to live in peace but now they see that his 'family' is being attacked – and we all know that in Italy, "family" is still seen as being sacrosanct. If left wing terrorists were organised enough to set off six bombs almost simultaneously in places associated with Ciano, without any of them getting caught in the act, or blowing themselves up in the process, don't you think that there would have been more casualties?'

'A child was killed!'

'Very convenient for them! They've got a martyr without losing any of their voters. Look…' She reached for the article she had read before and, having quickly located the paragraph she wanted, pushed the paper over to him, finger next to the paragraph, 'Read that.'

'Lorenzo M. eight years old, was killed instantly by a shard of glass from a loose window pane dislodged by the blast. His father…'

'You see? Even the death was only indirectly the result of the blast! This isn't left wing terrorism; this is a political strategy by the right, worthy of Machiavelli.'

Ciancolini leaned back in his chair and tilted his head further back to look up at the ceiling while a flushed Francesca glared at him apprehensively.

'Go back to your office,' he said, suddenly letting his chair rock forwards. 'I need to think, and I need to speak to the President.'

'But…'

'No buts. Do as I say.'

Francesca picked up the unopened case file and, without another glance at him, left the room.

Back in her office, she felt too agitated to sit down and pretend that everything was normal so, without sitting down, she grabbed her bag and said to Maria-Carla and her other colleague, Stefania, who had now arrived, 'I'm going for a coffee. Back in ten minutes.'

Maria-Carla looked at Stefania and raised an eyebrow, 'Looks as if Ciancolini's being trying it on; whoever would have thought it of him!' Stefania giggled.

They were waiting for Marco when he got back to his flat in Via Topini and this time there were no warning signs in the street to prepare him. He had assumed that they would be irritated at having lost him earlier in the day and half expected that, at some point, he would receive another talking to; but he did not expect to be arrested. The same officer as before, with his two sidekicks, was again waiting for him, but this time, as soon as he walked through the door, his wrists were grabbed from each side, his arms pushed up his back and his ankles expertly hooked backwards so that he collapsed heavily and painfully to the floor.

A pair of snap-cuffs were placed on his wrists and a heavy boot pressed down on his neck banging his left cheekbone heavily against the marble tiles. A second boot, presumably belonging to the other officer, crashed into his ribs, driving all the breath out of him and causing excruciating pain. His pockets were turned inside-out and their contents either discarded on the floor or passed across to the officer in charge who calmly studied the items passed over to him.

After what seemed to Marco like ages, the officer looked at him and gave a little wave of his hand; the pressure on his neck was relieved and powerful hands got hold of his upper arms, pulled him upright and moved him roughly over to one of his own chairs, which had been moved from the table and placed in the middle of the room. His arms were placed over the back of the chair so that most of his weight rested on his strained shoulders rather than resting on the seat of the chair. He wanted to scream with the pain but was determined that he would resist as long as he could without.

'You've been wasting a good deal of our time, Antognoni, as well as not telling us the truth – not very wise tactics, as my men and I have important work to do, and I get a little upset when someone messes me around.'

Marco tried to be defiant, 'You can't…' The man nodded and a fist arched around from Marco's right hand side and caught him centrally, just below the ribcage.

'You appear not to fully understand your position, Antognoni,' said the man, shaking his head as Marco struggled to breathe. 'We do not have time for games and you need to make sure that there are no negatives in your answers to us and that you do not, in any way, presume to tell us what we can and cannot do. When you decided to spy on members of the government, you made yourself an enemy of the state and placed yourself beyond the protection of the law. You have no rights and you are going to give us all the information you have about what you have been doing with Petrini and Mecocci, and who you have been doing it for.'

Marco desperately tried to ignore the pain and gather his thoughts – Raffaele! They knew about Rafa as well. How? Had he been tailed to the Villa Borghese after all, despite his precautions? And if they had, did that mean that they'd tailed him to the basement in Via Favino? He didn't have to wait long before he knew the answer as, after a brief pause, the officer continued, 'Just so that you're not tempted to make up any more stories and waste more of our time, you may as well know that we know everything that Petrini knows already, but it appears that you are the one with the explanations we really want,' he smiled, 'and you're going to give them to us.'

Nico! It wasn't possible. 'I don't believe it.' he managed to get out through the pain that felt like shards of broken glass in his lower chest. He tried to slow his breathing down to put his ribs under less pressure.

'You know, I take it, that your friend Petrini has a child. It's curious how quickly people will tell you what you want to know, if their children are at stake. When he was shown a live CTV link to his son's nursery and when we pointed out the large car with the heavily tinted windows parked just by the point where his partner will cross the road after she's picked their son up, he became very talkative.'

'You bastard,' moaned Marco. The fist of one of his guards was pulled back to help improve his manners but a shake of the head from the officer in charge, caused it to be relaxed.

'Now that you can be under no more illusions, I think it would be a good idea if we got started. Now,' he said, turning over Marco's phone in his hand,' why don't you start by telling me how to get into the memory on this phone of yours.' Marco said nothing and the officer nodded at one of his assistants and glanced down at Marco's feet.

The heel of the man's foot came down hard on the top of Marco's foot and he groaned as waves of pain began to shoot up his leg. 'Our technicians will be able to extract all the information, but it would save everyone time, and you a great deal of pain, if you co-operate now.'

He knew that what he said was true; any IT professional, and many amateurs would be able to crack the security on the phone within minutes – if not seconds. But he also knew that the longer he was able to hold out, the more chance there was that the others would become aware that he had been arrested. He raised his face, noting as he did so, that the extra pressure that this put on his armpits and shoulders seemed to lessen somewhat the new pain in his foot. 'Go fuck yourself,' he said, almost hoping for more pain which he hoped would make him pass out.

The officer, however, knew his job too well to allow his victim to pass out. For the next three hours he inflicted constant pain on Marco, but occasionally poured water into his mouth to keep him conscious. Marco knew that he mustn't say anything at all; even if he told them things that they already knew to make the pain cease, he was aware that he wouldn't be able to stop himself continuing for fear that the pain would return again. He couldn't tell them how he had lost his tail in the morning because he hadn't suspected he was being followed; no, he couldn't tell them how he'd passed the day as he'd just wandered around aimlessly, thinking about the olive grove he wanted to buy one day – and no, he wasn't going to tell them why he'd been bugging ministerial offices.

Finally, Marco sagged and his head dropped forwards. The officer indicated to one of the other men that they should lift his head up again and, as he did so, roughly after grabbing a handful of Marco's hair, a trickle of deep red blood could be seen coming out of his mouth while the eyes were wide-open but apparently unseeing.

The officer frowned. 'Get a wet sponge from the bathroom and bring him round.' One of his assistants did so but, despite the sponge and a number of lighter slaps, fifteen minutes later they had to admit defeat.

'Alright. Let's get him down into the back of the car then, Di Livio, come with me to take him in, and you, Bertone, clean this place up then make your own way back.'

Di Livio went out of the door and returned five minutes later with a large zip-up canvas bag which he opened up on the floor next to the chair supporting Marco's slumped body. Marco was placed in the bag which was zipped up and then made its way, on Di Livio's shoulder, down the stairs and outside, where it was tipped into the back of an Alfa-Romeo 156.

Chapter 27

As Francesca bustled her way out of the *Palazzo di Giustizia*, barely acknowledging the doorman's friendly smile as she did so. She was seething inside. How could he? How could Ciancolini get cold feet now? Now, when they must be getting closer to the decisive point – now, when they had come so far, made so much progress, now that they were on the verge of preventing a coup. Ignoring the kiosk not far from the entrance where she was sure to have to make small-talk with people she knew who had slipped out for a crafty fag-break, she hurriedly crossed Viale Guidoni, attracting one angry gesture from a motorist who was forced to reduce his speed slightly as she crossed in front of him. The force with which she slapped her right palm into the crook of her left elbow, bringing the forearm up in the rudest gesture she knew, helped relieve a little of the tension she felt and, having walked along past the schools and the ethnic burger bar at the first junction, she felt much calmer by the time she entered the Amici Tuoi Bar where she ordered a cappuccino and a custard filled doughnut.

'OK if I take them outside,' she asked the bartender, who gave a shrug which she interpreted as acquiescence. A structure resembling a low budget conservatory had been erected across the pavement in two and a half of the spaces marked out for cars at the side of the road – she wondered how much it had cost to persuade the municipal police to turn a blind eye.

There was no-one else inside the structure and she sat at one of the five small white plastic tables facing back towards the *Palazzo di Giustizia*. As she began to eat her doughnut, she reached across to the next table for the newspaper that had been left there, and turned it round to face her. The headline on the front page was predictably to do with the bombings, and was one she had noticed back in the judge's office. What she hadn't noticed before, however, was the photograph of the blast scene below the fold on the front page.

The blast scene formed the background to the photograph, but in the foreground was the corpse of a young girl, a smile incongruously still on her face even though her body was transfixed by a long shard of glass. She placed the doughnut on the table, resting on the serviette with which it had been passed to her, and next to the *cappuccino*. She had seen pictures of bomb sites before and managed to maintain the emotional detachment she needed to do her job properly, but this was different. The smile on the child's face somehow made it impossible to remain detached – this was as striking as the award winning photo by Nick Ut of nine year old Kim Phuc running away from the South Vietnamese napalm attack; now she could understand why Ciancolini had been so nervous.

She knew that when she got back into the Palazzo she should go up and talk it through calmly with him. He wasn't doing this from any political motivation; she knew that he had agreed to take over the case from Arturo because he felt that it was the only way to uphold justice and the rule of law. She doubted whether, under normal circumstances, he would even consider voting for Prodi and The Olive Tree grouping. If she'd been able to put money on it, she would have guessed that ten years previously he'd been a died-in-the-wool Christian Democrat voter, although he would have scrupulously refused to admit it believing that the judiciary should be above politics. Just to be on the safe side, she decided to give Cecco Busoni a call; hopefully he could persuade the President to give a little encouragement to Ciancolini.

'Ciao, Francesca. This is an unexpected pleasure. Everything OK?'

'Everything's better for hearing your voice, Signor Busoni… Actually, I was hoping you could do me a little favour.'

'If I can, I will. Go ahead and ask.'

She explained about the effect the coverage of the bombings had had on Ciancolini and, while saying that she was sure he'd soon get over it, felt that a word of reassurance and encouragement from both his old friend and from above wouldn't go amiss.

Busoni immediately agreed with Francesca's hypothesis about the bombings and was just saying that he would have a word and find a way of getting through to the President again when Francesca stopped him. 'Wait!'

'What is it? What's wrong?' he asked, startled.

It's a raid! I'm not sure. I can't…' She gathered herself, 'While we were talking, six unmarked police cars drove up fast. Three went to the main entrance of the Palazzo and one to each of the others on this side – I assume more cars must have arrived at the back. They stuck one of the magnetic blue flashing lights on the top of cars and then four armed men got out of each car and rushed the entrances. One of them has stayed at each entrance to make sure no-one goes in or out.'

'Francesca,' said Busoni urgently, 'Where are you calling from?'

'I'm in a bar just down the road.'

'Ring off and go and mix with a crowd of onlookers until you know what's going on. Do not try to go back in, or go anywhere near those doors until you're sure it's safe to do so. Get out of the bar quickly so you don't run the risk of getting trapped in there. Ring me again when you know what's happening.'

'Alright. Thankyou.'

'Go. Now!' and he hung up on her.

Once outside the bar, Francesca moved back along the road until she could mingle with a group of parents which had formed outside one of the schools. Many were around her age, or not much older so she did not feel conspicuous. There was much excited muttering and shrugging of shoulders as members of the group enquired whether anyone knew what was going on. She heard several far-fetched theories advanced but none which seemed to have any ring of plausibility.

A navy-blue van of the type used by the prison service to transport high-security prisoners, but not bearing any markings, pulled in next to one of the unmarked police cars in front of the main door, and four more officers jumped out. One went inside, to exit again a couple of minutes later accompanied by one of the earlier arrivals. This latter evidently gave some instructions to the man from the van and then returned inside.

The instructions were clearly passed on to the other officers from the vehicle, one of whom stood by the driver's door while the other two opened the rear doors and stood, one to each side, sub-machine guns resting menacingly on their arms. Excitement and speculation were reaching fever-pitch amongst the small crowd that Francesca had joined and this became even more animated as first Ciancolini, and then, to her surprise, his tearful secretary, were led out of the building wearing handcuffs.

Ciancolini was helped up into the back of the van, where he was joined by the two guards who had been standing by the rear doors. The doors were then closed by the driver who returned to his place and, after activating blue flashing lights that were set into each corner of the van's roof, started the engine and pulled rapidly away. Ciancolini's secretary was taken to one of the other cars where the remaining guard from the van opened one of the rear doors and, placing a hand on her shoulder, guided her inside. The guard then also got in and sat to one side of her while one of the original officers opened the door on the far side and hemmed her in from there.

Once the van containing Ciancolini had pulled out, the crowd of onlookers began to gradually disperse and Francesca decided it was wise to drift away with them while trying to keep the Palazzo in view for as long as possible. As she began to move away she saw several of the original officers exit the Palazzo from the entrances at either end, cross the road and begin to check the few shops and businesses on the other side, including the bar where she had previously been. Fortunately, having already moved along the street she was able to escape their pincer movement although she had no doubt that they were looking for her.

Taking out her phone, she tapped in Marco's number; the phone gave three rings and then her display indicated that it had been answered, but there was no friendly voice at the other end. She was about to say his name then she stopped; although his phone would not show her name, it would show which phone was calling – there was something very wrong. She pressed the red button to end the call and, after stepping off the road into a side entrance back against the wall to try and get her thoughts together.

There was something wrong, something very wrong. She closed her eyes and took a number of deep breaths. The only explanation she could come up with for Marco's phone was that it had to be in someone else's possession and that... that, she realised with a burning sensation in her chest, could only mean that he had been arrested. She had to shut down her emotions and try to think rationally: Ciancolini definitely and probably Marco – who else could they get to?

They came for Paul much more discretely than they had come for Ciancolini and Francesca. Arrests made at the *Palazzo di Giustizia* were going to be noticed so they might as well be dramatic to maybe panic other people into making mistakes, and to allow them to control the news agenda. The arrest of a part-time photographer and junior member of staff at the university however, offered much less scope for propaganda and could therefore be done quietly and efficiently.

He had walked into the university rather than using his bike as the weather was fine and sunny but not yet so hot as to make walking unpleasant. Passing through the large gateway in Piazza Brunelleschi he gave a moment's consideration to popping into the faculty's bar for a coffee, but decided that he'd rather get his lesson out of the way first and then treat his coffee as a reward. Entering into the main building on the other side of the former cloister, he nodded a distracted *buongiorno* to the caretaker in his glass cubicle and began to climb the steps behind.

The small room set aside for the use of the *lettori* was almost at the end of the corridor to the left and, as he walked towards it, he pulled out his keys and selected the correct one. He was surprised to find that the door was unlocked and had been left ajar. One of the other *lettori* must have forgotten something the previous evening and popped in to get it – he wondered which one it was.

'*Buongiorno*. You're early this morning…' he began cheerfully as he pushed the door wide open – then he stopped. There were two people he didn't expect in the room: one of them - a man he didn't know – had his back to the door and was going through the contents of his locker, having already dropped half the contents onto the floor. The other, a slim woman with close-cropped short hair of indeterminate colour and a slightly hooked nose over a narrow pointed chin, was the woman who had interrogated him after the explosion. The woman's right hand was resting on the desk, and in it, pointed generally in his direction was some kind of a gun. Paul stopped, unable to refocus his mind quickly enough from the lesson he'd been mentally rehearsing on the disappearing subjunctive mood in English, to be able to react immediately to the new situation.

'Sit down Mr Caddick' said the woman, almost tonelessly, flicking the barrel of the gun casually towards an empty chair as she did so.

'But what the…'

'I said, "sit down",' she interrupted brusquely. Paul sat down.

The woman pushed an ID card across the desk, identifying her as a Colonel Nicolini of SISMI; Paul gave her a puzzled look.

'What's SISMI?' he asked.

She ignored the question, replacing the ID into her pocket. 'How well do you know Marco Antognoni?' She fixed her eyes on him.

Paul pursed his lips and shook his head, hoping that he was managing to convey regret at not being able to help her.

She looked down at her lapel and, with the tips of the fingers of her free hand casually brushed away some miniscule speck of dust that she had spotted on her uniform. Then, she looked Paul directly in the face again and placed her hand inside her jacket, from where she extracted a small plastic pouch. Without taking her eyes away from his, she turned the pouch over revealing a photograph which she placed in front of him.

'Let me give you a word of advice Mr Caddick,' - she managed to make the English title sound both out of place and threatening, - You will shortly be coming with us to answer some questions in a more formal setting – but, it will be much easier for everyone if you begin by demonstrating your willingness to co-operate immediately. Marco Antognoni is the man in the picture. Please look very carefully and then try to answer my question again.'

Paul looked down and saw a fairly clear photograph of Marco and Francesca talking together and holding hands at what appeared to be a table in a bar. He felt his chest constrict, 'That's my sister-in-law,' he said, confident that, if they'd got this far, they surely already knew who Francesca was.

'I didn't ask about the woman, Mr Caddick; I asked about the man.'

Paul shrugged, 'He must be a friend of my sister-in-law. Why, has he done something wrong? He hasn't done anything to Francesca, has he?' he asked, in an attempt to feign anger to cover up the fear he was feeling.

Again she ignored his question and, reaching into her pocket, pulled out two more photographs. The first was a very grainy still picture, presumably taken from a CCTV camera of Marco entering the small restaurant near Trastevere. She did not immediately turn over the second photograph but Paul knew what it would show. He raised his eyebrows in surprise – how could they possibly have been keeping them under such close observation for so long, and not have done anything.

As if she read his thoughts, the woman said, 'Although we're not as obsessed as you English about watching every move that our citizens make, we do use technology during appropriate investigations and we have suspected for some time that this restaurant has been used as a place to deliver consignments of drugs. Imagine our surprise when we identified amongst the clients this man, who has done time in prison although not for drugs.' Paul was silent. 'Do you take drugs, Mr Caddick? … No? … No, I didn't think you did – and I don't think Antognoni is involved with drugs either. That's not why you met him there, is it?' She flipped over the last photograph: even grainier than that of Marco, but undeniably him.

'I chose that restaurant by chance. It was just in the right place at the right time; I didn't take any notice of any of the other customers.'

Nicolini rolled her eyes and turning her head towards the other man in the room said, 'You done yet?'

'I am. I've got everything that might be useful, Maam.'

She turned back to Paul. 'I could cuff you, but we don't want to distract the students, do we, so I suggest that we leave the building nice and quietly. I'll go in front, and my colleague here will bring up the rear.'

'I need to put up a notice cancelling my lesson.'

Nicolini shook her head. 'It's all been taken care of – your lessons have been cancelled... indefinitely.'

Five minutes later, Paul had been taken through the rear entrance of the building, into the underground car-park where he was unceremoniously bundled into the back of a waiting Giulietta. He was sat behind the driver, who had been waiting by the car; Nicolini sat in the front passenger seat, half turned so that her revolver was pointing vaguely in his direction, and the other man sat alongside him, now linked to him by a pair of hand-cuffs.

Once in motion, the Giulietta smoothly took the ramp up to ground level, turned left and slowly covered the forty metres to the barrier, which rose automatically as the vehicle approached and then turned right onto Via degli Alfani and sped away, using headlights and the occasional blast of the horn to clear bicycles and pedestrians out of the way.

At the end of the road, the driver slowed and then, turning left, sped up again giving a long blast on his horn before making his way alongside Piazza d'Azeglio to the Viali. As usual there was heavy traffic on the Viale so, as soon as he had eased out into the flow of traffic, he lowered his window and reached out to fix a magnetic blue-flashing light onto the roof. As soon as he had withdrawn his hand, he swapped hands on the wheel and, with his temporarily free right hand pressed a button to activate the car's siren.

As the car cut through the traffic on Viale della Giovane Italia, Paul wondered if they were heading for the motorway on their way to Rome, but almost immediately after reaching the Arno, the car pulled to the left, cut through a gap in the verge between two trees, and across a service road to two high metal gates. A *carabiniere* appeared on the other side and then hurried back inside when he recognised the car. Ten seconds later the gates began to swing open, admitting the car to a small courtyard. Inside, they turned right and squeezed through a small arch leading to a second courtyard, completely surrounded by high buildings and, because of this, in deep shade everywhere.

Nicolini and the driver both got out of the front and the driver walked round and opened Paul's door. The guard to whom he was handcuffed indicated that they should slide across and get out of the opened door.

Once out of the car, a firm hand on his shoulder guided Paul towards a doorway where the Nicolini was already being admitted; reluctantly Paul moved towards the doorway, glancing upwards as he did so at the rectangle of open sky above. As he did so, a bird flew across the rectangle appearing to emerge precisely from one corner, trace a perfect diagonal and then disappear from the opposite corner. It was the first bird he could recall having seen above the city that year and he wondered fleetingly what people who believed in omens might have made of it.

As they entered the building, the single bulb hanging from the ceiling in the small reception area was not much of an improvement on the gloomy, high-sided courtyard outside and the walls, which looked urgently in need of a new coat of white-wash did little to bring any cheer to the area. There was a young carabiniere behind the desk, watching straight-backed as Nicolini replaced the desk's phone on its cradle, presumably having announced their arrival to some higher power.

The only embellishments on the fading whitewash were the obligatory photograph of the current President of the Republic, a crucifix that wasn't quite hanging straight and a small notice-board to which three pieces of paper were attached with drawing pins. Paul felt sorry for the young carabiniere if he had to pass his whole day there.

'This way,' said Nicolini without looking at him, moving over to the far wall and opening a door which, apart from a small, worn brass handle, had been over-painted with whitewash and blended in with the rest of the room.

As the door was opened, Paul glimpsed a long corridor beyond. Again lit by artificial light and surmounted by a series of intersecting barrel vaults, indicating that the building had either been part of a monastery at one time or its architect had been inspired by cloisters, the corridor offered little indication that this was going to be a pleasant experience. The officer who had driven the car, removed the handcuffs and, placing a hand on his shoulder, indicated that he should follow Nicolini without delay.

To the right hand side of the corridor, the archways formed by the columns supporting the arches had been bricked up, each around a metal door and two small windows about fifty centimetres long and thirty deep. Below each window was a shelf holding a machine that looked like a tape-recorder with two pairs of headphones attached. The shelves also held note pads and pens. Paul realised that the windows must contain one-way glass and that there was probably an interrogation cell behind each of the doors. The first of the cells was in darkness but realising what the rooms were, he tried his best to get a glimpse through the other windows as he passed.

The second cell was also empty; he got a quick glimpse of a man sitting with his head in his hands in the third room and in the fourth room was Rosa.

He stopped suddenly, causing the following guard, who still had his hand on his shoulder, to walk into the back of him. 'My wife!' he exclaimed, considerably more worried than he had been a few moments before.

'Move on,' said the guard, increasing the pressure on his shoulder. With a concerned glance back over his shoulder towards the second of the two small windows, Paul complied. Seconds later, Nicolini pushed open the heavy metal door of another, identical room and stepped to one side allowing her colleague to guide Paul through the doorway which was quickly filled as the door clanged closed behind him, echoing around the bare walls.

Left on his own, Paul's reflex reaction was to try the door which, he was not surprised to find was firmly locked and without a handle on the inside. Then, he looked carefully at the room he was in. About three metres wide, one end was dominated by the grey metal door through which he had entered and the two grey rectangles flanking it; although he knew that they were windows, he found it difficult to think of them as such as they were completely opaque from the inside. The room, or cell, was roughly four metres long and the only furniture was a plain metal table that appeared to be anchored in the floor about two thirds of the way down the room and an uncomfortable looking metal chair, similarly anchored to the floor, that had been placed on the far side of the desk. As if the one-way observation windows were not enough, he noted that high up in one corner of the room was a camera with what he assumed was a microphone just below it. Apart from the two grey rectangles and the camera, the walls and ceiling were bare except for a bright strip-light parallel to the wall with the door and about a metre into the room. Assuming that the anchored chair was for the interviewee, the light would shine fully on the prisoner while making it difficult for the prisoner to see the faces of the interviewers clearly.

He wondered whether any communication with Rosa would be possible and tried knocking on the wall that separated them, but found that it had been papered, or coated, with some soft material that would not only deaden the sound of any knocking but which would prevent other noises from passing as well. Not knowing how long he would have to wait before he was questioned, Paul began to walk circuits of the room, occasionally turning round and changing direction to relieve the boredom. The only thing he could do was to stick to his agreed story; all he had done was to take photographs for a prospective book. Francesca had insisted when he'd made his first trip to Rome, that he mention the book somewhere it would be remembered on the basis that it gave him an alibi should he need one later on. He'd not been convinced by the plan originally, but now, he was glad that, if necessary, he could tell his interrogators to check out his story with the police who had been on duty at the Defence Ministry in Via Castro Pretorio. It was unfortunate that both he and Marco had been picked up by the CCTV cameras going into the same small restaurant but he would just have to try and pass that off as coincidence; it was lucky that they hadn't had CCTV cameras inside the restaurant. Even if they weren't convinced that it was coincidence, he had to keep insisting that it was. Fortunately, he didn't think that he'd mentioned the meeting to Rosa, so she would be able to respond with genuine surprise if she were questioned about it. Surely, even if they kept him in custody, they would have to let Rosa go.

Heading away from the *Palazzo di Giustizia* area, Francesca decided that it was not a good idea to head directly towards the centre, and she knew that to either go home or to her parents' house was out of the question. Reluctantly she jettisoned both her phones in a convenient rubbish bin; she had a vague idea that there were ways of tracking the locations of mobile phones even when they were not in use and knew that she couldn't take the risk. She would somehow have to procure herself another. The other thing she knew that she needed to do urgently was to withdraw as much money as should on her cards before they were blocked – if they hadn't been already.

She was lucky; both her credit and debit cards were still functioning when she tried them in the *bancomat* at the Banca dei Monti dei Paschi di Siena on Via di Novoli five minutes later, managing to withdraw four hundred and twenty euros to go with just over a hundred she already had in her purse. At least now she had enough money to be able to survive for some time without giving away her location. After leaving the bank, she doubled back through a park, passing close by the Palazzo di Giustizia again, reasoning that close to where she had started would probably be the last place they would be looking for her. In fact, as she recrossed Viale Guidoni, she could see that all the unmarked cars except one had now left the Palazzo and there only appeared to be one person left guarding the main entrance.

Once she was away from the Viale and threading her way through the working class residential area of Firenze Nova, she felt safer and could turn her mind to deciding where to go, and what she could do next. Fortunately, not having used the bike that morning meant that she did not stand out because of her clothing and should be able to get around without being noticed, unless she were very unlucky. Several old school-friends had lived in the Rifredi area beyond the railway and she thought that, as was fairly common in Florence, many of them would have stayed fairly local. The problem was, of course, deciding which ones, and knowing whom she could trust.

Maybe Elena, she thought. When they'd been at the *scuola media*, twenty years earlier, they had been inseparable for a couple of years, before the different academic paths that they had chosen had gradually loosened the bond as each had made new friends. But they'd never had any kind of falling out and, on the rare occasions when they had bumped into each other over the last few years they had always got on well and promised each other that they would meet up when they had more time. The other advantage with Elena, she thought was that she knew where to find her; from an early age, Elena had known that she was destined to take over the family business, running two shops that sold electrical goods. One of the shops was on the other side of the city but the original, and larger outlet was not far from Piazza Dalmazia in the heart of the Rifredi area.

Her hopes high, she threaded her way through the perpetual heavy traffic of the Piazza and made her way up the first part of the wide *viale* leading towards Careggi hospital until she could turn left into the short road where the shop was situated. Then she stopped, dismayed. Where 'Mattolini Elettrodomestici' had proudly stood since the nineteen-fifties, there was now an internet cafe.

She stood for a moment, completely disoriented, then realised that it must be over a year since she had last passed that way and even longer since she had last seen Elena. With a sigh, she went over to the door where red plastic letters had been applied to the inside of the window informing her that the 'café' was open from seven in the morning until midnight and that she could also do her printing there.

With an even deeper sigh she pushed the door open and stepped inside. A glass sided cubicle had been erected just inside the door on the left, for the use of the manager, if that wasn't too grand a title for him. As in other internet-cafes that she had noticed around the city, the man who looked her over as she entered was of North African origin, probably Tunisian or Algerian and, to judge by his clothing, was probably not particularly well-paid. The keyboard of the master computer that shared the cubicle with him had been pushed to one side and, in the space which it normally occupied was a pile of forms that he had clearly been in the process of completing together with two other young North Africans who were sitting on a pair of old bar-stools facing the cubicle. To her right was a row of eight well-used desktop computers, each faced by a red plastic-backed chair and separated from its neighbour by screens made out of plywood. Behind the cubicle was a cluster of telephone-booths where a sign told her that internet calls could be made to over fifty countries for less than fifty cents per minute. One of the computers and three of the phones were in use as Francesca looked around. None of the users appeared to be Italian.

'Computer or telephone?' asked the North African, looking up from the pile of forms.

'Francesca gave an apologetic smile. 'Not at the moment I'm afraid. I was wondering, do you by any chance know what happened to the people who ran the Electrical shop that used to be here?' she asked although without much hope of success. He raised a shoulder slightly and pursed his lips to indicate that he couldn't provide the answer.

'OK Not to worry. Sorry to have troubled you.' and she left the shop.

Taking stock of the situation outside, she noticed that there was a baker's across the road which she was fairly sure had always been there – or at least for as long as she remembered. With a bit of luck they would be able to tell her what had happened to Elena's family, as well as giving her the opportunity to buy a sandwich for her lunch.

There was only a single girl working in the shop and, as she didn't look to be much over twenty, Francesca's hopes sank again as she entered, but this time she was to be pleasantly surprised. She had to wait while two other customers were served and took the opportunity to chat with each other about a range of subjects from the "scandalously" high price of fruit to the difficulty of parking near the hospital. Finally, after they had pronounced on all the major issues of the day and paid for their purchases, they left the shop leaving Francesca alone with the girl behind the counter.

'Could I have a slice of that rustic pizza please?… Yes – that one – the one with the *salamino* on top… thanks.'

'Anything else, signora?'

While cringing slightly at having been addressed as though she were a middle-aged matron by the younger woman, Francesca gathered herself together, 'Yes please. I'll have a *budino di riso* as well.' As the girl reached down for one of the rice-based cup-cakes, Francesca added, 'Maybe you could help me.' The girl looked at her with a smile. 'I used to know the family that owned the Electrical shop across the road… the one that's now an internet-cafe…' she gestured towards what had formerly been Elena's shop. 'I don't suppose, by any chance, that you happen to know where they are now, do you?'

The girl's smile broadened as she carefully placed the *budino di riso* in a paper bag on the counter next to the slice of pizza. 'Oh, you mean the Mattolinis. I didn't really know the old couple; I saw them occasionally when I was a girl but they'd retired and passed the shop onto Elena before I started working here regularly – it's my parents' shop really. I think they live somewhere over beyond Scandicci now, towards Vingone.' Francesca's heart sank. 'That's the old couple of course, Elena got married just before they sold the business, and they've got their own place towards Cercina.'

The shock of finding out how out of touch with her old friends she had become, was almost greater than the shock of everything else that had happened that morning. She was speechless for a moment and then. 'I hadn't realised how long it must have been since I last saw Elena… as far as I know, she didn't even have a boyfriend last time I saw her, let alone a husband.'

The girl looked carefully to each side, even though they both knew that they were alone in the shop, and then leaned forward conspiratorially towards Francesca, 'They say that it was one of these internet dating things – can you imagine!' With the benefit of an extra fifteen years' experience and having seen how difficult it could be for busy people to meet potential soulmates, Francesca thought that, yes, she could imagine it but, instead of destroying the girl's youthful romantic illusions she limited herself to making an indistinct sound that could be interpreted however the listener wished.

'It's a shame they're not there anymore… I'd have liked to have seen Elena again. What do I owe you?' she said, pushing a five euro note across.

The girl rang the amounts for the two items into the till and, as she sorted out the change, said, 'I can give you Elena's phone number, if that's any help.'

'That would be fantastic.'

'Just give me a minute,' said the girl, handing Francesca her change, 'I'll have to get it out of the book in the back; I don't think I've got it stored in my phone.'

No longer the possessor of a phone and not wishing to make the call from a public phone in a bar, Francesca found a *tabaccaio* where she could purchase a ten-euro phone-card, and then, at the third attempt, a phonebox in working order. With a feeling of excitement, she tapped in the number.

'Pronto,'

'Pronto. Elena?…. *Sono* Francesca… Francesca Conte.'

There was a brief pause and then what seemed to be an explosion at the other end of the line, 'Franci! Where are you? What are doing? When are you coming to see me? Why haven't you rung for so long … I've got so much to tell you.'

When she managed to get a word in edgeways, and after apologising profusely for having lost touch, Francesca agreed that she would come and see her friend that evening and, yes, she'd be delighted to stay the night. As the house was more than a kilometre away from the bus stop in Cercina along several tiny side-roads and tracks, it was agreed that Elena would get her husband to pick

Francesca up from the entrance to the small private carpark next to the parish church of Saint Pius X at about half past six. Francesca got the registration number of Elena's husband's car from her and assured her friend that she would be there at quarter past six, just in case traffic was surprisingly light, and that she would not worry if he was held up before he got to her. She also asked what she could bring along with her and was told not to be ridiculous, a reaction she determined to ignore and instead bought the best bottle of *prosecco* that she could find.

She easily recognised the little green four by four Panda as it pulled into the little carpark just after ten to seven; the four by fours had never been a common sight in the city and now that the new, curvier version was available, even the standard Pandas seemed to be disappearing rapidly. The driver, who was dressed in a smart business suit that seemed out of place in the rustic vehicle, leaned over and wound the passenger window down to check he was picking up the right woman.

Once she was inside and they had introduced themselves, she was able to study him as he pulled back out into the traffic. He was a tall man, although it was hard to judge exactly in the cramped car and, from his profile, seemed to have an angular face which, although not handsome had a reassuring air about it. His hair was swept back and she was fairly sure that he was thinning on top; she guessed that his age must be somewhere between forty-five and fifty – probably closer to the top end.

He turned off the busy road almost immediately and made his way carefully past the area of sixties housing and along the narrow lanes that led to the Medicean villas of Castello and La Petraia before doubling back past Villa La Quiete and dropping down almost to the rear of Careggi Hospital. Instead, however, of following the road around the rear of the hospital, he turned off to the left and began to climb the narrow road that led up towards Cercina on the slopes of Monte Morello.

They spoke little as driving along the narrow lanes, which were often flanked by high walls or banks, and seemed to have countless blind-bends, required maximum concentration from the driver. At one point, Francesca commented that if she had to drive there she'd be worried about meeting someone coming the other way on one of the bends. He smiled and, without looking at her, replied that it wasn't the cars that were the problem, as most drivers using that road were aware of the care required; the problem was the wild boar which would occasionally wander out of the trees at dusk. Although they would usually scramble away and try not to be seen, just occasionally, particularly if they had young with them, they would see cars as a threat to be challenged. She understood why, despite the smart suit, he had decided that an old Panda four by four with the incongruous looking bull-bars on the front was a wise choice.

When they reached the romanesque church at Cercina with its rough stone bell-tower, Fabrizio, as she had discovered his name was, swung to the left along an even narrower road that passed along the side of the slope between olive groves and clusters of trees. After a while he slowed right down and turned onto a rough track between the trees. Almost immediately the track dropped down and emerged below the group of trees into a paved area by the side of a large converted barn.

A large terrace ran all along the side of the barn that faced down the slope with an outdoor table and chairs sitting in the shade of two large fig trees. Below the house were about twenty mature olives and a number of other fruit trees that appeared to have been planted more recently. Several smaller outbuildings were set against the hillside behind the barn and, at the far end, a large sun-lounge had been added on. Through the olives, she could see that there was a large flat paved area with a tarpaulin covering what must be a pool in the middle. Fabrizio glanced round at her and smiled. 'Come on. Let's not keep her waiting.'

Elena had heard the car, or the dogs had, which amounted to pretty much the same thing. As Francesca turned from closing the door of the Panda, she found herself enveloped in an enthusiastic hug and her cheeks covered in kisses, while at the same time staggering against the weight of the labrador that jumped up against her. 'Ginger! Down!' she heard Fabrizio shout, and the weight was removed.

'Franci. I can hardly believe you've come. You can tell me all about all the exciting things you've been doing. You're looking wonderful as always. When are you going to get married? Have you met the right man yet?'

Francesca laughed for what seemed like the first time for ages, and managed to hold her friend at arm's length. 'Never mind me. What's this?' she said making a gesture with her left arm that encompassed the house, the grounds and Fabrizio, 'and even more importantly, what about this?' she asked, her eyes falling on Elena's belly. Elena flushed with pleasure and pulled Francesca gently towards the house.

'Come on, we can start talking while I finish getting the dinner ready.'

Francesca knew that there was no escape from everything that had happened and that before the end of the evening she would have to ask for Elena's help, and probably Fabrizio's too, but for now she felt she owed it to her friend to let her enjoy telling her all her news, and so she insisted that wanted to be brought completely up to date before she would say anything about herself.

'… Sales had been steadily dropping off for some time. It started even before Mum and Dad retired and passed the business on to me. The repairs side was doing alright but hardly anyone was buying new machines anymore. There were plenty of people coming into the shop and they'd ask all about the different types of washing-machine or fridge, have a look and try and imagine them in their own houses, then we'd never see them again. Of course, what they were doing was coming in and making use of our knowledge to help them decide on the models they wanted and then ordering from one of the big national mail delivery stores. I spent ages trying to think of some way of turning the business round without coming up with anything – and then I met Fabrizio.'

'He seems nice.'

Elena smiled, ' "Nice" doesn't really do justice to him. I met him through the church; Don Ostelio had set up a computer club in the Parish room and we met there. I wanted to learn how to make a website because I thought it might help the business, and a friend of Fabrizio had dragged him along because he hadn't been going out since his first wife had died.'

'Did you know her?'

'No. She died two years before I met Fabrizio and she'd been ill for several years before that – Motor Neurone Disease – he doesn't like talking about it so I don't push him. Every so often he'll tell me a bit more about her but I think he's worried I might feel jealous.'

'And do you?'

Elena laughed, 'Not in the least. I don't begrudge him any happiness he had in the past, so long as he's happy with me.'

Francesca leaned over and gave her friend a kiss on the cheek, 'How could he not be. Anyway. Go on. I want to know the whole story.'

Elena, who was a naturally outgoing person, had made an effort to talk to Fabrizio as he always seemed to hold back from the rest of group and she thought he had looked sad. The first time, she had been politely rebuffed but when Elena thought she was doing something worthwhile she persisted. There had been no thought initially of developing any kind of deeper relationship but, once they had broken the ice and begun to talk about things that were not computer related, they had found that they enjoyed each other's company and things had developed from there. One day, Fabrizio had told her that there was something he wanted to show her and, without telling her where they were going, he had driven her up to the almost complete barn conversion.

The conversion, and the landscaping had been undertaken by an uncle of his, who he didn't really know but who had died both childless and intestate eighteen months earlier. The notary dealing with the estate had eventually tracked down Fabrizio and two cousins, both of whom lived abroad and had no interest in owning property in Tuscany. By using all his savings, Fabrizio had enough money to buy out the interests of the two cousins, but he didn't really fancy moving up into the hills if he didn't have someone to share his life with. Elena had continued to gush about how wonderful the place was and wax lyrical about the view and the potential for the house, until he had got hold of her shoulders and told her to shut up and listen. She had still not believed that he really meant it until he had produced an elegant diamond and ruby ring and slipped it onto her finger.

She had expected some opposition from her parents, mainly because Fabrizio was twelve years older than her, but they were delighted when they met him, especially when Fabrizio agreed to play chess with her father at least once a week. They also raised no objection when she had suggested closing down the business and selling off the properties. She had done everything she could to make it a success so that they would not see the business they had spent so many years building up disappear, but they both assured her that it would be a weight off their minds knowing that she was free of the responsibility and hard work while the sale of the properties should make her financially secure for life. As for the news that they were to be grand-parents, well that had been the icing on the cake for them – her mother rang at least twice a day to check on her progress and offer advice.

Francesca did her best to push thoughts of Marco, Ciancolini, and her family to the back of her mind as Elena told her story as they finished preparing the dinner and then ate their way through the magnificent array of food, but when they reached coffee and Fabrizio got out a bottle of grappa, she knew that she could put it off no longer.

'Look, Elena, I know we should have got together ages ago and had an evening like this, and I know it's my fault that we haven't, but when I rang you today, it was because I knew I could trust you probably more than anyone else. But I want to be honest with you so you can tell me to go if you want.'

She felt nervous and knew that she had expressed herself very badly. Elena looked puzzled but Fabrizio looked at her and said calmly, 'You're in some sort of trouble, aren't you,' it was a statement rather than a question.

'Big trouble,' she sighed, 'although I haven't done anything wrong... certainly not morally.' Elena reached out a hand and placed it over Francesca's while her other hand moved unconsciously over her belly, as if to protect her unborn child.

'You can rely on us absolutely. I know you well enough to know that you'd never do anything that would hurt other people. Anything we can do to help you, we will.'

'Thankyou. But you'd better wait till you know everything before you make statements like that.' She smiled and turning her hand over underneath Elena's, she squeezed her friend's hand. She looked around, 'You don't have a television here, do you?'

'We do,' said Fabrizio, but the signal is so bad that we never bother putting it on.'

'Well,' said Francesca, 'I'm pretty sure that on the regional news bulletin, if not the national one, there will be news of a raid this morning at the *Palazzo di Giustizia*, carried out by Special Forces. Depending how much information they decide to give, it may well also say that during the raid they arrested Judge Ciancolini and have made other arrests through the city. They may also say that they are looking for at least one other person – If they do, then that other person is me.' She paused and studied their faces: Elena looked pale but Fabrizio was impassive.

'Last year, when I was working on a corruption story involving a government minister, I came across information that suggested that there was a group of people including some members of the current government who would stop at nothing to ensure that the country returns another right wing government at the next election – and by "nothing" I mean that defamation, blackmail and even murder, form part of their tactics.'

'Surely not,' said Elena, 'You must have misunderstood somehow.'

Francesca shook her head sadly and continued, 'Do you remember the judge blown up in a car-bombing a few months ago here in Florence? Yes? Well that was part of it. Remember Loredana Cabrini-Pellé? Well that was murder! Have you heard of the Mitrokhin Commission that's meant to be investigating claims made by a Russian defector and who keep leaking information to the press that's damaging to the leaders of the left? Well that's part of it as well.'

'I think we'd better sit somewhere more comfortable,' said Fabrizio, 'I suspect that this is going to be a very long evening.'

'Alright,' said Fabrizio nearly three hours later, glancing at Elena who had fallen asleep on the settee some time before, 'If I've understood you correctly the key points are these; firstly, at any time after Prodi publicly agrees to lead the left coalition there may well be an attempt on his life which, the right will portray as the result of left-wing infighting and betrayal, justifying a harsh crackdown; secondly, the people will be so frightened by the prospect of a return to the 'years of lead' that they will overwhelmingly vote in an extreme right-wing government and, last but not least, you, your boyfriend, your friend the judge, your brother-in-law and a number of other people who you have quite sensibly avoided naming, will either meet with accidents or spend the rest of your natural lives on some high security prison island. Have I got it right?'

'Yes. That's about it.'

'But,' continued Fabrizio, holding up a finger to stop her, 'the President of the Republic,' is aware of the situation and would be prepared to stick his head above the parapet if you can assure him that you have evidence that would stand up in court, and you do have some people who you know you can trust within the security services.' Francesca nodded.

'Right,' he said, planting his feet firmly on the floor and pulling on the front of the arms of the high-backed rocking chair in which he'd been sitting. 'First thing to do is to make sure that we all get enough sleep… in sensible positions, ' he added, looking at his wife in the corner of the settee. 'And then, in the morning, I'll try and find out what's happened to your judge and the rest of your family.'

Francesca shook her head as she rose and glanced towards Elena, 'No. You've got them to think about. I don't want you getting involved any further – you've been really helpful already, giving me somewhere to stay for the night, and an opportunity to talk things through and get them clearer in my own head. But...' she said, cutting him off as he was about to object, 'there is one thing you could do for me... I need the home address of a police commissioner, if that's at all possible.'

In the morning, before Fabrizio left at half past seven, Francesca made them both promise that if the police or other security forces came asking, they should not deny having seen her because if the police came it would mean that they already knew. What they should tell the police should be as close to the truth as possible, leaving out only the explanation that she had given them and the fact that Fabrizio was trying to obtain Vichi's address. 'It was,' she said, highly unlikely that she would be traced there, but that if she were, then the more honest they appeared, the better it would be.

After Fabrizio had gone, she persuaded Elena to cut her hair for her and borrowed a very unflattering jacket and an old pair of reading glasses of Elena's. When she tried them on, Elena stepped back and looked her up and down with a frown, 'My God, you look awful!' she said.

Francesca turned and looked in the mirror for a few seconds and then, pulling a face, said 'Good,' both girls then broke out laughing before a final embrace.

The old Piaggio that Elena had retrieved from one of the outbuildings wobbled alarmingly as Francesca ascended the rough trackway through the trees to the road, but she managed to hang on while cursing the fact that she no longer had access to her Ducati. When she reached the road, which now felt reassuringly smooth, instead of turning towards Cercina, she turned to the left and made her way slowly along the winding road until she found another that she was sure would lead her down to Sesto Fiorentino. Once in Sesto, she parked the moped in the underground carpark below the big Esselunga store and bought herself a few essentials that she needed, relying on the anonymity of the big store.

After finishing in the store, and before returning to her moped, she walked along the road back towards Castello, until she found a bar with a telephone available for public use. It was still a few minutes to eleven so, before she rang Elena, she ordered herself a cappuccino and began to browse the daily paper.

"Spring Cleaning in *Palazzo di Giustizia* – series of arrests as Police swoop on corrupt officials" was the somewhat unwieldy headline on the front page of *La Nazione*, over a not particularly good photograph of a figure being pushed into the back of the police van outside the *Palazzo* – a picture that she assumed had been taken on a mobile phone. The short, accompanying piece next to the image informed her only that the previous morning, police had made a surprise swoop on the *Palazzo di Giustizia* to arrest a number of officials suspected of having acted in ways intended to pervert the course of justice. Readers were then directed to turn to page five for the continuation of the story. Despite the seriousness of the situation she gave a wry smile at the classical news-reporting style; as every schoolchild told to write a newspaper article about anything would be instructed, the first paragraph should give the who, what, why, where and when of the story, and nothing else. This, however, was almost too perfect and its vagueness suggested that either very little information had been released to the press, or that the press had been warned off the story.

Turning to page five and reading the supporting story attentively made her believe that while the first of these two options was almost certainly the case, it was equally likely that pressure had been brought to bear to ensure that journalists did not dig too deeply into the background to the story. Although the story contained statements from eyewitnesses who had observed the raid from the nearby streets, only one person who had been inside the *Palazzo* was quoted and they had clearly been instructed not to reveal the names of those arrested. Francesca knew the employee quoted by sight but had not had any dealings with him either personally or professionally. She had never really known or, she admitted to herself, even considered what his actual role was in the *Palazzo*, and now assumed, from the fact that he'd obviously been presented to the journalists as a reliable source, that he was actually there to spy and report on the *Palazzo* employees.

She was surprised when she saw the journalist's by-line as the report was written by a journalist whose work was usually thoughtful, probing and considered. This article displayed none of those qualities. She would somehow need to speak to Gian-Marco again but was loathe to talk to him at the newspaper offices; she would somehow need to get him away from his desk.

Just as she was about to go to the phone and call Elena, an elderly man with curved shoulders and wearing a grey herringbone overcoat asked the barman if he could use the phone and so she had to wait a few minutes before she could ring her friend. While she waited her turn, she flicked idly through the rest of the paper although she didn't see much that relevant to her own situation: more than three thousand ethnic Serbs were being evacuated from their homes in Kosovo after disturbances in which twenty eight people had been killed and more than six hundred injured and the Russian president was making menacing noises about possible intervention which were giving rise to predictable warnings from the western powers; there had been protests around the world against the war in Iraq on the first anniversary of the invasion, most memorably in London where two Greenpeace activists had been arrested after scaling Big-Ben; in Italy, there was concern that the price of petrol had risen above a euro and ten cents per litre for the first time, while the sports pages were reporting on Fiorentina's hard fought away victory against Verona and looking forward to the mid-week home match against Bari; a suspected drug-dealer in Rome had been shot while attempting to evade capture and there were glowing reviews of the new Jim Carrey film *"Endless Sunshine of the Spotless Mind"*.

Finally, the old man finished informing whoever he was talking to about the progress of his many and various ailments, and the amount it was costing him for the barrage of tests that had been advised but not prescribed, and she was able to make her call.

Elena was very apologetic when she picked up the phone as Fabrizio had been unable to find an address for Commissario Vichi.

He had, however, been able to make some discreet enquires about Francesca's family but it wasn't good news.

'I'm not expecting good news, Elena; just tell me, please.' There was a pause and Francesca could imagine her friend nervously clearing her throat.

'It sounds as if both Rosa and your brother-in-law have been arrested. He was seen being taken away from the University, and all his lessons have been cancelled until further notice and they came to the house for Rosa just after half past eight yesterday morning.'

Francesca tried to think; she was not surprised that they'd been able to link Paul to her and to Ciancolini, but she'd hoped that they hadn't got anything against her sister – maybe they'd just taken Rosa in so that they could check what Paul was saying against what she could tell them. If that was the case, then Rosa should be OK as their story should be pretty watertight.

'Franci?' came Elena's slightly quavering voice, 'Franci; are you still there?'

'Yes. I'm here.'

'I'm afraid that there's more… They arrested your parents as well.'

'My parents!' Francesca felt as if someone had just slapped her hard. What had her parents got to do with anything? They didn't know anything.

'I'm afraid so. Although they were sent home again last night and are being held under preventative house arrest.'

That was a small relief, anyway, she thought – then another doubt assailed her. How had Fabrizio found all this out? If he were noticed asking questions it would place suspicion on him and on Elena as well. If SISMI started digging in the right places, it wouldn't take them long to establish that she and Elena had once been virtually inseparable, and the girl in the bakery would probably remember their conversation.

'I'm amazed he's managed to find out so much. Is he sure?' she asked, hoping that Elena would be able to allay her fears on their behalf.

' 'Fraid so. He didn't even have to ask to find out about Paul and your parents. The office-gossip lives somewhere near your parents and he was regaling everyone this morning with the story of how the City Councillor who lives near him had been arrested. You know how everyone is: always ready to spread any malicious gossip or rumours about people who they know are better than them because they do things for other people. At that point, one of the others chipped in to say that her daughter's tutorial at the university had been cancelled and that one of her friends had told her that the *lettore* who was supposed to be giving it had been seen leaving in a police car. Fortunately, the neighbour of your parents wasn't paying attention at that point, so no-one made the link between your parents and your brother-in-law.'

'What about Rosa? How did he find out about Rosa?' asked Francesca anxiously.

'Ah, he had to be a bit cleverer there. One of his firm's clients has an office very close to where Rosa and Paul live. Fabrizio gets on well with this client so he rang and said that he'd been trying to get hold of Rosa about a piece of glasswork that he'd commissioned, but couldn't get hold of her – maybe her phone was out of order, and he was a bit concerned as he needed the piece fairly urgently for another client. Well, his client said that of course he'd pop round and ask Rosa to get in touch with him. When he rang back a few minutes later, he'd been told by the old lady in the flat opposite that Rosa had been taken away by the police yesterday morning and hadn't been seen since.'

After resting her forehead for a moment against the wall to which the phone was attached, Francesca thanked Elena for all that she and Fabrizio had done, reminded her of what she should and should not tell anyone who might come asking about her and insisted that there was nothing else they could do at the moment. She could tell that Elena wanted to do more but was determined that her friend with her new found happiness should not be dragged any further into her affairs. With a vague promise that when everything was sorted she'd be in touch again, she rang off, paid the barman for the call and left the bar.

She really wanted to speak to Marco, but she knew that if the secret services had picked up those who were working with her in Florence, it was almost certain that Marco had also been arrested and, even if he hadn't, any attempt to contact him at the moment would only risk compromising him.

Gian-Marco Piovanelli raised an eyebrow slightly as Francesca slid into the seat alongside him but gave no other indication that he was surprised by her changed appearance.

'Caffé?' He said and, at her nod, half turned and called over to the barman, 'Two more coffees and two glasses of water, *per favore.'* Then he leaned back and looked at Francesca, waiting for her to speak.

'I'm glad you were able to get out… Thanks… it's important.' and then she too sat back until the barman had delivered the two coffees and glasses of water to the table and withdrawn again. 'By the way; that story I asked you about last time we spoke – you remember – about the thwarted assassination attempt on Guzzanti – well, I was right. It was a plant and, even though they'd made the arrests, there wasn't really a plot – or at least there was no plot that was intended to succeed.'

The sub-editor from *La Nazione*, nodded, 'I worked that much out once you got me curious about the story, but I couldn't work out what the possible motive for it was; I know that Guzzanti's committee is likely to be critical of several leading figures on the left, but bumping him off wouldn't be very good PR.'

'Exactly. Guzzanti was never going to be bumped off, as you so eloquently put it. What this was meant to do was to raise his profile and that of his committee, so that anything that comes out is given greater importance – if something is worth killing for, then it must be important.'

'But,' he objected, 'you know, and I know that his committee – this Mitrokhin Commission isn't going anywhere; there's no way of telling what's truth and what's not.'

'You're right,' she said, 'we know that, and a lot of the people we know, know that, but does the barman over there? Does his partner?

Do his parents? Do his friends? … You know that the answer is "almost certainly not", and there are a lot of people out there like him… in fact, there are a lot more people out there like him than there are like us… And what have they been reading in the papers recently, and been having piped into their living-rooms and kitchens, by our completely impartial media? Leaks, slurs, and off-the-record briefings about how the evidence the commission is gathering indicates that senior left-wing leaders have actually been working in the interests of foreign powers and against the interests of patriotic Italians for years.'

Gian-Marco had begun to stir the sugar into his coffee while she spoke and, distracted, he now continued to stir while his mind was elsewhere. 'OK. Let's say you're right. Who's behind it and what have they got to gain? And possibly even more important will be, are you able to prove any of it?"

'We can prove a lot of it, but not yet all of it… and I don't think that we've got a great deal of time before we get to crisis point… that's why I need your help.'

He looked at his watch, 'Look, there are a few things that I've got to finish off in the office, but once I've done them, I can get the rest of the afternoon off; I've got the impression that this is a bit complicated for a coffee break...can you give me a couple of hours?'

'I'm the one who's asking the favour here, so of course I can. There are just a couple of things I need in the meantime…' He looked at her with a raised eyebrow indicating curiosity. 'I need to know where I can get hold of an unregistered phone quickly… and I need the home address of a Police Commissario.'

Gian-Marco's eyebrow raised even further; 'Are you sure that's wise? Your somewhat amateurish attempts at a disguise and the fact that the place where you work was the target of a police raid yesterday, would suggest that it might be in your best interests to stay as far away from the police as possible.'

She reached across and placed her right hand over his and gave a little smile, 'I'm touched by your concern but not all the Police and security officials in this country are on the wrong side… I'm pretty sure that I can trust this one to do what is right.'

'Alright,' he said, 'on your head be it… What's his name?'

She told him and he asked her to ring him on his direct line in about half an hour. As for the phone, he suggested that she went to one of the stalls in Piazza San Lorenzo selling primarily covers for mobile phones. If she asked for Zdravko, she should be able to able to get what she needed. Once he had corrected her attempt at practising the Bulgarian's name, he got up, paid for the coffees and set off towards the main offices of *La Nazione*, while she, after paying a visit to the toilets, headed off in the opposite direction across the centre of the city towards the San Lorenzo market.

As usual, the market was full of tourists keen to stock up on their 'genuine' florentine leather shoes, bags and jackets, the vast array of t-shirts of very variable taste and quality, and the piles and piles of tacky souvenirs, amongst which brightly coloured wooden Pinocchios and shiny white miniature versions of Michelangelo's "David", made out of reconstituted marble or resin mixed with plaster were ubiquitous. The stall she was looking for was at the far end of the market, close to the junction with Via Nazionale.

'You want very nice cover for phone,' asked a swarthy man with a false smile in heavily accented English, as soon as she stopped in front of the stall.

'Sono Italiana,' she corrected him, 'and, no – I don't want a nice cover for my phone. What I want is a new phone; I was told that Zdravko would be able to help me.'

He glanced around furtively obviously wondering if it were some kind of sting. Presumably, Francesca, even a Francesca with badly cut hair and an odd pair of glasses, didn't look like his typical clients. 'I'm sorry, ' he said, 'I sell covers for phones – not phones.'

'That's not what I heard,' she said smiling sweetly. 'I heard that it would be possible to buy a phone cover with a phone inside it – a phone with an unregistered SIM.'

He looked around again, this time looking more anxious. 'Just a moment,' he said and sold a set of three interchangeable coloured covers to a teenage American who was strikingly underdressed for the time of year.

As the American moved off, Francesca remarked, more to herself than to the stall-holder, 'You can understand the British, but you'd think that Americans would realise that a "continental climate" means that it can be very cold in early spring.' The swarthy man, whom she assumed was Zdravko, just gave a dismissive shrug.

When the man was sure that there were no other customers within earshot, he looked at her again and said, 'Two hundred euros.'

Francesca shook her head, pulled her purse out and taking two fifty-euro notes between her fingers said, 'Too much, I have a hundred here,' hoping that the desperation she felt wasn't showing in her voice. Another group of tourists stopped at the stall and looked at the different designs on the phone covers. Francesca closed her hand around the two notes and pretended to do the same.

'Was costen das?' finally asked one of the tourists, holding up a cover which showed a close up of the penis from Michelangelo's statue of David. Francesca wondered whether the phone cover would end up discarded in a drawer after the German got over his holiday and returned to whatever staid job he did every day in Munich or Berlin or Hamburg.

'Zwanzig euros,' said the stall holder.

'Nein,' said the German, putting the cover down.

The stallholder spread his hands wide, palms upturned in a gesture of submission, and then, in a mixture of English and German, said, *'Warten!* I like you so I give you *zwei* for *dreizig.'* He smiled and, with his right hand gave a sweeping gesture across his stall. 'Your *frau;* she like this one maybe?' and his brought his hand to rest where it indicated a cover illustrated with the central section of Bronzino's "Venus, Cupid and the folly of time".

A look at his companion, who was pulling gently on his sleeve, was enough to convince the German that this was not a good idea so, resisting the pull, he shook his head, held up one finger and said, *'Ein für, funfzehn.'*

After a show of reluctance, the stallholder accepted the offered fifteen euros and handed over the original cover, at which point the German's companion finally managed to move him on.

Little more than a minute later Francesca was the possessor or a fully charged, very basic pay-as-you-go phone pre-loaded with ten euros credit, to which she very soon added a further twenty euros after purchasing a *ricaricard* in a *tabaccaio* around the corner in Via Nazionale.

'Sono io,' said Francesca as soon as Gian-Marco picked up his phone.

'OK. I should be able to get away from here just before four. Where do you want to meet?'

Having already thought about this, Francesca had no hesitation in suggesting that the should meet in the Cascine Park, partly because she knew that for Gian-Marco it was vaguely in the direction of home and partly because it had several entrances, plenty of shady corners and was not particularly well lit. He agreed to meet her on the site of the faux-Roman amphitheatre as soon as he could get there, which he assumed would be about half past four, and where she knew that she could observe him arrive unobserved to make sure that he wasn't being followed.

'The address you wanted is in Via Cocchi. Number 63; second floor.'

'Where's that – I've never heard of Via Cocchi?'

'I'm not surprised. It's just a quiet residential street, so unless you happened to know someone who lived there, it's not the sort of place that gets mentioned in conversation. The top end of the road, where your man lives, comes off Viale Volta, almost opposite the entrance to the gardens of Villa "Il Ventaglio".'

'Alright. Thanks for that. I'll see you later,' and she rang off. She really wanted to ring Marco, or her sister, or even her parents but, after holding the phone in her hand with her finger poised over the keyboard for a few seconds that seemed far longer, she resisted the temptation and slipped it into her pocket. For the moment, she knew that anything she could do, she would have to do alone – however terrifying the idea might be.

With almost two and a half hours to go before she was due to meet Gian-Marco, she had plenty of time to locate Vichi's house in daylight so that she could minimise any risk later on. It also meant that she did not have to just hang around, killing time, and feeling conspicuous before it was time to make her way to the park. Forcing herself to stop every so often and look in shop-windows to blend in with the crowds, she gradually made her way through the centre of the city, past the Duomo, then across from Piazza della Signoria to the large square in front of the imposing marble facade of Santa Croce.

As she walked past the statue of Dante who surveyed the occupants of the square from his pedestal just in front of the church, she wondered what the great thirteenth century poet would have made of the current political situation; to which circles of Hell would he have consigned the leaders of the planned coup, and would he have seen her and her friends as being at least worthy enough to escape Hell and only be condemned to a few thousand years in Purgatory? She tried to remember what she had learnt about the Guelphs and Ghibellines when she'd been at school to try and work out which side, as a White Guelph, Dante would have favoured in the current crisis, but soon decided it was impossible to decide which side were the modern Guelphs and which the Ghibellines.

The Piaggio was where she had left it, chained to a railing. Unchaining it and slipping the open faced helmet on, she pushed it off its stand and braved the almost constant flow of traffic on the Viale to head towards the Arno. As the Viale met the Lungarno she followed the traffic round to the left, past the high walls of the Carabinieri barracks and then headed east, ignoring the mass of traffic that tried to push her over towards Ponte San Niccoló and the road up towards her parents' house. At the next major junction she put her left indicator on and then, when the lights changed, turned into the long straight road that crossed over the railway lines and continued northwards towards the hills.

Following the road to the very end, opposite the Youth Hostel, she then swung to the left and shortly after joined Viale Volta where it began to level out after descending from Fiesole. She continued past the entrance to the gardens of "Il Ventaglio" until she came to a small square on her left where she propped the Piaggio on its stand in the middle of a cluster of parked cars and small vans.

She walked casually back up Viale Volta, past the end of Via Cocchi and then along to the next right hand turn, which she followed until it met Via Cocchi again forming a triangle. She then again turned right and made her way slowly back up to the Viale so that she could get a good look at the outside of the house. She was pleased to see that, unlike its neighbour which had a high locked gate, there was only a low metal gate set into a hedge to separate the small garden to the side and rear of the house from the road. Although she couldn't see it from the road, she knew that to comply with safety regulations there had to be a rear entrance to the block and she was confident that making her way into Vichi's house later would not present too many difficulties.

Leaving the Piaggio in the midst of at least thirty other motorini and motorbikes belonging to students, and possibly staff, of the university's Agronomy Faculty, she made her way across the park to the Piazzale delle Cascine and then carefully selected a spot in the trees from where she could see the main access road and the bus stops on Piazzale Kennedy and the main avenue through the park.

After about fifteen minutes, she saw a figure walking briskly along the elm lined avenue leading into the park from the city and, as it came closer, she could clearly distinguish Gian-Marco's features. As he approached, she saw him slow a moment as he tapped the end of a cigarette packet enabling him to take the tip of the cigarette that emerged between his lips and, after replacing the packet in his jacket pocket, strike a match with his right hand while holding the box in his left and protecting the flame from the breeze in one fluid movement as he raised it towards the cigarette.

As he continued, more slowly, along the avenue, she kept pace with him for a couple of minutes along the parallel bridleway, with half an eye on him but most of her attention given to the road behind him to make sure that he hadn't been followed. Finally, when she was satisfied that there was no immediate risk, she pulled out her phone and tapped in 'Turn left.' Moments later she saw him reach into his pocket, extract his phone, flip open the screen, give it a quick look and then, replacing it in his pocket, leave the avenue to cross the rough grass to his left.

'You do know,' he said with a smile as he approached her, 'that this place still has a bit of a reputation for prostitution, don't you? If there are any over-zealous policemen about, they'll arrest you for soliciting and me for intention to commit indecent acts in a public place.'

'If soliciting were the worst they could come up with, then I'd be happy with that; as for indecent acts in a public place, I'll have to disappoint you. I never commit them anywhere with smokers… Now. Put your arm through mine and walk. It needs to look as if we have a reason for meeting here, well away from the crowds.' As he took her arm, she began walking, guiding him through the trees towards a less frequented avenue at the edge of the park where occasional benches had been placed between the roadway and the bank of the Arno.

'Now. Tell me everything you can and tell me what I can do to help,' he said, becoming serious as they sat down on one of the benches.

'It's quite a long story so I'll keep it as brief as I can.' He signed his assent and, in as much detail as possible, while being careful not to compromise anyone else, she filled him in on how she had originally discovered the plot, how dell'Omodarme had originally taken on the investigation and how Ciancolini had been persuaded to take over after dell'Omodarme's murder. While being careful not to name Capuano, Busoni or the Brigadier, she explained what they had discovered about the supposed plot to assassinate Guzzanti, the murder of Loriana Cabrini-Pellé, the involvement of Fogazzini and the proof that their surveillance equipment had assembled against other leading politicians and members of the security services. She did not tell him that the hold they had over Fogazzini was the threat of publicly exposing her brother as, if he were exposed anyway, they would lose their hold over her.

'So you want me to try and make sure that at least some of the truth gets told.'

'That's one thing; although you'll have to decide what it's safe to publish and then see what you're allowed to publish.'

He laughed, 'You think we're censored at *La Nazione?*'

She looked at him, mildly irritated, 'Don't be naive. You know as well as I do that it's the owners of all papers who set the tone and decide the parameters of what's acceptable and what's not – and *"La Nazione"* is not exactly known for its radicalism, is it?'

'That's a bit unfair. Although it's always been a moderately centre-right paper, we try to take a pretty centrist line, reporting both national and local issues and we're free to criticise politicians on either side providing that we offer balance.'

She snorted, 'Balance within accepted parameters. When was the last time you did a really in-depth analytical piece challenging accepted viewpoints and slaying a few sacred cows? I'll tell you when – it was during *Tangentopoli,* when the whole of the media felt it was not only safe, but expected, for them to bring down politicians by accusing them of taking bribes! And do you really think that *Tangentopoli* really got to the root of the problems rather than just clearing out the dead-wood so that the power-brokers behind the system could start afresh?'

He shrugged, 'We do our best. You know there are some very good people who work for the paper.'

'Of course there are… and you're one of them. But you know that you can't go outside editorial guidelines, and the editor – who is it now? - Carrassi – has to stick to guidelines set out by the board of directors – and who do they represent? Take a good look at who your shareholders are; the two biggest are both owned by consortia of large companies and if you trace through the complicated web of ownership you'll eventually realise why *La Nazione,* like almost every other Daily Paper is never going to rock the boat too much.'

He held up his hands in a gesture of surrender in the face of her passionate speech, 'Alright. So tell me what I can do, if I can't write about anything.'

She softened, 'Sorry. I didn't get you out here to have a go at you. I'm afraid I'm a bit on edge at the moment – I know you're one of the good guys… There are some aspects of what I've just told you that don't look quite right to anyone and, it would be quite legitimate for you, as a serious journalist, to raise questions – Guzzanti and Cabrini-Pellé are obvious examples as well as the arrest of Ciancolini. But maybe the main way you could help me is by keeping me up to date with what's coming in on the wires: any anti-Prodi briefing that you get; any news about government ministers and…' she paused and swallowed nervously, 'and any news you hear about my family and Marco Antognoni.'

Gian-Marco assured her that he would do all he could and, after a long hug, they left the bench and made off in different directions.

Brigadier Bernardo Casini closed the secure line and sat drumming his fingertips on the edge of his desk with a frown on his face. Finally, the frown disappeared and he focussed on the Major who was waiting respectfully on the other side of the desk.

'Sit down, Sandro,' he said, gesturing towards the chair facing him and then, when his junior officer had complied, continued, 'You are a good officer and one in whom I have complete faith, and as such, I feel that I have to be completely open with you about what's going on.' He indicated with a gesture that he didn't want interrupting. 'You've been present during some of the interviews with Salvatore Stiappa, and it won't have escaped your attention that the information we have got out of him is political dynamite. It also won't have escaped your attention that most of the people who've been incriminated by what he's told us are very powerful and very influential, and you know what that means.'

The major gave a small nod to indicate that he was fully aware of the sensitivity of the matter in which they were engaged.

'At the moment, it appears that the people for whom Stiappa has been working have momentum behind them and it is possible that we will be unable to bring them to justice. The Judge who had been personally authorised by the President of the Republic to carry out an investigation into this affair has been arrested along with most of those who have been working alongside him. At this point I don't know which side will come out on top but, I want you to know that, should this turn out badly, I will take full responsibility for the arrest of Stiappa and for everything that has been said and done since his arrest. I also want you to know that should you wish to distance yourself further from this matter and have no further involvement, I am prepared to transfer you to another unit of your choice with a commendation for your exemplary service while under my command.'

The major's shoulders were drawn further back and he sat upright in his chair with a determined look on his face.

'Permission to speak, Sir.'

The Brigadier indicated with a gesture of his right hand that the Major should continue. 'If you are satisfied by my work and my attitude, Sir, then I wish to remain under your command. I am happy to state that at no time have I been asked to do, or say, anything, which does not appear to me to have been in the best interests of justice and the State whose values it is my sworn duty to uphold. Will there be anything else, Sir?'

'Yes, Sandro,' said the Brigadier with a slight smile, 'before you go and check on the prisoner, I would consider it an honour to shake your hand.'

Chapter 28

As Commissario Vichi hung up his service overcoat on the first of the hooks in the wide entrance hall of his two bedroomed flat to become, for a few hours at least, plain Giacomo Vichi, there was a light knock on the door he had just closed behind him. Thinking that a parcel delivery must have been left with the neighbour, he turned back to the door and slid back the bolt he had just pushed into place for the night. *'Un momento.'* he called.

On the landing in front of him, dimly lit by the single forty watt bulb was a youngish woman with shortish dark hair and glasses. *'Si?'* he said in a rising tone that indicated surprise, 'Can I help you?' Then he caught his breath as she stepped forward and the light from the hallway behind him illuminated her face.

'*Buonasera*, Commissario. Do you have a few minutes you can spare – or do you have to arrest me?'

Before he could reply, his wife's voice came from the kitchen, 'Is that you, Giacomo. Is there someone with you?'

Vichi opened the door wider and gestured to Francesca to enter and then, as he closed it, called, 'Yes, it's me… and there's someone with me who I need to talk to.' and then to Francesca, 'Please have a seat in the living room while I go and explain to my wife who you are and why you're here.' He ushered her through a doorway and indicated that she should sit on a comfortable looking two-seater black-leather sofa, pointed to the TV remote control and said 'Feel free,' before leaving the room again.

Hoping that her instincts were correct, and that she could trust Vichi, she tried to distract herself by looking around the room. As well as the sofa she was sitting on, there was another, more worn looking black sofa at right angles to the first, with a glass coffee table, almost completely covered by books and magazines, standing on a circular Persian-style rug over the white ceramic tiles in the space between the two sofas. A mid-sized grey combined television and VHS system was placed on a triangular pine table in the corner of the room facing the two sofas. A few framed photographs hung on the wall: one of a younger Vichi posing in police uniform, presumably on the day he was admitted to the force; one where Vichi and a serious looking woman who Francesca assumed to be his wife had been posed with two teenage boys; and one of each of the boys as young men. The only other decoration on the wall was a painting of the Arno which Francesca thought was of good quality.

When Vichi's wife popped her head round the door a few minutes later, the serious look in the photograph was softened by little wrinkles around the eyes which made Francesca think that she spent much of her time smiling.

'Hello; I'm Gianna. We'll be eating in a few minutes and we'd be delighted if you'd join us. The bathroom's just across there if you need to freshen up.'

Francesca opened her mouth to refuse the offer then, as she did so, realised how hungry she was, having eaten nothing more solid than a cappuccino since leaving Elena's in the morning. Instead of refusing, she smiled and said, 'That would be lovely, if you're sure it's no trouble.' Signora Vichi just smiled and returned to the kitchen.

The meal was a very simple one as the Vichis had clearly not expected to have a guest. For the first course Signora Vichi placed a large bowl of steaming pasta in the middle of the table and invited Francesca to help herself. *'Penne al arrabbiata,'* she said apologetically, 'I always try to make my sauces a bit spicy as it masks the taste of the gluten-free pasta. Giacomo claims it tastes very similar to the real thing, but that's because he hasn't eaten any real pasta for more than four years. I get to eat proper pasta when we go out, so I get to compare the two.'

'It will be fine. A friend of mine only ever cooks rice pasta, so I'm used to eating pasta *senza glutine.'* This wasn't quite true as the few times she'd eaten the rice based pasta at her friend's house, she'd always found it very disappointing. However, she soon realised that she was so hungry that she wolfed it down without really caring what she was eating.

The main course was a pork stew to which Francesca was fairly sure that Gianna Vichi had added an extra tin of cannellini to make it stretch to three people.

It was only when she had cleaned the last drop of stew off her plate with her last bit of the deliciously fresh rosemary-topped focaccia that Vichi leaned back in his chair and looked at her seriously. 'Well, Signorina, I think it's time that you told us your story – all of it. I assume that that is what you came for.'

Francesca cleared her throat nervously feeling suddenly tongue tied. She looked across at Gianna wondering whether it was wise to reveal everything in front of her. Vichi correctly interpreted her glance; 'Feel free to say whatever you need to say in front of

Gianna. I have a feeling that if I'm able to help you there may well be consequences that have an effect on her as well as me, so it's only fair that she should hear what you've got to say too – and in anycase, I value her advice.' Gianna put her hand on Vichi's forearm and gave Francesca a reassuring smile.

'If you really feel you can't say what you need to say with me here, then I can go and load the dishwasher.'

Francesca managed a smile, 'No; please stay. I didn't want to suggest that I didn't trust you.' She took a drink of her water and, for the second time that day, began to tell her story.

Vichi listened attentively, interrupting on numerous occasions to get her to clarify points or repeat again details of the evidence they had gathered. He was particularly interested to hear what they had discovered about the way the dell'Omodarme bombing had been reallocated and then brushed under the carpet. As the investigation should really have been his, it still rankled that it had been taken away from him. 'And you have evidence to show that this Stiappa organised the bombing itself?'

'More than just evidence; we have his signed confession which also confirms which politicians and members of SISMI he was in contact with. His confession was videotaped so there can be no question that he was coerced into making his confession.'

Vichi shook his head, 'That's good, but the Public Prosecutor would never allow it to be used in court. Once he's been arrested, a court will look unfavourably on any declaration a prisoner makes when he's not accompanied by a lawyer. Although you haven't said so, I'd wager a lot of money that the confession wasn't extracted from the prisoner by entirely legitimate means.' Francesca didn't reply. 'I believe you, Signorina, but I can understand why the President of the Republic insisted that Judge Ciancolini had to put together a case that would stand up in any court of law. You have to assume that those who are behind this conspiracy will have plenty of friends in the judiciary who will be only too pleased to throw the case out if they are given any pretext.'

'What about the politician – Fogazzini?' asked Gianna Vichi, with an encouraging smile to Francesca.

'She'll testify, if necessary.'

Vichi shook his head again, 'She resigned on health grounds. The rumours in the newspapers – rumours that haven't been denied – are that she had a nervous breakdown. Again, a good lawyer – and you'll be sure that they will have the very best – will destroy her testimony. There's prejudice against mental illness, and there's still prejudice against women; you've really got to have more or they'll destroy you.'

'Surely,' said Gianna Vichi thoughtfully, 'you're losing sight of your primary objective.' They both looked at her. 'You're not doing this in order to put Stiappa and Fogazzini and Marelli and the others in prison – or at least that's not the most important thing. What you're trying to do is firstly to make sure that the country's next government is a fairly elected one, and closely linked to that, you want to stop them killing, or at the very least destroying the reputation of Romano Prodi… Putting the conspirators in prison is a desirable consequence of that, but it's not essential.'

'So what you're saying is that the information Francesca has, while it might not be enough to convince a potentially biased court, it would be enough to alter the public's perception.'

'And at the very least, they wouldn't dare harm a hair on Prodi's head as that would confirm that the accusations had been justified.'

Francesca, feeling exhausted after all the emotion of the last thirty-six hours was glad to sit back and listen as the confused thoughts and voices that had been debating the issue inconclusively within her head were replaced by the rational and relatively dispassionate voices of the Vichis. On the whole it was Gianna who prodded, coming up with ideas and possible ways forward, while Vichi was more practical, looking for the flaws and potential pitfalls in her suggestions.

At first she was disappointed in the commissario, seeing him as unnecessarily pessimistic but the more she listened the more she realised that he was on her side, recognising that the situation was so critical and the stakes so high that she could not afford to make the slightest mistake. When it came to the role of the Police, he agreed that success would be impossible if the conspirators were able to retain the loyalty of the various Police forces around the country. But, this time, it was Vichi himself who looked to find the solutions.

There was no point, he said, in looking to identify individual officers who could be trusted without nullifying the potential for interference from above and, while he was sure that the majority of Questori and Vice-Questori were people of the utmost integrity, he was also certain that there would be plenty of bad apples amongst them. Unfortunately, due to the nature of the system, one didn't reach the higher echelons of the Police, or other security forces, without being adept at playing the political game. While that didn't necessarily mean that they were corrupt, it did mean that there had to be question marks, particularly over those with the most highly prestigious positions.

Lower down the pecking order, while there were plenty of mavericks who, at times, were prepared to by-pass the official channels if they thought that they were an impediment to justice, they only survived because they achieved results and because they retained the loyalty of their men. Unfortunately, as one of the ways in which they retained the loyalty and respect of their men was by taking all responsibility for bending the rules on their own shoulders and not risking the careers of those who worked under them, it meant it would be difficult for them to play an effective role.

'Unless, of course,' interjected Gianna, 'their orders came from higher up, from a source of unimpeachable authority… if you can achieve that, then the whole of the police force will see it as their duty to take action, even if there are no orders from their immediate superiors.'

'But,…' interjected Francesca, 'the Police are responsible to the Ministry of the Interior, and we know for certain that both Rossi, and Marelli at Justice, are two of the leading members of the conspirators and I can't imagine that anyone at or near the top of the force is going to risk opposing the ministers they work for.' She shook her head but Gianna wasn't discouraged.

'I wasn't thinking of people at the top of the force, and certainly not of anyone in the ministries. I was thinking of going above that.'

'Innominati! The President of the Republic!' said the *commissario*, surprised.

'Why not?' responded Gianna and then, turning back to Francesca, 'Didn't you say that Innominati was already aware of the situation?'

'Yes, but… but he didn't actually say he'd do anything. He just gave Ciancolini permission to keep investigating with the promise that he'd back him, provided he could produce evidence that he could guarantee would stand up in court.'

'And would the evidence you have stand up in court?

Francesca closed her eyes and tilted her head back for a moment, then looked at them again and gently shook her head before saying, 'The evidence we have is strong evidence but not all of the evidence was acquired legally.' Vichi raised his eyebrows, 'A fair amount of the evidence we have is the result of illegal phone taps and bugging devices. Evidence either comes directly from those taps or has been extracted by using evidence gained from them to apply pressure to suspects. I think I'm right in saying that a defence counsel could apply to have such evidence struck from the court records.'

'They could also, apply to have the case heard in camera as it would regard vital state interests… and once the evidence can no longer be heard by the public then you are at the mercy of whatever judges are appointed. But,' said Gianna, 'I don't want to be too pessimistic. If the President can be persuaded to make a stand for what we all know is right, then I think that there is a chance that this could be resolved without having to rely on the courts.'

'Go on,' said the commissario, 'tell us how you envisage the situation working out.'

'Your first task, is to get Innominati fully on board, and I think that it won't be as difficult as you envisage.' She smiled, 'Think about it. He was elected as President as a compromise candidate; no-one really wanted him, but at the same time, because he's never really done anything major in his political career, no-one had any strong objections to him. Now, he's eighty six years old with only two years to go before his mandate ends and he'll quickly be forgotten by everyone. He has absolutely nothing to lose by making a stand, and a place in history to gain. If he can be made to see that, then there's no reason why he should continue to sit on the fence. As President he is the number one representative of the Republic and, when he took office, he took an oath to serve the Republic. Will he really want to be remembered as the President who sat back and did nothing when it was in his power to save the Republic? Can you get to see Innominati again?'

'I can't,' said Francesca, 'but I know someone who can.'

'Good. If Innominati is prepared to make a stand, then I think it can be done.'

'But how? Isn't the President just an expensive figurehead with no real power? I always thought that the Constitution had been deliberately written that way to avoid another Mussolini appearing.'

'It was,' said Gianna with a smile, 'but it's incredibly difficult to write a legal document without loopholes – especially when it's put together by a committee. You're right in saying that the President has no real power, but the Constitution does give him obligations and responsibilities. So long as his mind is focussed on the relevant articles of the constitution then he could argue that he has a duty to intervene.'

Vichi smiled, 'I told you that I valued Gianna's advice. Being married to an Associate Professor of Constitutional Law has its advantages. She can tell you which articles of the Constitution give Innominati the authority to intervene, but I don't think that there's any chance of him being prepared to stick his neck out unless he's sure that there's strong backing for his position. In military terms, I think you would probably argue that there's no point making airstrikes unless there are boots on the ground prepared to consolidate the position.'

'Which brings me back to the point I was making. With specific orders from the President of the Republic, Rossi and Marelli and those close to them would be bypassed and the regular Police officers would do their duty.'

'Hmmm. The theory's sound, but if those orders were countermanded by others in the chain of command, I'm worried that what you would get would be paralysis.'

'Which would give Rossi the excuse to declare a State of Emergency and put SISMI in charge of operations,' added Francesca.

For the next two hours they kicked around various ideas without coming to any definite conclusions; Gianna explained how, in her view, parts of Articles eighty-seven, ninety-one and one hundred and four gave the President the legal authority to intervene while article one hundred and nine gave him the means to do so, if he could be persuaded to use it. Vichi assured Francesca that if there was a coherent plan of action backed up by a commitment from the President then there would be enough serving police officers on side to at least ensure that the force remained neutral. In the meantime, he personally, would do his best to find out what was happening to those who had been arrested and see who else was at risk. Francesca, having been reassured that the Brigadier had not been arrested - Vichi was certain that he would have heard from his colleagues in Viterbo – said that she would contact him as soon as possible both to get an update on the Stiappa situation and to establish how much of the organisation remained at liberty and active.

Finally, when Francesca stood up to leave, Vichi asked her where she was planning to stay, and when she said that she intended to stay in an empty garage owned by a friend of her father, said that he did not think that that was a good idea. It was very likely that whoever was controlling the SISMI operatives in Florence had been going through all known acquaintances of the family, and any properties belong to them with a fine toothcomb.

Gianna suggested that she should stay there, but Vichi opposed this idea on the grounds that they needed to keep contact to the bare minimum if they were to have any chance of success. 'Do you know Via Fanfani?' Francesca shook her head.

'Good,' said Vichi, 'I'd have been surprised if you did. Head out towards the start of the Firenze-Mare motorway but before you get there, take a right towards Castello just before you get to the airport. At the first set of lights, don't turn right but move slightly to your right and make sure you get onto the narrow road that runs parallel to the one you've just come off. That will take you under the railway branch line and then towards the main line. At the point where it reaches the high wall separating you from the railway line, it turns ninety degrees to the right and changes its name to Via Fanfani. There are a few industrial units along there that have been thrown up fairly haphazardly but, until the Second World War, it was all agricultural land there and my grandparents had a *casa colonica* and a few fields there. After the old man died, the fields were sold off but the family could never agree what to do with the house. As a result, it just sits there now, half ruined, and various members of the family use it to meet up occasionally for get togethers and barbeques, but no-one lives there. My uncle has a few vines on the remaining bit of land but the wine he makes is so awful that even he hardly bothers going there anymore.

The house itself is pretty run down but there's a barn next to it and we keep our camper-van in there. There are sleeping bags stored under the seat and there should be a nearly full gas bottle. The one thing that works properly in the house is the toilet and there's a well next to the barn. I think that you'd be fairly safe there for the next few days.'

'That will be fantastic, and will make life a lot easier. I'll probably need to go down to Rome or Viterbo, but to know I've got a safe base here in Florence will make a big difference. I don't know how to thank you enough.'

'Just stay safe, and don't get arrested,' said Gianna. 'Let me just put a few bits of food together in a bag for you to take with you.'

Thirty five minutes later after having ridden past the entrance first to make sure that she had a good understanding of the layout, Francesca chained up the moped two hundred metres back along the road where a few cars had been left overnight, and cautiously approached the entrance to the *casa colonica* on foot. Ignoring the high locked gates, a further ten metres took her to a point where a large bush appeared to be draped over the wall from the inside. Prising the edge of the foliage away from the wall, she found that, as Vichi had explained, part of the wall had collapsed inwards, the loose mortar destroyed by the tendrils of the bush. Although, with the bush in place, the wall appeared intact, with the foliage pulled back it was clear that it was possible to scramble over and into the property.

Once inside and no longer exposed to the lights of the railway line, everything seemed very dark and Francesca stood for a minute with her eyes closed to help them get used to the low light level. When she opened them again, she could just make out the outlines of two buildings: the large mass of the house and the smaller one of the barn.

Cautiously, she made her way to the far corner of the house and then took eight hesitant paces along the back wall before crouching down and feeling around her with her hands. Nothing. She shuffled a few inches forwards and tried again – Yes. That must be it. Her fingers closed over the edge of a terracotta pot then moved towards the centre and gripped the stem of the plant that was growing there.

After an initial reluctance to move which was resolved by rocking the stem gently from side to side to break the seal that had formed between the inner and outer pot, the plant came upwards with its compost filled pot liner. Reaching into the bottom of the outer terracotta pot, she felt a key-ring with two keys attached inside a polythene bag which she pulled out and slipped into her pocket before carefully placing the plant next to the pot.

Straightening up, she turned and slowly made her way across to the front of the barn where she soon located the padlock securing the door.

Inside, even closing her eyes again for another minute did nothing to help with the blackness and she very carefully shuffled around the barn, with the fingers of one hand trailing lightly along the wall and her other hand stretched out in front of her to reduce the risk of walking into any stray garden implements. Eventually, after what seemed like an age, she came to a smaller door in the sidewall towards the back of the barn. Halfway down she located the inside latch of a yale type lock, which she turned and then fixed in the open position.

Surprised by how light it now seemed outside after the blackness of the barn, she went out and carefully replaced both the plastic bag with the keys and the plant, back into the terracotta pot, before re-entering the barn through the side door, flicking the catch so that it locked when she closed it and then, with arms outstretched again, locating the camper van in the middle of the barn.

Working her way around the van, she found the magnetic key box she was looking for, tucked inside the second wheel-arch that she came to and, when she had located the keyhole on the driver's door, was able to retrieve the torch that Vichi had told her was on the parcel-shelf below the steering wheel.

The inside of the van was clean and tidy with everything stowed away in the numerous cupboards so that it was ready whenever the Vichis managed to get a couple of days free. Underneath the rearmost seat she found two all-seasons sleeping bags, one of which she pulled out of its compression bag and shook to loosen up the fibres, then she unclipped the table from the side of the van, folded up its leg and rested the top on the ledges at the edge of each seat. Once the rear cushions from the seats had been placed over the table top, she was left with an adequate double bed.

Before sleeping she considered ringing the Brigadier but dismissed the idea, deciding that it would safer to ring from a public phone using a phone-card in the morning. Although she was fairly confident of the safety of the phone she had purchased from the Serb, she couldn't be a hundred percent sure; Vichi hadn't seemed at all surprised when she'd mentioned how she'd acquired the phone, and she realised that if the police were aware of what was going on, there must be a reason why it hadn't been clamped down on.

Finally, although she felt like just lying down and sleeping, she forced herself to go outside again to the well, bring up some water and, after washing herself as well as she could beside the barn, filled up the water container from the van and took it inside for use in the morning.

She was so tired that she fell asleep instantly and slept deeply and, as far as she could remember, dreamlessly until after seven, which was far later than she'd intended. Even though she was anxious to telephone the Brigadier as soon as possible, she made herself meticulously restore the Volkswagen, as she now saw that it was, back to the state in which she had found it, including replacing the key in the keybox. For the side door of the barn, however, she carefully placed a small fragment of wood that she picked up off the floor in such a way that the latch didn't quite click shut. The way it was left, the lock would still turn if someone inserted a key but it would be easy to slip in a credit card and push the catch back without using a key.

Fortunately, there was no-one in sight on Via Fanfani and she was able to squeeze through the overhanging bush and make her way out onto the road without any problems. The motorino was where she had left it, although most of the cars that had been parked there had now gone, and ten minutes later, she had topped it up with two-stroke at one of the large garages just before the airport and the start of the motorway. As she had expected, there was a public phone at the garage and she dialled in the number she had memorised for the Brigadier's direct line.

'Casini…'

'Buongiorno. Chiamo da Firenze,' she said, hoping that he would recognise her voice and that she would not have to say her name out loud,

There was a pause, then she heard, slightly muffled as though the Brigadier had moved the phone away from his mouth, 'Could you come back in ten minutes please, gentlemen. I need to take this call.' There were indistinct voices in the background, the sound of scraping chairs and the metallic thunk of a door closing.

'Thank God you're still at liberty. What happened?'

'They just swooped on the *Palazzo di Giustizia* without warning. Luckily I'd just gone across the road for a coffee, so I was able to get away, but I saw them take Judge Ciancolini and his secretary away. I know that my sister and brother-in-law have also been picked up and I'm worried about Marco – I haven't dared risk calling him and I had to get rid of my phone as I assume it was compromised.'

'Very sensible. Well done. The question is, what now?'

'I've spoken to a Police commissario, who I trust. He thinks that if we can get clear backing from Innominati, the Police will either back us, or at the very least turn a blind eye until the outcome is known.' She could almost feel the Brigadier frown through the receiver of the phone.'

'I wouldn't have thought there was much chance of that. He's got where he is by perfecting the art of sitting on the fence, why should he change now?'

Francesca decided to treat the Brigadier's question as a rhetorical one and responded with one of her own' 'What about Stiappa?'

'Stiappa is singing like a bird. He's sure that a large part of the money is already in his bank account and we've already filled up two video-tapes with him telling us everything he knows about politicians, civil servants and some members of the security services. It's not all relevant to what we're interested in, but there's plenty that is – including arranging the explosion that killed dell'Omodarme.'

'OK Keep him safe and don't let him talk to anyone.'

'Don't worry, he's nice and snug here, and he will be until we transfer him to somewhere more permanent.'

'I'm going to try and talk to someone who may be able to help us with Innominati. I'll ring again this evening and then again at this time tomorrow, in the meantime, is there any way you could find out anything about Ciancolini, or Marco?'

The brigadier's voice was surprisingly tender when he replied, 'Francesca, I'd really like to – I'm concerned about them as well – but, probably the worst thing I could do would be to show an interest. They will know that there are other people involved and they'll be on the lookout for anyone asking questions who hasn't got a legitimate interest in them. - I'm sorry – I really am.'

'Alright. I understand. I shouldn't have asked. I'll speak to you tonight.'

As she left the filling-station and made her way round the one way section to head back in towards the centre of the city, she looked longingly at the entrance to the motorway beyond the airport; 'Motorcycles below 150cc prohibited' read the sign by the entrance. If only she had her Ducati, she thought with a sigh, she could have been in Rome in three hours and find out for herself what had happened to Marco. Instead, with a maximum speed of just over twenty miles an hour, the Piaggio whined its way through Novoli towards the centre, where she could see Brunelleschi's dome dominating the skyline.

She had decided that the best place to 'hide' was in the centre, in the middle of the crowds where no-one would pay her any attention and the occasional police officer who might be walking around would have their eyes fixed on people's handbags and pockets rather than having the time to study people's faces. All she needed to do was make sure that she didn't attract any attention to herself and try and avoid meeting anyone she knew well. She left the motorino with the dozens of others parked haphazardly outside the *Facoltà di Lettere* of the university and made her way through to Piazza Santa Croce where she found a space on one of the benches and took her phone out.

Four rings and the phone was answered.

'Si?'

'I need another address if you can.'

'Good morning to you, too.'

'Sorry. *Buongiorno.*'

'That's better. Now tell me what you need.'

'Susanna Busoni, daughter of Francesco Busoni an architect from Tavarnelle and grand-daughter of Giorgio Busoni, one time member of the Senate. She may well live in Tavarnelle as she works with her father.'

'It shouldn't be too difficult. I'll text you as soon as I've got it.'

'Grazie… Oh, and Gian-Marco…'

'Si?'

'You're a treasure!'

'Get lost,' and he closed the phone, as she'd known he would.

When she had placed her phone in her lap so she could pick it up as soon as the address came through, she shook the newspaper to open it fully, and gasped. On the bottom half of the front page was a photograph of her face reproduced, she assumed, from her personnel file at the *Tribunale*, and alongside it was the heading, 'Further suspect sought at *Tribunale*', followed by, 'Following Wednesday's raid at the *Palazzo di Giustizia,* a spokesman confirmed yesterday that a further person is sought in connection with the operation. The public are urged to the utmost vigilance in looking for Francesca Conte, aged 35, who works as an administrative assistant in the family law section.

During the initial raid when Judge Bettino Ciancolini and his Personal Assistant, Loretta Milazzi were taken into custody, it is believed that Conte had temporarily absented herself from the building. The spokesman stressed that Conte, who is suspected of involvement with a subversive group acting against the interests of the state, may be armed and should not be approached. Anyone with any information should immediately telephone the operations team on 055.852300 with all relevant details.

It is believed that, given his profile as a leading Investigative Magistrate, Ciancolini will be transferred to Rome once initial investigations have been conducted in Florence. Signorina Milazzi has been released on remand following preliminary questioning.

Conte, a former journalist, is the daughter of City Councillor Guido Conte of the controlling 'Democratic Socialist Party.' A spokesperson for the Mayor said that there would be no statement released until the position was clearer, but that in the meantime Councillor Conte would not be taking any part in the running of the Council. Councillor Conte was not available for comment.

Councillor Conte was elected in....' the article continued to summarise her father's political activities to date, indicating to Francesca that only a limited amount of information had been released to the press.

She turned back to the front page and scanned the other leading articles, then felt her phone vibrate against her thigh. 'Il Fienile, SP49, Locality Marcialla (follow signs towards Certaldo from Tav. 3k) Get paper – urgent – Report bypassed sub-editors' room.'

A bit late to tell her about the paper, she thought: a good job she'd cut her hair. Three kilometres from Tavarnelle; it would take her about an hour on the motorino and it was just after ten-thirty now. She knew that Susanna Busoni had a young daughter and was banking on her picking her daughter up from nursery and taking her home for lunch. Visiting Busoni at his office again probably wouldn't be wise, but she was sure that if she could catch Susanna, she'd be able to get through to the old man.

She knew it was the right house almost as soon as it came into sight along the road, just before the village of Marcialla. A large old hay-barn had been mainly rendered in white and had several tall thin windows inserted into the side, recessed at an angle so that, unless one was fairly close, they didn't break the visual line of the sides of the barn, while making the most of the spectacular views to the South-West. The typically Tuscan terracotta air-bricks on the front of the barn had been left in place to retain the effect of a rustic building, but she imagined that there was now a large pane of glass behind the terracotta.

Unlike the majority of the larger houses in the countryside closer to the city, the land around the house was not fenced off and she was able to run the Piaggio off the road and round the back where she placed it out of sight by some bushes.

A wooden bench had been placed against the wall of the barn near the back door and Francesca sat down there to wait until Susanna got home. As she waited she closed her eyes and leaned her head back against the wall and tried to remember some of the poems she had learnt by rote when she was at school, to try and stop thinking and worrying about Marco, her parents, Rosa, Paul and Ciancolini.

'Mamma! Mamma! There's a lady near the door.

The child's voice awoke her and, for a moment, she struggled to remember where she was and why she was there, before recognising her surroundings. What had changed since before she had dozed off was that now there was a little girl of, she guessed, three or four years old standing in front of her looking at her.

'Amalia. Come here – now,' came the slightly anxious voice of Susanna Busoni from around the corner. Francesca managed a smile as she began to rise and the child turned and ran back to its mother.

When Francesca turned the corner of the house, she saw Susanna Busoni crouching by the side of the child who was talking to her animatedly and pointing back to where Francesca now stood.

Susanna rose and stepped between Francesca and the child, 'Who….? And then, as she recognised her, 'What are you doing here?' She looked round anxiously and Francesca, realising that Busoni may not have told her what was going on, held her hands out in a peaceful gesture and smiled.

'I'm sorry if I've startled you by coming here. I know you've probably read what's written in this morning's paper but, if you check with your father, he'll tell you that none of it is true.'

'Sorry. I didn't mean to seem unwelcoming…. It was just the surprise… I think I probably felt a bit guilty about letting this one just wander round the back on her own – It could have been anyone there. My father's told me more or less what's going on, but I didn't recognise you at first…. Come inside.'

As soon as they were inside, Francesca was about to speak but Susanna glanced towards her daughter and put her finger briefly on her lips and then, 'Amalia, take your coat off then go and sit on your potty and wait for mummy.' Amalia laughed, slipped off her coat and let it fall on the floor and then ran out of the room.

'OK' said Susanna, 'She's such a little chatterbox, and at that age. You can never be sure that they won't repeat something they've heard at the wrong time; the kids at the nursery go home and chatter and it only takes one to repeat something innocently and you' can't tell where it will end up.'

'It's alright; I understand. You've probably realised that things aren't going well and the next few days are likely to determine how things turn out, one way or the other. I know I've no right to drag you into this, but I need to speak to your father fairly urgently.'

'You could have gone to the office and you wouldn't have had to wait.'

'I did think about it, but I wasn't sure if there would be clients there and, with everything that's happened over the last couple of days I'm getting a bit paranoid about other people's safety. Out here in the open I can be absolutely certain that I wasn't followed, but in a built up area that I don't know particularly well, it's much more difficult. I really am sorry about disturbing you here.'

'No, that wasn't what I meant; I was just thinking about you and you having to waste time waiting.' Francesca smiled her thanks and Susanna continued, 'OK When I come back with Amalia, ask her to read one of her books to you – No, she can't read yet, but she knows her favourite stories off by heart, so she'll follow the pictures and pretend to read – While she's doing that, I'll ring my father and she'll be too busy concentrating on the story to pay me any attention…. Right, let me go and sort her out. - I'll be back in a minute - Make yourself at home.'

Francesca did so. She sat on a comfortable settee that was loosely covered with a throw, obviously intended to offer some form of protection from a lively child and the inevitable attendant risks of *nutella* and home-made jams. The settee also had the advantage of offering its occupants an oblique view of the driveway to the house so that she would be aware if any other visitors approached.

A few minutes later, mother and daughter returned, Amalia with a collection of books and toys clasped in her arms. 'Now, this lady doesn't know the story of *Capucetto Rosso*! Can you imagine that?' Amalia looked at Francesca with her eyes wide open, and Susanna bent down and whispered something in her ear. A big smile spread across the little girl's face and she put her treasures down on the settee beside Francesca.

'Would you like me to read you a story?' she asked earnestly.

'That would be lovely. Come and sit next to me… or on my knee, if you prefer.' Amalia climbed up and, book in hand, found a comfortable position on Francesca's lap.

'Now,' said Amalia in a very grown-up way, 'I want you to listen very carefully,' Francesca nodded gravely, trying not to laugh, 'Open the book please.' Francesca did so and saw that the first two pages consisted of the first few lines of the story facing a picture of *Little Red Riding-Hood* being given a basket in her mother's kitchen.

'What's your name?' asked Amalia and Francesca saw Susanna shake her head in warning.

'Maddalena,' she said, thinking of her grandmother, but you can call me Maddie because I like it better.' She saw Susanna smile and wondered if Busoni had told his daughter about the Campolargo family.

'Alright, Maddie. I'm going to start now.' She smiled at Amalia. 'Once upon a time…' Francesca settled back to listen while she watched Susanna put a couple of things away in the kitchen and then, after checking to see that Amalia was fully engrossed in her story-telling, pick up the phone.

'*Ciao*. It's only me….. Listen, I need you to do me a big favour…. The plans I've been working on for the new houses in Via delle Mimose….. Yes. That's right. The four maisonettes. Well, I've got a meeting with the client first thing in the morning and while I was driving back, I thought of a slight amendment I need to make to the drawings….. No. That's really sweet of you, but I really need to do them myself; I'm not sure I could explain it properly over the phone….. No, I can't. I don't really want to take Amalia out again. I think she's got a bit of a temperature…. No. No. Nothing to worry about …. Would you? …. About an hour? That would be fantastic….. OK. See you soon….. *Ciao, ciao*!' She looked over at Francesca who nodded to show that she had understood and then gave her full attention to Amalia and *Little Red Riding-Hood*, thinking that as soon as all this was over, she wanted to start a family with Marco.

After *"Little Red Riding-Hood"*, Amalia demonstrated the virtues of almost all her toys to Francesca before her mother finally came over and said, 'Time you went for a little nap I think, or you'll be too tired later on.'

Amalia's bottom lip came out in a little pout, 'I'm not tired and Maddie wants to play, don't you Maddie?'

Before Francesca could answer, Susanna, who had obviously expected a similar response, continued, 'Grandad's coming later, and he won't be very happy if you fall asleep when he's playing with you, will he?'

'I won't fall asleep,' insisted Amalia, but Francesca could tell from her voice that the argument her mother had made carried some weight with her. She appeared undecided about whether or not to resist, then turned to Francesca, 'Will you still be here when I wake up, Maddie?'

Francesca glanced at Susanna who indicated that she should say 'Yes'. 'Of course I will. I couldn't possibly leave without saying good-bye to you. You do what Mummy says now and go and have a nice little sleep.' Amalia looked up and then stretched and kissed her on the cheek before slipping off the settee and running out of the door at the far end of the room.

'Excuse me a minute, while I just go and make sure she's really gone to bed. She won't sleep, she'll only pretend, but we need her out of the way when Dad arrives, otherwise you won't get chance to speak to him. He always said that he wouldn't spoil grandchildren and he'll try to be stern when he arrives but we all know that in less than five minutes she'll have him twisted round her little finger.'

While Susanna was gone, Francesca amused herself by thinking about when she would have her own children and wondering what sort of father Marco would be and how her own parents would interact with their new grandchildren. She tried to remember how they had been when Alessio and Mati had been little but realised that she hadn't really paid much attention at the time.

Susanna was back in just over five minutes and sank down on the settee next to Francesca. 'Phew. I don't know about Amalia, but I could do with a rest.'

'She's lovely. What does her father do?' The question was innocent – just making conversation while they waited for Busoni to arrive, but it clearly touched a nerve; Francesca saw a hardening of Susanna's look which she failed to hide as she turned her head towards the window.

'Her father does pretty much whatever he pleases. He has his own business selling computers and spends most of his time travelling around, visiting clients and designing tailor-made systems for them. About a year ago, a friend kept dropping hints that, for some of his female clients, regular servicing had taken on a whole new meaning. I thought it was just malicious gossip at first but then someone else told me and, after that, when I worked up the courage to challenge him, he admitted it – said he didn't think I'd mind and that he was always careful that there were no complications. I kicked him out there and then; the house is mine anyway.'

'I'm sorry,' said Francesca.

'Don't be. I don't know what I saw in him in the first place.'

'What about Amalia?'

'Luckily, he never really paid her much attention when he was here. Now he turns up once a month with a tacky toy for her, sits for half an hour looking bored as she tells him what she's been doing and then says he's really sorry but he's got to rush off and he'll try and spend more time with her next time.' She shook her head. 'Anyway. Let's not talk about him; he was just a bad mistake. His only redeeming feature is that he gave me Amalia,' she raised her eyes towards the ceiling and smiled as she did so. 'Now. Let's make sure that we intercept Dad before he gets to the door. It would be better if she didn't hear him arrive.'

They moved into the kitchen, near the door, and drank water while they waited, chatting about anything but the reason for Francesca being there. When they saw Busoni's red Fiat Sedici turn off the road and onto the driveway, Susanna slipped off her seat and stood in the doorway waiting for him. As he approached, she held a finger to her lips to indicate that he shouldn't call out.

'Is she asleep?' he asked with a worried look on his face as he came closer.

Susanna smiled and shook her head, 'Probably not but I don't want her to know that you're here yet. There's someone else who needs to see you first... Come in, and let's shut the door.'

As he came in, he caught sight of Francesca and stopped dead, surprise written across his face.' I'm afraid I got you out under false pretences,' said Susanna, 'There's nothing wrong with Amalia, but this seemed like the most natural way to get you out here.'

'Buongiorno, Signor Busoni,' said Francesca with a half-smile, 'It's good to see you again.'

'And you, of course. But, tell me, what's actually going on at the moment? I only know what I've read in the papers and I don't believe a word of that... Are you alright?'

She assured him that she was fine, except for the worries she had about the others, but that overall they seemed to be at crisis point with the possibility of thwarting the conspiracy hanging by a thread. The authority to act, written out by the President, had been written out for the benefit of Ciancolini and, with his arrest, it was now unlikely that the letter of authority had any more validity. As quickly as possible she gave him the gist of her conversation with Vichi, leaving the bit about Busoni contacting the President again until the end.

'So, unless you can think of a better alternative, the only chance we have seems to lie in persuading the President to put himself in the firing line and make a stand.' She stopped and waited while Busoni processed the information and assessed the options.

'Franco Innominati has never been known for his decisiveness,' he mused, 'he'll take quite a bit of persuading. He looked at Francesca.

'And the only person we can think of who has any hope of succeeding is…' she returned his look without blinking.

Busoni sighed, 'is me, I think you were going to say,' he said resignedly. 'Well' I can't promise that I'll succeed but I'm prepared to give it a try… Now, what do we know about the people who've been arrested?'

She set out what she knew about the arrest of Ciancolini, including how she herself had been lucky to escape capture, and then told him the little bit of information that Vichi and Fabrizio had been able to give her about the rest of her family.

'I'd be pretty sure that your parents aren't in any danger; apart from the fact that neither of them knows anything about what's being going on, you father is too well known and respected around the city for anything to happen to him or your mother. As for your sister and Paul, things look a bit more complicated; Paul, in particular, has broken plenty of laws while I'm sure it would be possible to make a good case out against your sister as an accomplice. Being your father's daughter will help Rosa a little bit, but as far as Paul is concerned, the only thing I can think of is to get the British Consul involved – I assume he is still a British subject, isn't he?'

'As far as I know. I've never really heard him say much about it. I think he considered himself as a European more than anything – except when there was a football match on or it was time for the Olympics. I'll try and find out how you get in touch with the Consulate about things like that.'

'I'm pretty sure it will need to someone who's a member of his family and whose face is not plastered over the front of the newspapers as a wanted criminal.' intervened Susanna. Are there any relatives in England who could be contacted, who would call the consulate?'

Francesca thought for a moment. 'His nephew, Luke, might be the best person. He's only twenty and still a student, but he's bright as a button and he speaks reasonable Italian. He usually spends at least three weeks with Rosa and Paul every summer, and he's been coming over most Christmases as well, since his mother died…. The only difficulty is that I'd need to go home to get his number; I don't even have my own phone now.'

'Going home is obviously out of the question,' said Busoni.

'I know his address,' said Francesca, 'but writing to him would take far too long.'

'Write down his name and address, and what University he's at, and leave it to me,' said Susanna, 'I'll track him down – don't worry.'

Francesca looked at her dubiously but did as she asked. Busoni put his hand over Francesca's free hand, 'Susanna's always been very resourceful; if she says she can get something done, it will get done. Now, what about that boyfriend of yours?'

Marco was the one that Francesca had avoided talking about because she was desperately worried and trying not to think about it. Despite her effort to remain detached, she found that her eyes filled up with tears and she shut her eyes for a moment to try and choke them off. Busoni and Susanna waited patiently, Busoni still with his hand on hers. She shook her head, 'I don't know. I haven't heard anything and I haven't dared to try and contact him, because if they've arrested him and have his phone then that would only make things worse. I don't know what to do.'

'Do you think he has been arrested? Couldn't he be on the run like you?'

That was what she hoped, but she knew it wasn't true, and hearing her thoughts put into words by someone else, made her realise just how unlikely that scenario was. 'They picked him up after we'd been to Naples because one of his assistants had been picked up near one of the ministries carrying a listening device, and with Marco's address in his pocket. They let him go after questioning but they've been tracking him and he was only able to make contact when he was sure he'd lost them. The problem is that, as far as I can see, the only way SISMI could have moved against me and Ciancolini and the others up here in Florence is if they had Marco's phone.'

'Nonno!' shouted an excited little voice from the doorway and, as they all turned round, Amalia came running towards them, a slightly dog-eared cloth rabbit held in one hand.

Chapter 29

While still desperately concerned about the others, Francesca felt a bit better after she left the Busonis – maybe there was still a chance that everything would turn out OK – Busoni had an air of calm about him that inspired confidence. The stalls by the side of the road near the Certosa were still open so, before returning to Vichi's motor caravan, she bought some *porchetta* and some fruit to take back with her along with a selection of the day's papers.

She timed her arrival back in Via Forlani after it was dark and she knew that the last of the businesses along the road would have closed and been deserted for the night. Despite this, she had to walk past the overhanging bush when she got there as there was an old Fiat 127 parked less than fifty metres down the road; from the way the windows were steamed up and from the way the car was rocking gently, she thought that she was unlikely to be noticed but decided that it was better to be safe than sorry and walked on along the road deciding to try again in half an hour.

In the event, she didn't have to wait that long for less than ten minutes later the car drove past her and she caught a glimpse of a young couple: the man driving and the woman with her head leaning on his shoulder. As soon as the car was out of sight, she turned round and made her way back.

Inside the van, she found a note from Vichi telling her that he would come to see her (if she were there) at about eleven, so that she shouldn't worry if she heard someone approaching at that time. Hopefully he would have good news for her she thought, and settled down to look through the papers. She had not bought *La Nazione*, having already seen the important parts in the bar the morning and was pleased to see that, although her photograph appeared in the other papers, it was in a less prominent position than it had been in the Florence based daily.

What concerned her, however, was the greater prominence given to the leaks from the Mitrokhin Commission in the other papers. The Milan based *"Il Giornale"* had a teaser-article on the front pointing readers to a longer article on an inside page that was full of unattributed quotes with authoritative sounding comments casting aspersions on the suitability of several of the leaders of the left to be entrusted with the future of the country. Silvio Cioni, the Minister for Public Works was quoted as saying that he did not feel it was appropriate to comment at the moment as those who appeared to be guilty of crimes against the state were currently occupying positions which made it impossible for them to respond to the committee's findings.

Francesca shook her head in disbelief when she read this. For someone who didn't feel it appropriate to comment, Cioni had stuck his boot in quite viciously; positions which made it impossible for them to respond was as clear a reference to Prodi in his role as President of the European Commission, as naming him would have been, and his use of the word 'findings' implied that the Commission's work was complete and that there was no doubting their conclusions. Surely, she thought, the bias in the article was so pronounced that anyone would spot it, but then she thought of the paper's target audience and realised that they were giving their readers just what they wanted.

Just after eleven she heard the sound of a car outside the barn and turned off the lamp just as a precaution. A minute later, light seeped around the van as the main door to the barn was opened and a figure holding a torch entered, pulling the door closed behind it. The figure stood still for a few seconds, flashing the torch around and into each corner of the barn, then she heard Vichi's voice softly call her name and she was able to relax.

She relit the lamp in the van as he entered and, as soon as the light fell on his face, she could tell that something was wrong. She sat and waited for him to begin, but before he spoke he pulled a quarter bottle of grappa out of his coat pocket and placed it on the small table. Francesca, looked at him, wanting to know but at the same time fearing the worst.

'I'm afraid I've got some bad news for you – some very bad news.' He knew that he shouldn't be affected by this, he'd had to deliver similar pieces of news several times as part of his job and thought he'd trained himself to be detached, but it didn't seem to be working this time. He looked at her but Francesca remained silent, unwilling or unable to help him. After a moment he resumed, 'Marco Antognoni was shot….'

She had no idea what he said next; she didn't even know if he finished the sentence; her mind was reeling from the blow; it was wrong, it had to be wrong; she and Marco were going to spend the rest of their lives together and have wonderful children; they were going to travel and see new places, meet new people and eat different foods. It was impossible.

'Signorina Conte… Francesca?…. Here; drink some of this.'

She took the plastic beaker he held out to her almost mechanically and tipped its contents down her throat before spluttering as the fiery liquid made its presence felt.

When she had recovered from the effect of the grappa, she found that she no longer felt emotional; shock, she presumed, but she knew that she had to make the most of the moment. 'I'm sorry. I didn't take any more in after you said that Marco had been shot. Tell me again what happened,'

Vichi shook his head, 'I can only tell you the official version; I can't tell you what actually happened because I don't know… Officially, Antognoni was shot when he pulled a gun on two officers who were carrying out a drugs raid on his flat.'

'A drugs raid,' repeated Francesca incredulously… but he never.'

'That was obviously only their excuse. They say that they went to his flat as the result of a tip off and that they recovered over a kilo of badly cut cocaine. There's been a lot of pressure on the Roman police recently to clamp down on the drugs trade, so there will be no calls for an enquiry into Antognoni's death.'

'The funeral… I must go to the funeral.'

Vichi grimaced, 'They shot him three days ago and cremated him yesterday… I'm sorry.'

'What about the ashes?' she asked helplessly. Vichi didn't reply as they both knew it was a pointless question. Even if there was a little urn somewhere, she could hardly walk up and claim it.

'There's more bad news as well, I'm afraid.' Her eyes opened wide and showed her fear. 'No, not as bad as before…. Does the name Don Adriano dei Sisti mean anything to you?' She inclined her head to indicate that it did. 'I thought it might. He was arrested at the same time as the others, officially for misappropriation of church funds… that sort of thing happens occasionally and I wouldn't have made the connection if it hadn't been for the timing and the fact that the arrest wasn't carried out by the regular police and he hasn't been brought into the Questura or any of the local Commissariats. Normally, if a priest is brought in, we have the Diocese on our back demanding their release before we've even finished transcribing their details; this time, there hasn't been a squeak from the church authorities.'

'So how do you...'

'His curate came in to the Questura because he was worried that he'd heard nothing since Don Adriano was taken away. He wanted to know if he needed to get a substitute in to take Mass.'

Francesca sighed, 'Poor Adriano. He's suffered as much as anyone in all this.'

'How was he involved? What does a parish priest have to do with what's going on?' asked Vichi, unable to allow his compassion to completely subdue his instincts as a policeman.

'Are you religious?' she asked, surprising him.

'I suppose theoretically, yes, like most people. It's just something I've always taken for granted.'

'And do you believe the Bible should be taken literally?'

'Well, no. Obviously not. It's allegorical, isn't it?'

'Unfortunately,' she said, there are plenty of people within the church who believe that it should be taken literally, particularly Deuteronomy... Adriano isn't one of them.' Vichi looked puzzled and Francesca gave a little smile, the first since he'd arrived. 'He believes that we all have a duty to love each other, regardless of race, colour creed or gender.... Unfortunately, his greatest love wasn't a love of which the church authorities, who would cite the Bible as their justification could approve.'

'But,' objected Vichi, there are quite a few people in the church who have secret families, even if the Church turns a blind eye and denies that there is a problem.'

'There are. And some of them, like Adriano, find that their greatest love is for another man. Adriano loved Arturo dell'Omodarme, and because of that he agreed to help us when we needed to get access to Fogazzini.'

'The minister? I still don't...'

'No. Not Maria-Grazia, her brother, the Bishop of Todi. We needed to be able to speak to him so that we had leverage over the minister, and we'd have found it difficult to get to him if we hadn't had a priest needing to see him urgently.'

'I see,' said Vichi thoughtfully. 'How much does he know about the others involved? What I mean is,' he clarified, 'could anyone else who SISMI aren't aware of be endangered by anything he may tell them?'

'No. There's no danger of that. The only people he knew about were me and my sister, apart from dell'Omodarme of course... I can't imagine that dell'Omodarme would have had any reason to tell him about anyone else. He was very protective of Adriano and wouldn't have wanted to put him in an even more difficult position... It was me who asked him to help with Fogazzini because I knew he'd want to help bring those who killed Arturo to justice.'

'If you're successful, they still will be.... And, I'm sure that Don Adriano will be alright. If his involvement has been as limited as you say it has, then keeping hold of him just causes another problem for them.' He reached out for her hand to comfort her, but she withdrew hers as she felt his touch.

There was silence between them for a while until she appeared to take a resolution and, pushing her shoulders back said, without any further signs of emotion, 'I've made sure that pressure will be put on Innominati to intervene. Hopefully, we should know whether he's agreed by the end of the week. Now, I think I want to be alone.'

Vichi inclined his head to show that he understood and put his hand on the door-handle to leave. 'Anything I can do....' his voice tailed off as he slid the door open, not expecting a reply.

Standing outside the van, he was surprised to hear her say, 'The report of Marco's death; can you get me a copy?' - her voice was toneless.

'I should be able to get a copy tomorrow. I'll bring it round when I come in the evening.'

'Earlier. I need to have it earlier in the evening. I have to go away for a couple of days.'

He shrugged, 'I'll do what I can, but I won't be able to get it here before eight.'

Finding her way through the vicoli of Naples was easier the second time, although she still had to take great care at some of the intersections. She was sure that some of the teenagers she passed sitting astride their motorini by the sides, or in the middle, of the alleyways were there to act as lookouts for any incursions by police, carabinieri or even rival Camorra groups but, although she felt numerous eyes following her, no-one approached her.

This time the dog didn't bark and only one set of eyes peered at her out of the gloom although she was fairly sure that a faint metallic glint on the edge of her vison was coming from the barrel of a pistol. As before she question thrown at her in the strange high-pitched voice was *'Cchi vulé?'* although this time it was followed almost immediately with 'You!' as she was recognised and the thug's eyes narrowed.

'Yes. Me. I need to see Don Adolfo – now.'

Without speaking he opened the door wider and took a step back to allow her to enter.

Without taking his eyes off her, the man pushed the door closed with his foot and indicated to Francesca that she should turn and face the wall with her arms above her head and her palms flat against the wall.

Knowing that an important boss like Don Adolfo needed to be well-protected, she did not complain even when he roughly inserted his boot between her ankles to push her legs further apart. With the barrel of his gun pressed against her back at the base of the spinal-column, she was aware that any false move would leave her paralysed for life and did not flinch even when he ran his free hand down the inside of her thighs to check for hidden weapons.'

When he was satisfied that she was unarmed, she felt the release of the pressure on her spine as he backed away to allow her to slowly turn round. He waved the gun barrel towards a chair at the side of the entrance hall and then took an intercom out of a side pocket as she sat down. He didn't take his eyes off her as he spoke rapidly in thick dialect that she found impossible to follow; the only words that she was fairly sure of were 'woman', 'Florentine' and 'here', although she could make a good guess at the sense of the communication he was making.

She was mildly surprised when the door at the far end of the corridor opened and a female figure was silhouetted in the aperture, and even more surprised when she was invited to enter in clear Italian but with an accent she couldn't place. The next room was dimly lit and Francesca found it difficult to tell exactly how it was furnished, but the woman opened another door to one side and showed her into the room where she had met Don Adolfo on her previous visit.

'I need to speak with Don Adolfo,' said Francesca as she lowered herself into the same chair she had sat in on her previous visit.

'That won't be possible tonight, Signorina Conte,' said the woman, emphasising Francesca's name to indicate that she was fully aware of who she was and why she was there, 'You have information for Don Adolfo.'

'Everything you need to know about who killed the Jaconos is on these sheets of paper. You've got names, places and times,' she said, pushing across two folded sheets of A4.

The woman, who had positioned herself so that the main light source was behind her, spent five minutes reading carefully through the notes while Francesca sat quietly studying her. Francesca estimated her to be no older than her mid-twenties and was surprised to see that she was dressed far more tastefully than she would have expected for a gangster's moll, as she assumed her to be. When the woman had finished reading she looked at Francesca and said, 'You seem to have paid your debt… what I don't understand is why you brought these yourself; the agreement was that Capuano would pass them on… I find it hard to believe that you were so excited by your last visit here that you were so keen to return.'

Francesca met the woman's penetrating look without lowering her eyes. 'I have a further proposal to make to Don Adolfo, which I think it would be better if Rita Capuano was unaware of.'

The woman contemplated her for a moment and then said, 'I'll hear your proposal.'

Francesca shook her head, 'With respect; this is for Don Adolfo's ears alone.'

The woman's mouth smiled but her eyes narrowed, 'That won't be possible. You'll have to deal with me… otherwise you may find that this area of Naples can be quite dangerous for a young northerner to walk through alone – even in daylight.'

Francesca thought for a moment, uncomfortably aware that she didn't really have a choice. 'Alright: have it your way... I assume that you have business associates in Rome…' she glanced at the other woman who sat impassively, ' Major Sergio Ramazzotti, currently attached to SISMI and based at the Ministry of Justice in Via Arenula, just north of Trastevere – I want him dead.'

'Then, why don't you kill him?' said the younger woman, 'As far as I'm aware, we have no interest in him.'

It was Francesca's turn to show a mirthless smile. 'Ramazzotti may well be one of the people pulling the strings behind Stiappa but, more importantly than that, if Ramazzotti were to meet with an unfortunate accident over the next couple of days, I would be able to tell you exactly where to find Stiappa.'

'And if he doesn't have an accident?'

'Then it will be up to you to find Stiappa and settle your affairs with him – but you won't find it easy.'

The woman's eyebrows raised slightly before she stood up indicating that the meeting was at an end. 'We'll consider your proposal and, if we decide to accept and fulfil our side of the bargain, we will expect to see you again when you will meet your obligations… should you fail to meet your obligations, I would advise you to look after your niece and nephew very carefully.' Despite feeling her heart rate increase at the mention of Mati and Alessio, Francesca managed to keep her features under control, nodded her acceptance of the terms and turned on her heel towards the door.

She needed to find out more about the woman, having been disconcerted by the other woman's knowledge of her own affairs, and the only person she could think of who would be able to help her was Rita Capuano. However, as she was almost certain that she would be followed when she left the home of Don Adolfo and she did not want Capuano to be in any way involved in the deal she had just done, she took the opposite direction and headed downhill. The vicoli were a maze but she knew that heading down would eventually bring her down to Spaccanapoli from where it would be easy to reach Corso Umberto and then the main station. Once she reached the Corso it would have been easy to reach the station on foot but instead she took a taxi in the knowledge that, if questioned later, the driver would be able to report that he had dropped her off at the station.

As she had hoped, there was a train due to leave shortly for the North and she was able to get on and settle into a seat as if preparing for a long journey. She made sure that she was in full view of the people milling about on the platform so that whichever of them was working for Don Adolfo would be able to confirm that she had left the city. When she heard doors begin to slam in the distance and knew that departure was imminent, she stood up and leaned nonchalantly against the window as if to get a last look at the city, but in reality to take note of any passengers who got on the train at the very last minute before the doors were slammed shut.

The train was a slow *'regionale'*, which suited her purpose perfectly as she had no intention of remaining on it for long. It would have been perfect if it had made the first of many scheduled stops at Napoli Gianturco station but that was too much to hope for and it was nearly a quarter of an our later before it came to halt in Aversa. She stood by the window, watching a handful of people get off and a few dozen enter the train until, just as the doors began to be slammed shut, she stepped out quickly onto the platform and behind a convenient pillar. From where she stood, she could see the full length of the train and was certain that no-one had descended after her, however, she waited another five minutes moving towards the exit, to allow those who had left the train before her to clear the station. Less than an hour later after two bus rides and a short trip on the underground, she was pressing the discretely placed doorbell outside Rita Capuano's home.

The older journalist displayed no surprise as she let Francesca in and ushered her through into the big room at the back. *'Caffè?'* she asked as she indicated a seat and Francesca smiled to indicate her gratitude.

When the coffee was ready and her host had taken a seat opposite her, she explained that she had been to deliver the information herself and described the precautions she had taken to avoid being seen coming to Capuano's afterwards, to distance Capuano from involvement with the Camorra. She did not tell Capuano that the real reason for visiting the house of Don Adolfo again was to try and get the Camorra to kill Marco's killers for her. She knew that what she had done breached every professional, ethical and moral code that she knew, except for the 'honour' code of the gangsters themselves, and she knew that she should be ashamed of herself, and that Capuano would be horrified if she knew.

As it happened, she didn't feel ashamed, she felt only a deep burning hatred towards those who had murdered Marco that she persuaded herself was determination to ensure that his death did not prove to have been in vain. She had originally intended to phone Capuano to let her know that the information, that was effectively Stiappa's death warrant, had been passed on to the Camorra, but meeting the woman instead of Don Adolfo had disconcerted her; she had to know that the woman she had met had the authority to make the promise she had.

Capuano raised an eyebrow when Francesca told her about the meeting with the woman and, when she had finished, said quietly, almost as if she were talking to herself, *'La Guiablesse!* So it's true then.'

As she did not elaborate, Francesca, puzzled more than before, had to prompt her, *'La* what?'

'La Guiablesse.' repeated Capuano in a voice that suggested a degree of awe that Francesca found strangely disconcerting in the older woman who usually radiated an air of world-weary cynicism. She gave Capuano a look that urged her to continue. 'In Caribbean and Central American folklore the *Guiablesse* is a she devil who

men find extremely beautiful – irresistibly so – but who has hidden claws with which she will rip them to pieces after seducing them.'

'But why… I don't understand,' said Francesca, feeling even more confused.

Capuano sighed. 'Back in the 1890s when the first waves of emigrants were making their way to the Americas, quite a lot of them ended up in Costa Rica where they were mainly employed in building the main railroad that runs all the way up the country, linking Nicaragua to the North with Panama to the South. One of these Italians, who I believe was a great-great-uncle of Don Adolfo, established himself as a sort of leader of the Italian community, protecting their interests and making sure that work was distributed fairly and that immigrant workers from other countries weren't undercutting labour rates. Obviously, once the main railways were competed, the Italians moved into other areas of life and Don Abbondio…' Capuano raised a hand in an apologetic gesture, '… Yes, I know… just like in *'I Promessi Sposi',* I'm not sure if that was his given name or if he chose it himself… Don Abbondio expanded his spheres of influence with them – the classic way in which Mafia type organisations develop. Have you read *'The Godfather'*?'

'A long time ago. I've seen the films much more recently.'

'Well, if you think about how Vito Corleone's business grew and gradually expanded into other areas, sometimes because the only choice was between expanding to control new sectors or being crushed by rivals, there are a lot of similarities with how Abbondio's business grew. By the end of the Second World War, it was clear that, if they wanted to retain their influence in Costa Rica, they would need to come to an agreement with the Mafia in the States. Drugs from Nicaragua, and particularly from Colombia, have to pass through Costa Rica if they're being transported in any worthwhile quantities and, as Abbondio's family continued to control employment on the Railways, the Mafia need either their co-operation or their destruction. Co-operation was the only sensible choice.'

'OK. I get that – but what's it all got to do with the girl?'

Capuano gave a thin smile, 'Be patient; I'm getting there. The current head of the Costa Rican family, Don Luigi, had five children; all of them, at some point were sent to spend time working with some of the main Mafia families in the States, I suppose you could describe them almost as interns while they were being trained in the business. The eldest, a daughter, I believe married into one the American families and never went back; the eldest son is now back working alongside his father as is the youngest son. The second son was killed in a shoot up and the second daughter is *La Guiablesse* who you met earlier.'

'But…'

'I'm getting there. My sources tell me that she was the brightest of the five and her father had promised her mother that she would be kept out of the business, so when she went to the States, although she was nominally living with one of the families with whom her father did business, she was also signed up to study medicine, which obviously gave her a good knowledge of anatomy. Unfortunately, Cristina, as she was then known, found the family business much more interesting than Medicine. Somehow - and the information I have from this point on is only hearsay – she got involved with the family in the States and was given more and more jobs to do by them. Now there was a disagreement with another local family and one morning the head of the other family was found dead in bed with his windpipe having been torn out. His two bodyguards who'd been sitting outside the door of his hotel room, were also found dead with their throats cut. Being in a hotel, the police had to be called which alerted the local press and, despite pressure from above, a few details leaked out. The most relevant of these details was that the three men had arrived at the hotel accompanied by a woman who the receptionist had the impression was beautiful, even though she positioned herself so that it was difficult to get a good look at her face.

Less than a week later, Cristina dropped out of university and reappeared several months later back in Costa Rica. Her reappearance coincided with one of the United States periodic attempts to clamp down on the drugs trade, and particularly to cut off the supply routes. Costa Rica has always maintained friendly relations with the United States and there's a lot of inward investment, particularly from pharmaceuticals companies. It abolished its army after the revolution in 1948 and relies on a fairly laid-back police force to keep order, which makes it an ideal place for the CIA to use as a base to keep an eye on Central America. In theory, all the CIA operatives who are based there are employees of the big pharmaceutical or IT companies which allows the Costa Rican government to turn a blind eye to their presence. The CIA station chief was a puritanical, humourless man in his late forties, with a wife and two kids back in Missouri, to whom he was meant to be devoted. Nevertheless, there were rumours that he'd fallen head-over-heels for a mysterious local woman which led to all sorts of gossip and speculation amongst his staff. Then, one morning, just before he was about to lead a major operation against the drug traffickers, he didn't turn up to work and wasn't answering his phone.'

'Don't tell me,' said Francesca, 'he was found in his bed with his throat ripped out.' It was Capuano's turn to give a nod to signify that Francesca had arrived at the correct conclusion, 'and, presumably both the CIA Boss in Costa Rica and the Mafia Boss in the States had had sex before they were murdered?'

'You've got it. She turned up here in Naples at the back end of last year and has either made herself indispensable to Don Adolfo, or may even have taken over from him as head of his family.'

There was a minute's silence then Francesca shook her head, 'I'm amazed. How can you possibly know all that?'

'To be able to write the sort of articles I write, I have to know what lies behind the stories even if there are a lot of things I could never write about. So long as I'm even handed and don't seem to be favouring or focussing on any particular group, I'm generally tolerated. Cristina Trocchia, as she's really called, made the mistake of allowing herself to be referred to as *La Guiablesse* in Camorra circles when she first arrived here, probably to create an aura and earn respect. When I first heard the name, it meant nothing to me and all I was getting were vague rumours from my usual sources, but when I checked out the name and discovered its Caribbean origin, a bit of cross referencing and speaking to colleagues in first the Caribbean countries and then in the States, helped me sort it out – but I've never seen her yet… If I were you, I'd make sure I never had anything else to do with her; because of the arrests that have taken place and the leaders who've been killed in feuds, the women are gradually taking on more active roles in the Camorra families, and they don't always play by the same rules. Most of the male gangsters could still be loosely described as 'men of honour', but the women….' she allowed her sentence to hang like an axe between them.

She caught the night train from Napoli Campi Flegrei and was lucky enough to be able to pay a supplement on the train and occupy a couchette which should have made the journey much more comfortable. Despite Capuano's warning that she should avoid *La Guiablesse*, she took a grim satisfaction, the first satisfaction she had felt since hearing of Marco's death, in the thought that revenge was now in the right hands. As she lay on the narrow couchette she tried to imagine *La Guiablesse* ripping the throat out of Marco's executioner until the steady rhythm of the train wheels on the rails gradually dulled the clarity of her thoughts and she dropped into an uneasy sleep.

The sex was as wildly energetic as any she could ever remember and involved positions and actions that she had previously only ever read about while researching articles, the accounts of which she had assumed were grossly exaggerated. At some point her viewpoint changed from that of an interested observer to that of *La Guiablesse* herself and she felt a surge of power as she experienced the blend of desire and hatred that the assassin was feeling. Finally, as she shuddered in ecstasy, and the man, whose face was blurred, moaned and tilted his head backwards, she thrust her long fingernails forcefully into the side of his throat, tearing through flesh and muscle until they curled round the trachea and tore it out through the hole her fingers had made in the neck. As she knelt above the body, holding the bloody trachea, which resembled a gigantic grey caterpillar, aloft in triumph, with grey blood dripping onto her naked breast, the dead man's face turned towards her and Marco's face glared into hers. 'We were fighting for what was right. Now, how are you any better than them?' Then Marco began to laugh, a harsh demonic laugh that turned her to ice and she woke up shivering, covered in sweat and with part of the tangled sheet twisted in her hand.

Chapter 30

Having flicked quickly through the pile of newspapers that his secretary had handed him when he arrived, Bernardo Casini picked out the one he felt would be most informative and began to look at the key items of news in more detail. The leading story told of the enthusiastic reception given to the Prime Minister at the first of a series of rallies that had been held in Milan the previous evening. It appeared that the Prime Minister intended to run a very long, personality centred campaign before the big Regional elections of the following year to provide a strong base for the next General Election. Yet again, masses of people seemed to have been taken in by the affable, anti-establishment, man-of-the-people, patriotic act which the Prime Minister, one of, if not the richest man in the country had put on for their benefit.

At the same time he seemed to be able to persuade them that the country was a far more prosperous, more moral and happier place than it had been when he had taken over, and blame the European Union for the fact that unemployment had risen and the money in their pocket bought less than it had done previously. This conjuring trick was achieved with the backing of the Church, who he was quick to praise for safeguarding the morals of those who may be tempted by the excesses of foreigners who were a threat to the established order. Despite some cuts he had been forced to make to prevent the country sliding into insolvency, he had steadfastly championed the Church's right to continue receiving a high proportion of the 0.8% of Income Tax destined for good works and, as a result, he was guaranteed the tacit support of the Church, despite that organisation's theoretical aims being more in line with those of the socialists. The previous evening it seemed as if all the vain boasts and meaningless promises he had made had been given wild applause by the Milanese public. Without naming names he had spoken about the threat posed to the nation by alternative leaders whose real loyalties lay elsewhere and implied that the nation's shortcomings under previous governments had been because it had not been led by true patriots.

Casini skimmed over much of the content of the Prime Minister's performance which, unlike the Milanese crowd, he found depressingly predictable and vacuous. He had always believed that the forces of order should be loyal only to the state and show no favour to any of the political parties, but he found that this Prime Minister stretched his tolerance to the limits, whether or not he were aware of the virtual *coup d'état* in which some of his leading ministers were involved. He found it depressing that the latest opinion polls showed increasing support for the Prime Minister and his allies and feared that this trend would only increase after further planned rallies to be held in Rome, Florence, Naples, Palermo and then finally Milan again, over the next ten days. All the papers except the communist *Manifesto,* which completely ignored the rally, the 'reformed' communist *Unità,* which reported that the rally had taken place without reporting anything the Prime Minister had said and the centrist *Repubblica* which reported what he had said without editorial comment, were unanimous in their praise of the Prime Minister and his stewardship of the country. All the other national papers not only took the opportunity to praise the Prime Minister but also used their reports as opportunities to remind their readers of the leaks coming out of the Mitrokhin Commission.

He pulled a pile of official reports towards him and picked up a pen with a sigh, then changing his mind, he pushed the reports to one side and pressed one of the buttons on his intercom. 'If he's in the building, could you send me Major Lo Verde, please,' he said as soon as a slight click told him that his adjutant had pressed the speaker switch and before he had chance to ask what he wanted. He lifted his finger, cutting off the conversation without bothering to wait for a reply.

When Lo Verde knocked and entered five minutes later, Casini had a file open in front of him next to a notepad on which he was writing a list of names. Quietly, Lo Verde closed the door behind him and made his way towards Casini's desk where his superior made a vague gesture which he interpreted as granting him permission to sit down, which he did.

'Things are looking fairly bleak,' said Casini, as he finally looked up from the paper in front of him; 'our judge is being held under house-arrest with tight security – there's no news of two of the others who were arrested, while officially, another of those who was working to expose this conspiracy was killed while resisting arrest during a drugs-raid… the young woman who you met when we were interrogating Stiappa is having to lie low as she avoided arrest by a miracle when they picked the judge up…. and I'm left with the problem of what to do with Stiappa.'

'If I may ask, Sir, how big is the group trying to prevent the coup?' asked the Major, calmly.

'A very good question, Sandro. Arturo dell'Omodarme was very insistent that nobody knew more than a handful of the others involved, to keep security as tight as possible. The problem now, of course, is that dell'Omodarme is dead, Ciancolini, who I assume knows all the key people, is beyond our reach, and it's going to be very difficult to arrange a meeting with Francesca Conte, particularly as she could be picked up at any moment.'

'With respect, Sir. It would be very difficult for you, not to mention unwise but, for a more junior officer, it would be less of a risk.'

Casini raised his eyebrows, 'And your reasoning is…?'

'If you were caught, or even just seen, with Conte, it would be an absolute disaster. Not only would that, at the very least, contaminate you so you could no longer do anything useful, but it would almost certainly lead to your replacement here, which would make it impossible to keep Stiappa under wraps. On the other hand, if a more junior officer who you can trust were arrested, he could claim that you knew nothing about what was going on.'

Casini, leaned back in his chair and looked at his junior officer for a minute, his eyes unwavering but his expression unreadable until Lo Verde began to feel uncomfortable. Finally, he seemed to make his mind up. 'You may have a point… Did you have anyone in mind for such a mission?'

Despite his military discipline and self-control, Lo Verde coloured slightly under Casini's penetrating gaze. He cleared his throat nervously, 'I thought, maybe… perhaps you could entrust me with such a mission. I've met her before, which would reduce some of the risks involved.'

Casini smiled, 'I'll think about it… In the meantime, I've got another important task for you,' and he turned around the sheet of paper on which he'd been writing and pushed it across the desk towards Lo Verde.

When Lo Verde left Casini's office twenty-five minutes later he had a new spring in his step as he moved towards his high-tech workstation. Whether or not he would be allowed out to meet up with Francesca Conte, he now had work to do that would enable him to put his considerable skills as a computer intelligence analyst to good use, and that hopefully would make a difference.

He had already encoded instructions in his computer so that it could take him quickly to the dark-web whenever he needed access and, in less than five minutes he had the recent banking history of the first of the names on the list on the screen in front of him. From there, by cross referencing locations at which she had made card-payments or used cash machines with military or police installations he was able to work out where the woman was working. From there, it was an easy task for him to access the hidden servers recording the ins and outs from the building of both staff and guests. She was there at the moment and records showed that, although there was some variation at the start and end of days, he could be certain of finding her there any day between ten-fifteen and four.

Committing what he had learnt to memory, he moved on to the second name on the list and, as far as possible, repeated the process.

By lunchtime, he had been through the whole list, occasionally being able to take shortcuts where Casini had added additional information, except one whose name he had passed over, and had managed to locate with a reasonable degree of certainty ten of the eleven he had searched for. After checking his watch, he pulled out his mobile phone and dialled the last name on the list, whom he knew personally and did not need to search for.

'Ciao, Marino. It's Sandro here, Sandro Lo Verde. How's it going?…. Yeah – I bet! ….. Oh, not too bad…. life goes on…. No! She was ages ago; we decided to go our separate ways…. Married to my work – you know me…. Listen – I'll be in Rome tonight. I was going to book into one of those cheap hotels near the station, then I thought there are much better ways to spend an evening than in a grotty hotel; I'll ring Mariano and offer to buy him a pizza… Yeah, and the wine as well!…. Are you sure?…. OK. I'll bring a toothbrush. See you later; I'll ring you when I'm in Rome…. Ciao, Marino.' He pressed the button to end the communication then, after waiting a few seconds, pressed the internal phone button labelled "Casini"…. 'Brigadier Casini, Sir. It's Major Lo Verde here. Could you spare me a minute? …. Yes, Sir. I'll be there straight away.'

Chapter 31

Commissario Vichi got off the bus in Piazza San Marco and, after a cappuccino and a glance at the day's paper which led with the story of the Prime Minister's forthcoming rally in Piazza della Repubblica, made the short walk to the Questura in Via Zara. He accepted the salute of the officer at the front entrance with a distracted nod and made his way up the stairs towards his office on the third floor, ignoring the lift.

'Commissario! Commissario Vichi!' came the slightly husky voice of the Questore's PA just as he was reaching out for the handle of his office door. He paused and turned with a smile; for some reason he always found that a smile was his instinctive reaction when he came across her in the corridor, even though, when she had something to communicate to him it was usually enough to wipe the smile off his face.

'I'm glad I caught you,' she said, 'I was just on my way to see if you were in your office.'

'Oh,' he replied, puzzled, 'Why didn't you ring?'

'Because, Commissario, you have a habit of taking your phone off the hook when you don't want to be disturbed, and it would appear that last night, you forgot to put it back on again.'

'I'll try to make sure that it doesn't happen again, Signora. I must have knocked it off the cradle when I picked my things off the desk last night. However, as I haven't been here overnight I won't have missed any calls. What can I do for you?'

'The Vice-Questore would like to see you in her office, at your convenience.'

'Questore or Vice-Questore,' he asked, puzzled.

'The Vice-Questore. Her secretary is at a funeral today and, as the Questore is out this morning, I'm covering for her.'

'OK Please tell the Vice-Questore that I'll be with her in five minutes. I just need to take my coat off and sort that phone out.'

The Vice-Questore had only recently been appointed and was one of the very few females to reach such a high level in the Police service and, he assumed, the first to be appointed to the role in one of the highest profile Italian cities. She had a reputation of being very austere but he had a feeling that that might just be a carapace to defend herself from the inevitable barbs of those who resented her appointment. So far, he had had very little contact with her, so it was with a certain amount of curiosity that he made her way to her door as he searched his mind for any recent cases that might have generated complaints or be dragging on too long.

As he came round the corner to the door of her office, fist already raised to knock, he was surprised to see that it was open, revealing the Vice Questore sitting behind her desk.

'Avanti,' she called, and then glancing at his fist, which in his surprise at finding the door open, he had forgotten to lower, 'have I done something to upset you, Commissario?'

'Sorry, Ma'am; I was expecting to have to knock at the door,' he said, giving a brief salute and then dropping his hand. 'You wanted to see me.'

'Yes, Commissario,' she said reverting to her usual austere self, 'Please close the door and take a seat.' He did as he was asked.

For a few seconds she returned her attention to the papers on her desk then, after initialling the bottom right hand corner of the top paper, pushed them neatly together and slipped them into a drawer. She looked at him thoughtfully for a while before speaking. 'I've been meaning to catch up with all the staff individually since I got here, but things have been a little hectic… Tell me, how's your current case load?' Her grey eyes, set in an angular face that was framed by medium length dark hair whose roots were overdue for a touch up, were penetrating but gave little away.

'Fairly run of the mill at the moment. I'm working with the *Guardia Fiscale* and our colleagues in Prato to try and strangle the supply chain for the recent flood of counterfeit bags, and we're still after the armed robbers who held up the Post Office in San Casciano…. but other than that, there's nothing major.'

She nodded, 'That's what I thought… So, if you were to be absent for a while the world of the Questura would not be thrown into turmoil with gangs of delinquents marauding through the streets of Florence.' Despite her words, her face remained impassive and Vichi felt a growing sense of uneasiness.

'I… I wasn't thinking of taking any time off at the moment, Ma'am.'

She reached into a drawer on her left and pulled out a sheet of beige coloured writing paper that had been folded in half. Pushing it over to him without unfolding it, she said, 'Read that.'

Puzzled, he unfolded the sheet of paper and turned it round to face him, with the Vice Questore watching him attentively as he did so. There was no need for him to feign surprise at what he read; he had half feared a letter of dismissal or a notification of suspension if he had been discovered or even just suspected of, helping a fugitive – almost anything – but not this.

'But why? Why me?' he couldn't help blurting out.

The Vice-Questore leant back in her chair. 'That's just what I wanted to ask you… I've had a look through your file and you've done a generally good over the years, but there's nothing to suggest why you would be picked out for this….' When he showed no signs of enlightening her, she continued. 'Without intending any disrespect, it is only usually officers with flawless records who are selected for postings such as this, and yet the comments made by my predecessor in your personnel file indicate that he harboured some reservations about your method of working and felt that you sometimes achieved positive outcomes despite your methods rather than because of them. Do you have any idea why you have been selected?'

Vichi shook his head, 'No Ma'am. None whatsoever… Am I,' he hesitated, 'able to turn this down?'

She snorted, 'I already rang to decline on your behalf, at least until after the Prime Minister's rally later this week, but was told that this was non-negotiable,' there was a touch of irritation in her voice.

'Perhaps the Questore…'

She slapped her hand on the desk with unexpected violence, 'The Questore will see it as a mark of respect towards him that one of his officers has been temporarily assigned to the President's own corps of guards. He won't be intervening on your behalf and I suspect that if you refuse to go, your head will probably be displayed on a pole in front of the Questura as a warning to others.'

They regarded each other warily for a few seconds then he asked, 'When do I leave?'

She sighed, 'The order says to report at once, but I don't think it would be unreasonable for you take the first train tomorrow morning. I imagine that both you and the three officers you're instructed to take with you will need time to pack and sort things out before you go…. I assume you'll be taking your Inspector.'

He considered; Preziosi was completely reliable and able to show initiative but, on the other hand, he knew that his marriage was under a considerable amount of strain at the moment and felt it wouldn't be fair to cause him any more problems. 'If you have no objections, Ma'am, I think it would be better if I chose three more junior officers – Preziosi knows the details of the cases I've been working on almost as well as I do, and would be the ideal person to take over as lead officer.' She nodded. 'If it's alright with you, I'd like to take: Venuti, Capezzi and Fazzi.'

The choice is yours, Commissario, but are you sure about Capezzi? I've heard that she can be a little… unpredictable at times.

He smiled, 'I'm sure. I've worked with her a few times; she's young, enthusiastic and opinionated. I think that occasionally some of my colleagues have felt a little threatened when she's offered her opinion… mainly because she's almost always turned out to be right. If I'm allowed to choose my own team, I prefer to have officers who aren't afraid to use their initiative… Will that be all, Ma'am?'

'Yes. Thankyou, Commissario… and make sure that Preziosi is fully briefed on your open cases before you go.' She watched him walk towards the door with a frown on her face. When the door was firmly closed she picked up her phone.

Vichi made his way quickly to his office and sat down to think about what his next move should be. After the initial shock of the announcement, he had had no doubt that the temporary posting was linked to Francesca and the efforts to stop the conspiracy, even though he didn't quite see how temporarily attaching him and three of his junior officers to the unit detailed to protect the President was really going to help – surely it was Prodi and other left wing leaders who were under threat, not the President.

His first call was to Gianna, although, as he'd expected, the secretary at the Law Faculty in Bologna claimed that she was unable to locate her and Vichi was not convinced that any effort would be expended in getting a message to her to ring their answer-phone at home. It did not seem wise either to be more explicit with the secretary or to leave any great detail on their own answer-phone so he limited himself to the bare minimum: 'Hi, it's me. I'm being posted to Rome temporarily beginning tomorrow. The good news is that it means I'll be home early today. Ciao.' The message felt very unsatisfactory but he hoped that its brevity would alert her to the fact that the matter was too serious to be discussed over the phone.

After leaving his message for Gianna, he rang down to the officers' room and asked for Venuti, Capezzi and Fazzi to be sent to him as soon as they were available. The officer who answered the phone promised to do his best to track them down, and Vichi decided to fill the time he had to wait by making sure that all the files he needed to hand over to Preziosi were in order.

Fazzi was the first to arrive, pleased to have an excuse to put to one side a report he'd been updating on kerb crawling in the industrial area between Calenzano and Prato. Each number-plate picked up on the security cameras had to be checked against vehicle registration details and then against the logs for previous evenings to try and differentiate between regular offenders and one-offs. The most experienced of the three officers Vichi had selected, he gave the impression of being lethargic but was actually astute and able to move surprisingly quickly when necessary. There was also the advantage that, as a divorced man with no children, he was unlikely to resent being told he had to be ready to go to Rome for an indefinite period the following morning. He raised an eyebrow when Vichi told him that the order to travel to Rome had come out of the blue and that he had no idea what it was about, but he had worked with the Commissario regularly and knew better than to ask for information that wasn't offered.

Venuti, the youngest of the three officers was the next to appear, having been called out earlier to a suspected burglary in a house just off Via Bolognese. Although he was still enthusiastic and keen to make an impression, he had asked the right questions before calling in the scientific support team and had discovered that there had not really been a burglary but that the husband had inadvertently left a window open allowing the wind to blow the curtains in, which had in turn swept some Capodimonte figurines that the wife considered as family heirlooms off a shelf and onto the floor. The wife had seen the mess, and immediately suspected burglars, while the husband, unwilling to disabuse his wife and take the blame on himself, had decided the best thing to do was to keep quiet. Once Venuti had discovered the truth, he had insinuated in the wife the idea that it could possibly have been her who had failed to close the window securely, thereby ensuring the safety of the husband.

When he was told about the temporary transfer to the President's staff in Rome, his eyes lit up at the prospect of becoming an essential part of the President's staff so early in his career. Vichi decided it was better not to disabuse him of the notion.

It was not until early afternoon that there was a brisk knock on his door causing him to break off from his conversation with Preziosi.

'Avanti!' he called and the door was pushed open to reveal a young woman with unruly shoulder-length hair dressed in a denim jacket and a pair of stone-washed jeans sporting several rips and patches.

'Permesso,' said the woman as she advanced into the room, 'you wanted to see me, Sir.' Despite her unusual attire, her manner was completely relaxed as though there was nothing unusual about her appearance. Inspector Preziosi was sitting in one of the chairs in front of the desk and he indicated that she should take the other one before turning back to Preziosi.

'OK. Thankyou, Giuseppe. If you could give me fifteen minutes with Capezzi, we'll finish going through these later.' The inspector nodded his assent and, after picking up a note pad and a handful of files, left the room.

'Is this the design for the new uniforms, officer?' he asked when the door had closed behind Preziosi.

'No, Sir. I've been on surveillance duty. I came straight in when I got the message saying that you wanted to see me.'

'Very conscientious of you, ' said Vichi dryly, 'May I ask what you were surveying?'

'I've been assigned to keep an eye out for pickpockets around the Duomo and in San Lorenzo Market, ' she replied in a studiedly neutral tone.

He raised an eyebrow, 'And is that really the best use we've been able to make of your talents at the moment, or have we been invaded by a higher level of pickpocket than usual?'

Capezzi was careful to keep any expression out of her voice as she replied, 'It's not for me to question the wisdom of those who allocate duties, Sir.'

Vichi looked at her, 'And whose team are you currently assigned to?'

'Commissario Capo Cabras.' She again kept her tone and expression carefully neutral.

'Ah!' said Vichi; just the name of the Commissario Capo was enough to explain everything. Cabras was rigid and inflexible in his methods. Working his officers hard and insisting that everything be done strictly by the book. He only had two or three more years to go until retirement and Vichi couldn't imagine him changing his ways now; Vichi could imagine the Commissario Capo looking back fondly to the time when he had joined the force and the only women in the Questura were secretaries or cleaners. The idea of a bright young woman in his team, particularly one who had been flagged up in the report sent by the Police College as a potential high-flyer, was hardly likely to be one that sat comfortably with him.

'Would I be correct in thinking that you wouldn't be too upset if I were to request your reassignment to a small team that I've been asked to set up?' He didn't give her time to reply before continuing, 'It would mean being away from Florence for some time performing special duties.'

She frowned, 'I'd be happy to be reassigned, Sir, but I'm not sure that Commissario Capo Cabras would agree to it.'

'Leave that to me. How long are you meant to be on surveillance duty today?'

'Until eight o'clock this evening,' she replied, this time only just managing to mask the disgust in her voice.

'Grab a bite to eat then go back there. I'll speak to the Commissario Capo about your reassignment and then I'll ring you to let you know who will be relieving you… You'll need to meet me, Fazzi and Venuti at the station at five-thirty in the morning. Wear your normal clothes but pack your uniform.'

While she had previously been careful to hide her feelings, there was now a smile on her face that she couldn't suppress and Vichi found it very difficult not to smile with her as he dismissed her. When she had gone he rang Preziosi's extension, 'Giuseppe. I need to go and speak with Cabras; can you give me another ten minutes… Oh… I don't suppose you happen to know what Capezzi has done to get on the wrong side of Cabras, do you.'

To Vichi's surprise, Preziosi laughed, 'I do, Sir.'

'Well?'

'I think it's probably better if you don't know, Sir.'

'Out of the question, Vichi. She needs to learn to do the basics if she's to survive in the force until she leaves to have babies. She can be assigned to your team from the beginning of next week, but not before.'

Vichi had hoped that a polite request to Cabras would suffice, but whatever offence, real or imagined, that Capezzi had committed, together with his own uneasy relationship with the Commissario Capo, had clearly knocked that idea on the head.

'I'm afraid that I'm going to have to insist. The Vice-Questore has instructed me to select a small group of officers for a priority task. Capezzi is one of the officers I need and, unfortunately, I need her now.'

'Ridiculous,' snorted Cabras and reached for the phone on his desk. 'Get me the Vice-Questore. Now!' he snapped. 'We'll see about that.'

Although Vichi felt calm, there was an uneasy silence for almost a minute until Cabras's phone rang. He snatched it up, 'Vice-Questore….. Yes, it's Cabras… I've got Commissario Vichi here with me. He wants one of my officers reassigned to him with immediate effect….. The officer is currently working on one of my operations….. I suppose so, but that's not the point….. Yes, Vice-Questore….. No, Vice-Questore, of course not…. Immediately. Yes, Sir.' He slammed the phone down and glared at it, as though it were responsible for his humiliation. After a moment his glare was transferred to Vichi, 'Take her, and God help you if you want to give her any real policing to do.'

Vichi breathed a sigh of relief when he was out of Cabras's office; he hadn't been a hundred per-cent sure whether Vice-Questore Morace would back him, particularly given the reservations she had earlier expressed over Capezzi's suitability. Somehow, he felt that working under one of the first female Vice-Questores to be appointed in a major city was not something that Cabras would find comfortable, and he wondered how long it would be before he requested early retirement.

Back in his own office, he rang Preziosi to ask him to send a very junior officer to relieve Capezzi and then to come up so that he could continue the handover of his current cases.

Florence's Santa Maria Novella station is surprisingly busy at half past five in the morning, despite most of the souvenir shops having yet to open. The majority of those calling into the station bar seemed to be businessmen, or occasionally businesswomen grabbing a quick breakfast before catching an early morning express either South to Rome or North towards Milan, with the occasional bleary-eyed tourist looking slightly lost. Capezzi and Venuti were there before Vichi, chatting and laughing together in the station bar as he approached, and Fazzi arrived shortly afterwards. Vichi ordered himself a coffee and a doughnut, bought himself a half-litre bottle of water for the journey and paid for the breakfasts of the others, before they made their way to the platform to catch the five forty train to Rome.

The train had the old-fashioned type carriages with separate compartments and they were lucky enough to find one which had just been vacated by passengers alighting in Florence. The three junior officers each put their holdalls or rucksacks up onto the luggage racks, while Vichi placed his next to him taking up one of the two free seats in the carriage. A middle-aged man dressed in a business suit opened the door and stuck his head in.

'Is that seat free?' he asked, in a tone that suggested that he was taking the answer for granted, and then looked put out as Fazzi held out his police identity card.

'Sorry. Reserved for police business.'

The man backed out, muttering, and Fazzi pulled the door to again and lowered the blind before sitting down and looking at Vichi.

Vichi gave a little laugh, 'It wouldn't really have mattered. I haven't been briefed myself yet so I can't give you any details of what we're going to be doing…. But, seeing as we're alone, I can tell you that when we get into Rome, the three of you are to make your way to this address,' he handed each of them a slip of paper, 'It's a farmhouse about five miles outside Rome, near the village of Setteville, just off the Via Tiburtina about three hundred metres after the Old Hall Hotel and Conference Centre. You'll need to get a bus to Setteville and then walk from there. You should get a preliminary briefing late this morning and then I'll be joining you this afternoon.'

'But you do have some idea of what this is about, don't you, Sir?' asked Capezzi shrewdly, making eye-contact with him.

'I have my suspicions but, as I may be completely wrong, I think it would be unwise of me to share them with you. We'll find out in a few hours anyway… Two other things: as we're not meant to be drawing attention to ourselves, it would probably be better if we avoid using our official ranks and titles while we're on our journey and, at whatever the last stop is before we arrive, I think it would be a good idea to split up so that we're not seen as a group when we arrive…. Oh, and if I were you, I'd pick up a book or a paper or something at the station, as you might be hanging around for quite a bit before the briefing.'

At Settebagni, the three officers left Vichi apparently dozing in the corner of the compartment and started to move along the corridors. Fazzi headed forwards until he found an open window in the corridor where a man in a slightly crumpled business suit stood ignoring both the 'Smoking Forbidden' and 'Do not lean out' signs, clearly unable to survive until the end of the journey without a dose of nicotine. 'Mind if I join you?' asked Fazzi, taking up a position alongside him. The man shrugged his shoulder and moved slightly to one side to make room for the newcomer.

Capezzi and Venuti made their way along the corridor in the opposite direction, looking like any young couple heading to Rome for a break. When they spotted a free seat, Venuti stuck his head in the compartment and asked if it were free but a woman told him that her husband had just gone to the toilet and they moved on. When they had travelled almost two carriage lengths without finding any free seats, Capezzi put a hand on Venuti's arm and suggested that they may as well just in the corridor as there couldn't be more than fifteen minutes left of the journey.

When they got off in Rome, they could see Fazzi ahead of them on the platform but there was no sign of Vichi. Fazzi made his way over to the newsagent stand to purchase a magazine and a travel card while Capezzi steered Venuti towards a nearby vending machine to avoid having to join the queue at the news-stand immediately behind their colleague. She kept an eye on Fazzi while purchasing another bottle of water from the machine and then moved over to the news-stand when he had moved off, telling Venuti to keep an eye on where he went. At the stand, she purchased two monthly travel permits, a copy of *Espresso* magazine and a copy of *Guerin Sportivo*.

'OK,' said Venuti when she rejoined him, 'Where are we going?'

'No idea. I'm assuming that Fazzi asked how to get to Setteville, so we'll just keep an eye on where he goes and only ask for directions if we need to… it would seem a bit odd if two people asked how to get to Setteville within two minutes of each other when, probably, no-one's asked the question for months.'

'Alright. You're the boss,' responded Venuti with a laugh.

Chapter 32

The walls of the cell were bare, with only two small windows, well above head height, to break the monotony. They were on adjoining walls so he could tell that he must be on the corner of a building, but he could see so little out of them that he had no idea which way the building faced – not that it made any difference of course.

He had been interrogated for nearly two hours on the day they'd brought him in before he'd been taken to his cell. That first time, the questions had been asked by Colonel Nicolini who'd arrested him at the university, and it had been very clear what they were after. She wanted everything she could get about his relationships with Francesca, Ciancolini, dell'Omodarme, Marco Antognoni, a Major Ameglia who he'd never heard of, and a professor at the university who he knew but who he wasn't aware was involved. Throughout the interview, or interrogation as he reminded himself it was, he had remained calm and tried to come across as someone who was willing to help the authorities as any good citizen should, but at the same time surprised and somewhat offended that anyone should suspect him of anything. Towards the end he had allowed this to become a clear, and what he thought would appear as a perfectly understandable annoyance at being held without any clear accusations being made against him, Secretly he was pleased by the lack of any specific allegations as he assumed that it meant that while they had enough information to link him with what was going on, they were unsure about what role he had actively played.

The session had begun with Nicolini questioning him again about the night that dell'Omodarme had been murdered and, as what he had told the regional director of SISMI on the night it happened had been substantially the truth, he had no difficulty in retelling exactly the same story. He did add that dell'Omodarme had suggested the possibility of him taking some photographs for a book that a friend of his was considering producing, which immediately led Nicolini to ask why he hadn't mentioned that when he'd been questioned earlier. At that he had shrugged his shoulders, 'I suppose, it didn't seem to be of any relevance at the time. You know, when some people mention "a friend" they're really talking about themselves and as it was only a vague enquiry, I just assumed that the idea had died with him and was of no relevance.'

'You were asked at the time about what the two of you had talked about, not what you thought was relevant.'

Paul had shrugged his shoulders at that, 'I'm not used to answering questions just after someone has been blown up on my doorstep and when my sister-in-law has just been rushed off to hospital. I did the best I could at the time.' Nicolini had returned to dell'Omodarme three times over the two hour period but each time she had received the same answers.

'And tell me about Professore Carrà.'

'What about Professore Carrà?'

'You can start by telling me, when you first met him then follow that up with how well you know him and when you last met and what you talked about.'

'Like me, Professore Carrà works at the university although our paths very rarely cross. After I first started working as a lettore, colleagues and sometimes students would point out who people were but I can't remember ever having been formally introduced to him. We will have been to the same receptions occasionally, but I can't remember there having ever been any conversations there that went beyond something like, "Could you pass the olives please.". The only proper conversation I can ever recall having with him was a couple of years ago, and that was just a general enquiry about the progress of one of his students.'

'Who was the student, and what was the enquiry about?'

Paul considered for a moment, genuinely unable to recall the student's name, then shook his head. 'I can't remember the name although I've an idea that it was one of the very common Florentine surnames. If I remember right the student had completed all their exams except one, which was preventing them from getting on with their thesis. As the missing exam was English, Professor Carrà was telling me what a wonderful student this was and suggesting that if the student was suffering from nerves on the day, I might wish to take that into account and be lenient. And that was it.'

'And what was the outcome?'

'Of the student's exam? He did alright: not brilliantly, but nothing to be concerned about, and I gave him the mark his performance deserved, as I would for any student. Since then I don't recall any other conversations with the professor. I'm sure that we will have occasionally nodded to each other on the stairs, or possibly even said *"buongiorno"* occasionally, but no more than that.'

The subject of Carrà had been brought up again later in the interview but again his answers were completely consistent and he denied having any knowledge of who the professor's closest associates in the university might be. As with Carrà, he was able to be completely truthful when he was questioned about Maggiore Ameglia, denying ever having heard of him.

With regard to Ciancolini, he was able to say quite truthfully that he had never knowingly met him, and slightly less truthfully that he was unaware of any connection between Ciancolini and Francesca. When the colonel suggested that he knew that Francesca was working for the Judge, he insisted that she had got her facts wrong and that Francesca actually worked for Judge Graziadei. He said that he'd heard of Ciancolini because his name was occasionally mentioned in the Florence section of *La Nazione*, but that he'd never met him.

The interview became more difficult when Nicolini moved on to Francesca and Marco. Francesca had insisted that whatever happened, if he were ever questioned he must stick to the story they'd agreed on, which in his case meant causing more problems for her. When she had gone over the story with him and he had objected that it would cause complications for her, she had made him promise that he would stick to the story come what may. She had pointed out that if he were arrested then it was almost certain that they already knew about her and that nothing he said would make her situation any worse. They had assumed, however, that the connection between Paul and Marco would be unknown, and that assumption had already been shown to be incorrect by the photographs they had shown him of the restaurant in Rome. He knew, however, that having already denied knowing Marco, he had to continue insisting that it was just coincidence that had resulted in them being in the little restaurant in Rome at the same time.

'And you seriously expect me to believe you just happened to be in the same very small Roman trattoria as your sister-in-law's boyfriend, just by chance and without being aware of it.'

'No,' said Paul, 'I think that if I were in your shoes, I would also find it very hard to believe. I'm sorry about that, but sometimes coincidences do happen… it's possible that this man is a close friend of my sister-in-law, but I've never met him and don't recall ever having heard his name mentioned. So I'm afraid I can't help you.'

'Tell me about your relationship with Francesca Conte.'

Paul sighed and looked up at the ceiling for a moment, 'She's my sister-in-law. That's it!'

Nicolini leaned back, arms folded, looking at Paul.

He knew what she was doing and he was fairly confident that he had the patience to sit quietly and wait for her to give up but, as there was nothing to be gained from antagonising her unnecessarily he decided to allow her a little victory. After waiting until the silence had become uncomfortable, he began again. 'Francesca is seven years younger than me; at the time we met she was only fifteen and the only person I was interested in was her sister. Because of the age gap, both Rosa and Francesca had their own groups of friends, so I never really saw much of her early on. More recently, she's been busy with her career and I've been busy with mine, and with the kids. She comes round occasionally and she and Rosa will have a gossip over a coffee and sometimes we're guests at my in-laws' at the same time. She's pleasant and I like her but more because she's Rosa's sister than for any other reason. I know it must sound odd but I wouldn't say I really know her as a person.'

Paul could read the disbelief in the colonel's eyes but wasn't really bothered; the story had enough of the truth in it to be possible.

'Although we don't have as many CCTV cameras as I would like in Florence, I sure that you won't be surprised to know that there is one near the entrance of the *Palazzo di Giustizia*... We've been having a look at that and it shows that on more than one occasion recently, you've picked your sister-in-law up when she's finished work.' The colonel stopped and looked at Paul.

'Was that a question?' asked Paul, forgetting for a moment his resolution to appear as co-operative as possible. Nicolini inclined her head slightly to indicate that it was.

'After the explosion that killed dell'Omodarme, my wife was worried about Francesca. I give a couple of private English lessons over on that side of the city just before lunch and, when Francesca started working in the *Palazzo di Giustizia*, my wife suggested that I should pick her sister up sometimes and give her a lift, on the pretext that I was just passing. Sometimes I remember and sometimes I don't, and sometimes she sends me a text to tell me that she's made other arrangements and not to bother stopping. Is that good enough for you?'

Paul knew that apart from the unfortunate photographs of the roman *trattoria*, the weakest point of the story was the justification for the photography trip to Rome. He had mentioned that the project had first been hinted at by dell'Omodarme, but then had to follow that up by telling Nicolini that Francesca had rung him a few days later to tell him that dell'Omodarme's friend really existed and wanted the project to go ahead. He told her that a representative of that friend had then visited him over breakfast at his hotel in Rome to give him a list of the buildings to be photographed. The man he had met had introduced himself as Emilio, had given him a generous cash advance on his expenses and taken his bank details to pay his fee when the project was complete.

Nicolini's scepticism about his account was clear to see but Paul pointed out that he had approached the officers on duty in the reception at the Defence Ministry to ask permission to take photographs, 'Do you really think that if I were doing something underhand, I'd walk up to the officer in charge of security at the

Defence Ministry, give my real name and ask for permission to take photographs?'

'Not unless you were either very stupid, or very clever,' Nicolini had responded.

Since that first interview, Paul had been questioned twice a day, every morning and every afternoon, by officers who, he was fairly sure, didn't really know why they were asking the questions, other than to check for inconsistencies when his answers were compared to previous ones. He asked for a lawyer and was told that as he was being held under emergency anti-terror regulations, that wouldn't be possible until he were charged. He asked for the British Consulate to be informed of his arrest and was told that as he had applied for, and been granted, Italian nationality by right of marriage some years before, for the time he was in Italy, his Italian nationality took precedence over his British.

On the tenth morning when his cell door opened, it was opened by the guard who usually appeared to lead him to the interrogation room. Usually he came alone, but this time, he was accompanied by two other men; one of them, a man in his late sixties dressed in a well cut linen suit was unknown to Paul, but his jaw dropped when he saw the other man behind the guard.

Francesca feigned sleep as the train stopped for five minutes at the Campo di Marte station on the northern side of Florence, with her head turned towards the wall to avoid any chance of recognition. To get off in her home city would be too much of a risk in the present circumstances while she hoped that it would be easier to blend in with the crowds at Bologna Centrale.

In Bologna, as she checked the timetables to work out the safest way to return home, her eye was involuntarily drawn towards the waiting room where the terrorist bomb had killed eighty-five mainly young people in 1981. She could not repress a shudder at the thought of how she had been in the city that weekend with her father visiting his elder brother who had just come out of hospital.

The blast, at ten twenty-five in the morning, had shaken the windows of her uncle's house even though it had been more than two kilometres away. She looked up at the station clock, set permanently at ten twenty-five as a memorial to those who died and thought of how they were still fighting the same enemies. In 1995, at the last of the big trials of those linked to the bombings, she had been shadowing one of the crime reporters from *La Nazione* and had witnessed the convictions of Licio Gelli and a number of SISMI officers for obstructing the original investigation into the massacre. Thinking of this reminded her that there had also been allegations that one of the SISMI officers involved had also had links with the Camorra, which maybe explained how the conspirators had managed to recruit Stiappa. The memory made her even more determined that those involved in the current conspiracy, who Paul had convinced her were somehow linked to the remnants of Gelli's P2 through their distant cousin, the Sienese lawyer Guerrini, had to be stopped.

Back in eighty-one, being unable to travel back to Florence from Bologna Centrale, she and her father had been forced to take an alternative route back to Florence, and she turned her attention to the list of departures from the city's San Ruffillo station and saw that there was a train leaving for Prato at twenty past eight. That would suit her perfectly as, from Prato, she could easily get a bus to the out-of-town Gigli shopping centre, and from there, the regular buses into Florence would give her more control over where and when she arrived in the city. Having taken her decision and realising that she had over an hour and a half before the train left, she decided she would walk the six kilometres to San Ruffillo which would still give her time for a cappuccino and a brioche in one of the bars along the route.

During the sixty-five minute journey to Prato she decided to change her plans slightly as she realised there was always a slight chance of bumping into someone she knew at Gigli, and it would probably be safer to get a bus from Prato to Sesto and from there into Florence. Before she did so, however, she sat down on a park bench with a bottle of water and the local paper to see if there was any news of any of her family. There wasn't.

When she rang Gian-Marco he addressed her as Maria, making it clear that he was not alone and could not speak freely, but at the end of the short conversation he suggested that 'it would be great to meet up again, maybe in the same place as last time,' a suggestion to which she agreed.

Late that afternoon, having retrieved the motorino from where she had left it, she made her way out towards the airport and then followed the little lanes from there until she found a suitable spot beneath the Viadotto dell'Indiano to leave the bike and cross the footbridge over the Arno into the park. This time, Gian-Marco was there before her and, as he saw her coming, he stood up and walked to meet her.

'I haven't got long. It's the Prime Minister's Florentine rally this evening, so I've got to be back in the sub-editor's office fairly soon… Let's walk.' and he took her by the arm.

'You must have some important news to come and meet me on a day like this,' she said hopefully.

'I have… There still isn't any definite news about your sister or brother-in-law, but an English nephew of theirs has arrived and he's kicking up a fuss. The English consul called the paper this morning and asked if we knew anything, and said that he'd be issuing a statement later if he didn't get satisfactory answers from the Italian authorities.'

'Well done, Susanna,' thought Francesca, although what she said was, 'Bravo Luke!'; even though she knew she could rely on Gian-Marco, there was no point involving Susanna Busoni in the story if it could be helped – she mustn't forget that Gian-Marco was a journalist with an eye for a good story.

'So what happens now? Surely, if the consul releases a statement, you'll have to publish it, won't you?'

'We've been asked to hold back for the moment: the official line is that there are issues which require clarification before we can publish.'

Francesca snorted, 'As if that ever stopped a newspaper from publishing before!' Gian-Marco ignored her interruption.

'What's really interesting is what the nephew's doing. Have you ever heard of social networking? … Not really? … Well, I think it's going to be a big thing. Now that more and more young people – especially students – are getting access to computers, there are more and more sites being set up. Most of them don't last very long, as you'd expect, but some just take off. Apparently the nephew has an account with a site called Friendster, a Malaysian based site that allows people to set up their own profiles, post items and comment on other people's items. He's put a comment on there claiming that his uncle and aunt have been snatched off the streets in Italy by government forces and are being held illegally. All sorts of comments have already been made in less than twenty-four hours, some by weirdos and serial conspiracy theorists, but plenty of them by more sensible people.'

'But most people haven't heard of this Friendly or whatever it's called, and there still aren't that many people with regular computer access except at work.'

'It's growing all the time and major news agencies like Reuters are now monitoring sites like this, as sometimes posts can lead to big stories. The important thing is that it's beyond our government's control, so the story has the potential to become big news.

She thought for a minute of the implications of what Gian-Marco had told her. If these social media networks caught on they were clearly going to revolutionise the way in which journalists worked and gathered information; more immediately, it meant that Rosa and Paul were at least safe from sharing the fate of Marco. 'I need to think this through, thanks for that,' and she hugged him and kissed him on both cheeks, 'Now, Go on; get back to work! … I'll be in touch.'

Later, when she went back to Via Forlani, the main gate was open and a bronze coloured Renault 5 was parked outside the door.

She remembered that Vichi had said that the house and barn were family properties rather than just his and hoped that this was just a relative dropping something off or picking something up from the house. At the very worst, she thought, some members of the family might have decided to meet up for a barbeque, which would mean that she would either have to wait until the early hours before going to the van, or find somewhere else to sleep for the night. She decided to give it half an hour and then ride past again before making up her mind. Luckily, when she returned forty minutes later after riding over the Viadotto dell'Indiano and then around Scandicci to use up time, there was no sign of the Renault and the gate was closed. Parking the motorino where she had on the previous nights, she walked back up the lane and, after checking that there was no-one around, slipped through the gap behind the overhanging bush.

She didn't expect to see Vichi until just before midnight and was surprised when she heard the gate being opened just after half past ten; if it wasn't Vichi then she would have a problem as, other than the main gate and the nearby section of damaged wall, there was no other way out. Quietly, she pushed her things under one of the seats in the camper van and slipped out of the door. There was a wheelbarrow and several lengths of wood in one corner of the barn not far from the side door and, as carefully as was possible in the inky darkness, she felt her way across and crouched down next to the wheelbarrow.

Whoever was coming had evidently left their car outside the main gate and Francesca only heard the occasional faint footstep as someone approached the barn. Vichi usually came through the main door but this time she was sure that whoever was coming was making for the side door. She felt around her and felt a thick piece of wood next to her; quickly she picked it up and stood poised to attack whoever came through the door. A key was inserted in the outside of the lock and she heard it turn and then the door was pulled open.

'Francesca… Francesca… it's me, Gianna Vichi… I'm alone.'

Francesca exhaled and released the breath and tension that had been pent up inside her as she lowered the piece of wood.

'Gianna… you gave me such a scare.'

'I'm sorry… I thought it was better to let you know who it was before I came in.'

'It's a good job you did,' said Francesca, indicating the piece of wood, 'I was just about to take a swing at you with this…. Come in.'

Inside the camper van, Gianna explained that she was there instead of Vichi because he had been called down to Rome; she had been the previous evening and waited for more than an hour for Francesca to turn up but without success. Vichi had told her to stress to Francesca that she must stay out of sight and not do anything until he was able to let her know what was going on. Gianna said that he had been sure that the call to Rome must be linked to the situation and that, hopefully, the President's intervention would prove decisive. Francesca promised that she would not do anything foolish, although she did intend to be in the centre of Florence the following evening when the Prime Minister was due to hold the next rally of his tour.

'He may not need these rallies, ' said Gianna, gloomily, 'there are rumours that Prodi may decide not to come back because of these reports from the Mitrokhin Commission. If he drops out, the left will be in even more disarray than usual and will struggle to find a convincing figurehead.'

When they had talked for a while, Gianna said that she ought to be going and promised to return somewhat later the following evening when hopefully she would have heard from her husband.

Although she had told Gianna Vichi that she intended to be in Florence the following evening to see for herself how the people were reacting to the Prime Minister's rallies, that was only partially true. She hoped that the massive police operation involved in managing the Prime Minister's high profile visit would distract them from some of their other duties. In particular, she hoped that they would relax their vigilance on her parents' house so that she could find some way of getting a message to them.

The following afternoon, surrounded by tourists of several different nationalities she got off from the *'Florence by bus'* tour when it stopped on the Viale just below the steps leading up to the Basilica of San Miniato. When she had made her way up the steps, she turned into the monumental cemetery rather than following most of the tourists inside the basilica. Often ladders were left by workmen carrying out repairs on the roofs of some of the private chapels just inside the high, fortress-like exterior wall. If she were in luck, she would be able to get a clear view of her parents' house from the top of one of the ladders. She was not in luck but consoled herself with the thought that as there was no policeman stationed on the wall, it meant that the only ones keeping an eye on the house must be stationed immediately outside. From the games that she and Rosa had played as they grew up, she knew that there was one point in the wood behind San Miniato, from where it was possible to see the windows in the upper storey at one end of the house, without being visible from the ground floor or the road outside. If she were lucky, she might be able to attract her grandmother's attention by using the small mirror in her bag to redirect the sun.

She did not, however, get to put her plan into action. As she began to walk round the far side of the basilica, her phone rang in her bag. Checking that there was no-one within earshot, she stopped and took out the phone. As soon as she pressed the green button the angry voice of the Brigadier came on the line;

'Francesca?'

'Si.'

'Where are you?

'In Florence, why?

'And where were you last night?

'I was here... What's going on?'

He was slightly calmer now, 'The SISMI Major who pulled Marco Antognoni in, was murdered last night. His throat was ripped out. All hell's broken loose with increased security everywhere.'

'Nothing to do with me, ' she replied, glad that the brigadier couldn't see her face, 'although I can't say I regret his passing.'

'Just make sure you stay low for now. A lot will happen over the next couple of days.'

'What...' but the communication had been cut off at the other end.

Knowing that she was not calm enough to safely carry out the plan she had set out with, she decided to abandon it and instead made her way deeper in to the wood until she found a tree stump to sit on. Taking out her phone again, she tapped in the number she had memorised that *La Guiablesse* had given her.

'Dica.'

'Tell your boss that Salvatore Stiappa is in the high security wing of the prison at Fossombrone.'

'Capito.' And again she found herself cut off.

'And thank you too,' she said as she slipped the phone back into her pocket.

Chapter 33

Fazzi was near the front of bus while Capezzi and Venuti, who had got on after him, ignored him and made their way towards the rear. The journey took over half an hour and, after the first few minutes when Venuti pointed out some of the monuments to her, they lapsed into silence.

As soon as Fazzi stood up and moved towards the centre door to get off at the stop outside the conference centre, Capezzi poked her colleague with her elbow to make sure he was awake. Fazzi gave them a quick glance as he got off and Capezzi winked to show that she knew what she was doing. She noticed that three other men who, to her, looked suspiciously like policemen wearing plain clothes also got off at the same time as Fazzi. When the bus set off again, she pressed the button to alert the driver that the next stop was required and then sat back hoping that they wouldn't have to walk too far in the opposite direction. As it happened, there was another stop just before an industrial complex less than six hundred metres after the farm entrance they were looking for, so they arrived only five minutes after Fazzi.

Their identity cards and police ID badges were checked in the yard by a soldier in his late thirties with close cropped silver grey hair who Capezzi thought looked remarkably like the footballer Fabrizio Ravanelli, while another soldier holding a sub-machine gun watched over them. Inside, there were about a dozen people, the majority of whom were male, taking together in small groups; Capezzi and Venuti went over to where Fazzi was talking with the three who had got off the bus at the same time.

'You made it then,' he said with a smile, 'I thought you'd changed your minds when you stayed on the bus.'

'It would have looked a bit odd with six of us walking up the road to an isolated farmhouse,' responded Venuti.

Fazzi introduced them to the other three, who turned out to be normally stationed in Ancona. Like the three Florentines, they had no idea why they had been seconded to work for the President along with one of their officers.

Several other officers arrived over the forty minutes or so until Capezzi could count twenty four in total, twenty men and four women. Shortly after the last of these arrived, a Carabinieri major entered the room and clapped his hands twice to call for attention.

'Thankyou,' he said when the buzz of conversation had died down. 'I understand that everyone who is expected has now arrived. Your officers are currently in a meeting with the President of the Republic and there will be a briefing for you all at fifteen-thirty. In the meantime, if you would like to make your way to the makeshift desk by the door where you came in, you will be allocated your quarters. If you could return here when you are sorted, a buffet lunch will be provided at thirteen-thirty.' He held up a hand again for silence as those nearest the door began to turn towards it. 'I must also request that, while you are here, you limit your mobile telephone usage to emergencies and that you do not reveal your location to anyone. Thankyou. That will be all.'

The four female officers were billeted together in a room with two bunk-beds, a small table and four metal lockers. Capezzi was the third to arrive and, as the two bottom bunks had been taken, threw her bag onto one of the top bunks. 'When I was a kid and we used to go on camps, it was always the top bunks that were taken first,' she said, in surprise.

One of the others laughed. 'I hope you're good at climbing – there are no ladders.'

'Ah,' said Capezzi as the last of the four female officers entered the room. 'It looks as if you and I get the bunks with a view but that need a bit of ingenuity to reach them.'

Capezzi was the youngest of the four and the only one who was not an officer. The closest to her in age was a rather severe looking Captain from the Forestry Police based in Turin who she guessed was in her late twenties while both the others were well into their thirties. One of them, a police inspector from Vicenza seemed to rival the forestry captain for seriousness, while the other, a police sergeant from Rieti who was the only one of the four who was wearing a wedding ring, had a twinkle in her eye that made Capezzi warm to her immediately.

Just before half past three, everyone reassembled in the large room where they had originally gathered and took their places on the chairs that had been set out in front of a large screen. The Carabinieri major re-entered the room and made his way to the front.

'Welcome back, and I hope you enjoyed your lunch. In a minute you will be briefed by President Innominati via direct video link.' There was a murmur of surprised comments amongst the assembled officers before the major resumed. 'If you have any questions of general concern at the end of the briefing, you will be able to address them to me; any questions which are of a more individual nature can either be asked to me in private, or will be addressed by your own officers who have already been briefed and will be with us later.' He checked his watch and then moved to the back of the room, pressed a button which turned the projector on, and then tapped something into a mobile phone.

Thirty seconds later the bulb was sufficiently warm for the somewhat uncomfortable looking figure of the President of the Republic to gradually come into focus in front of them.

The President waited another twenty seconds or so before someone off camera obviously advised him that he would now be visible.

'Ladies and Gentlemen, I'm aware that this briefing is very unusual and will come as something of a surprise to you but, unbeknown to almost everyone, we are entering into a period of deep national crisis.' He paused and took a sip from a glass of water. 'I myself found it very hard to believe when I was first informed, but it appears that there is a plot to undermine the very fundamentals of our democracy. You may think that, unfortunately, that is not so unusual in this great nation of ours. You may be asking yourselves why you and your colleagues are being informed of this and why the matter can't be dealt with by the forces of law and order and the various branches of the security forces in the usual way…. That is a legitimate demand and one which I originally asked myself when I was informed of the problem…. Unfortunately, we know that some of those involved in this conspiracy hold positions of great power and influence and while clearly the vast majority of your superiors are beyond reproach, we do not believe that all the conspirators have been identified and cannot risk our countermove being sabotaged by even a single false friend.' He paused again, took another sip of water and glanced at someone who was off camera before continuing. 'Your immediate superiors, with whom I have met today, have all amply demonstrated their loyalty to the State and to our Constitution and each was asked to select three of their most trusted officers to form a temporary elite corps with the sole purpose of putting an end to this conspiracy. It is essential that each of the eight leading enemies of the state are arrested at precisely the same time to avoid the risk of others escaping the net. Each of these people is so influential that even a single failure could result in the overthrow of the State as we know it. There are a number of other conspirators who we are aware of who can be dealt with in a second wave of arrests but who must not be allowed to coalesce around any of the eight leaders.

Your officers have each been told the target of their own group. The decision has been taken, and minutised, that you should not know who the targets are until the very last minute; this decision has been taken so that, should our attempts to defend the existing State and Constitution fail, the State which will take its place cannot accuse you of disloyalty or of plotting against that State.

Gentlemen… and ladies… if we succeed, and I believe that we will, most of what is done will remain unknown, as even to acknowledge that people such as the leaders of this conspiracy could aspire to dismantle our democracy would weaken the faith of many people in the State. The parts you play will, therefore, remain unheralded, but they will be known by those who matter, and you will be proud in your own true Italian hearts. Thankyou.'

The President left the desk from which he had addressed the officers and walked off camera. The Carabinieri major returned to the front and waited for the sudden burst of animated chatter to die down.

'Before I take any questions, there is one piece of information that I would like to add.' The last murmurs from the officers died away. 'For the duration of this operation, each of you has been temporarily upgraded by three levels. Once the operation is over you will revert to your current grades, although clearly what you have done will be taken into account in any future applications for promotion… Now. Any questions on matters which affect everyone?'

After the major had left the room and the officers broke up into their groups, Fazzi said, 'I don't really see the point of the temporary promotions. If we're only here for a short time, the difference to our pay will be insignificant.'

'That's not why they've done it,' said Capezzi quietly, 'The higher the salary we're on, the more money gets paid out to our next of kin if anything happens to us.'

There was a sharp intake of breath from Fazzi and Venuti seemed to go several shades paler. Capezzi gave a wry smile and shrugged a shoulder.

When Capezzi was woken up by the alarm of one of her colleagues on the Friday morning, her first instinct was to roll over and try and go back to sleep. The longer this period of activity with almost double pay went on the better. Vichi had warned them that there might be a lot of waiting around and that it might be boring, but she would far rather be bored in a comfortable farmhouse than in the centre of Florence looking for pick-pockets. Having nothing in common with her female colleagues other than her gender, she had spent most of the previous day and a half chatting to Venuti who, despite his impatience to get into action, had turned out to be more cultured and sensitive than she had expected. She knew she would have to be careful as he had let slip that he found her much more attractive now he'd seen her out of uniform. Workplace relationships were not a good idea in her opinion and she had no intention of being any more than good friends, but she had to admit that she was enjoying his company. Fazzi, who was a few years older, seemed either relaxed or fatalistic – she couldn't decide which – and had spent most of the preceding day and a half playing cards with a handful of officers from other cities.

Her three room-mates had wasted little time after the alarm had gone off; one had gone out to the bathroom, while the other two, in various states of undress, were sorting their clothes out. Capezzi decided that she would wait for a few minutes until the bathroom was free before making a move.

The door to the room was pushed open and the Forestry Captain re-entered the room.

'Everyone is required for a briefing at seven thirty,' she said brusquely, 'Come on Capezzi, no time for beauty sleep now – wakey, wakey!'

'Don't worry, I'm awake. I was just doing some mental exercises while I wait for my turn in the bathroom,' she lied, not wishing to give the other woman the satisfaction of being able to tell her to get up.

'Today's the day that everything will come to a head,' announced Vichi after they had been divided up into their teams in the main hall. 'Romano Prodi is flying back from Strasbourg this evening, and we've been picking up rumours that a plan to assassinate him has been brought forward to tonight. We think that those involved in the plot must have become aware that measures are being taken to thwart their plans and have decided to act immediately to pre-empt any action being taken against them. It means that we need to move very quickly, quicker than we would have wished, but it also means that they may not have all their security measures in place.'

'When do we get to find out who our target is?' asked Venuti eagerly, even forgetting to add 'Sir' in his excitement.

Vichi gave a little smile, 'We're not meant to tell you until the last minute, but I think it's only fair that you should know, particularly as we've been allocated two of the more unpredictable targets.'

'Two?' asked Fazzi, 'I thought Innominati said that action had to be taken against each target at the same time, to avoid any escaping or contacting others who may be involved.'

'He did. But, very conveniently, at six o' clock this evening, two of the targets have a meeting with each other scheduled. On the positive side, it means that one team can be deployed elsewhere; the downside is that while one person is likely to offer little resistance, two people may each feel that they can't lose face in front of the other – particularly the Commander in Chief of SISMI and the Regional Commander for Tuscany…. Now, before I go on, is there anyone here who wishes to pull out of this operation? I'll fully understand if there is.'

There was silence for a few seconds then Fazzi asked, 'Do we need to put our uniforms on now or do we travel to wherever we need to go without drawing attention to ourselves?' No-one else spoke so Vichi took it as confirmation that no-one wished to drop out.

'I knew I'd selected a good team. Thankyou… Now, the scheduled meeting will take place in the Questura di Lucca: SISMI have an office on the third floor.'

'I know it,' said Venuti, 'the Questura I mean, not the SISMI office: it's very close to the station.'

'It is, but we won't be arriving by train. We'll be going as far as Pisa by train, and then we're going to use this piece of paper signed by the President to commandeer a car from the Police station and use that to get to Lucca. There's a train that leaves Rome at one fifty seven and gets into Pisa just before half past four. I think it's best if we don't put our uniforms on until we get to Pisa.'

'Sir?'

'Yes, Capezzi?'

'Are we allowed to know who the other targets are?' Vichi paused to think while Capezzi and the other two colleagues appeared to wait with bated breath.

Finally, he sighed and, looking around to double check that no-one else was within ear-shot, replied, 'The other principal conspirators are: the Interior Minister Mauro Rossi; Giacinto Marelli, who as Justice Minister is notionally our boss; Silvio Cioni, the Minister for Public Works; Giancarlo Caprai, the Communications Minister; and the Beneventano brothers, both Leandro the Undersecretary for Reform and Devolution and more importantly, Dino who, as I'm sure you know is both President of the Campania region and owner of Tele-Campania. Rocco Lesine, the media magnate is also deeply involved but he's out of the country at the moment.' Even Fazzi looked impressed by the list.

'But that must be half the government!' said Venuti, eyes staring ahead.

'Not quite,' said Vichi, 'but not far off, and there are a few other, more junior, ministers involved as well, who we'll have to deal with later.'

Chapter 34

Just after six, Mauro Rossi, replaced the phone in its holder on his desk, having just assured the American Ambassador that the risk of Italy electing a left wing government in the foreseeable future was so small as to be insignificant. The Ambassador had been concerned that the regular drip-drip of negative publicity about the Prime Minister's sexual peccadillos and somewhat irregular business deals could lead to a surprise victory by the left with the implication that, if that were to happen, inward investment from America might be less forthcoming. Rossi had assured Ambassador Palin that the information that was leaking out of the Mitrokhin Commission was causing the opinion poll ratings of the leaders of the opposition to plummet. When Palin had pointed out that the Americans had little faith in Mitrokhin and had declined to purchase his archive, Rossi had reminded her that it was not in the best interests of either of their countries for these doubts of America to be made public. He was fairly sure that even if any intelligence about what was about to happen had been picked up by the CIA, they could be counted on not to make any sort of fuss.

After telling his PA that he was not to be disturbed under any circumstances, he turned on the computer on his desk and logged onto the site monitoring the security cameras outside the main entrance to Bologna's Guglielmo Marconi Airport where, in less than an hour, the private jet carrying Romano Prodi, who was still President of the European Council, would touch down.

He made no attempt to disguise his eye movements as the generously endowed young secretary shifted her position on the corner of his desk and recrossed her legs. As he had stopped dictating, she smiled, casually flicked her hair back over her left ear, and then slowly licked the tip of her pencil before positioning it back above the note-pad ready to continue taking down his letter.

'Ready when you are,' she said leaning slightly forwards to accentuate the swell of her breast against the black silk blouse.

'Hmm, ahem. Yes. Where was I,' said the Prime Minister, trying to combine thinking about the letter to the President of the Veneto Region with working out how much time he would have between finishing the letter and his next appointment. He wasn't sure that he had any more of the blue pills with him, so it was probably better to put it off. 'Your request for additional funds for flood defences has been passed to the appropriate ministry for evaluation and will be dealt with expeditiously – actually, Barbara, when you type this up can you find out which is the appropriate ministry and put the name in the letter – You will of course be aware that.... Now what is it?' He jabbed his finger down on the intercom button next to the orange light that had begun to flash. 'I said I wasn't to be disturbed for any reason.'

'I'm sorry, Sir. It's the President. He says he needs to see you urgently.'

The Prime Minister rolled his eyes, 'Well tell him that I'm in a meeting and will ring him…' he broke off as the door to his office was pushed open and the President of the Republic entered his office accompanied by a soldier wearing what he thought was a brigadier's uniform and two sergeants. 'What… I don't… Mr P..p..president. I didn't expect…'

The President ignored him and spoke to the secretary, 'That will be all for now signorina, but we may need you later, so please don't leave the building.' He sat down opposite Prime Minister Pannunzi with the Brigadier alongside him; the two sergeants took up positions just inside the door.

'Now, Roberto. I need you to listen very carefully – without interruptions – and then do exactly what I say – Is that understood?' asked the president in a very calm voice.

'What the Hell do you think you're doing? Have you gone completely mad? You can't just come barging in here and start giving orders. The Constitution…'

'The Constitution says that the primary duty of the President is to represent the national unity. It also says that I have the right to dissolve one or both Houses of Parliament and to appoint state officials in circumstances set out by law. I've read it, Roberto, I doubt very much that you have. Now, if I recall, I said that you needed to listen to me without any interruptions, but before I start, send a message to Marelli telling him that you need to see him in your office immediately; I expect it will take him about twenty minutes to get here…. Now – if you don't mind.'

The Prime Minister, who had gone very red, looked for a moment as though he might refuse but then he pressed a button on his phone. '….. Gianna. Contact the office of Minister Marelli and tell them that I need to see him in my office immediately…. No, nothing else.' 'You'd better have a very good reason for this Mr President.'

'Now, Roberto. You are in the middle of a publicity campaign at the moment: one which appears to be going remarkably well. Unfortunately, while you have been performing to your public around the country, several of those who theoretically work for you but who actually are the ones who really run the country, have been plotting to undermine the democratic process and ensure that "your" government is returned with a large majority.'

'Of course my ministers are…'

'Please be quiet, Roberto. Almost all the leaks that have come out of the Mitrokhin Commission have been carefully co-ordinated to do maximum damage to the leaders of your political opponents, partly to ensure that they are not trusted but also so that there will be no danger of public unrest when Romano Prodi is assassinated.'

'But… Prodi assassinated… You're mad.' He pushed himself to his feet with his hands on the edge of the desk.'

The two sergeants inside the door raised their automatic pistols slightly and the Brigadier hissed, 'Sit down.' The Prime Minister sat down.

'I do not believe that you personally are involved in this conspiracy; you just provide a convenient shield behind which some of your colleagues are acting for their own interest. Several of your ministers are involved, however, as are some members of the security forces. This gives me somewhat of a dilemma; I should order the immediate arrest of all those involved and, in my role as President of the High Council of the Judiciary and Supreme Council of Defence, make sure that they are made an example of.... However, were I to follow that course of action, it would appear that I as President were interfering in the political process and the whole country could degenerate into near civil war. Consequently, what I propose should be done is the following…'

'…and make sure that Macri is available after Prodi's plane lands. I want maximum coverage of the protests against him. They say that a big demonstration has been organised -we need interviews, incisive analysis that doesn't appear biased, and we need good quality footage…. Make sure it's done.' Dino Beneventano leaned back in his soft leather chair and away from the speaker-phone on his desk. He knew that Rocca Lesine would have made similar arrangements for the many channels that he controlled and had been assured that functionaries at the Communications Ministry would have held back as long as possible before granting permits to journalists from "less reliable" outlets.

He went over in his mind the emergency address he would make later that evening to the viewers of Tele Campania. He would deplore the assassination while subtly expressing understanding for the motives that had driven a "patriot" to deliver justice to someone who he saw as being a tool of the former eastern bloc and as such an enemy of the state. The regional assembly would be called for an extraordinary sitting that night and he would regretfully have to propose emergency powers within the region to enable police and carabinieri to take potential troublemakers into protective custody until matters had settled. It was best to also arrest a few right-wing thugs to create an illusion of even handedness. He had, of course pre-warned the right-wingers to be arrested so that they would not oppose any resistance, other than verbally of course; hopefully, the left-wing activists who would be taken by surprise would resist arrest, reinforcing the impression that they were the true dangers to peace in the country.

It wouldn't surprise him if his younger brother, Leandro, rang to check that all the arrangements were in place. Leandro had always been a worrier and he hoped that, after the election, when he was rewarded for the part he had played by being promoted from Undersecretary to Minister, he would be more relaxed. As President of the Campania region, he had already benefitted from measures that his brother had guided through Parliament, giving more autonomy to selected regions, and when Leandro was even more influential he hoped that he would be able to position himself to make a future bid to become leader of the party nationally.

The speaker-phone began to buzz and its green light began to flash. He glanced at his watch – six-fifteen – Leandro was so predictable sometimes! He laughed and then composed himself before pressing the button below the green light and speaking to his PA.

'*Si*, Renata – what is it?'

Salvatore Stiappa kicked the door of his cell and shouted out angrily, although he wasn't sure whether anyone could hear. 'How much bloody longer? This was only meant to be temporary… I was promised good treatment – *Cornuti!*' He gave the door another vicious kick and then retreated to the narrow bed with the lumpy discoloured mattress on the other side of the small cell.

As he sat on the bed he realised he hadn't drunk the coffee they'd brought him earlier. He picked up the tiny cup and tipped its barely lukewarm contents into his mouth and grimaced. The coffee was never good quality but barely lukewarm it tasted even fouler than usual. He hurled the empty cup across the room at the door and yelled, 'And get some fucking decent coffee!' as he watched the cup fragment into tiny pieces with the violence of the impact.

Feeling suddenly tired, he lay back on the mattress and, putting his hands behind his head, closed his eyes to rest.

General Tacchinardi, the head of SISMI, entered the Questura of Lucca through the side door, showed his ID to the officer stationed at the small desk just inside the door and, as the officer snapped to attention, nodded and made his way up the rear stairs of the building. He was dressed in a plain, though well-cut, business suit, and had not attracted any attention as he had made his way from the hotel near the Duomo, where he had booked in under an alias.

He met no-one as he ascended the stairway, which pleased him. The less people who knew he was there the better. He mentally congratulated the regional director for having had the foresight to site her headquarters in Lucca rather than the regional capital, Florence where you couldn't go anywhere without being recognised. There was no nameplate or even a number on the plain grey door half way along the corridor on the third floor – nothing to identify it as the base for one of the most influential, and yet least known, people in Tuscany. 2-3-4-7-0 he tapped into the small keypad below the door handle and pushed.

'At ease.' he said, making a calming gesture with his right hand, as Regional Director Marusa Nicolini, and an immaculately dressed captain, whom he seemed to remember was called Bolano, began to rise.

'You know Captain Bolano, I believe,' said Nicolini and Tacchinardi inclined his head in confirmation, 'He's been instrumental in running operations on the ground.'

'Go over the precise details for me again, Captain; we need to be a hundred percent sure that nothing can go wrong.'

Bolano cleared his throat, 'As you know, we have agents planted within all the significant groups of political activists, and many non-political groups as well – just in case. We estimate that there will be an angry crowd outside the main entrance of Bologna Airport when Prodi emerges. There will be a police cordon holding them back but at one point the cordon will break because of the pressure of the crowd and, at the point the cordon breaks one of the demonstrators will pass through with a petition in one hand, which will be concealing a knife. Hopefully the demonstrator will be able to slip back into the crowd and get away in the confusion.'

'What if he's caught?'

'He's been well paid and he thinks that this has been organised by the 'Ndrangheta, who are not known for their leniency with anyone who betrays them.'

'Thankyou, Captain. Your work won't be forgotten. Now Marusa, I need to brief you on what will happen afterwards… No, it's alright, Captain, you can stay, then the Commander won't need to repeat things to you later…. Caprai, has made sure that the most awkward of the RAI's journalists are otherwise engaged this evening so we don't have to worry about too many awkward questions being asked before we have everything completely under control. Rossi will go to the Prime Minister and insist that a State of Emergency is declared, which will enable Marelli to introduce emergency security measures including detention without trial… What's the situation here in Tuscany? Have you managed to remove the flies from the ointment?'

'Most of them are already in custody; as you know we anticipated Marelli's new regulations somewhat. Judge Ciancolini is prepared to admit that he has been investigating threats to the constitution but so far he hasn't provided any details other than that he was working with the security consultant in Rome who met with an unfortunate accident. My impression is that once everything is done and dusted, he can be persuaded to keep quiet as to do otherwise would seriously damage the country's standing. The couple we arrested in Florence are, I believe, fairly insignificant. He seems to have been recruited solely to take photographs of the outside of government buildings and continues to maintain that story. There is a slight complication in that as he's originally a British Citizen, a relative who's arrived from England has been kicking up a fuss about his disappearance and has got the British Vice-Consul involved. The wife, again seems to be only peripherally involved; unfortunately she's the daughter of a popular city councillor in Florence, so again we need to consider our moves carefully.'

'OK,' said Tacchinardi, 'Make sure things are sorted and keep me updated. Now..' he glanced at his watch, 'put the CCTV from Bologna Airport on the screen and we'll watch what happens.'

Two floors below, in a small room at the corner of the building, a grim-faced sergeant took off his headphones, glanced at the shorthand notes he had been making and said to the colleague who sat next to him, 'I need you to get me Casini on the phone now.'

Minister of Justice, Giacinto Marelli was irritated by the peremptory summons to the Prime Minister's office; he had far better things to do with his time than listen to the fool's self-glorification and wouldn't have bothered going if the others had not always insisted that they needed to keep Pannunzi in place as a figurehead. Well, Pannunzi could have five minutes of his time and that was it.

He nodded curtly at the Prime Minister's secretary and made straight for the door of the office as the secretary picked up the phone to announce him. 'He's expecting me,' he said over his shoulder as he pushed the door open, and then, as the door swung shut and he turned to face the Prime Minister. He stopped.

There was an armed soldier on each side of the room holding some kind of guns. Another army officer was standing to one side of the Prime Minister's desk while he could see the back of an elderly man sitting facing the Prime Minister who looked deathly pale. Why had Pannunzi summoned him if he already had visitors? It didn't make sense. It made even less sense a moment later when the elderly man turned towards him and he recognised the President of the Republic. 'Mr President,' he croaked after a moment's pause, wishing he'd cleared his throat before speaking.

The President stood up and turned towards him, unsmiling. 'It's over Marelli, we know everything and the time has come to put an end to this madness.'

Marelli considered; it was after quarter past six. Prodi's plane must have landed by now and the security channel he would be taken through was under their control. There was nothing the President and whoever else was involved could do to stop what was going to happen.

'I'm afraid I don't know what you're talking about, Mr President. Perhaps you'd like to explain.'

It was the army officer, who he now saw was a brigadier who spoke, directing his words first to the President, 'With your permission, Signor President, I'll explain.' The President acknowledged the brigadier's request and sat down. 'Take a seat, Signor Marelli – unless you'd rather stand… We are aware of what is meant to happen in the next half an hour in front of the Guglielmo Marconi airport. Fortunately, that will not now happen; Commissioner Prodi is being directed back within the airport from where he will be taken to the President's official helicopter and from there to a safe location. In the next five minutes a number of your associates will be taken into custody and more arrests will follow over the next twenty-four hours.'

"I must tell you, Mr President,' sneered Marelli, 'that you're too late. Prodi has been so discredited with the public that it doesn't matter whether he lives or dies. Being sneaked out of the airport by helicopter will only damage his reputation even further by showing that he's afraid to face his critics. When what has happened here tonight is made public, you will be impeached. By arresting me now, you're effectively offering your resignation.'

The heavy double door of Mauro Rossi's sumptuously decorated office, swung open, the dampers on top preventing it from crashing back against the wall. He took his eyes away from the screen and looked towards the door, irritated that his order not to be disturbed had been ignored.

'Off the seat. Hands above your head. And on your knees,' barked out a harsh female voice with a slight Genoese accent, 'Quickly.' He complied, bewildered.

'Mauro Rossi, you are under arrest for conspiring against the State and for the attempted murder of Romano Prodi, President of the European Commission.'

'There… there must be some sort of desperate mistake,' he said, 'Don't you know who I am.'

A smile appeared on the face of the female police officer who had spoken previously and who seemed to be in charge of the other two who had burst in, but the smile chilled the Interior Minister more than her words had. 'Let me assure you, that there is no mistake, Minister, and how you behave in the next few minutes will determine whether you spend the next ten years under house arrest or the next thirty in solitary confinement in a high-security wing.'

Rossi could feel the sweat trickling down from his armpits and down the middle of his back, staining his shirt. The Genoese officer nodded to two of the officers who accompanied her and they grabbed him under the armpits and pulled him roughly to his feet, pushed him across the room and dropped him in one of the chairs. The officer picked up a cordless phone from Rossi's desk, scrolled through the stored numbers and thrust the phone into Rossi's hand. 'Tell Vercellese not to move from his home until he hears from you again.'

Nervously and with a slight stutter, Rossi conveyed the message and then the Genoese took the phone from him and cut the communication before he could respond to Vercellese's perplexed query as to what was going on. Nicola Maroni, the Vice Questore of Frosinone was next to be contacted and he was informed that he was suspended from duty with immediate effect and, for the moment, should return to his home and remain there. The officer was careful to keep Rossi under pressure at all times, rushing him and barking orders at him so that he did not have time to reflect that if he were being asked to contact other conspirators it meant that the other side had very limited manpower. Finally, to his surprise, he was told to call his driver and tell him to be outside the door of the ministry in ten minutes.

Vichi had been assured by the Inspector who had planted the listening device in the SISMI office that the door was not substantial. Nevertheless they took a ram from the store-room up to the third floor with them, the inspector silently leading the way. Once they were in place, the inspector stepped to one side and Fazzi, who had the heaviest build, got into position to use the ram. Vichi checked that Venuti and Capezzi were immediately behind him and when he was sure they were all ready gave the signal for Fazzi to swing the heavy ram.

The door gave way immediately and Fazzi's momentum carried him forward into the room with Vichi immediately behind him shouting *'Mani in alto* – nobody move..' His pistol was trained at the male and female who sat more or less facing the door. The third occupant of the room was standing to one side and as Venuti who, due to the width of the door frame, was slightly behind the others, burst into the room he realised that his colleagues were between him and the third man.

Bolano, who had moved over to the window for a moment, sized up the situation immediately and went for his gun. One of the intruders had his hands occupied by a ram, one was almost covered by his colleagues and he couldn't get a clear shot at the obvious leader. That left the woman, and if he could take her out he'd have a clear shot at the leader. As he whipped his gun up, the last officer to have entered saw what he was doing and thrust across at his female colleague to knock her out of the way as he took the shot.

Capezzi was buffeted from her right hand side and then reeled as both men got off their shots at the same time. There was an excruciating pain in her left shoulder and for a second everything went black. The sound of another shot came from behind her and noise echoed around her head for a few seconds before her vision cleared and she found herself on her knees but still holding her pistol.

A pool of blood was slowly spreading from underneath the SISMI officer who was spreadeagled against the wall, but what stunned her most was the sight of Venuti lying by her side with part of the left hand side of his face missing. Vichi was still covering the two seated SISMI officers while Fazzi, who she realised must have fired the last shot had dropped to his knees beside Venuti.

There was the sound of running footsteps in the corridor outside and then the order came for everyone to drop their weapons.

'You're too late. In less than five minutes roughly a quarter of the adult population will be either watching or listening to news bulletins, learning about how the leader of the left was unwilling to face questioning by the crowds and reporters outside the airport in Bologna. Give it another half an hour and the news will have spread by word of mouth drowning out the voices of those who wish to prevent us from stopping the moral decline of the country. We might even be forced to reintroduce the death penalty – and make it retrospective, Brigadier.' The Brigadier remained impassive, as if he hadn't seen the Minister's jabbing index finger or heard his words. The Prime Minister's face was ashen as he sat slumped in his chair.

'Sit down, Marelli. We'll watch the news together, shall we? Then I think there will be arrangements to be made.'

A mobile phone rang in the Brigadier's pocket and he pulled it out, pressing the green telephone icon as he lifted it to his ear.'

'Casini…… *Si*. OK…… Soon as you can.' He pressed the red button and dropped the phone back in his pocket, his face expressionless. He glanced at one of the two officers who had remained guarding the inside of the door and the officer moved over to the television at the side of the room, turned it on and selected RAI Uno.

On the screen, popular variety-show presenter Carlo Conti was enthusiastically signing off from his audience as the final credits began to roll. The officer muted the volume and stepped back as the credits were replaced by the first of a series of adverts. The four main protagonists, who temporarily appeared to have nothing to say to each other watched the silent screen as if mesmerised by the images. Finally the logo of the early evening news bulletin appeared and the officer raised the volume and moved back to his position guarding the door.

Francesca placed her black tea down on the formica-topped table and turned her attention to the television. Lo Verde had passed on the Brigadier's instruction that she must remain hidden, but had told her that everything would come to a head this evening. He had not told her what was planned but had advised her to watch the early-evening news bulletin, saying that if the bulletin did not give clear signs that the conspirators had been defeated, she should assume that the most sensible course of action was for her to get out of the country as soon as possible.

There were very few people in the bar near the wholesale fruit and vegetable market in Novoli and no-one seemed to be paying much attention to the television in the corner. She had chosen the bar knowing that most of its clientele used it in the morning during the busiest hours of the market.

As the opening credits died away, a young, unbelievably well-tanned for the time of year newsreader appeared. Perched cross legged on the edge of the desk in what appeared to be the new casual mode, she wished the audience a good evening with a big smile and then began by delivering the main headlines before moving on to the main story. The RAI's Europe correspondent took over to report on five arrests made in Spain connected to the recent train bombing in Madrid; pictures of the devastation caused by the bombing were shown and, in a voiced over interview, the Spanish Security Minister expressed the hope that the entire Al Qaida cell had now been destroyed.

When the camera returned to the studio a picture of Bologna's Guglielmo Marconi airport was showing on the screen behind the presenter with an inset picture of Romano Prodi in one corner. 'President of the European Commission, Romano Prodi, who is a strong favourite to win the primaries to become leader of the left wing Unione at the end of his term in Brussels, has landed at Bologna airport within the last hour to launch his campaign. Large crowds had gathered outside the airport demanding that Prodi respond to the charges that he was 'the Kremlin's man in Italy' during the cold war. Mr Prodi…' here she paused and put a hand over her ear, clearly receiving an unexpected instruction through her ear-piece. 'I'm sorry,' she said, looking discomposed, 'I'm hearing that there are important updates to this story just coming in… I'm also hearing that this bulletin is being interrupted in order that the Justice Minister can make an important live announcement…. We're going over to studio three now.'

Francesca watched, spellbound, as a camera zoomed in on a shiny desk behind which a haggard looking Mauro Rossi sat, holding a sheet of paper between visibly trembling hands. As the camera stopped zooming in, Rossi was obviously given a signal to begin by someone off camera. He cleared his throat nervously, glanced down at the paper in front of him and then back to the camera again.

'Good evening… This evening I have to make a very important announcement to the nation… As you will know, the newspapers have recently been full of rumours, in many cases even accusations against European Commissioner Romano Prodi. I have to inform you that these allegations are completely without foundation and have been spread by rogue elements sitting on the Mitrokhin Commission. There is incontrovertible evidence to demonstrate that a number of people, many occupying positions of trust and responsibility, have knowingly orchestrated a campaign intended to defame Commissioner Prodi – and other leaders of the left – and in so doing create a situation of instability which would justify the declaration of a State of Emergency and the suspension of rights granted to all Italian citizens particularly by articles thirteen and twenty-two of the constitution.

'During this campaign, a small number of people have been detained unlawfully and, as soon as I have completed this broadcast, I will be issuing immediate orders for their release and for any pre-existing charges against them to be dropped. That will be my last act as Secretary of State as I will be tendering my immediate resignation to the Prime Minister, and will no longer be playing any part in public life.

'Finally, I would like to thank you for your attention and for having supported me during my time as a member of the government. Goodnight.' The image of Rossi faded away and a screen wipe returned viewers to the main studio and the young newsreader who had clearly lost some of her poise.

'Welcome back to the studio. That was clearly breaking news and we will provide you with further updates and analysis later in the evening. Meanwhile, to return to the day's other news....' The rest of the news bulletin, which had lost all relevance passed in a blur, and if anyone had asked Francesca what it was about she would have been unable to tell them a thing. Finally, when she had gathered herself together enough to rise out of her seat and make for the door, there was a change of tone that attracted her attention again. 'We are getting more breaking news, this time from Lucca. It appears that the sound of gunfire was heard coming from the Questura just over half an hour ago and that there are now three ambulances outside the doors. The Police have not, so far, released any information and a cordon has been erected keeping everyone, including our reporter, Gian-Luigi Battistuta, at least fifty metres away from the building. Gianni, what can you tell us?'

'Very little at the moment, Katia. We received a phone call at about twenty past six telling us that shots had been heard coming from inside the Questura. When we called the police, they declined to comment and I was despatched to the scene. Viale Cavour, which for those who know Lucca is the road just outside the main station, has been blocked off, as has another road which runs down the side of the Questura. Three ambulances arrived almost immediately, one of which has already departed carrying a woman who was escorted out to the ambulance with a blanket draped over her shoulders.'

'Do we know whether the injured person was a police officer?'

'I'm afraid not, Katia. That's all I have at the moment. Hopefully, I'll have more details next time you're able to come back to me. For now, I'll hand the line back to the studio.'

Outside, Francesca leaned back against the wall feeling exhausted: she was surprised to find that she was crying and tried to brush the tears away from her eyes, but they kept coming. Finally, when she felt she was more or less in control, she made her way to where she had left the moped and directed it towards the Viali and then to her parents' house.

She remembered nothing of the fifteen minute ride, couldn't remember stopping at any red-lights or seeing any police cars – she just knew that home was the place to be and that at that moment, home meant her parents' house, not her own little flat on the Poggio. She leaned the moped against the wall next to the door and, realising that she'd left her keys on her desk in the Palazzo di Giustizia what felt like a lifetime ago, rang the bell.

It was her mother who opened the door and both women broke down in tears as they hugged each other fiercely.

Chapter 35

'You're not going back to the University then?'

Paul shook his head, 'Certainly not now. With the compensation they've promised us for the wrongful imprisonment, we can afford to take three months away in your parents' camper-van. We've decided that as soon as this award ceremony is out of the way, we're going to drive north and take a tour around Scandinavia. It's a shame we won't get to see the Northern Lights, but at least we'll get plenty of daylight.'

'Probably too much,' said Francesca, 'when I was hiding away in the commissario's camper-van inside that barn, it was the exact opposite, just the odd glimmer of light during the day where there was a loose tile. I've had quite enough of campers for one lifetime.'

'I took a bit of convincing. I still don't feel entirely happy about abandoning Mati and Alessio for all that time, even though neither of them is bothered and Mati says we'd be mad not to do it "while we're still young enough".'

'She's got a point you know, big sister; it must be terrible being in your forties!'

'Huh! You just wait. It comes to everyone.' All three laughed.

'Did you say that Luke was going with you?' asked Francesca.

'Not exactly. He's going to get the Eurostar out to Lille and meet us there. Then he'll be with us for a couple of weeks as we move north.'

'How much did you tell him about what happened, in the end?'

Rosa glanced at Paul before replying. 'We decided to tell him more or less everything – not about the interrogations obviously, but more or less everything else – I hope that was alright.'

'Yes. At least he won't have any starry eyed romantic notions about the purity of the Italian state – I still can't get over the fact that Marelli was allowed to retire gracefully on a full ministerial pension and no-one is supposed to ever know how deeply involved he was. Cioni, Caprai and the Beneventano brothers as well. The only politicians who'll go to jail will be Rossi and Vercellese.'

'That's politics. It's dirty and grubby but both Innominati and Ciancolini are sure that the repercussions of exposing and jailing half the previous government would create too much instability. Apart from Dino Beneventano who's got another year to go as President of Campania, the political careers of the others are finished. Pannunzi's agreed to look at a complete reform of the security services, but I think we may have to wait until after the next election before anything meaningful happens. Prodi's indicated that the first thing he intends to do, if it isn't sorted by the time he's elected will be to place someone like Admiral Brandiforte in temporary charge to wind it up before responsibility for security is transferred to a new agency. At least Tacchinardi and Nicolini and half a dozen other senior SISMI officers are going to spend a long time behind bars, so there'll be some sort of justice.'

'I know. But it's not enough, is it? It still leaves you with a nasty taste in your mouth. What about Guerrini?'

'Try and forget about Guerrini,' said Rosa. 'He's gone. Fled the country, and he won't be able to risk ever coming back.'

'He was warned,' said Paul, 'he's got friends in high places and someone tipped him off – and if he's got friends in high places then Franci's probably right; I'm sure a blind eye will be turned whenever he needs to slip back into the country.'

'Maybe we should have dealt with him ourselves – family business,' said Francesca.

'That's not the way our side of the family goes about things… is it?' responded Rosa, giving a penetrating glance at her sister. Francesca could not avoid colouring slightly, but did not reply.

Rosa was fairly sure that her sister had taken matters into her own hands in revenging Marco's death, but decided not to push the point, and instead asked, 'What are we meant to wear for this ceremony on Friday?'

Paul rolled his eyes, 'I'm just going to the kitchen to get a beer.'

The ceremony was to be a very private one, held well away from any prying eyes, and Ciancolini had explained that it had to be kept a complete secret for the foreseeable future. 'The President feels – and I agree with him – that the less the public gets to know about what's been happening the better. Given some of the methods that were used to secure evidence, we're hardly on very solid legal grounds ourselves and, even though this planned coup d'état has been thwarted, there will always be enough fascists around to want to stage another one. Letting them know that illegal methods have been used to remove so many influential figures will only encourage their warped sense of being in the right.'

Francesca had objected strongly and there had been a heated argument, but in the end, Ciancolini had told her that she had no choice but to accept. There would be some aspects that she could write articles about, but some of the politicians who had nominally been allowed to remain in office until the election before "retirement" could not be exposed. She was still simmering as they drove up the Passo della Consuma towards the President's secret mountain retreat where they were to be invested with the insignia of the *Cavalieri di Gran Croce Ordine al Merito della Repubblica*

Italiana, the highest civic honour which lay in the personal gift of the President of the Republic; a special dispensation was required for the honour to be conferred on Francesca as it was only usually awarded to over forties, but Ciancolini had informed them that in the circumstances Pannunzi had agreed that he could personally validate the dispensation.

Chapter 36

A captain wearing full dress uniform held a velvet tray with gold tassels out towards the President of the Republic. Innominati picked up the first of the medals that rested on a furled green silk sash on top of the cushion and turned to face the four people who stood in a row facing him. Ciancolini stepped forward from the row and stood facing the President with his head bowed slightly.

'In the name of the Italian Republic, I, Alessandro Ignazio Oscar Innominati, *Gran Maestro dell'ordine di Merito della Repubblica Italiana*, hereby bestow on you, Bettino Pietro Ciancolini, the grade of Cavaliere of the Order of the Grand Cross of Merit in recognition of services performed for the honour of the Republic.' As he spoke, Innominati allowed the sash to unfurl and carefully placed it over the judge's head and right shoulder so that the medal was just below his heart on the left side of his body. The President saluted and Ciancolini stepped back into the line.

Francesca waited patiently as the process was repeated for Paul and Rosa before it was her turn. Despite the resentment that was still simmering within her for what she saw as the cowardly decision to let several of the leading conspirators "get away with it", she still felt a huge swell of pride as the green silk sash with its narrow red border was slipped over her head. She glanced down at the flared white cross around the circular centre-piece with the emblem of the republic and smiled as the gold of the entwined olive and oak fronds that separated the arms of the cross caught the light.

So lost was she in contemplating the medal and thinking that Marco should also have been there that she lost the rest of the formal declaration that Innominati made to bring the ceremony to an end. It was only when Rosa nudged her that she was able to refocus and move through, with the others, to an adjoining room where a buffet and glasses of champagne had been set out.

A handful of the President's official advisers had also been invited to the ceremony and Francesca had to accept their congratulations as she gradually picked her way round the buffet. After a while she found herself next to Innominati himself and, when he had finished talking to Paul, she put a hand on his sleeve and said respectfully, 'Signor Presidente. Could I possibly have a word in private?'

'Of course, my dear,' said the President, 'this is your day and I'm entirely at your disposal. Let's go and sit over there by the window,' and he led the way over to a window alcove at the far end the room which contained two chairs.

'Sir – With respect – I would like you to reconsider your decision about the futures of Caprai and Marelli… and I would also like to see increased efforts being made to bring Avvocato Benito Guerrini to justice.'

Innominati looked out of the window and sighed before he replied. 'Signorina Conte, you are fortunate enough to be still young and you can see your path lit up for you by the flame of justice. One thing you still have to learn, and sometimes it can be a very painful, as well as a salutary lesson, is that the very flame of justice, like all other flames, casts shadows, and sometimes those shadows can be very dark. I don't like the idea of Caprai and Marelli enjoying comfortable retirements, praised by many for their years of dedicated service to the Republic any more than you do. But sometimes we have to take a decision about what's best – and that isn't always the same as what's right. All causes – particularly extreme ones – benefit from the presence of martyrs and I don't intend to create any.'

'I'm not sure that I can accept that,' responded Francesca, 'I believe that failing to expose them now, makes them free to come back onto the scene at a later date, possibly when their supporters are even stronger.'

'I'm afraid, Signorina, that my decision has already been taken and is irrevocable and that... that little bauble round your neck indicates your acceptance of the authority of the Grand Master of the Order which, for as long as I'm President, is me.'

She could see she was getting nowhere and so reminded him of her second request, 'What about Guerrini? He's been pulling the strings all along but he's not well known enough to be viewed as a martyr.'

'We have no concrete proof of his involvement, or at least nothing that would condemn him in a court of law, particularly as I'm sure he has many friends throughout the legal system. You should also know that over the last half century there have been many occasions when the Advocate has been very helpful to the State, and a certain amount of gratitude has to be placed in the scales when evaluating his case.'

Francesca was horrified, 'You can't be serious... Sir... Guerrini supported the State for as long as he felt that that was where the power lay. As soon as he saw the chance of returning the State to how it was in his father's day, he switched his allegiance, returning to his true colours. He's one of the members of P2 whose name was never discovered, and he's been working to fulfil their objectives – you can't possibly let him get away with it.'

The President shook his head and rose, 'Thankyou for giving me your opinion but I must continue circulating amongst my other guests – If you'll excuse me.'

Chapter 37

As Francesca and the other awardees were about to leave, the President asked Ciancolini if he would remain behind as there were other matters that he needed to discuss with him. The judge accepted and embraced the other three before they made their way to Rosa's two-door Fiat Panda.

Paul slid into the back, hoping that the five glasses of champagne he had drunk would help him drop off to sleep as Rosa negotiated the twisty road down into the Arno Valley where they could get the motorway for the last few kilometres into Florence.

'I suppose we have to keep these hidden,' said Francesca, fingering the medal that still hung around her neck, 'bit difficult to explain, otherwise.'

'I think I'll keep it hidden until Mati or Alessio get married, then I'll wear it to their wedding. Probably by then, everyone will have forgotten about Innominati. If he's still alive, he'll probably thank us for telling the story then.' Both sisters laughed.

'Enough about all this, tell me more about this fantastic holiday that you and Paul have got planned, well away from politicians.'

'Much better idea,' came Paul's voice from the back.

'Well,' said Rosa, 'When it gets to July and everyone in Florence starts moaning about the heat, and the mosquitoes and the tourists, we're going to head north. I want to swim in one of the lakes before we leave Italy, and then do some glacier skiing the same day. After that, I fancy a couple of days near Annecy before we start heading north again.'

'I went to Annecy a few years ago. It's stunning with the old town set between two rivers at one end of the lake. The central bit is absolutely full of restaurants, although you'll pay a lot less if you find somewhere in one of the nearby villages that are a bit less touristy… Careful!'

'It's alright. I've seen it,' said Rosa, slowing as they approached a tractor that was stationary on their side of the road just before a blind bend.

'They could hardly have found a worse place to stop,' said Francesca, 'You should be OK if you give a long blast on your horn before you pull out.'

'I know,' muttered Rosa as she dropped the car into second gear and put her hand on the horn as she began to pull out, craning her neck in an attempt to see around the tractor's big wheel. Paul, who was half asleep, just kept his eyes shut and let them get on with it, knowing that Rosa didn't appreciate any advice from him when she was driving. Francesca, in the passenger seat, unclipped her seat belt and raised herself up, hoping to get a better view.

Intent, as they were, on peering ahead, neither of them were aware of the logging truck that rolled silently backwards down the steep bushy bank to their right until it slammed into the side of the car. Rosa's right arm and leg were trapped against the steering wheel as the driver's side of the car buckled inwards; Francesca was flung violently against the far side of the car knocking all the breath out of her and breaking several ribs against the inside of the door.

There was a gap in the guard-rail at that point and the car came to a halt with two wheels hanging precariously over the top of a steep slope that fell away through the trees towards a small fishing lake. In what seemed to her in her dazed state like the far distance, Francesca heard a large diesel engine and the car began to move slowly sideways again before catching on a tree stump. The sound of the engine altered, the car seemed to move slightly back again then there was a jolt as the truck rammed them again.

Just over two miles away, across the valley, an elderly silver-haired man wearing an expensively cut camel-skin coat watched calmly through a pair of Zeiss hunting binoculars as the white Panda began to first slide and then, after evidently catching on some obstruction, roll down the slope. Part way down, one of the occupants was thrown clear when one of the doors became detached but the other two were still inside when tongues of flame began to curl out from under the car a few seconds after its carcass came to rest just short of the fishing lake. He watched the flames spread until the car was completely engulfed and then lifted the binoculars higher and focussed on the body that had been thrown clear. It was still in exactly the same position with limbs splayed out at normally impossible angles. Looking still higher, he saw that both the tractor and the logging truck had now disappeared.

Without even allowing himself the smallest smile of satisfaction, he turned and pushed his way back through the bushes and walked with a slight limp back to the silver-grey Audi that awaited him. Seeing him approaching, the driver jumped out and held open the nearest rear-door for him. He entered without a word, as did his driver, who then set off carefully down the road.

Epilogue - October 2009

A wispy, silver, autumn mist was still lingering in the distant valley bottoms, where the late October sunshine was only just beginning to make headway. Higher up, however, the mountain peaks and east-facing slopes were bathed in light and a keen-eyed observer would have been able to distinguish minute details over a distance of several miles.

The old lady, sitting in her wheelchair on the sun-bathed hotel terrace was no longer a keen eyed observer but could see enough to appreciate the overall view and memory allowed her mind to fill in the minute details that her eyes couldn't see. A childhood, however distant, spent roaming the mountain slopes around the Val d'Aosta, either on her own, or accompanied by her older sister, was not something that one easily forgot. She could have brought the mountains into better focus by putting on the glasses that the optician had prescribed and that her daughter had insisted on buying, but she wasn't going to – certainly not today. She had worn them once or twice to stop her daughter complaining, and she regularly wore them when she was on her own, in her own sitting-room, looking out over the whole of the city of Florence. Never in public – and certainly not today.

The table by which she had had her wheelchair placed was the one which would catch the most sun, and it sat on the south-eastern corner of the upper terrace, just a few metres from the top of the steps that led down to the lower terrace with its heated pool. On the top of the table was a small coffee pot, an empty espresso cup and a sugar bowl, alongside which lay a small pair of silver sugar-tongues. On the edge of the table nearest to her was a light fur muff inside which she kept her left hand while her right hand, with its elegant calfskin glove rested in her lap clutching an embroidered silk handkerchief.

She saw the distinguished looking elderly man, before he saw her, as he emerged from the double-doors of the hotel on the other side of the terrace. Despite a slight stoop, she guessed that he must still be around six feet tall and the expensively cut camel-skin coat, the carefully arranged cashmere scarf and the hat that he held in his left hand all exuded wealth, power and a sense of self belief. As he turned his head to look around the terrace, for a moment she saw something in his profile that reminded her of her father and an involuntary shudder passed through her.

As he spotted her and began to make his way over, walking with a slight limp she noticed, she pushed the handkerchief into her bag and placed her right hand inside the muff with its twin.

He stopped, three yards away from her, obviously wondering how to begin the conversation. Before he had chance to decide, she helped him out. 'Good morning, Beni. Take a seat and call a waiter over, would you.' He did as he was told and then sat without saying anything, caught off his guard by the use of his childhood name, waving in the direction of a waiter as he did so.

'A cup of your luxury hot chocolate for me, and my nephew will have the same, although without the whipped cream on top – he never did like that.' The waiter bowed his head in acknowledgement of the order and retreated.

'Your memory is very good, Aunt.'

'I'm sorry, Beni; you'll have to look me in the face when we speak – my hearing isn't what it was, so I need to be able to see your lips when you speak to me.'

He lifted his head, suddenly aware that he had been avoiding his aunt's eyes and, clearing his throat, repeated, 'I said that your memory is very good, Aunt.'

'Yes, it is,' she replied, looking away from him for a moment and out over the mountains, 'it's just my body that lets me down these days – although sometimes I wish it were the other way around.'

He waited until she turned back towards him and then said, 'And why is that, Aunt?'

She glared at him for a moment and he fought an impulse to recoil from the hatred in her look, and then her eyes returned to normal, 'There are many painful things that I would rather forget amongst the good things that made life worth living.' Then she was silent.

'Why did you ask me to meet you here?' he asked, as the silence began to become uncomfortable.

'I think you can probably work out the answer to that question. I suppose a more interesting question would be, why did you agree to come? You can't have expected this meeting to be a pleasant one.'

'I came because I was curious. I wanted to see to what state you've been reduced and how much you regret having rejected the family all those years ago.'

They were silent as the waiter brought out the hot-chocolates and then withdrew again.

'Regret! Of all the decisions I ever took in my life, I thinks that's the one I'm most proud of, although it's a close call between that, helping my sister to elope and shooting my husband.' She looked at him, curious to see how he would react, but he had recovered some of his poise now and showed no surprise.

'Mother said that she was sure it wasn't an accident and that you were responsible. It was far too convenient otherwise. You were lucky it was during the confusion of the liberation, otherwise you'd have had to swallow your pride and come back to the family to get you out of trouble.'

Oh, Beni. You haven't changed since you were a spoilt little boy, have you? Despite all your obvious intelligence, and your ability to get people to do what you wanted, you never understood what motivated people who weren't self-centred, did you? … If I'd gone back to the family at that point, it wouldn't have been to get me out of trouble, it would have been to get more revenge… What did I care about getting out of trouble? I didn't even know I was pregnant then, and even if I had, I'd have killed both myself and my baby rather than go back to the family.'

'So why did you come here? And how did you find me?'

She smiled for the first time during their meeting, 'Now that is a better question with a much more interesting answer. Your first question has a very short and simple answer so, I'd prefer to leave that for a while.' She paused and drank half the cup of chocolate in one go. 'You know, as well as anyone, that all of us with Campolargo blood in our veins have been steeped in intrigue for centuries, and we can be very resourceful. I may have rejected the family because the way we had behaved over the previous century made me ashamed, but that doesn't mean that the ability to plot and scheme isn't there somewhere in my character, maybe even in my genes, so that I could pass it on, as could my sister Chiara.' She paused again.

'Go on,' he said coldly.

'You thought, when you had my sister Chiara's grandson and one of my grand-daughters killed and left the other one an invalid, that you'd eliminated the risk from the 'honest' side of the family – but you miscalculated badly,' She smiled again and her smile seemed to cut him like a blast of arctic wind. 'Rosa and Paul had two children who I've spent a lot of time with over the last five years, and one of them, my great-grand-daughter is something of an expert with computers.'

He raised an eyebrow, and managed an expression that would have convinced most people that he was perfectly at ease, if it hadn't been for the way his grip tightened around the handle of his untouched cup of hot chocolate.

She continued, 'Mati also has an English cousin, my sister's great-grandson who, despite only being twenty-five, has already established something of a reputation for himself with the English Police Force, and has apparently been fast-tracked. It took them more than four years, but together they managed to track you down and find out what name you were living under – then it was just a case of keeping track of you and waiting for the right opportunity.'

'The right opportunity for what?' he asked with an edge to his voice.

'The opportunity provided by my health to persuade my doctor to recommend that I must get away from the city and get some mountain air at a time when it wasn't possible for my daughter and son-in-law to accompany me.'

'And why didn't you want them to accompany you?' he asked, no longer bothering to hide his curiosity.

She smiled, 'Not only do they not know all the details about you, but the last thing I want is for them to be involved in what I have to do; I think you would agree that to do so would be unwise and would lead to a lot of tiresome complications.'

He rolled his eyes and placed his right hand on the edge of the table to push himself up, saying, 'I think it's time I was going, Aunt. I don't think you really have anything to say that would interest me, and I have better things to do that sit here and drink chocolate.'

To his surprise, she smiled again and lifted her hands slightly together with muff that covered them. "Good-by, Beni,' she said as she pulled the trigger of the small revolver that Luke had procured for her.

'That was easy,' she thought, as he slowly slumped sideways, blood oozing out of a small hole just to the right of his nose. Before there was any reaction to the muffled shot from the other guests on the terrace, she pushed her wheelchair slightly back from the table and then rolled it the short distance to the top of the steps where it toppled over and cast her head-first down the steps.

*****

Thankyou for reading 'Affairs of State'. If you enjoyed it, please take a moment to leave a review at your favourite on-line bookstore and on my Facebook page.

Thankyou

Phil Whitney

Contextual Notes

Giorgio Amendola: 1907-1980 – Writer and Politician. Communist Member of Parliament 1948-1980. Argued for Euro-Communism and for separation from the Communist Party in the Soviet Union.

Giulio Andreotti: 1919-2013 – Writer and Politician. Leading figure in Christian Democratic Party (CD). Prime Minister 1972-73, 1976-79, 1989-92. Various senior ministerial positions between 1954 and 1992. Regularly accused of Mafia links and involvements in conspiracies but nothing proved. Subject of Sorrentino's film "Il Divo" (2008), and loosely represented in "Godfather lll".

Enrico Berlinguer: 1922-1984 – Leader of the Italian Communist Party (PCI) 1972-1984. Separated the PCI from the Communist party in the Soviet Union.

Amadeo Bordiga: 1889-1970 - Marxist theoretician. Founder Member of Italian Communist Party. Believed in Dictatorship of the Proletariat. Criticised Stalinism as the culmination of bourgeois democracy. Imprisoned by Mussolini in 1923. Expelled from PCI in 1930. Viewed representative democracy as bourgeois electoralism. Joined Communist International in 1949.

Bettino Craxi: 1934-2000 – Politician. Italian Prime Minister in coalition with the Christian Democrats and others August 1983 to April 1987. Admitted accepting bribes but fled to Tunis before he could be sentenced. 'Doing a Craxi' refers to escaping justice by fleeing the country.

Massimo D'Alema: Born 1949 – Journalist and Socialist Politician. Italian Prime Minister October 1998 to April 2000. Like Prodi, D'Alema was targeted by the Mitrokhin Commission.

Antonio Gramsci: 1891-1937 – Journalist, Philosopher and Politician. Socialist then founder member of Italian Communist Party. Arrested and imprisoned by Mussolini in 1926. Released on health grounds in 1934.

Paolo Guzzanti: Born 1940 – Journalist and Politician. Member of Senate May 2001 to April 2008. Member of Parliament April 2008 onwards. President of Mitrokhin Commission 2002-2006.

Vasili Mitrokhin: 1922-2004 – KGB field officer then archivist. Defected to Britain in 1991 with 25,000 documents allegedly copied from the KGB archives. References to Mitrokhin and to the Mitrokhin Commission set up by the Italian Government are, as far as I am aware, correct.

Giorgio Napolitano: Born 1925 – Actor, Writer, Political Economist, Resistance Fighter, Politician. Member of Parliament 1953 to 1998; Member of European Parliament 1999 to 2004; President of Italy 2006 to 2015.

Romano Prodi: Born 1939 – Economist and Socialist Politician. Italian Prime Minister May 1996 to October 1998 and May 2006 to May 2008. President of the European Commission September 1999 to November 2004. There were regular attempts to smear and discredit Prodi during his time in politics – some of these attempted smears are referred to in the novel.

Mario Scaramella: Born 1970 – Lawyer, Security Consultant, Nuclear Expert and "Advisor" to Mitrokhin Commission. Present at meeting when Alexander Litvinenko was poisoned with polonium. Reported plot by ex-KGB officers in Naples to assassinate Paolo Guzzanti. Later arrested and charged with 'calumny'.

Palmiro Togliatti: 1893-1964 - Politician. Founder member of PCI. 1927-1964 Party Leader. Member of Provisional Government 1944-1946; Member of Parliament 1948-1964.